Three-times Golden Heart® Award finalist **Tina Beckett** learned to pack her suitcases almost before she learned to read. Born to a military family, she has lived in the United States, Puerto Rico, Portugal and Brazil. In addition to travelling, Tina loves to cuddle with her pug, Alex, spend time with her family, and hit the trails on her horse. Learn more about Tina from her website, or 'friend' her on Facebook.

Deanne Anders was reading romance while her friends were still reading Nancy Drew, and she knew she'd hit the jackpot when she found a shelf of Harlequin Presents in her local library. Years later she discovered the fun of writing her own. Deanne lives in Florida with her husband and their spoiled Pomeranian. During the day she works as a nursing supervisor. With her love of everything medical and romance, writing for Mills & Boon Medical Romance is a dream come true.

NURSE'S SECOND CHANCE AT FOREVER

TINA BECKETT

FESTIVE REUNION WITH THE DOCTOR

DEANNE ANDERS

MILLS & BOON

First published in Great Britain 2025
by Mills & Boon, an imprint of HarperCollins*Publishers* Ltd,
1 London Bridge Street, London, SE1 9GF

www.harpercollins.co.uk

HarperCollins*Publishers* Macken House, 39/40 Mayor Street Upper, Dublin 1, D01 C9W8, Ireland

Nurse's Second Chance at Forever © 2025 Tina Beckett

Festive Reunion with the Doctor © 2025 Denise Chavers

ISBN: 978-0-263-32524-9

11/25

MIX
Paper | Supporting
responsible forestry
FSC
www.fsc.org
FSC™ C007454

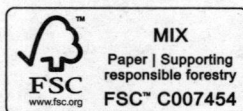

This book contains FSC™ certified paper and other controlled sources to ensure responsible forest management.

For more information visit www.harpercollins.co.uk/green.

Printed and Bound in the UK using 100% Renewable Electricity at CPI Group (UK) Ltd, Croydon, CR0 4YY

NURSE'S SECOND CHANCE AT FOREVER

TINA BECKETT

MILLS & BOON

To my 'opposites attract' husband.
It's still true, even after all these years!

PROLOGUE

LOUISA MELIA WASN'T sure what was worse: the finality of death, or the fear that cracked open her chest and found her heart whenever one of her family members went out on that racetrack. Maybe they were both equally bad. As she sat in the very same emergency department waiting area that she'd cried in when her husband was pronounced dead, she shut her eyes. First Brad and now her brother, who had idolized her late husband. Who had learned all of his tricks, who had practiced each of his shortcuts. And had wound up paying the price for them.

Her mom held her hand with a tightness that didn't quite equal what was in her own gut. Lou leaned closer. "He'll be all right. He *has* to be."

"From your lips to God's ears." The saying in their family was repeated anytime something went terribly wrong. Like her husband taking a curve too fast and crashing into an embankment. Or Silas being hit by another driver and flipping his stock car over several times. She only hoped whatever divine being was up there was listening this time.

The doors that led to some other area of the hospital opened, and there stood a man in scrubs. He was tall and lanky, and she was pretty sure he was the same trauma

surgeon who had worked on her husband. Lou was a critical care nurse herself, so she tended to remember faces in the medical field.

"Mrs. Halford?" He glanced around the crowded room. Her mom seemed frozen in place, so Lou stood up and walked over to the man.

"I'm Lou Melia, his sister. How is he?"

The doctor glanced in the direction of her mom before nodding. "He's still with us. He's broken several bones including a compression fracture of his L2 vertebra and will need intensive rehab, but we're cautiously optimistic."

She sagged and then took his hand, which was comfortingly warm. "Thank you. When can we see him?"

"He's still recovering from surgery. But once he wakes up, you can see him briefly. He'll be intubated and under sedation, so he probably won't respond, but I think he'll know you're there."

Lou let go of his hand. "At least he's alive."

"He's one of the lucky ones."

"I know." How many casualties of racing had this surgeon seen? Probably more than his fair share, since the hospital was close to the track.

He must have recognized something in her face because he stared at her. "You're Brad Melia's wife?"

"I was. Yes." Brad had been well-known in the race circuit, but she was surprised the surgeon remembered him. The accident had been four years ago, after all. Their daughter hadn't quite reached her first birthday when it happened.

"I worked on your husband. We did the best we could, but…" His voice trailed away.

"I know. Thank you again for all you did. I'm just glad Silas is going to be okay."

This time. But what about the next time?

She suddenly realized she couldn't sit around and wait for that next time. She needed a change of scenery. And the timing was perfect, since Cara was getting ready to graduate from preschool at the end of May.

With that seed planted inside her heart, she needed to figure out how to tell her mom she would be taking Cara and moving away. Far away. Away from the memories of Brad's accident, which still flashed across the news from time to time when there was a similar wreck on a nearby racetrack. Away from the constant images of racing that were inevitable in this part of Alabama.

But she would break that news once Silas was well enough to come home. And once her emotions had had a chance to settle. As if that were even possible.

But maybe in a new setting, where there weren't memories of heartache and loss, she'd be able to start over. And to give her daughter a life without turmoil or the complications of a huge publicity machine where reporters just didn't want to let go. And next year would be the five-year anniversary of the great Bradley Melia's untimely death. The interview requests would start coming in, just like they always did. Maybe if she were no longer in the area, they would finally leave her alone and let Brad rest in peace. A peace he had never seemed to find while here on earth. He deserved that. And so did she.

Maybe now they would both have that chance. She would cling to that hope with all she had in her. And prayed she was making the right decision.

CHAPTER ONE

DANE CRIGHTON HAD been doing chest compressions for five minutes straight. He knew that because the newest member of his team kept on giving him a countdown after each minute had passed. Her voice was right in his ear, the headsets necessary to combat the noise of the chopper, but he found it distracting, even though he knew it was standard protocol for their air rescue squad. Most people knew that he wasn't fond of the constant reminders, however. Dane was able to keep a mental countdown that helped him keep track of how long he'd been going.

"Let's switch."

This time he frowned. This was the second time she'd offered to take over, her Southern drawl identifying her as being from a different part of the country. Dane was well aware that CPR fatigue was a real thing, but he worked hard even on his days off to keep himself up to par in the stamina department for just this reason. But it would interfere with his concentration if he had to keep telling her he was fine, especially since this time she hadn't phrased it as a question.

He glanced at her, aware that it was more of a glare before saying, "Okay, switch."

She ignored the pointed look. As if perfectly synchronized, they switched positions, with Dane now on the Ambu bag and the nurse doing compressions. And her rhythm was spot-on. He'd found himself critiquing each and every thing she did. He wasn't sure if it was because she was new or because something about her vaguely irritated him. Maybe it was her self-assurance. Maybe because he'd noticed her in a way that was other-than-professional ever since they'd first been introduced yesterday.

Today, her hair was pulled up in a clip, one dark strand falling free and bouncing to each timed thrust of her hands. Something about that caught his attention and fascinated him, although his mental computer of what they needed to do to save this man's life still worked flawlessly in the background.

Their patient was thirty-four year old Matt Harrison, who'd suddenly collapsed while hiking in a more remote area of Flagstaff with three buddies. One of them had thankfully started CPR immediately while another called 911. Because of the terrain and distance to the nearest hospital, it was decided to airlift him out rather than try to evacuate him by rescue squad.

Dane's gaze flicked to his watch, and because he knew she was expecting that countdown, he said, "One minute."

They'd tried defibrillation and two doses of epinephrine, and they'd gotten him back once, only to have him revert to V-fib.

They were still a few minutes from landing at Flagstaff Memorial, where they could do more diagnostics to try to figure out how to fix the problem. Matt was

young, and Flagstaff's cutting-edge cardiac care unit was his best shot at a decent recovery.

"Two minutes."

He had to admit, the new nurse was making CPR look easy. Her cheeks were flushed, but she kept counting, the numbers sounding as strong as when she'd started.

He squeezed the Ambu bag twice for every thirty compressions and glanced again at his watch. Fifteen seconds left. The second hand slowly moved forward until it was time. "Three minutes. Let's reassess, then switch."

He knew she would immediately agree, as opposed to him. She seemed to be a by-the-books player. Not that this was a game. It was deadly serious.

Just as she stopped compressions, Dane was surprised to hear a blip on the heart monitor. He held his hand up in a signal to wait as his gaze jerked upward to the read-out. Holding his breath, he watched as the familiar cadence of a true sinus rhythm scrolled across the screen. It was followed closely by a couple of chaotic beats, but then seemed to settle back in. When he glanced at his partner for this trip, he saw she was also staring at the monitor. Neither of them moved for close to a minute.

The rhythm stayed in place, and Dane blew out an audible breath, a sense of exhausted relief washing over him. Getting out his stethoscope, he placed it against the patient's chest, even though he knew the odds of the machine malfunctioning were almost nil. The second dose of epinephrine they'd given at the five-minute mark had evidently taken a little longer to act than he'd expected. But at least it had kicked in. Now they just needed to land. And that steady beat needed to stay in place.

As if reading his thoughts, the chopper pilot's voice came through his earpiece, letting them know that they were getting ready to land at the hospital. He saw the nurse's lips move as if praying. Or maybe she was just breathing out a thank-you to the universe. Whichever it was, he sent up one to add to hers just as he felt the helicopter's landing gear touch down on the helipad.

Even before the rotors had finished powering down, a team of three people burst from the doors of the hospital, wheeling a gurney. He recognized one of them as the head of cardiology who had received national recognition for tweaking the way valve replacement surgery was done. He'd transferred from one of the country's top teaching hospitals, saying he'd needed a slower pace for the sake of his family. Dane had overheard the term *silver fox* used by one of the nurses in the ER when talking about the surgeon. But if Jake Norden was aware of those whispers, he gave no sign.

All he knew was that their patient was damned lucky to have landed on Flagstaff's doorstep.

"Hi, Dane. What have you got?"

He gave Jake a rundown on what had transpired as they transferred the patient to the gurney and power-walked back to the hospital. He was vaguely aware that the nurse who'd been on the flight was following behind at some distance as if she felt her part in the patient's care was done. As if relegating herself to a lower spot on the team. But that didn't settle right with him.

"Can you keep me updated on his condition?"

"Sure thing. Thanks." With that, Matt's new team bustled through the door, bypassing the ER and heading

straight to the elevator, where they would undoubtedly go to the cardiac wing on the second floor.

Dane waited at the door, holding it open for the pilot and the nurse, who were walking together, talking about the case. He'd tried to remember her name the whole flight and had come up empty. Something that wasn't like him either.

He could blame it on swearing off relationships after a recent breakup had ended up...well, volatile on his ex's part. But that didn't mean it was okay to brush off niceties, like learning someone's name.

The pilot smiled. "Well, Lou, welcome again to Flagstaff Memorial. It was great working with you."

Ahhh, that was it. Her name was Louise. Or was it Louisa?

"You too. Thanks!"

Chuck, the pilot, nodded at him as he walked by. When the nurse followed, Dane said, "Er... Lou, could I speak with you for a moment?"

Her eyes widened, and a trace of uneasiness entered her gaze. "Sure. Is something wrong?"

Now that he had her attention, though, he wasn't exactly sure what it was he wanted to say. But he gave it his best shot. "No. Everything's fine. I just wanted to thank you for what you did up there."

Her brows went up, and her lips curved slightly. "You mean...for doing my job?"

But that sexy accent held no hint of reproach, so at least she didn't think he was being an ass. At least, he hoped not. He felt one side of his mouth twitch up in response. "I just didn't want to breeze past you without at least saying something. Do you want to grab a coffee?"

And why he'd asked that, he had no idea. He decided to tack on some kind of explanation so she didn't think he was hitting on her. He definitely wasn't. "I don't know about you, but my adrenaline is always pumping after every rescue."

This time she laughed. And that low-throaty sound… something bottomed out in his abdomen.

"So you're going to add caffeine to the mix?" One of her brows arched.

He smiled back. "Doesn't everyone?"

"Not me, but to answer your question, yes. I could go for something, sans caffeine. Is there a cafeteria in the hospital?"

"Yep, just off to our right." They started walking. "Do you prefer Lou? Louise?"

"Lou or Louisa is fine. Most people just call me Lou, though."

"Okay, Lou it is. And you can call me Dane."

"Dane. Sounds good." She glanced at him as they walked. "How long do you normally perform CPR?"

"As long as it takes. Why?"

"No. I mean, do you have a preferred length before you hand off to someone else? I noticed you didn't want to switch that first time. And since we'll probably be working together on runs, if we're both on duty when the call comes in, it would be nice to know."

He'd been kind of gruff the first time she'd offered to step in, and he knew it. "Sorry about that. I can normally do two or three cycles without fatigue setting in."

"I see. Is that what you prefer to do?"

"It is."

They made it to the cafeteria and got in line, which

wasn't as long as it could have been. He ordered an espresso, and Lou ordered a frozen decaf coffee drink. When the attendant asked if she wanted any flavoring in it, she asked if they had mocha.

"We sure do." The young guy behind the counter gave her a brilliant smile, and Dane almost rolled his eyes. He was probably all of eighteen, and Lou had to be at least… He wasn't going to touch that. Not that she looked like she was out of her teens herself, but to become a critical care nurse took a few years. So he was betting she was in her early thirties.

They got their drinks, and Dane sat down at one of the tables that had a view of the San Francisco Peaks in the distance. She glanced out and took a drink of her coffee. "This is so different from Alabama."

Her voice was soft, almost as if she was mulling something over.

"Ahh, that explains your accent. What part of Alabama?" It was normal small talk that usually meant nothing, but he found he was interested. Flagstaff probably did seem different from the Southeast.

"About fifty miles east of Birmingham." This time she looked at him but didn't offer anything more or the name of the actual town.

He didn't want to pry, so he offered up another question instead. "That's quite a journey. How did you decide on Flagstaff Memorial?"

"Actually, I needed a change, and I saw the ad posted in an online nursing journal."

"So you applied."

She smiled again, and this time the curving of her lips hit him somewhere in the midsection, setting off a

warning bell in his head. He needed to be careful. Jana had left a bad taste in his mouth—her expectations of what a relationship should be had been far beyond what he was willing or able to give—and the last thing he wanted was to give off vibes that signaled interest.

"I did. And the rest is history, as they say."

"How do you like it so far?"

"The hospital is great, but Flagstaff itself isn't how I pictured it. I thought there'd be long stretches of desert and hundred-degree temperatures."

"We don't get as hot as other parts of Arizona, but we are in a drought and have been for a while. July usually brings monsoon season, which helps, but it evaporates so quickly that in recent years, it hasn't raised the water levels by a whole lot."

She looked out the window again. "Well, it's beautiful. And…it's not Alabama."

Said as if that were a good thing. But this time, he decided to just let that go without commenting on it.

"Well, I'm glad you like it here."

"I do, so far. We'll see when the school year rolls around if that continues."

When he tilted his head in question, she went on. "My daughter will be starting kindergarten this year. Another reason I thought this was a good time to move."

His eyes went to her left hand. No ring. And the skin on her ring finger wasn't any lighter than the rest of her hand.

Divorced? Or just a single mom?

None of his business. And he'd do well to remember that.

"I see. I hope she likes it." He downed the rest of his espresso in one swallow and set the cup on the table.

"So do I." She gave a shrug with one of her shoulders. "My in-laws weren't super happy about my leaving, but… I just couldn't stay under the circumstances."

So maybe it was a divorce situation. Another reason to be thankful that he and Jana had broken it off before having kids, which she had been pressing for recently. But he hadn't been ready, and he wasn't sure why. Maybe because his own upbringing had been fraught with conflict, his mom doing her best to police his activities and control what sports he could participate in. Just like she'd done with his dad. And Jana…well, she'd given off some vibes that made him wonder what their future would be like. Whatever the reason, he was happy with his life the way it was. And it was certainly different from the corporate life his dad had led. But Dane wasn't interested in sitting behind a desk. He was a self-proclaimed adrenaline junky, and emergency medicine suited Dane's personality to a T. He shook himself back to the present, remembering what he was going to say.

"I'm glad you landed at Flagstaff. You're certainly good at what you do."

"Thanks. It's a little different from my last position, since my former hospital didn't have an air rescue unit. But I talked to a friend who was involved in CareFlight, which is one of the major air ambulance services in my area of Alabama, and she loves it, so I decided to take the plunge."

That surprised him. He assumed that she *had* done it at her last job, since she'd seemed at ease with the con-

fined space and didn't seem nervous about being in the chopper. "You must not mind air travel."

"Air travel, no. But skydiving or anything involving being in the air while outside a plane, yes."

"So no hang gliding or parasailing for you."

"Nope to both of those. You?"

Dane happened to love hang gliding, but he could understand why a lot of people were afraid of the sport, especially here in Flagstaff. The only good launch site was on Mount Elden, and wind conditions and landing could be tricky to navigate. Jana hadn't been thrilled with him going up.

"I've done both and enjoy them."

Something in her face changed. Grew harder, if he was reading her right. But he wasn't sure why that would be. Maybe her ex had been a hang glider?

He didn't even know if she had an ex. She hadn't referred to her in-laws as "former," so maybe she wasn't divorced. Again, not his business.

He decided to try to end their conversation. He needed to get back to the ER anyway. "I'm sure plenty of people will offer, but if you ever have any questions about Flagstaff, feel free to ask. I was born and raised here, so I'm pretty familiar with the ins and outs of the city."

"Thanks, I will. At the moment, though, I need to go and finish out my shift. I'm sure I'll see you around."

"I'm sure you will."

With that, she got up and threw her trash in the receptacle, while he bided his time by pretending to answer messages on his phone so they didn't have to leave together. He wasn't sure why, though. The ICU wasn't on the ground floor, so they wouldn't actually be headed

in the same direction. Maybe it was the way she made him feel off balance, as if he couldn't figure out what she was thinking. Or maybe it was just that damned accent. And the nagging wonder if it deepened while in the midst of...

Oh hell, he'd never find that out, so why did it matter?

It didn't. But now that the thought had been birthed, it was going to be hard as hell to get rid of it. Still he waited until she was out the door before he tossed his own trash and headed back to the emergency department—a place where things were rarely ever dull. Just like hang gliding. Or dirt bike courses.

And that's the way he liked them.

Dirt biking?

Lou had to read the flyer twice before realizing it wasn't some kind of joke. This hospital really did have a fundraiser that involved dirt bikes racing through a course and partway up a mountain. And this was the fourth anniversary of the event.

What were they thinking?

Her eyes widened at what was at the bottom of the flyer. *For more information, please contact Dr. Dane Crighton.*

Dane Crighton. Who also loved hang gliding. Goose bumps broke out across her arms. She could remember the exact second that her husband's car went up in flames. Wasn't dirt biking up a mountain road even riskier than racing around a paved track?

She knew there was a reason she'd sensed nervous energy bouncing around Dane on the chopper and again in the hospital cafeteria.

Maybe he didn't ride in the event. Maybe he just organized it.

The man said he. Loved. Hang gliding. Wasn't that enough reason for her to proceed with caution around him, even if he didn't ride dirt bikes?

What if the bikes referred to in the brochure were simply mountain bikes that used pedal power? Would she be just as scared of that?

Probably not, because there wouldn't be a motor involved. Or speeds that were off the charts.

There wasn't an engine in hang gliding either, and yet she was thinking about how dangerous that was.

They're not asking you to sign up, Lou. It has nothing to do with you.

But it might if she didn't step up and voice her concerns. What if someone was injured or killed?

Like Brad had been?

She'd spoken up with him, too, after a near miss the year before his fatal crash, asking him to give it up, or at least race at safer tracks. He'd looked at her like she'd grown two heads. Like her concerns were of no consequence. She'd been pregnant at the time, but even that argument hadn't swayed him. But at least she'd done what she'd felt led to do.

So maybe she should try to talk to Dane and see what this was about. After all, the brochure had said to address any questions to him. And if that didn't work? Should she go to the hospital administrator?

As a new employee? Did that seem wise? She was still an outsider who probably hadn't earned a right to be heard yet.

Was that something that really needed to be earned? Shouldn't she speak up for what she saw as right no matter if she'd been here one day or ten years?

Maybe she should take a breath and think about it for a day or so. At least until the shock of seeing what was on that flyer wore off. Her previous hospital had sim-

ply had a gala every year. Strapping on a pair of sky-high stilettos was about as dangerous as that event got.

Brad loved seeing me in heels.

A cramp settled in her chest before she quickly shook it off. She couldn't afford to sink into a funk like she'd done the year after her husband's death. Until her mom had reminded her that Cara needed her to be present in her life. That had done the trick. Realizing that her daughter's life was passing by in milestones that couldn't be recaptured had jerked Lou back to reality. And Cara was the only biological child Lou would ever have…and not just because Brad was dead. This was *literally* the only child she would ever give birth to since a complication had meant an emergency hysterectomy minutes after Cara's birth.

And that had been followed by Brad's death a year later.

She would hate for another person to lose a loved one to something that could easily be prevented. So yes, she was going to have a conversation with Dane and see what he said. And if he brushed her off like Brad had?

She didn't imagine he would thank her for bringing her concerns to his attention or asking him to change course and come up with something safer. But at least she'd know that she'd done what her conscience dictated. With that in mind, she started her day in ICU, surprised when Matt Harrison wasn't in his room anymore.

Had he died?

She asked one of the charge nurses. They said that no, he was simply doing so much better that he'd been moved to a regular room after only two days in critical

care, starting out in the cardiac unit and then moving over to ICU.

"That's so great. And fast."

"It was a surprise to us all, actually," said Betsy, a matronly figure with a heart for her patients, from what Lou had seen. "They still haven't figured out an exact cause for his sudden V-fib, so he'll wear a Holter monitor to see if they can catch any abnormalities. And they've ruled out hypertrophic cardiomyopathy. They're going on the assumption of myocarditis at this point, since he had Epstein-Barr a few months ago."

Myocarditis was an inflammation of the heart muscle and could be caused by an infection, like Epstein-Barr. It could be life-threatening without treatment. But judging from how quickly Matt seemed to be bouncing back from his potentially fatal cardiac event, Lou held on to the hope that he would make a full recovery.

"That makes sense. Also why it happened while hiking, since the exertion would have put additional stress on his heart."

Betsy eyed her. "Hey, I know you're new here. Do you want to meet for dinner sometime? I know what it's like to move to a strange place. I did that after my divorce five years ago. I felt lost for a while when I first got to Flagstaff. Then I fell in love with the place. I hope you will too."

Lou hesitated. She didn't know very many people yet, and although Cara was in a daycare program that was highly rated, she wasn't sure she knew anyone well enough to trust them to watch Cara at night. Especially when it wasn't something required for work. "I don't know. My daughter—"

"Bring her with you. I know a great place that's family friendly."

"Are you sure? She can be loud."

"Of course I am. I don't have children of my own, so I always enjoy being around them when I get the chance. I miss my two nieces who still live back home."

Lou bit her lip before saying, "If you're sure you don't mind."

"Not at all. What's her name?"

"Cara. Short for Caralee."

"I love that. Does Cara like pizza?"

"Loves it." She couldn't believe this was happening, that she was getting to go out for dinner with a colleague. "Thank you for offering. Let me know when and where."

"How about Adagios this Friday. It's on the south side of Flagstaff. It's about ten minutes from here."

"Thank you, Betsy, that sounds great, and I'm sure Cara will be thrilled."

"I can't wait to meet her."

Lou entered the date onto her phone along with the place. It felt good to be making connections, since it was something she wasn't always the best at doing. Nor had she needed to be. Brad's fame had meant having more people rooting around in her life than she wanted or needed.

Pushing all of that away, she threw herself into work with a gusto that felt good. She hoped there were more days like today: days where she felt like she belonged and was wanted for herself. Not for her connections to her husband. There were days in the last year of her marriage when she hadn't even felt like she was wanted.

Brad undoubtedly hadn't meant to make her feel like that, but it hadn't changed the reality.

Maybe this would be different. Maybe she would make new friends and adapt to Arizona better than she could have dreamed possible. Maybe her meeting with Dane would go just as well, and he would hear her concerns and take them seriously. She wasn't asking him to cancel the event. She was just...

Well, she kind of would be asking him to. Or to at least modify it and make it something safer. Maybe mountain biking instead. Something where you couldn't go any faster than your feet could pedal.

Thinking about that, it seemed kind of ludicrous, even to her own brain. Mountain bikes could reach speeds that were pretty damned fast.

But all she could do was try. And hope for the best.

Dane was in the middle of transcribing his digital notes when a knock sounded on the door of his office. He pressed Pause, irritated at the continued stream of interruptions. This was the fourth person who'd needed to speak with him, or so they said. Most of those requests could have waited until he was on the floor.

This time, rather than invite the person into his office, he decided to meet them at the door and see if he could avoid a protracted discussion about things like latex allergies. Once someone sat in that chair across from his desk, it had been quite a chore to uproot them again.

Sighing, he opened the door, knowing the frown on his face was not the most welcoming thing, but he couldn't force himself to smile at this point. He'd been

off the clock for the last two hours, and it had seemed impossible to get anything completed in all that time.

He blinked at who it was. It wasn't one of his interns or a nurse with a question about a patient, but Lou Melia. He'd finally looked up her last name on the list of hospital staff. Now it was engraved in his subconscious.

"Lou. Hi. We don't have a run right now, do we?"

"A run?" She looked puzzled before her gaze suddenly cleared. "Oh, you mean a medical run."

"What else would I have meant?"

She shook her head. "Never mind. Do you have a minute?"

He would have sighed again, except he had a feeling that she wasn't here with a simple question that could be answered in the hallway, unless it was about their cardiac case. "Sure. Come on in."

Come to think of it, Lou didn't look all that thrilled to be here. If anything, she seemed apprehensive. Was she opting out of the air rescue unit? She'd mentioned that she hadn't known it was part of the job description until after she'd applied. But she wouldn't need to come to him with that request, although it would make sense that she might think she needed to inform him of her decision since they'd worked together before. Holy hell, he hoped it wasn't due to something he'd said or done.

She sat in the chair across from him, perching on the very edge as if she couldn't wait to get out of there. Her hair was pulled into a high ponytail, but there were several strands that fell around her face as if she, too, had had a long, hard day. Despite that, she was still beautiful.

He blinked. Damn. This day was just getting better and better. First he'd lost a patient who'd been only five.

She'd been unrestrained in the back seat of a car that had hit a guard rail. Then he'd learned that the little girl's dad—who'd been behind the wheel—had been high on meth. It had been a kick to the gut that had ached all day long. Those were the notes he was transcribing, in fact.

"What can I do for you?"

She put a piece of paper on his desk. He glanced at it and realized it was the flyer about the annual fundraiser. Why would she be…

Ahhh, he was the contact person for the event. Last year, it had been the hospital administrator, even though Dane was the one who planned the route and so forth. This year they'd asked him to be the go-to person.

"You want to enter the competition?"

"Me?" The word came out strangled as if that were the last question she'd expected from him. "No. I'm asking you to make it into something different."

He sat back in his chair. "Different. Different how?"

"As in a walking event. Or even a bicycling event."

Okay, that was the first time someone had ever suggested that.

"A…*walking* event." He couldn't prevent the sardonic lift of an eyebrow. "Any particular reason for that?"

"Dirt biking is…well, dangerous."

Oh Lord. How many times had that word been thrown at him during his childhood? Too many times. One of his friends had overheard his mom use that argument about football and had dubbed her the Squasher of Dreams. He hadn't been wrong.

Dane worried that if he ever did become a father, he might let his child take risks that were way out there

just to avoid being like his mom. He eyed Lou with exasperation.

"So is air rescue." He tried to say it in as reasonable a voice as he could. But this was just…

"I know, but…" She seemed to search for the right words. "Is the fundraiser a race?"

"Kind of. As in it's a timed event, but it's more about getting out there and completing the course rather than winning. Like a marathon. Most people run just to complete the event and say they did it. The majority aren't trying to take first place."

She sat there. Maybe she was processing his words. Maybe it wouldn't even matter. He already knew she didn't like hang gliding or things like that. Maybe she was just hypersensitive to her own mortality. But surely she wouldn't try to press others to change because *she* was scared.

Hadn't his mom done just that?

"Has anyone ever been killed doing it?" she asked.

"As in dirt biking? Or as in our event specifically?"

"In this event."

"No. Never. It's not about taking undue chances. It's about completing the course, just like I stated. Has anyone ever been injured? Yes. Just like you can twist an ankle crossing the street. No one has ever been seriously hurt outside of being bruised up. We have pretty strict rules about bike inspections and protective headgear."

"But the course goes up the side of a mountain?"

The exasperation morphed into sheer frustration that made his head feel like it was trapped in a vise that was slowly tightening. "It does, but…listen. Would you like to go see the track for yourself?"

Her brows went up. "Could I?"

Relief washed over him. Okay, maybe this wasn't going to be as bad as it originally seemed. "Yes, absolutely. How about Friday?"

"Yes, that would be…wait. No. Um, I have plans that night."

Did she have plans? Or did she have *plans*? As in with a man. Plans that involved the use of that soft, sweet drawl?

Why did the thought of that make him cringe? Because he was tired and not thinking straight.

She went on. "But maybe we could another day. I'm off on Monday. Are you working then?"

"I am, but only until six in the morning. How about at eight?"

"Could we make it nine?"

So she wasn't an early riser. Something about that thought made him smile. "Sure. Nine it is." It would mean him getting to bed a little later that day after coming off an overnight shift, but he'd done that plenty of other times without any problems.

She breathed a big sigh. "Thank you. It's just that any kind of racing brings back some pretty hard reminders of what can happen."

"You know someone who was hurt dirt biking."

"No. Not dirt biking. And killed. Not hurt."

The gears in his brain kicked to life, spinning. She was from Alabama. East of Birmingham, right? The home of stock car racing. Oh hell, that's why her last name had seemed so familiar. Surely she wasn't… "Are you any relation to Brad Melia?"

She bit her lip hard enough to turn it white. Suddenly

he knew that was exactly it. Exactly why she'd relocated to Flagstaff from Alabama, where one of the most famous NASCAR tracks was. Exactly why the idea of dirt bike racing made her shrink away.

"He was my husband. And yes, that's why I'm concerned about the fundraiser."

"I'm sorry, Lou. I had no idea. He was a great guy."

"Was he? Did you know him personally?" The words were sharp, but then she shut her eyes. "I'm sorry. Of course he was."

He reached over to cover her hand before he could stop himself. "Go with me and see the course. Walk it with me, or better yet, ride it with me. It's nothing like a NASCAR event. The people who come out aren't entering to win. At least, the vast majority of them aren't. They're just there to have fun and have the thrill of completing the course, like I said before. Once you've seen it, then you can talk to me about whether or not you still think it's more dangerous than, say…walking in Central Park after dark. Okay?"

"Okay." She squeezed his hand and then withdrew hers. "And could you avoid telling anyone who my husband was? It's part of the reason I left Alabama. It just hurt to hear his name bandied about in the news every year on the anniversary of his death."

"Of course. I wouldn't dream of it."

"Thank you. And thanks for listening to my concerns. I already feel better about it."

He was glad she did. As for Dane, he suddenly had a lot of concerns. And one of them involved inviting Lou to what he thought of as his mountain. The place he went when he needed to clear his head after a hard

day at work. Where he was thinking of going as soon as he was finished writing this report about a child's unfortunate death.

He wondered if there was anything that would alleviate Lou's concerns. Or how much it would bother him if she still insisted he tweak the event into something completely different.

He wouldn't. It had become much too popular over the past four years to do that without a lot of hell being raised, including by the hospital administrator and board members, some of whom participated in the event every year, as did he.

But he could listen. And maybe help her see things in a different light. One that didn't involve reliving the pain of the past.

Dane hadn't had anyone die, but he had caused a lot of hurt in his family. Hurt that his father had never gotten over until just before his death. But there was nothing he could do about that now. And since his dad was gone, his brother was the sole owner of the family business. Without Dane, there was no backup if something happened. Dane had tried to talk both his dad and Allen into selling the company. They wouldn't hear of it. But Allen let Dane know every chance he got that he should be in there helping him.

But it wasn't what Dane wanted out of life. He didn't want to sit back and play it safe—like his dad had always done—and then wake up one day and wonder where his life had gone. He and his brother would just have to agree to disagree. Because neither of them was willing to change their minds. It looked like that was the way it would have to be.

And as far as Lou went, he'd better stick to a serious hands-off policy. Because after losing her husband like she had, he could imagine she wanted nothing to do with men who flirted with danger. Wasn't that where this concern about the dirt bike race originated? What she needed was a man like his brother. Or even his dad. Men who played it safe no matter what. What she didn't need was someone like Dane who wouldn't be happy sitting on the sidelines, nor did he intend to. Not that she would ever be attracted to him.

So yes. Hands off. He knew that in his head. Now if he could just convince his heart of that before it got him into big, big trouble.

CHAPTER THREE

DINNER WITH BETSY on Friday had been great. It turned out they had a lot in common. Betsy was from Atlanta, so they were both from the South and shared some funny anecdotes about foods that their families ate that others thought were disgusting. Like hot boiled peanuts and greens cooked with bacon. They both even came with local Southern accents. The other difference was that Betsy had divorced an abusive husband and had finally shed his stalking when he started dating another woman, something that she'd had trouble coming to terms with. But a simple background check would show that he'd been convicted of domestic violence and had served three years in prison for what he'd done to her.

So both of them had experienced loss in different forms. And Lou was pretty sure they were going to forge a fast friendship. Which she truly hoped was the case. She'd told Betsy of her concerns about the dirt bike racing. The other woman had listened, nodding periodically. "I'm glad you're going with him to see it. But I do understand why it would concern you. Let me know how things go, okay?"

She'd also offered to watch Cara, which alleviated one

concern right there. She didn't really want her daughter to see her arguing with Dane if it came to that.

So on Saturday, she dropped Cara off at Betsy's apartment, promising she would be back in a couple of hours, to which her friend had replied, "Take your time. We're going to make cookies, if that's okay with you."

"Cookies!" said Cara. "What kind?"

While the pair walked off discussing which type of cookie was their favorite, Lou left to go meet Dane at Flagstaff Memorial. He'd said it would be easier to drive out together than to explain how to reach the site.

Once she got to the hospital, she found his Jeep parked in one of the patient parking areas. The hard top had been removed, leaving the interior open to the sun. She parked next to him, stiffening when she noticed he was towing a trailer with a motorcycle strapped to it. Did he expect her to ride on that thing?

She got out of her car and went over to his. "Um… why do you have that?"

"What?" He said it in a nonchalant tone that told her he knew exactly what she was talking about.

"Never mind." She felt huffy and argumentative, and she wasn't sure why. But she'd told herself she was going to approach this with an open mind, and she needed to hold herself to that.

She got in his vehicle, and they took off down the road west, away from downtown Flagstaff and toward the mountains she'd seen outside the cafeteria window. She had to admit the warm breeze blowing across her face felt good. She was very glad she'd caught her hair up in a clip, though, or it would be whipping around

her head and turning into a giant knot. "Is that where the course is?"

"It's not up the main mountain, but one of the smaller slopes. It doesn't look all that impressive, actually. At least, not to a serious dirt bike enthusiast. But like I said, it isn't meant to be a hardcore course, just a fun time being together and supporting a good cause."

So was Dane one of those serious dirt bike enthusiasts who preferred hardcore courses? She didn't ask because she was pretty sure she didn't want to know the answer to that question. But then again, really…what was it to her if he were? He was a grown man who could make his own decisions.

Like Brad was?

And that was the problem. Yes, she'd let Brad make his own decisions. But those decisions had come at a great cost. In some ways, she was still angry at him. She'd heard anger was part of the grieving process, but how long was too long to stay mad at someone who wasn't here to talk things through with? Who wasn't here to defend his decisions?

Is that why she was here asking Dane to defend his decisions? To explain why he was promoting an event that she felt was dangerous? It was a hospital, for heaven's sake. If this were truly a huge risk, wouldn't the powers that be shut it down?

She felt a little silly now that she had time to think it through. And the fact that the ER doctor was using his time off to basically prove himself to her made her feel guilty. He'd been on duty all night from the sound of it.

"Hey, if you don't want to do this, you don't have to."

He glanced at her. "Do what?"

"Take me out to the site."

"We're already on our way." He smiled. "Besides, I have a feeling that the only way to make you feel better about it is to show you what it's all about."

So far it wasn't working. If anything, she felt worse.

The fact that Dane hadn't just brushed her off and told her to mind her own business was a credit to him.

She studied him under her lashes, taking in his strong profile with its deep groove down his cheek, the long fingers that wrapped around the steering wheel and gripped it. The way his dark hair, with its light sprinkling of gray, was pushed off his forehead in a casual way, the wind causing it to ruffle. He looked tanned and healthy and completely at ease. Unlike Lou, who felt like she was wound so tight she could explode at any moment.

He caught her looking and frowned. "Too much wind?"

And if she said yes? There was really nothing he could do about it now. "No. It actually feels good. And maybe I needed to have some cobwebs blown away."

"I very much doubt that. I can't see you sitting around waiting for them to gather."

"Ha! Sometimes they gather whether you sit around or not."

They rode in silence for another five minutes or so, and then Dane pulled into a large cleared area at the base of one of the mountains. There was a sign that read Cinder Hills OHV Area.

"OHV?" she asked.

"Off-highway vehicles. It includes ATVs, dirt bikes, Jeeps, and other vehicles that are made to go off-road."

"And your motorcycle?"

"It's heavier than a dirt bike. But I brought it to show you around a little bit. It can tackle most of the flat areas safely. And it'll give you an idea of what's possible." He smiled. "The key word here is *safely*. Don't worry. I won't do anything crazy with you on board."

"On board? What does that mean."

"Pretty much what it implies." He lobbed another grin at her.

Her stomach twisted. "If you're planning to go fast, count me out."

"Safely. Remember?"

"Good to know, since I do have a daughter to think about."

"I did take her into consideration." He turned left into a parking lot. "We can unhook the trailer and take my Jeep up to the trail instead, if it'll make you feel better."

It would. But if she was truly here to assess what the course was like, wouldn't it be better to experience it on two wheels? Probably, but her nerves were now kicking in, and suddenly she wasn't sure of anything.

"It's safe to ride double on the course?"

He reached over and covered her hand, his fingers warm and reassuring. "Safer than driving through the streets of Flagstaff. And we won't do the uphill portions. I'll take it slow and easy, okay?"

Something about the deep timbre of his voice as he murmured that promise made her stomach slip sideways again. In a completely different way this time. In a way that made her wonder what slow and easy with him would be like.

She shook that dangerous thought away and somehow managed to squeak out the word "Okay."

He must have taken that to mean she was completely nervous, because he covered her hand with his and gave it a light squeeze before switching off the vehicle and pocketing the keys. Then they got out, and she watched as Dane unhooked the strapping that held the motorcycle on the trailer. It was smaller than the kind of touring motorcycle she'd expected him to have, but maybe that was because it needed to be lighter to handle off-road conditions. Truth be told, she knew very little about motorcycles. In the early days of her and Brad's courtship, she'd ridden on his bike with him and had thought it was okay, although she'd never been totally at ease with it, since he'd always felt a need for speed. But after they got married and he became a household name in the racing industry, his main goal in life had become retaining that status. He took chances that seemed unnecessary, and they'd begun arguing about it on a regular basis. She'd hoped her getting pregnant would help in that area, but it didn't seem to make a difference. At any rate, she no longer wanted to ride his bike with him, and he'd finally sold it.

Dane set the bike on its kickstand, then opened a compartment at the front of the trailer, taking out two helmets. "I have a leather jacket in here if you want one."

Her nerves kicked in all over again. If he was planning on taking it slow and easy, why the need for all the protective gear? Although the helmets were understandable. Or maybe it was the thought of wearing something that had his scent clinging to it that was making her insides knot in a way that had nothing to do with fear. It was becoming an all-too-common occurrence around

him, and she needed to make it stop. Somehow. She just wasn't sure how to do that.

She'd survived life with a man who loved being in the danger zone. She didn't think she could go through that again. With anyone.

"I'm good without your jacket." She hadn't come dressed for a motorcycle, but she did have on some rugged shoes that were good for hiking as well as jeans and a T-shirt. Was she really going to get on that thing with him?

Evidently, since she hadn't screwed up the courage to tell him no. So she was just going to have to sit back and hope it didn't last too long. Except a tiny part of her knew that was a lie. She was afraid she might want it to last longer than was strictly necessary. Maybe even long enough to plant his scent deep into her skull, where she could revisit it from time to time.

Oh God, she was in trouble. Deep deep trouble.

The second she settled in behind him and Dane felt her arms wrap around his waist, he knew he'd made a tactical error. He'd brought the vehicle half as a joke, thinking she'd refuse to get on. But she hadn't, even though it was clear she was nervous as hell about it. He told her the truth. He was very aware of the fact that she had a child, but holding to that truth, he would have been just as careful with her if she didn't have one. He'd brought her here to reassure her, and he wasn't about to take chances that he didn't need to take.

"You've been on a bike before, right? So you know how to move with me?"

There was silence for a split second before her shaky voice came back. "I have, but it's been a while."

"Just put your feet up and relax." As soon as he said the words, a mental image appeared that he couldn't erase. And he hoped to hell she hadn't caught his gaffe.

"They are up. But as far as relaxing, I can do that after we're done."

The sexy image in his head squelched into oblivion.

"Here we go." He put the bike in gear and released the brake, and off they went. He kept his speed as slow as he could without putting them at risk of falling over and rode on the lower portion of the trail. Her arms tightened around him as they went into the first turn, a gentle curve that was tame. This part was pretty wide open, so he was able to swing around and rework the same portion of the trail. His helmet had a mic and receivers so he could talk to whomever was riding tandem, not that he often took women with him. "Okay so far?"

She pressed closer as if startled to hear his voice. Then she responded. "Yes. Doing fine."

He took the next curve, and they continued on their way, picking up a little speed. There was just one other car in the lot, and so far, Dane hadn't seen anyone else on the trail. The first switchback came up, and he took the curve smoothly. She moved with him in a testament to the fact that she had indeed been on a bike.

With whom? Her late husband?

A sliver of some unidentified emotion crawled under his skin before he could stop it.

Dane could understand why she might be fearful of anything that involved chances, though, so he continued to take things slow and easy. The day of the race, there would undoubtedly be a few hotdoggers—people who wanted to show off for the crowd—but there were

strict rules about keeping your distance from other riders and always giving a wide berth when passing fellow participants. So far they hadn't had a problem. There were contingencies in place if anyone got out of hand. But he'd told Lou the truth. This fundraiser was more like a big picnic gathering than anything else.

They had a few more turns to go through before the next portion of the trail began, along with an uphill climb. So he kept to the course, and as soon as he saw the terrain change, he slowed the bike and stopped. "We'll go on foot from here since there's a scattering of hills before it begins to truly climb."

When she didn't let go of him, he frowned, wondering if she was frozen in fear. "Everything okay back there?"

"Oh, yes, sorry." She took her hands off his abdomen and scrambled off the bike, waiting as he turned the machine off and put down the kickstand.

Then he turned to look at her. She was fumbling with the strap under her chin, and her hands were shaking. His frown grew, and he reached for the buckle and popped the snap open. Then he eased the protective gear from her head and looked at her.

She'd said she was okay, but she didn't look that way, and her blue eyes met his only to jerk away again. He stowed her helmet and then reached for her hands. "You don't have to ride back. We can walk."

"I'm okay. Seriously. It's just nerves. But it's not nearly as bad as I thought it might be."

He studied her face. A wash of color marked both of her cheeks, and she still wouldn't quite meet his gaze. "Was your last experience on a bike a bad one?"

She shook her head. "No, it was just…it's complicated. And a very long story."

In other words, she didn't want to talk about it. He got it. Jana had ridden with him a time or two, but she seemed bored by the whole experience, so it ended after the second run. And he'd never felt her press her cheek to his back the way Lou had done, as if she couldn't get close enough.

It had made him a little shaky himself.

Realizing he was still holding her hands, his right thumb stroking over the soft skin he found there, he let her go under the pretext of unbuckling his own helmet and stowing it away. He then pocketed the keys. If he hadn't had his helmet on, he might have been tempted to kiss her. That realization shook him more than the ride itself had.

He shook himself back to reality. Hands off…remember?

"Are we going to leave your motorcycle here? Couldn't someone steal it?"

"We're not going far. And they'd have a tough time getting it out of here without a trailer nearby."

He'd originally chosen this course because it was one of the easiest in the area. Enough that even a novice should be able to complete it with care. The flyer urged participants to travel the course at least once and told them that the safety of everyone was of the utmost importance. That folks should just come and have fun. There were no prizes given for time placements, but everyone did receive a commemorative patch for participating.

"I just want to walk up the next hill so you can see

what the rest of the course will be like. The trail loops around and then travels back over the same path we came in on."

"The trail is a lot wider than I thought it would be."

"Yes, it's so folks can pass each other when coming from opposite directions. And the course is long enough that there shouldn't be large clumps of people all vying for the same space. Come on, I'll show you."

They walked a couple of hills and then up the first section of the climbing portion of the course, which let out on another flat section. They stopped and looked over the trails.

"I have to admit, this is nothing like I thought it would be. No cliffs or obstacles someone would have to jump over."

"There are trails that have both of those things, but I never would have selected one of them for something like this. Feel better about it?"

"I do. I may have jumped to conclusions."

"Understandable under the circumstances." What circumstances were those? That she'd lost her husband to an accident on a racecourse? Maybe. He could see how that might color her perceptions of anything that had the word *race* attached to it. But the reality was that this event wasn't intended as a race, and the brochure's wording had been carefully scripted to get that fact across. But even the Boston Marathon, while not mentioning it was a race in the title, could still be perceived as one. And there was still a "winner"—the person who crossed the finish line first.

She glanced at him. "It's probably the way I'm wired. I'm a cautious person by nature."

So was his mom. And yet Lou had married a stock car driver and even though she didn't know about the air rescue when she got the job, she stayed with it even after she found out.

"I don't know that I would classify you as cautious."

"You might be surprised. I am. I'm constantly second-guessing the decisions I make about my daughter's safety, knowing that being too protective can sometimes be as damaging as being too permissive. There has to be a balance. And I don't feel like I've achieved that yet."

"I'm sure most parents feel that way." Hadn't Dane himself been worried about being a too-permissive parent as a reaction to his own upbringing?

"I suppose so. But because of Brad—her father—I know I'm more likely to keep her from doing things that are the slightest bit risky."

"I can understand that."

Could he really? He had no idea what life for her had been like in the aftermath of her husband's death. But whatever it had been, it was enough to make her hyper-careful. The way she'd clung to him on that motorcycle could probably be chalked up to that, whereas many men—him included—might assume she was just trying to get closer. It made him see her cheek pressing into his back in a whole new way. Which meant he too needed to be careful around her, and to try to see things through her filter.

Which would be pretty damned impossible, since his mom had also been vigilant of their safety. She'd constantly questioned her husband's water hobbies, like diving. And when Dane's adventurous nature had presented itself as he reached his teenaged years, she'd relentlessly

nagged him about being careful. It had probably sent Dane in the other direction. Rather than reining that side of him in, he'd let it off the leash. Sometimes way off the leash.

He glanced at Lou. "You ready to head back?"

Thinking about his childhood wasn't going to do him any good. His dad was gone—dying of cancer nearly five years ago—and his mom had sold their home and moved into a huge fifty-five plus village less than a year later. Her life was simple…and safe. Everything she could possibly want or need, from grocery stores to programmed activities, could be found on the streets of that village. It was up to Dane to go visit her, since she rarely ventured out of that community. And he almost never shared aspects about his life with her, as it would only cause her to be anxious.

"Yes. Thanks for bringing me out to see it."

"Do you feel better about it?"

"I do now."

He had no idea if she was just saying that because she thought it was what he wanted to hear or if she was being sincere. But for now, he was going to take her at her word.

And if Dane knew what was good for him, he was going to keep his distance. As much as their job allowed, anyway. Because he felt like he had just opened Pandora's box. Attraction and warning swirled in a misty dance that could spell disaster. And as much as he might want to stuff it all back inside and slam the lid shut, he wasn't sure it was possible. So right now he was going to ignore it. And only when that became impossible to do would he stop and deal with it.

CHAPTER FOUR

LOU WAS PRETTY sure she'd ticked Dane off somehow during their jaunt to Cinder Hills. He'd been charming and communicative on the trip there and during their ride on his bike. He'd also seemed at ease as they'd stood looking out over the view. But once they headed back to Flagstaff, he'd seemed quiet and moody, becoming almost a different person. And she had no idea why. The relief she'd felt in knowing that the course wasn't overly dangerous wasn't reflected in Dane's attitude as they got closer to the hospital.

And when he pulled up next to her vehicle, it was as if he could barely wait until she got out. She'd thanked him again, leaning down to look in the window, making an attempt at a smile only to have him nod and tell her it wasn't a problem, asking if she needed anything before he headed out.

She refrained from saying she needed an explanation, deciding it probably wouldn't do her any good. And maybe his long shift had finally caught up to him.

But when she passed him at work the next day, he'd barely acknowledged her, looking like he was in a big hurry. It made her feel like he wanted to be anywhere but where she was.

It was unsettling, but she had no idea how to ask him about his behavior without turning something that might be nothing into a big deal. So she just let it go and did her job.

Betsy asked her how things went when Lou picked Cara up, and she shrugged. "I'm not sure. I thought it was going well. And then changed my mind. I don't know if I'm just overthinking the trip or what. But he got really quiet on the way back."

"Did anything happen?"

"Not that I know of, but..." Her left shoulder hiked up again.

"Maybe he's interested in you and isn't sure how to approach it."

Lou couldn't hold back a laugh. "That definitely wasn't the vibe I got. I'm going to just assume he was tired. He'd just come off a night shift, and we went straight out to the course."

"I bet that was it." Betsy paused. "He did get out of a relationship a few months ago. But I have to say he probably dodged a bullet with that one."

Lou didn't ask what she meant by that. She didn't have to. It was pretty obvious that her friend wasn't a fan of whoever the woman was. And maybe that was it. Maybe he'd thought Lou might be interested in him for some reason and had done his best to shut her down. Well, there were no worries on that front. She had no interest in getting into another relationship right now. Especially with Cara added to the mix. And the fact that Dane reminded her a little of Brad didn't help. In the early stages of their romance, he'd been so attentive and loving, but then as he got more and more involved

in racing, she'd seemed to become an afterthought, especially when she questioned the risks he began taking to stay at the top of his game.

The arguments had been draining and awful, and Brad had started drinking more, both after his races and at home.

She didn't see that side of Dane, but the quick flip-flop in his attitude had reminded her of her late husband. One minute happy and the next inscrutable and broody with long periods of silence.

She sighed and tucked the sheet around one of her patients, giving her a smile and a reassuring pat on the arm. "Is there anything you need?"

Dorothy Tucker, a sixty-five-year-old patient who'd had a massive stroke less than twenty-four hours ago that had left her unable to speak and paralyzed on her left side, shook her head. It was touch and go, and as much as Lou wanted her to make it, Dorothy had to want to live. Right now, it just seemed like she didn't. And there was nothing Lou could do to force that on Dorothy or anyone. So she pressed the call button in the woman's right hand, holding it up so she could see it.

"I'm just a call away, okay?" And although she had several patients right now and was stretched pretty thin, she added, "Even if you just want to see a friendly face."

Dorothy's eyes watered, and one side of her mouth moved, but nothing came out.

"It's okay. Just give it some time." There was no guarantee she would regain any function, but Lou had told her the truth. It was still early. And she'd been given a clot-busting drug that had done its job. Now it was a waiting game to see if the affected areas of her brain

would recover or if they'd been deprived of oxygen for too long. But she'd been healthy and active up until the clot, so hopefully she could overcome this.

Betsy opened the door. "Lou, you have a call. Go. I'll finish up here."

She nodded and squeezed her patient's hand again. "Betsy will take good care of you."

Then she was off, racing down the hall toward the helipad. Their hospital had kind of a unique setup where available staff were matched to the situation at hand. A heart attack would sometimes get a cardiologist if one was available. If not, an ER doc would be pulled. She could only hope it wouldn't be Dane this time. But if it was, she was going to do her job to her best ability, and if he had a problem with her, he could just get over it.

Of course when she saw him push through the door ahead of her, her stomach sank. She might have given herself a pep talk, but the reality of seeing him had made her heart jolt in her chest.

She hesitated for the briefest second before shoving the door open and moving with swift feet toward the chopper, whose rotors were already beginning to spin.

Thankfully that meant they would be on their way. Due to their headgear, the mics would be open between both them and the pilot, so there would be no personal talk on the trip, which was fine with her. She climbed into her seat and nodded at Dane before strapping in and putting on her headgear.

Dane spoke, giving them a rundown on what they would find. A head-on collision on I-40 had stopped all eastbound traffic. There was one injury that was deemed life-threatening and in need of a medical evac-

uation. "Wind conditions?" The question was aimed at their pilot, who was the same one from their last run.

"I should be able to get you down without a problem. They've cleared the highway near the accident."

"Good."

Within five minutes, they were there. She jumped off first, followed by Dane. Police and EMTs were on the scene and were working with several injured people at once. They were directed to a patient who was still in a vehicle, whose door had been pried open with the jaws of life. Inside, Lou caught sight of a female patient slumped over the wheel.

One of the EMTs was next to her, taking vitals, although there was no sign that she was conscious. "What have we got?"

Dane's voice rose above all the noise around them.

"Looks like the airbag failed to deploy or was disabled. Steering wheel caught her in the chest. Respiration is depressed. We haven't moved her yet because we knew you guys were en route."

"Get the back brace."

Although he'd voiced it as an order, Lou wasn't offended. There often wasn't time for niceties on these runs. She hurried back and got what she knew she'd need and came back to join Dane. Together with the EMT, they eased the accident victim back in her seat, and the ER doc cut her shirt to see what they were dealing with.

"Dammit!"

The second the word was voiced, she saw why. Paradoxical breathing was clearly evident across three ribs on her left side. When the patient breathed in, instead of those ribs moving outward, they sank due to the pres-

sure difference. It was a life-threatening condition because the ribs could easily pierce a lung and cause air to be trapped in the abdominal cavity. A pneumothorax, which no one wanted to see.

She glanced at him, waiting to see what he wanted to do. "Let's get her braced and out of the car."

It was a hard and awkward job with three of them working within a limited space while trying not to do anything that might further compromise the patient's breathing.

Soon the patient was on the ground with the back brace beneath her. The compromised rib area was already turning dark, and the fractured areas were moving independently of the rest of the chest wall.

"Pulse ox is eighty-four. We need to get that up."

Which meant they were going to intubate. Since trying to do that in flight was difficult due to space constraints and the movement of the aircraft, they would need to do it here on the ground.

Lou got the equipment ready and then handed Dane the endotracheal tube. He moved to the woman's head. Tilting it back, he slid the tubing smoothly into place, and she handed him tape to keep it there. Then she hooked up an Ambu bag to the tube and started respirations.

Either the patient's lung tissue was bruised and was impeding the exchange of oxygen, or there was already a pneumothorax in play from a punctured lung. They would soon know.

"It's inching up. At eighty-seven. Eighty-eight. Let's get her in the air."

An EMT took one end of the gurney, Dane took the

other, and they started moving her toward the helicopter. Lou kept squeezing the bag, an internal count going on to keep everything steady and even. Two minutes later, they were inside and had secured both the gurney and the patient to the floor of the aircraft. Then they lifted off and raced toward the hospital.

While flying was always inherently dangerous, Lou didn't pause to think about that when she was working. She was too busy trying to help save someone's life. And this was one kind of race that she wanted to win—so maybe she was like Bradley in that way. But this wasn't for glory. This was for someone else's good. And she loved her job. Always had. Even the flying part, which was still new to her.

The trip hadn't required any talking other than about their patient, and for that she was glad. At least she knew that she and Dane could still work together effectively. And if that ever changed?

She glanced at the doctor as he continued to monitor the accident victim. His hair fell over his forehead in a way that made her fingers itch to push it back. To take her mind off it, she said, "Did you get a name on her?"

She was sure they must have that info, but she'd been so busy trying to get things ready that she'd somehow missed it.

"Jenny Carter, age thirty-six."

The clinical way he said it made her jerk her attention back to the doctor. But he didn't even glance her way. So he was still giving her the cold shoulder? Or was he simply too busy to pay attention to anything other than their patient?

She wasn't sure, but she was now doubting her earlier

thoughts about being able to work with him. Maybe she needed to actually talk to him and see what was going on. And if he wouldn't tell her? Then that was on him. She was willing to reach out first and try to put whatever had happened behind them. But if he wasn't open to that, then she was going to continue on as she normally did. She was not going to change the way she did business with people.

Why? Because she'd learned that it didn't help anything. She'd tried everything she could think of with Brad, and in the end, it had changed nothing. The angst she'd felt over that had made her physically ill. It affected how she behaved around Cara when she was an infant—not letting her own child get past the wall of armor that she'd erected around herself. It had taken her mom to help her realize that no matter what was going on between her and Brad, Cara needed her desperately.

So she was not going through that again. She was not going to let another person change how she related to those around her. She couldn't. For her sake and for the sake of her daughter.

They landed, and then there was the rush to get the patient into the ER, with a team surrounding them. Each member knew their assigned task and did it without hesitation. Soon they had Jenny stable enough to send her down to imaging, and a surgical suite was being readied to repair her damaged ribs and any other injuries that might need tending to.

She and Dane stood aside as they wheeled the patient down the hall. He glanced at her and started to move away, but she put a hand on his arm to stop him. "Do you have a minute?"

His eyes shut for a brief second before reopening. "Sure. What do you need?"

"Coffee. Right now I need coffee. How about you?"

For a few tense seconds, she thought he might refuse. Then he nodded. "Coffee it is."

They walked in silence in the direction of the cafeteria. And now she was second-guessing this decision as well. How often would they actually be called on to work together? Maybe not that often, but today had proved excruciating. She'd been very aware of him on every level. Enough to interfere with her work? Maybe not today, but if it got worse, it might. And if it was something she could fix, then wasn't it better to tackle it now?

They got their coffee, then went outside onto a terrazzo that featured a clay-tiled floor and colorful sailcloths to provide shade over the seating areas. There was also a tiled pathway that meandered through the stuccoed space, past drought-loving plants and a small prayer chapel where patients' loved ones could go for peace and solitude away from the noise and busyness of the hospital.

Dane moved to one of the concrete tables scattered through the main courtyard and set his coffee down, waiting for her to join him on the bench. She did, not quite sure how to begin, but knowing it was something she needed to do. She'd only been here a week but had been hoping to settle into the area for years to come. So the sooner she dealt with this, the better.

"Have I done something to offend you?"

Her question didn't take him by surprise, although he'd hoped she hadn't noticed the way he'd tried to dis-

tance himself from her after their trip to Cinder Hills. But obviously she had, and for that he was sorry. Especially since he'd been just as aware of her on their run today. Every move she made reminded him of the way her arms had wrapped around him on their bike ride, which had been relatively quick in the scheme of things. And it wasn't fair to her.

He was an adult. He should be able to manage his impulses and feelings better than that. But ever since Jana, he'd been cautious. Very cautious.

Which was pretty funny, since Lou had basically accused him of being reckless before their trip to the park to see the course. Now she'd come around to seeing things his way—at least more than she had before—and he'd gone in the opposite direction.

"You haven't. I've just been preoccupied with things at work." Which was true. Especially since she was part of that work.

"Are you sure? Because you seemed to change halfway through the trip to Cinder Hills. I just assumed…"

Obviously it had bothered her. A lot, since days later she'd decided to talk to him about it. If he told her it had nothing to do with her, he'd be lying, and that was one thing he'd always prided himself on: being honest whenever he could. Even if it hurt.

"I could tell you were nervous when you were on my bike, and I don't want you to think I plan to make that a regular part of our interactions." Okay, so that was technically true. But he was walking a line here that could be easily crossed. Because the real unvarnished truth was that having her pressed against his back in those moments had done a number on him.

Her head tilted, and she studied him for a moment as if she didn't really believe him. "Of course I don't. Although I wouldn't mind taking my daughter up there. I think she would absolutely love the scenery."

"You want to take her dirt biking?" That shocked him.

She laughed, her nose crinkling in a way that made something hum low and deep in his midsection. That crazy sense of awareness. And the thought that maybe she wasn't as fearful of risks as he'd first thought. After all, she was part of an air ambulance service, wasn't she?

"Let's not get carried away. I've never even driven a dirt bike or any other motorized two-wheeled vehicle, for that matter."

"It's not that hard. If you can balance on a normal bike, you can balance on a dirt bike." The words were out before he could stop them. And they carried the hint of an invitation that he hoped she hadn't caught.

"Are you sure about that?" One of her brows went up, and she smiled again, the act carrying just as much kick the second time as it had the first.

"I am. And I'm prepared to prove it."

She blinked. And he couldn't blame her. Because this time the invitation wasn't just implied. He'd thrown it into the universe as if it were a kid's ball. Only this wasn't some child's game. This could turn into the very disaster he'd been hoping to avoid.

He could mitigate the damage by offering to give her the name of a driving school that offered motorcycle lessons and pretend that had been all he'd meant by his comment. But then there was that whole lying thing again.

In all honesty, Lou hadn't shown any romantic interest in him. Even now, she was talking to him in a way that she'd probably talk with any other human being, male or female. She was just being friendly. And kind. He'd seen that in her treatment of their patients. Maybe she just didn't like being on the outs with anyone and wanted to make sure things were okay between them. Were they?

He didn't think so, but right now, he couldn't think of a way to remedy that situation. Unless… Going back to that hill might not be the worst idea he'd ever had.

"You don't have to do that. I'd probably be a terrible student, anyway."

"I doubt that. My dirt bike is a lot smaller than my motorcycle and would be easier for you to manage. It would also be a good vehicle to learn on."

"Would we go back to Cinder Hills?"

"That would probably be the easiest place to learn, honestly. And a lot more forgiving than asphalt, if you did happen to fall."

"Are bicycles allowed in the area?"

So maybe she was going to chicken out after all. That would probably be for the best. "They are."

"Could I meet you there and bring my daughter—and our bikes?"

A few of his muscles relaxed, making him realize how tense he'd been about her agreeing to his offer. "I'm sure she would love it."

And a child would also provide a good buffer between them. Or at least a good buffer to keep him from noticing things about her, like that megawatt smile. And that slow Southern drawl. Well, he might still notice those

things, but he'd be less likely to act on anything if there did happen to be a "moment."

"And I wouldn't mind trying to ride your dirt bike, if you're game."

"I am." He couldn't stop a smile at the way she pronounced the word *game*. The *a* came out more like a long *i* sound than anything. He found himself mentally trying to reproduce the sound and failing.

Hell, her words—accent or no accent—probably had more to do with trying to rebuild the bridge he'd purposely set aflame the last time they'd been at Cinder Hills than any real desire to ride his bike. But in a way, she was right. It would be hard to work as a team if he was doing everything in his power to keep them from getting too close. Physically, emotionally, or any other way.

So maybe instead of worrying about it, he should allow himself to get involved, just like he would in the life of any other colleague. Or any other friend. And then trust that nothing else would happen. Even if he might secretly entertain hopes that it would.

CHAPTER FIVE

CARA WAS MORE excited than Lou had seen her since moving to Arizona. And it was all because of Dane. She'd done the right thing, hadn't she? By confronting him and trying to improve the atmosphere between them?

She hoped so. In the week since they'd had their talk, they'd had two more runs together, and he'd seemed so much more relaxed than he had for their flail chest patient, who'd not only survived but had asked to meet the medevac team who'd worked on her. Dane, Lou and Chuck, their pilot, made time to meet with her in her room the day she was being discharged from the hospital. They didn't always have the chance to do this with patients, but it helped make it all worthwhile. And made Lou even more relieved that Dane seemed to have gotten past whatever was bothering him. Even if she still didn't know exactly what that had been.

She and Cara arrived at Cinder Hills to find it empty of all but a couple of cars. And neither one of them was the Jeep that she'd ridden in the last time they'd come here. She glanced at her smartwatch.

They were five minutes late, actually, and there was no sign of him. She checked her phone to see if he'd

texted and found it quiet except for a text from her mom, reminding her that Silas had a race today and to wish him luck. She closed her eyes. She'd moved here to forget about all of that, but it seemed she was destined to be reminded of everything over and over again. And instead of wishing her brother luck, all she wanted to do was beg him not to race again. Not to become another statistic.

Except not everyone did. If they did, the racing industry wouldn't be what it was today. Most drivers lived to see another day. Including Silas. In fact, lots of drivers spent their whole careers climbing out of their cars unscathed year after year.

The ones that were the most vulnerable were the ones who were willing to risk it all—even their lives—chasing the next win. That had been Brad.

But not Silas. At least, not yet. She could only hope his accident had made him more circumspect. And their mom did worry. Silas knew that. Hopefully it would matter enough to make him think hard before taking too many chances. But just in case...

She pulled out her phone and sent her brother a message, wishing him good luck and telling him to be careful. The same message she sent every time he ventured out onto that track. She waited. Normally he responded right away with some kind of quip to lighten the mood. But this time there was nothing. Was he already in the midst of the race?

Just then a familiar Jeep pulled up, towing a trailer with what looked like a much smaller version of his motorcycle. It was bright red like his other bike, but far

less intimidating. This must be what he'd called a dirt bike, earlier.

She held Cara's hand while Dane got out of the vehicle and said hello, kneeling down to the child's level to introduce himself. The act made something in her chest melt.

She forced herself to address him, sneaking a glance at her phone once more and finding nothing that made the worry in her stomach kick up another notch. "I'll unload our bikes if you want to do what you need to do."

She was having second thoughts about bringing Cara, especially when Dane's dirt bike was involved. But to *not* bring her would be giving in to her fear. And despite her cautious nature, she didn't want to protect her daughter so much that she made her afraid of everything.

You mean like you, Lou?

Dane got up, winking at Cara and telling her he'd be right back.

Lou busied herself with opening the hatch of her little car and pulling her bicycle and a smaller one from the interior and setting them nearby along with their bike helmets. Cara's training wheels had been removed last year, but she hadn't ridden in six months. Lou wanted to review the steps with her before allowing her child to get on.

And maybe she should remind herself of the steps on how to keep their relationship friendly but impersonal when it came to dealing with Dane. She was glad things were better between them. But she didn't want to cross that line and make things too good. Or she would be in worse trouble than she'd been before. Yes, she wanted to introduce Cara to experiences that were outside Lou's

comfort zone, but getting involved with Dane wasn't one of those experiences. If Cara got too attached, she could be hurt even if it wasn't either adult's intention.

Dane unloaded his dirt bike, then opened the back hatch to his Jeep and surprised the hell out of her by bringing out a bicycle of his own. An actual no-motor-involved bicycle. A sliver of pleasure went through her. That was incredibly thoughtful of him. It meant that he was thinking about Cara and wanting to include her in this venture.

Even Brad had rarely...

No. She couldn't change the past, and he'd been a new father at the time. She'd like to think that he would have made the time to be with his daughter if he'd lived long enough to see her as she was today.

And she wasn't here to compare Dane to her late husband. That wouldn't help anyone.

Still, she couldn't hold back a smile. "Wow, so you have a motorcycle, a dirt bike *and* a bicycle? Do you own a yacht too?"

"Yes, but it's currently parked in Florida."

For a split second, she thought he was serious, until she saw that line in his cheek deepen. She laughed. "You had me going for a second."

"I've never actually been to Florida. But maybe someday."

"What? You've never been to Florida?" Maybe it was because she'd lived just a few hours away from some of the most pristine beaches in that state, but she sometimes forgot that her new town was a long way from any ocean.

"Nope. I was born and raised in Flagstaff, remember?"

Said as if he'd never ventured outside his own hometown, and she doubted very much that was the case. He was an adventure-seeker.

"You really should go sometime. The panhandle has some of the clearest water in the United States. It's gorgeous."

"Hopefully I'll get there one day."

Even though she'd been born and raised in Alabama, she'd traveled to various parts of the United States, mainly due to Brad's racing schedule.

"I hope you do. I think you'd love it."

"Probably." He nodded at the dirt bike. "So, what do you want to do first? Ride our bicycles over the terrain? Or learn a new skill?"

She was trying to figure out how she was going to do that when Cara was right here. Not that she didn't think her daughter would stay still and let her try to ride the dirt bike, but she also didn't want to make this all about her. She wanted Cara to have fun too.

"Do you want to ride first?" She kept her voice low, addressing her daughter.

"Are you going to learn to ride that?" Cara pointed at the motorbike.

"I want to try. But don't worry, we're still going to ride our bikes."

"Can I try too?"

That was one thing she'd been afraid of. That her daughter would want to copy her. But at least she'd thought of what to say ahead of time. "Not until you're

a few years older and are really good at riding your own bike. You have to practice."

Okay, so she'd handled that the right way, yes? She hadn't ruled out dirt bikes altogether. She'd just made it conditional to doing something else first.

"Okay." The sudden defeated slump of shoulders made Lou laugh.

"Don't worry, honey. The years will go by faster than you can imagine." Something Lou needed to keep in mind as well. Because she could not have another biological child, and she wasn't sure she would ever have any more kids, whether through adoption or foster care. That meant she didn't want to rush through Cara's stages of childhood. Because she'd told her daughter the truth. Once gone, those years would never come back again. For either of them.

Dane wheeled his dirt bike over. "Why don't we let your mom try this out, and then we can all ride our bikes on the course here."

Lou frowned at him. "Do you think it's too advanced for her?"

"It's pretty beginner-friendly."

While the track had seemed easy enough the last time they were on it, she would withhold judgment. At least for now. And now that the moment had arrived, she was nervous about riding the dirt bike. She'd never even ridden an e-bike before. But judging from what Dane had said earlier, it wasn't that much harder than riding a bike. Hers had hand brakes, and the gears were all on the handlebars. She was used to shifting and so forth.

She glanced at him. "Be honest. How easy is this? Will I be able to ride in a few minutes? I don't want to

take all of Cara's time with me fumbling for an hour on your bike. Or have her witness me running it into a bush."

"There aren't that many bushes out here." He smiled. "And it's not that hard. There is some shifting of gears involved. Have you ever driven a stick shift?"

"As in a car? Yes."

He nodded. "Then that's half the battle. The principle is the same. You'll just be shifting with your left foot rather than your right hand."

"Hmm…left foot." It already sounded complicated. "Is the clutch not operated by a foot pedal?"

"No, it's operated by your left hand, where one of the brakes lines would be on a manual bike. You'll clutch with your left hand and shift with your left foot. And there's a saying, 'Gas and brake go hand-in-hand.' That's because your gas control is located on the right hand grip. Rolling it forward gives you more gas, and rolling it backwards reduces the amount of fuel."

Okay. She wasn't sure she had it, but maybe she'd just compare it to the car she'd once had. "Is the principle the same? Clutch, then shift…then add gas while easing off the clutch."

"Yep. The difference is that the left hand clutches and the left foot shifts. Push down on this peg—" he pointed at a lever above where the footrest was "—to shift to first gear, and then push it up with your toe to cycle past neutral and into second gear. I think we'll just work on those today. If you give it too much gas, you'll wind up on your bu…behind."

She grinned. He'd been about to say *butt*. Because of Cara, he'd changed it to a softer term. Something that

surprised her. He was a quick learner in that regard or maybe he'd been around kids before. Hopefully she'd be just as quick as far as the dirt bike went. "Got it. And if I pop the clutch, I'll stall it? Just like a car."

"Yes. Watch me the first time." He put on a helmet and climbed on his bike, starting it and revving it up a couple of times. Then he raised his voice to be heard above the sound of the motor. "It starts off in Neutral, so you won't need the clutch until you're ready to put it in gear. Then clutch, shift it into First, and slowly add gas while letting up on the clutch." He did so, lifting his right foot off the ground as the bike started going. He went a few yards, then circled back to her and stopped. "To stop, you cycle back to neutral, just like you would in a car. Your brake is the lever on your right handlebar."

Cara clapped her hands. "That looks fun!"

Fun? She didn't know about that, but it wasn't as horrible as Lou had imagined. Or maybe he just made it look super easy. "Can you show me one more time?"

"Yep." He repeated the steps while she watched intently. On the third try, she thought she might be ready to attempt it. Maybe.

They switched places, and she started the bike, trying to find the foot peg without having to look at it. Okay. God, if she fell off in front of Cara, she wasn't going to be happy. But why? Cara had fallen when she'd first learned to ride a bike. And a dirt bike wasn't nearly as heavy as a full-sized motorcycle would be. If she could just get moving, she was pretty sure she could balance the thing. Hopefully.

"Ready?" he asked.

"Come on Mama, you can do it."

Lou smiled at her daughter. "I hope so." She turned her attention to Dane. "So…clutch, shift to First, and then ease off on the clutch while adding gas." She raised her brows to make it a question.

"Yes."

Lordy. Here she went. She squeezed the clutch, and when she pressed the foot peg, it went down smoothly. Now… Slowly releasing the clutch while rotating the gas control, she started crawling along, having to add more gas to actually take her foot off the ground, but then she was going. Elation swept over her as she tried to keep her rpm's low enough that she wouldn't need to shift to a higher gear, since she hadn't asked how to do that. She did a big circle, making sure she was nowhere near Cara when she went to stop the bike, forgetting for a second where the gear shift was before remembering. She squeezed the clutch and pushed up on the peg, stopping the bike.

And she hadn't fallen off!

He came over. "I'm impressed. I think it took me a while before I figured out where everything was. And I wound up in the dirt of this very site a time or two before I was able to keep my balance."

She climbed off and handed the bike back to him. "I bet you can throttle through those gears using only muscle memory now."

He smiled. "Yes. But I enjoy the process, so I try to savor ramping up my speed…taking each click at just the right time to hit that sweet spot."

There was something about the way he said those words that made her heart skip a beat. He hadn't meant anything by them, she was sure, but still… Wowsa. She

was picturing dirt biking in a whole new way. And it had nothing to do with being on a vehicle.

Not something she should be thinking of with her daughter standing right next to her. Still, her face heated, and she looked away, hoping he hadn't noticed.

But when she glanced back a moment later, he was busy taking the bike over to his Jeep and loading it up again. She guessed the lesson was over, and she thought it was just as well. This man was danger with a capital *D*. And it had nothing to do with the dirt bike. It was more the sexy self-assurance that oozed from every pore of his body. It could go to her head so, so easily. Once it did, it would be hard to undo those gears. Just like the ones on his dirt bike. And she might just find herself right on her butt if she tried to give things too much gas.

Clutch it down, sister. Put that libido back in Neutral, where it belongs.

She was definitely glad they'd each brought their own transportation. Once he returned to where she and Cara were standing, she was pretty sure she had herself under control again, putting her arm firmly around Cara's shoulders. "Ready for that bike ride?" she asked her daughter.

"I am, if you guys are."

Somehow it made her feel better that Dane had brought along a bike helmet for himself, although maybe it was for Cara's benefit more than because he believed in them. But no matter the reason. At least it showed he was willing to use protection.

Gah! And just like that, she was chasing another rabbit and following it to a place she had no business going.

She jerked her own helmet on, yanking the strap and

fastening it. Then she helped Cara with her own protective gear and handed the child her bike. "Why don't you ride it around for a few minutes and get used to it again, honey. It's been a while."

"Okay." As usual, her daughter was cheerful about the request and climbed on, nearly falling off the bike before getting her balance. Then she proceeded to ride it all around the dirt track, where there was no danger of being hit by a car, until Lou motioned her back over.

Looking at Dane, Lou asked, "Do you mind leading us? I'll let Cara follow you, and I'll bring up the rear so I can watch her."

"That's fine. Yell at me if you need me to slow down or stop."

"I will." She got in position behind her daughter. "Follow Dane, okay? And be careful."

"I'm always careful."

Her conscience twinged, and she again wondered if she was too overprotective when it came to her daughter. But who could blame her?

Dane gave her a look that she couldn't decipher before turning to the front. He started off on his bike, keeping it slow until he knew that Cara was behind him. She kept her eye on both Dane and Cara, trying not to think about how they probably looked to anyone who might happen by. Like a little family on a fun outing.

And that's how it should have been, if only Brad hadn't…

Thinking that way was not going to change their circumstances. It would only make her miserable and bring back those feelings of rage and helplessness she'd harbored for far too long after the accident. Silas's own

mishap had dredged those memories up from the grave, and it had taken a giant force of will to push them away again.

Speaking of Silas. She reached for her cell phone in the back pocket of her jeans and pulled it out, glancing at the screen.

There! He'd responded, thanking her and telling her he'd call when he was done. When her gaze came up again, she had to jerk the handlebars to keep from colliding with a shrub just off the path. Damn. That was all she needed—to have an accident of her own. Thankfully neither Dane nor Cara had noticed, but when she went to stuff the phone in her pocket again, she missed, and it fell to the ground. Oh hell!

"Stop!"

Dane braked, and so did Cara, putting her feet down like a little expert. Both of them looked at her as she scooped up her phone and put it back in her pocket.

Cara tsked. "No phones while driving. Isn't that what you always say, Mama? Safety first."

Caught in the act. By her own child. She couldn't help it—she started laughing, partly out of relief that her brother was okay and partly at the absurdity of being chided about a rule that she normally lived by. But Cara was right. Whether on a bike or in the car, she'd had no business taking her eyes off the road. Or trail, in this case.

When she got herself back under control, she saw that Cara wasn't laughing. And neither was Dane. Okay. So it evidently wasn't as funny as she was making it out to be.

"You're right. I shouldn't have had it out. And I won't again."

It was one thing to expose her daughter to acceptable risks, like riding her bike through a beginner-friendly course. It was another thing to teach her that it was no big deal to text and drive.

"Can we go?" Her daughter had already moved beyond what had happened. And so should Lou.

"Yep."

Dane hadn't said a word. He simply started pedaling again, and she got an uneasy feeling that he'd slid back into his silence of a week ago. But why? It made no sense.

But she could be wrong. Maybe he simply hadn't wanted to add to Cara's chiding. And she could understand that.

They went around the switchback that they'd reached the first time Dane had brought her out to the course. They'd stopped riding soon afterwards the previous time, since the terrain had turned hilly. But this time, they kept going. The first incline was a gentle slope that even her daughter was able to easily manage. As was the second hill. When they got to the bottom of it, Dane slowed before stopping.

She followed suit. "What's wrong?"

"The next incline is steeper. I thought we might want to walk our bikes to the top of it, if you think Cara is up to it."

Lou looked at the hill. It was steeper. She and her daughter had hiked slopes higher than this one, but Cara had not been pushing a bike while doing it. "Is it possible to leave the bikes down here and walk up without them?"

"I can push hers and mine," he said.

"I can do it, Mama."

She studied her. "I don't want you to fall."

"Let her try." Dane's voice was low, but there was a tension in it that made her bristle and tilt her head. She was trying not to glare at him but wasn't entirely sure she was successful.

It wasn't that she was against Cara pushing her bike. In fact, she wasn't sure why she'd said what she had, other than the thought that walking up without the bikes would make it easier for everyone, not just her daughter. A mere hour ago, she'd wondered if she was being overprotective—a knee-jerk reaction to what she saw as Brad's recklessness. It was making her second-guess every decision she made. And it looked like she wasn't the only one who thought her parenting style was that of a hovering…didn't they call them helicopter moms? She could definitely picture herself and Brad having the same kind of arguments if he'd lived.

She ignored Dane for the moment and addressed her daughter, acknowledging what she'd said. "I know you can do it, Cara. So let's go. Walk on the side of it like I showed you when you were first learning to ride."

The path was made out of what looked like black sand, but they walked through it at a steady pace. Even Cara. When they got to the top, however, Dane wheeled his bike over to Lou and touched her arm. "Sorry. I shouldn't have said what I did."

"It's okay." She wasn't sure that it was, but she did know she'd been oversensitive and was still lingering in that zone. But she wasn't sure how to explain it to him without him thinking she was crazy for letting Brad's

death affect the decisions she made for her child. "And obviously, she was capable of making it up here."

"She was. She's a great kid."

That broke through her prickliness. She looked over at where Cara was bent down, studying some creature. Then she turned back to Dane, the warmth of his fingers against her skin a steadying force in what recently had felt like a chaotic world. Rather than pull away from his touch, she leaned against him for a second. "Thank you."

She toed the black sand and looked up, catching his brown eyes on her. "The color of the terrain is interesting. Is there a reason for it?"

"They're cinders from the volcanic rock in the area. Hence the name of the park. Sunset Crater Volcano is just to our left."

"Of course. Now it makes sense."

"Mama! Come here and look."

Cara's voice made her realize that not only were she and Dane staring at each other, she was still leaning against him, their shoulders and upper arms pressed tightly together.

Giving a squeaked laugh, she moved away and went to where her daughter was pointing at something. Some kind of small crab-like creature with little pinchers in front and a curled tail with—

Realizing what it was, she jerked Cara up. "Get away from that!"

Her daughter started to cry, and Lou picked her up, hugging her close. "Sorry, baby, but he could sting you. That's not a nice insect."

Dane came over as the creature was scurrying away toward a nearby stand of shrubs. Rather than killing it,

he let it go on its way. "It's not dangerous, but it wouldn't have felt good if she'd touched it."

She knew Arizona came with its own set of venomous creatures, but it was the first scorpion she'd seen here. Betsy had warned her to be careful about just stepping into her shoes without dumping them out first, although for the most part, the Flagstaff area was cooler than most scorpions liked. But obviously some still found their way here.

That was the second time Dane had seen her have a knee-jerk reaction to something her daughter did. But this time, at least he hadn't argued with her. "Everything about Arizona is still new to me."

"I know it is. But you'll get used to things."

Right now, she was wondering if she would. Or if she'd made a mistake in moving here. It had been yet another impulsive decision born of circumstances that had felt out of her control. But so far, she loved it here. Despite what had just happened. And Alabama had its share of dangerous creatures, from gators to rattlesnakes and all manner of things in between.

Now that the scorpion had moved on, they looked over the scenery. It wasn't a vista lush with greenery like where she was from, but it held a beauty all its own. She set Cara down again, just as a pair of horses came into view, their riders obviously enjoying the day. They moved over to the side to let the equestrians pass, but the couple stopped when Cara oohed and ahhed at the sight. The man got off and asked if it was okay to lead his mount over and let her pet him.

There was just a moment's hesitation. She got past it, picked Cara up yet again, and walked over to him. She

knew enough about horses to instruct her daughter to pet the animal's neck, which she did, asking, "What's his name?"

"Poncho," the man said. "And he loves kids."

The woman, who was still on her horse, patted the animal's neck. "And this is Ida. She's an Appaloosa. See those white spots on her rump?"

Cara nodded and patted Poncho one more time before Lou moved her away from the pair. "Thank you for taking the time to let her see them."

The man put his boot into the stirrup and swung himself effortlessly into the saddle. "You're more than welcome. We're camping just around the corner for the weekend. Feel free to stop by on your way out."

"Thanks again."

The pair moved away, and she noticed that Dane hadn't moved. If anything, he looked out of sorts.

"Do you not like horses?"

"It's not that I don't like them. I just don't trust them enough to ride around on them."

"And yet you'll get on a dirt bike and race it up a mountain?"

He gave a sideways grin that made his dimple dance and sent a rush of warmth spiraling through her abdomen. "A dirt bike doesn't weigh two thousand pounds or have a mind of its own."

"I'm pretty sure neither of those horses weighed that much."

But still. She'd actually found something that Dane was afraid of? Somehow that made him seem almost…human.

"They weigh enough to scrape me off on the nearest tree trunk."

That mental image of him slowly sliding down a tree made her laugh.

Cara seemed amused too. "Mr. Dane, Poncho is nice."

He seemed to take a deep breath. "You're right. Poncho is very nice. And so are our bikes. Are you ready to go?"

It looked like this was the end of the discussion. But she'd found a chink in his armor. And she intended to hold on to that nugget and keep it tucked away for a time when she needed a reminder that he wasn't superhuman.

Or immune to fear or worry. Because Lou was definitely not impervious to either of those things. And evidently neither was Dane.

CHAPTER SIX

DANE COULDN'T HELP but smile when he thought about yesterday. Lou's daughter was absolutely adorable with her blond hair and sweet smile. The very picture of her mom, except for the blond hair part.

So did that mean that he also found Lou adorable? She could be. When she wasn't either being maddeningly efficient about the way she handled CPR or acting like everything outside of her job should be feared.

Like the hospital fundraiser?

Well, she seemed to have come around on that front. She'd even gotten on his dirt bike and ridden a big circle around him. Only in first gear, but still. He was pretty sure he could talk her into doing it again and shifting into higher gears.

But the question was whether or not he should. He'd enjoyed their day together far too much.

He stared at himself in the mirror as he trimmed the scruff on his face, the words tattooed across his chest catching his attention. They were where no one else could see them, but where he would have to face them each and every day as he brushed his teeth in the morning or undressed to shower every evening. They were the last words penned by his father. The hospice nurse had

handed Dane an envelope with his name on it shortly after his father's death.

With a shaking hand, Dane opened it and found three words. Three words that his father had denied himself, that he evidently wanted Dane to take to heart. *Dare to Live.*

It had taken him a while to figure out what the message meant. His dad had always tried to allay his wife's fears and worries, tried not to do anything that might spark anxiety in her. He didn't fly unless he couldn't avoid it. And he'd stuck to his life as the CEO of a company he'd founded, trying his best to get both of his sons to join him. Allen had followed him into the business, but Dane had rebelled, making both his father and his brother angry. He'd become the official black sheep of their family.

So the words his dad had written didn't make sense. Until they did. Dane was the only one in their family who had truly followed his heart. And those three words were, in essence, his father's blessing over his life. And his permission to continue on as he was. He hadn't realized how much he'd needed it until the very moment he read his father's words. And so he'd had that message penned on his skin in indelible ink, in his father's handwriting. As a reminder to be true to himself. To not let himself be trapped in a life he didn't want. Dane hadn't done that. At least not yet. But that message was meant for his future self.

His mom had been afraid of anything and everything. And as much as he loved her, he saw how her fears had colored the lives of both his dad and his brother. In essence, his dad had given him permission to carve out

his own path. Not that he hadn't done that. He'd just always felt like the outcast for doing so.

But not anymore. And now it served as a reminder that he shouldn't try to make himself someone he wasn't. Not for anyone. It wouldn't be fair to them, and it wouldn't be fair to him. Doing so would only bring heartache to him and the other person.

Was he thinking of Lou?

Absolutely not.

He finished shaving and stowed the trimmer away in a drawer before walking into the bedroom and pulling out his clothes for the day. It was to be a busy one, since he was scheduled to be on call for the medevac unit today. He would work in the ER unless they needed to fly a patient to Flagstaff Memorial, usually from the scene of an accident. But they'd also been known to have to go and get a critical patient from a neighboring hospital who needed the specialized care they could only get at the larger teaching hospital.

Dane loved his job. Well, both of them. He loved the unpredictability of the ER. And he loved medevac, because it gave him the opportunity to make a difference in a patient's life. When minutes counted, it helped them to even up the odds for survival. That made the harder parts of his job worthwhile. When they lost a patient, he had the assurance that everything within their power had been done.

Once he was dressed, he put on his watch and headed for his garage, glancing from his Jeep to his motorcycle and trying to decide what he was in the mood for. Up went his chin.

Motorcycle.

Once that was decided, he strapped on his helmet, backed his bike out of the garage and headed for the hospital and the day at hand.

It was three o'clock before the call came in. The one that hit his phone with the text telling him to head to the helipad. So he got another doctor to take over his current case—someone who'd severed a tendon in their thumb while trying to pry apart frozen steaks with a butter knife.

Chuck Randall, his pilot, was already in the chopper, doing his pre-flight checklist. Chuck gave Dane a look before patting his stomach. "Man, that mushroom sauce from last night is trying to do me in."

He frowned at the man. "Are you sick?"

"No. Just a royal case of heartburn. I'll be fine."

"You sure?"

"Yep. As soon as Lou gets here, we're off. She texted that she's on her way." He glanced out the window. "Here she comes now, in fact."

Lou hopped on the aircraft and dropped into her seat, buckling herself in. "Do you know what we have?"

"I'm pretty sure it's not a severed tendon." He muttered the words more to himself than anything, but she glanced at him.

"Big case, huh?"

"Yep."

Chuck listened to his headset. "Okay, folks, we're off. We've got an unconscious first baseman who got hit by a fly ball. Possible skull fracture."

Lou's brows went up. "I thought baseball players wore helmets."

"This wasn't an official team. It was just a pickup game in someone's backyard. For a birthday party."

"Hell." That was pretty much a worst-case scenario. "Is there space to land?"

"They've got an acre of open land, so yeah. I've mapped it out, and we've got plenty of room."

"ETA?" Dane asked.

He put the chopper in the air and said, "Three minutes, tops." He paused, then burped and said, "Damn that mushroom sauce, anyway."

Lou glanced at Dane, a question in her eyes. He put his hand over the mic and leaned close to her ear, speaking loudly enough for her to hear, but not wanting Chuck to catch his words. "I'll tell you later."

There was no time for any other conversation. True to Chuck's comment, they were at the site in no time. He and Lou jumped from the chopper, medical bags in hand, including a neck brace. Baseballs that struck the head with enough force could cause catastrophic injuries, including skull fractures and neck injuries, not to mention fractured orbital sockets and facial lacerations. The fact that they were medevacing the patient rather than trying to send help by roadway spoke to the seriousness of the situation.

Someone waved them over. "He's here. Please hurry."

There were probably twenty people around a young man who looked to be a teen. The figure was lying on the ground. True to what the dispatcher had relayed, there was no movement from the victim. While Dane assessed the injuries, he listened to the eyewitness accounts of what had happened. The ball had been hit—hard—toward first base, which the teen had been

guarding. He'd been glancing at his phone and had been struck in the temporal region so hard that it had knocked him down. He hadn't been moved from where he fell.

Which was good news.

Dane turned the kid's head to the right and immediately saw the injury. The area was angry and purple, and there wasn't any external swelling that he could see. Not good. Because it could mean the swelling had gone inward rather than outward and might indicate a severe hematoma or a brain bleed. The fact that he was unconscious was also a bad sign.

He checked the kid's eyes, flicking a light toward each pupil. The right one was blown. Another indicator that there was bleeding in there somewhere. He was breathing on his own, and his heart rate was strong. The sooner they could get off the ground, the better for the patient's prognosis.

"Let's get him in the air."

They secured his neck with a brace just in case and got him loaded on the gurney. He let the kid's parents know where they were transporting him and told them to meet them there.

Out of the corner of his eye, he saw a man standing off by himself, face in his hands, and instinctively knew it was the guy who'd swung that bat. Dane's chest squeezed. It wasn't his fault. But then, it wasn't the kid's, either. No one thought it would ever happen to them. Until it did.

They got the patient in the air, and Chuck, who was normally relaying information to the hospital, was unusually silent. The chopper seemed to falter and dip before recovering. Lou glanced at Dane, her face turn-

ing white. "I've got the patient," she said. "Go check on Chuck."

Was the pilot feeling worse? He moved to the second seat up front and knew immediately that something was very wrong. Chuck was still controlling the chopper, but he did not look good. This was more than just mushroom sauce.

"Are you going to be able to get us in?"

"I-I don't think so. Feels like an elephant's sitting on my chest."

"I'm taking the controls. Hang in there, Chuck." Fortunately, Dane had his pilot's license and was able to fly. He'd gotten it before deciding to become a doctor. More to piss his family off than anything. But now he was glad he had.

He tapped his mic so that Lou could hear him. "Chuck's having a possible cardiac event. I'm going to take us in."

"Can you fly this thing?"

"Yes. Hold on. We may be in for a bumpy ride, but I'll get us down. Do you have the patient?"

"Yes. We're fine. Just do what you need to do."

The rest of the short flight passed in tense silence with Dane trying to keep track of Chuck's condition while flying the chopper. The pilot didn't look good. He was an ugly shade of gray. His eyes were now closed, his hands nowhere near the controls. If Dane hadn't been on call…

He hated to think what could have happened to Lou. To their patient. To Chuck. But they weren't home free yet. He still needed to find that helipad. He instinctively flew in the direction of the hospital, and there!

He saw the big white circle painted on a concrete pad next to the hospital. Taking them down, he tried to keep the chopper as steady as possible as he aimed for the circle, surprised by how much smaller it seemed now than when Chuck was in charge of the aircraft. Down, down, down… The helicopter's twin skids touched the ground, and he immediately cut the engines so that the rotors would power down.

They'd made it. Somehow.

People from inside the hospital came running with their own gurney, and Lou opened the sliding door to give them access. "We need help for Chuck too. Possible heart attack."

"Got it."

They lifted the first patient out and rushed him through the doors while Dane climbed out of the seat next to the pilot's. Between him and Lou, they got Chuck out of his seat and onto the gurney their other patient had occupied. "His blood pressure is through the roof, and I'm hearing bursts of tachycardia."

A second later, Jake Norden himself rushed through the doors, followed by a couple of orderlies. The head of cardiology reached them and asked for an update. Dane gave it to him, including the early symptoms, as they transferred Chuck to the gurney.

"Mushroom sauce, huh? Let's get him inside."

Dane and Lou hurried alongside the pilot as Jake continued to talk while assessing his patient. "I hear you landed the chopper?"

"Thank God for muscle memory."

Lou hadn't said anything. When Dane looked at her, she seemed almost in shock. She was there and yet not

there. He finished up with Jake and asked him to keep them informed of Chuck's condition, then let the team hurry away from them. He slowed his steps and then reached for Lou's wrist and turned her to face him. "Hey, are you okay?"

"W-we could have died." Her lips barely moved, and he could feel the shivers that were racing through her frame. She'd seemed so calm as she cared for their young patient, but it was probably the adrenaline that had kept her on task.

"But we didn't. We're okay."

Her eyes closed. "Oh God, I don't know if I can… I think I'm going to be sick."

"Sit down."

He helped her put her head between her knees, massaging the back of her neck with gentle fingers as he waited for her body to settle down.

She took a couple of long, shaky breaths and let them hiss through her teeth. "I'm sorry. I've never lost control like this before."

Her eyes came up and met his, the blue irises swimming with moisture.

"Hey, you didn't lose control. You held it together until you didn't need to anymore. You did a whole lot better than most people would have done."

"Not you. You flew the helicopter like you'd done it before. How…"

He squeezed her hands and helped her back to her feet. "Okay?"

"Yes."

"To answer your question, I have my pilot's license. I've flown choppers before, but not in the last year or so."

"You have your license." She bowed her head and shook it. "Is there anything you *can't* do?"

"I can't ride horses."

She looked at him and laughed. "Are you freaking kidding me? You can fly a damned plane, Dane."

"What can I say?" He held his arms away from his sides, palms out, as he gave a half shrug.

Her laughter stopped as abruptly as it had started. "If you hadn't been there…"

"But I was. It's *okay*, Lou. *We're* okay."

"Are you sure about that?"

He nodded, his hands cupping her face. "Yes. As sure as I am of anything."

Her eyes stared into his, looking for he wasn't sure what.

Then, with a suddenness that held him immobile, she went up on tiptoe and kissed him as if her life depended on it.

She owed him her life.

She wasn't quite sure how her lips had found their way to his, but once there, she didn't think she'd ever be able to leave them again. And when his palm curved around her nape, long fingers burrowing through her hair to find the sensitive skin of her scalp, she made a sound. Something halfway between a sigh and a plea for more.

It was a reaction to what had happened up in the air. That gladness that she was still alive and that need to express the gratefulness in whatever way she could. She knew it for what it was, but she still couldn't pull herself

away. Maybe because Dane just seemed so…impervious to anything bad happening.

Someone could see them if they came out that door, but since it was reserved for medevac situations only, it was doubtful. Because right now, there wasn't an emergency. Except in her head…in her body and anywhere else he might touch. Anywhere she hoped he might touch. This was Dane. And right now, the attraction she'd felt had somehow gotten loose and was on a rampage that couldn't be stopped.

It was hot outside, but it didn't compare to the fire that was raging inside her. She knew they should be checking on Chuck, but she couldn't bring herself to stop this train. Instead she let it continue to race down the tracks. Because surely Dane could control that too. Just like he'd taken charge of the helicopter. Like he'd controlled his motorcycle…his dirt bike. Anywhere he went, it seemed he could master whatever task stood between him and what he wanted.

And by the way he was now returning her kiss, it looked like he just might want her.

She knew that she wanted him. With a fierceness she hadn't felt in many years. Was it just her penchant for bad boys? Probably. And she wasn't even sure where that came from. Her mom had never stopped her kids from doing anything they wanted to do, as long as it wasn't illegal or immoral. And so she'd found Brad—who walked that line each and every day. But he'd always seemed to venture into territory Lou would consider selfish by risking his life in ways that seemed so foolish. It wasn't the racing itself. It had been his need to

stay at the top no matter the cost. And he'd paid the ultimate price.

So had she.

And Dane...

Just how far would he go?

That was what finally made her listen to her head rather than her heart. She hadn't seen him do anything she would consider reckless, but that didn't mean it wasn't in there. Because he hadn't hesitated even for a second before taking over the controls of that helicopter. What else would he not hesitate to do?

She put her hands on his shoulders and nudged, hoping he would take the hint and back off. Despite everything her brain was telling her, she still didn't have the power to pull her mouth from his.

He stepped back immediately, and just as immediately, she missed the warm pressure of his lips on hers. That was different from Brad, who would have been slow to leave. Slow to stop. He would have. It just would have taken a few extra seconds.

"I-I'm sorry." She put the back of her hand to her mouth, which still tingled, still wanted him back. "I think it was just adrenaline...and gratefulness."

He nodded, his own mouth suddenly tight and unapproachable. "You don't need to be grateful."

Yes, she did. But what she didn't need to do was kiss him. Because when she had, all her fears had melted away and become nothing. And that was a mistake she'd made once before. Brad had been able to coax her and placate her into letting him do what he wanted. Until one day, he'd come home sloppy drunk. She'd finally had enough and had stood on her own two feet and said,

"Enough!" And then the arguments had started. By then, she'd already been pregnant. And although Brad was just as excited as she was to finally conceive, it hadn't shifted his behavior one bit. He didn't seem to take any extra care on the track. If anything, it just made him more determined than ever.

He wanted his child to be proud of him, he'd said. But Lou didn't think it was as much about that as it was his own ambition.

"Yes, I do," she finally said in answer to Dane's comment. "But what I shouldn't have done was throw myself into your arms."

He dragged a hand through his hair. "Why don't we consider this one of those situations where being happy to be alive makes us do things that are out of character. Deal?"

"Deal." He was letting her off easy, and she knew it. Yes, he'd kissed her back, but she'd had no business putting her mouth to his in the first place. She would learn from that mistake and keep a tight rein on her wayward emotions in the future. If not for her sake, then for Cara's. She wasn't old enough when Brad died to remember how things had been. But she was old enough now.

She'd noticed when there was tension between them at Cinder Hills, when Dane had urged her to let her daughter try to walk her bike up that hill. She wouldn't put her in a situation where her young brain had to work through the foolishness of people who said and did things they later might regret.

"Let's go in and see how Chuck and our skull fracture patient are doing," he said.

"Okay."

They walked together through the door that separated them from what had just happened on that helipad. And Lou was glad to be leaving it, honestly. She still felt a little shaky, and she was pretty sure she was going to be a mess on their next run. But how often did medevac accidents really happen? Yes, there was the occasional accident involving medevac transports, but those instances were few and far between. The same thing could happen to a rescue squad that traveled on roads rather than in the air.

The hallway just inside that door was quiet. But she knew that once they reached the main floor of the ER, it would be loud and noisy and probably full of people that needed to be seen. The benefits of being one of the area's top medical centers was that they were the best at what they did. The downside was everyone in the area knew that, and they tended to converge on Flagstaff Memorial anytime they had a medical problem, even ones that could be handled at an urgent care center.

There was no sign of either the teenager or Chuck when they finally reached the hospital's hub. Dane went over to ask one of the charge nurses. When he came back, he said, "This way. The teen is in imaging, and Chuck is up on the second floor. As far as they know, Jake is still with him. We'll pop in and check on him, and then I have to write up an incident report about what happened."

"Do you need me to do anything for that?"

"Probably. I'll let you read it and add anything you feel is necessary, and then we'll both sign off on it.

Would you rather I come to ICU, or do you want to come to my office?"

"Probably your office, if it's all the same to you." She wasn't sure why, but she didn't want Betsy to see them together, which she knew was ridiculous. She and Dane worked together. It was natural that they would be seen by lots of people at the hospital. But Betsy also knew that she, Dane and Cara had gone to Cinder Hills together, and Betsy had watched Cara the other time they'd visited the site.

"That's fine."

They got on the elevator and took it to the second floor. As soon as they got off, they spotted Jake Norden at the nurses' desk reading over something. He glanced over at them and handed the paperwork back to one of the nurses before heading over.

"How's Chuck?" Dane asked.

"He's getting an echo right now, but I'm pretty sure there's a blockage in one of his arteries. He may need a stent, and we'll check his enzymes for damage to his heart muscle, but I don't think this was an actual heart attack. I'm hopeful he'll have a complete recovery."

Lou clasped her hands together. "Can we see him?"

"As soon as the tech is done, I don't see why not." The doctor smiled at her. "I don't think he'll need a stay in ICU, so he probably won't be down on your floor."

"That's a good thing, right?"

"Yes. I would consider it a very good thing."

He knew where she worked? That kind of surprised her, but there were probably memos that went out listing new hires.

"Are you liking the hospital so far?"

"Actually, I am. It's been… interesting."

Rather than as a stock question, he seemed really interested. Why couldn't she be attracted to someone like him? He was amazingly handsome, his salt-and-pepper hair containing more salt than pepper, but there were still dark strands sprinkled throughout. The cardiac surgeon seemed steady and by the book. Even his speech was slow and measured. And although he'd been a bigwig at one of the country's leading research hospitals, he seemed surprisingly content at Flagstaff Memorial. He didn't need to keep building his name brand, although she had a feeling he hadn't built it at all. It was what he'd accomplished that had made him famous in medical circles.

Jake smiled at her. "Maybe we could meet for coffee sometime and you could tell me about your last hospital and why you made the change."

She tensed, although she kept her smile in place. Surely he was still just being nice.

Although how could she know what kind of man he was when he wasn't on duty? Maybe he was all about the recognition. And for all she knew, he could throw wild parties at his place. But he just didn't have that vibe. When she looked at the ring finger of his left hand, there was nothing there, although a lot of surgeons didn't wear rings due to the risk of bacteria lurking underneath. But she'd heard other nurses talk about how they'd love to get one date with the man.

"Sure. Maybe on a day it's not quite so busy."

"Sounds good."

If Lou was smart, she would not join their ranks. Al-

though why not? Was she planning to stay single the rest of her life?

Maybe not her entire life. But for right now? Yes. She planned on letting Cara grow up a little more before introducing anything more than a pet to their little family. Because significant others had their own minds and weren't always predictable—just like Dane had mentioned about horses.

And someone like Dane was a complete wild card. She had no idea what went on below the surface. He might be completely different from how he portrayed himself. Although she had a feeling that what you saw was what you got with him—no apologies given.

He'd dated casually up until his last girlfriend. Betsy said she was surprised when they broke up a few months ago. Since then, there'd been no one that she knew of. Although why her friend had even shared all of that was beyond her. Lou wasn't interested. Despite that kiss. Despite admitting to herself that she was attracted to him. None of that meant she would get involved with someone like him.

Right?

If she were smart, she'd do what he suggested and just chalk it up to the aftermath of a stressful situation. Just like it had been.

Now that it was over, things should settle out. Just like Dane had said. And she was going to hold on to that thought until it was no longer an option.

CHAPTER SEVEN

THEY HAD A new pilot.

At least, they had for the last two runs, which had taken place over the course of three days. Dane knew Mike from seminars that he'd attended for the medevac team. He'd been a pilot for a long time, but in recent years, he stayed more on the coordinating side of the equation rather than actually going out on runs. But with Chuck still recovering from his stent surgery last week, they'd needed someone to step in.

He was a widower, his wife having died in a car crash a few years back. Mike had never remarried.

The man had also seemed to take an unusual amount of interest in Lou, which made Dane…itchy. Not literally itchy, but there was a weird prickly sensation he'd gotten whenever Lou and Mike chatted after their runs. It was as if they had a lot in common, which wasn't true. Mike was from this area, and Lou was not. And Mike had never had any kids with his wife, whereas Lou had a little girl.

But Dane had learned that Lou couldn't have any more children, something else that Mike and his wife had struggled with.

Had the man asked Lou out?

He wasn't sure, and it was really none of Dane's business. So he'd purposefully vacated the helipad area as soon as their patients had been taken inside, leaving the pair to discuss whatever it was they talked about.

Again, it was none of his business.

And yet he and Lou had kissed without him knowing any of those things about her. He found himself reliving those moments again and again despite his best efforts at banishing that particular memory. There'd been no indication that it would ever happen again or that she'd even given any more thought to it, unlike him.

He needed to take a page from her book. She was friendly with everyone, including Jake and Mike. So whenever she expended any of that friendliness on him, he needed to make sure he didn't take it personally. Because as he'd seen with other men, it meant nothing. At least, he didn't think that it did.

And as he'd seen from her reaction to him taking control of the chopper, it had almost done her in. She'd been in a state of panic. Not that anyone wouldn't be. But this was something different. A raw fear that was visceral and damaging.

Probably a result of her husband's death. But he was pretty sure that panic was just beneath the surface even on a good day. And Dane did not want to be the one who triggered another episode. So the more professional he could keep things with her, the better for not only him but her too. There were any number of men who would be good for her. Who were steady and true. Men like Jake, the competent cardiac surgeon. Men like Mike, the affable helicopter pilot.

Except she hadn't kissed either one of them. That he knew of, at least.

Dane checked on the signup sheet for the dirt bike race that was coming up next week. It seemed so long ago that Lou had expressed her concerns over the fundraiser. Concerns that had led to him taking her on site to explore the area.

Since then, he'd taken her yet again, along with Cara. Even that seemed like forever ago, when in fact it had happened just a week ago. And now the race itself was almost upon them.

He saw the usual names on the list. Most of the participants he knew from the hospital or from other area dirt bike events. And there was no one on there who surprised him. Lou hadn't signed up. Nor had Jake. Or Mike or anyone else like that. Neither Jake nor Mike seemed like risk-takers to him. Nor was Lou. He'd seen that firsthand.

And she didn't encourage her daughter to take risks either.

You're being ridiculous, Dane. How many moms urge their kids to take risks?

Certainly not his. And Allen was cut from the same cloth. Married with two children of his own, he and his wife were two of the most stable non-risk-takers he'd had occasion to meet. Their daughters were involved in ballet and tap. No gymnastics. No sports. Nothing that could be considered risky. And although he went to their recitals the way a good uncle should, he and Allen weren't close. They hadn't been since Dane had decided not to follow his older brother into the family business.

Allen was wealthy in a way that defied expectations.

And Margo, his wife, was a socialite born to old Arizona money. Two wealthy families that had come together and created a kind of supernova. It afforded their mom the opportunity to live in that fancy retirement village where she wanted for nothing.

Dane was comfortable, but he had no desire to be wildly rich. He spent what he wanted when he wanted and answered to no one. Well, no one except for those who were his supervisors and bosses. But they gave him pretty much a free hand to do what he wanted and needed to do—especially with the medevac program—to keep things running smoothly.

He'd even been offered the pilot's position on the team, something he wasn't interested in. He wanted to be in the thick of things, not sitting on the sidelines waiting for the other medevac members to bring the patients back to the chopper. He wanted to treat patients, patients that were a challenge and needed him to think on his feet. He'd often thought both of his jobs had been tailor-made for him. He loved the challenge of both medevac and emergency medicine. It was probably how Jake felt about his job and why the cardiologist was the top in his field.

He was so deep in thought that he passed Lou in the hallway before realizing it and turning back to walk after her. He touched her arm.

"Oh, hi," she said as if she hadn't noticed him either. Well, it wasn't quite the same, because he had noticed her. It had just taken a few seconds to register.

"What do you think of our new pilot?"

He wasn't sure why he'd asked the question, but to retract it now would seem weird for sure.

"I like him. I mean, I miss Chuck and will be glad when he's back, but I'm surprised Mike gave up flying in order to become the medevac coordinator. He just assigns the teams now, doesn't he?"

"You probably know more about that than I would."

"Meaning? You've been here longer, so you know how things work. And you've known Mike longer than I have."

He knew he should let it go and wasn't quite sure why he was goading her like he was. And that's what it was, if he wanted to really dissect it and see it for what it was.

"Just because you've known someone longer doesn't necessarily mean you know them." Look at him and Allen. He might have known his brother at one time, but that time had long passed. And other than being invited to birthday parties and special events, he almost never had contact with him. It was Margo's doing that he was invited at all.

And that time at one of his niece's birthday parties when his brother's wife's hand had wound up on his ass?

Damn. He did not need to be thinking along these lines. He had definitely not encouraged Margo to do that. He had stopped her from taking things any farther.

And with Lou's kiss? Could he say the same about that? No, dammit, he could not. Because the urge to press her back against that door to the hospital and get real and personal with her had been nothing like the disgust he'd felt at his sister-in-law's unwanted advances.

And hell if he wasn't feeling a touch of jealousy over Mike's blatant interest. And over the fact that Jake had asked her out for coffee while Dane had been standing

right there. She hadn't gone. But if Dane hadn't been there, would she have?

He had no idea. Nor did he want to know.

"Dane?"

He realized she'd said something, and he'd missed it completely. "Sorry. I was thinking about the dirt bike event and what still needs to be done. What did you say?"

She studied him for a minute before shaking her head. "Never mind. It wasn't important."

"Sorry." He stopped for a minute. "Hey, do you want to help me do something for the fundraiser? That is, if you have any extra time." Then he rolled his eyes. "Forget I asked. I know you have Cara, and I'm sure between her and the hospital, you have your hands full."

"I do, but ask anyway. If it's something I can do, I will. If I can't, I won't."

He hesitated. He really shouldn't ask, but his refreshments coordinator had just discovered she was pregnant, and the mere thought of food made her nauseous, so she'd dropped out.

"The person who was getting the refreshment list together for the fundraiser is battling a mean case of morning sickness and asked me to find someone else. She has a list partly done, but it's not complete. Can you look it over and see what you think? Maybe it's fine as-is, but since I'm not sure how much food she planned last year, I'm kind of lost."

All of that was true. But really he'd asked because he didn't want her to feel like she was an afterthought. She wasn't. He hadn't heard what she'd said because

he'd been too damned busy thinking about that kiss. Not for any other reason.

"Sure. I can take it home and go over it tonight if that will help."

"Yes, it absolutely will. I'll owe you."

"No, you won't. You saved my life once. The least I can do is save your hide. Or at least try to. No guarantees, though. I wasn't here last year, so I'm not sure what was done. How many folks showed up last year for the event, do you remember?"

"Close to a thousand."

Her eyes widened. "Seriously? That's a lot of food. Give me the list and I'll check it out."

"Do you have time to come to my office? I have a printout of it on my desk."

"Sure."

They walked back to his office, which was just down the hallway from the ER. She'd been there a couple of times before. Like for the incident report they'd had to sign.

"Do you know how the kid with the baseball injury is doing? I keep seeing that poor soul's face who hit the ball. He looked utterly wrecked." She glanced up at him.

"He's actually fine. He had a hairline fracture, which was a lot better than it could have been."

"Really? With the blown pupil, I expected a whole lot worse."

"Sometimes the nerves just get stunned from trauma and don't react the way we expect them to react."

Like the trauma of thinking the chopper was going down and having to switch pilots midstream? Lou had

been visibly shaken from that event. Was that all that was behind the kiss?

The kiss! Dammit. He needed to stop trying to figure out why that happened. It had, and that's all there was to it. He'd basically told her it was nothing. He needed to remember that and be done with replaying every second of it in his head.

"True. I guess we should be thankful that's all it was."

Which was exactly what Dane had been trying to do about that other thing, the kiss. He should be thankful that was all it was. That it wasn't an invitation for more, like with Margo. Or even Jana, who'd wanted to start trying for a child.

At least there was that. If something had happened between the two of them, there would be no possibility that Lou could get pregnant.

But nothing had happened. And it wasn't going to, if he had anything to say about it.

"I guess so." It took him a second to realize she was still talking about that blown pupil.

Arriving at his office saved him from having to come up with any kind of response. He motioned her inside and then searched on his desk for the neat sheet of paper that had a list of businesses and hospital employees who had offered to bring food.

"Here it is."

She sat down in his spare chair to look over the list. Dane had kind of hoped she'd just take it and go, but it made sense she'd want to go over it with him. And he had nothing pressing to do right now, so he went to his own chair and watched her as she perused what had been written.

"You have two local grocery stores who are providing fried chicken and several hundred subs. That should take care of around four or five hundred people, not all of whom will eat, right?"

"I'm not sure."

Her eyes moved lower to see who in the hospital was bringing food. "There are chips and several dips as well as taco meat and supplies for taco salad. That will take care of another fifty to a hundred people." She glanced up. "You said there were a thousand last year, right?"

"Yes."

"Okay, I can work with this. I don't see anyone in my department listed, and it doesn't look like cardiology has been hit up yet either."

He could understand her knowing the names of the folks in her department, but how often was she in Jake's area? Enough to know everyone's names, evidently. But again, it was none of his business. To let it get stuck in his head wasn't going to do either one of them any good.

"I know obstetrics has been contacted. That was where the lady who's been doing this the last two years worked. I'm not sure how many other departments have been missed, though."

"I have some time on my hands. I'll run floor by floor to see which ones she had time to get to and which ones she didn't. We may be good as far as businesses go. Especially since it's next week, right? I don't think a grocery store or any other business would be able to pull things together that quickly. And I can make something too."

"I wasn't hinting you needed to."

"It's fine. It'll be fun. I'll have Cara help me. She'll love it."

He bet she would. He could picture the child standing on a chair at the counter and helping to mix up batter. It made something tighten in his chest.

"Are you sure you don't mind?"

"I don't. Especially since I kind of pooh-poohed the idea of the charity event earlier. It'll help me make up for being suspicious about it."

"Nothing to make up for. I would have been suspicious, too, if I'd been in your shoes."

She had been suspicious. So suspicious that he thought she might try to have the whole event shut down. And now here she was trying to help the cause. What a huge shift in her attitude.

And he had to admit, there'd been a shift in his as well. She was competent and cautious. The fact that she'd come over to his side was a testament to her ability to change her mind rather than stubbornly stand her ground no matter what.

Talk about grateful. He was. She could be a huge asset if she liked what she saw at the event. He could see her stepping up and agreeing to take on an even bigger role next year if that happened.

"Maybe you would have been. But I can admit when I'm wrong. At least sometimes. So I do want to help. As long as you're okay with it. I'll run everything by you before implementing anything."

"Actually, I trust you. And it will be a huge weight off my shoulders if you'll just take charge of this portion of it. You can ask anyone you think might like to help to come alongside you."

"I'm pretty sure Betsy would love to be a part of this too."

"Sounds good."

He waited to see if she had anything else to say, but there was silence for about thirty seconds before she climbed to her feet. "Well, I'll let you get back to work. I'll give you a report by the end of the day."

"Do you want to just meet for dinner maybe? I skipped lunch, so by five o'clock my stomach is probably going to be in sad shape."

"Let me get back to you on that. If I can find a sitter for Cara, I will. If not…"

"Bring her along. It'll be fine."

"I'd rather not. We won't get anything done otherwise. As you've seen, she can be pretty talkative, and it's not easy to cut her off once she starts."

"I haven't minded."

He hadn't, which surprised him. Dane felt like he and his dad were just starting to find their way with each other when cancer had taken him from them. It had taken not only his dad but his mom, too, who still seemed lost in grief. She'd done everything in her power to shield her husband from harm…to keep him with her, but in the end it had all been for nothing. Kind of like Brad being taken from Cara. No one wanted it to happen, but it had anyway. And there was no way Dane would ever do anything to hurt that little girl. Getting involved with her mother would almost assuredly result in that happening. Because things would go bad, he was sure of it. And if Cara got too attached to him, she'd lose him just like she'd lost her own father. So maybe it was better if she didn't come with them to dinner.

"Maybe you haven't minded," Lou said, "but I do. So I'll let you know in about an hour or so. Otherwise we

can discuss it sometime tomorrow at work? Although the sooner I can pull this together, the sooner people will be able to plan what they're going to make."

He stood. Not to push her out the door, but because he knew she was in a hurry to get her task started. And he could see just a touch of Cara in her. Not in how talkative she was, but in how her drawl came faster when she was excited about something. And he thought she might just like playing a role in the event. "Okay, I'll be waiting to hear from you. Thanks again."

"You're more than welcome. Thanks for thinking of me."

No problem. He had been thinking about her. But in an entirely different way than what she was talking about. He needed to figure out what to do about it. And soon.

Betsy had leaped at the chance to spend more time with Cara. Since it was Friday and Cara had no school tomorrow, Betsy had offered to keep her for the night. "Please," she said. "I know being in a new place, you probably haven't had much time to yourself. Treat yourself to a massage or something."

Lou wrinkled her nose. "I'm not a massage type of girl, but maybe I'll pop some popcorn and sit and watch a chick flick after my meeting with Dane."

"Or maybe you could ask Dane to join you."

"Not hardly. This is a business meeting and nothing more." She couldn't afford to let it be anything more. At least, that's what she kept telling herself. Not just for Cara's sake, but for hers. Now, if Jake asked her out, she might be more willing to say yes.

Because he's safe, and you're really not interested in him.

She knew her subconscious was right about that. But did that mean that she saw Dane as someone she *could* be interested in? She cut off her inner voice before she piped up and gave her opinion yet again. Because Lou was pretty sure she didn't want to hear whatever she had to say. Especially about Dane. Just like she'd cut off Betsy before she could voice even more of an opinion than she had.

So she gave Cara a bath, which her daughter griped about, but once she learned that she was going to have a slumber party with Aunt Betsy—when had she started calling her that?—she became super animated.

Dear Lord, Betsy was probably never going to offer again.

Then once she had everything together, she dropped her daughter off at her friend's house and headed to the street taco place that Dane said he had made reservations at. You didn't need a reservation to eat there. You needed one to be seated on the side of the restaurant that looked out over the mountains and had a spectacular view of Mount Elden. It was yet to be seen if she agreed with that assessment.

She got to the restaurant two minutes ahead of schedule and saw that Dane's Jeep was already there. She knew it was his because he had a hospital parking permit glued to his front window. Just like she did.

Making sure she had everything she needed in the folder, she climbed out of her car and headed into the restaurant.

A thousand scents assailed her senses the moment she

stepped foot inside the eatery, each one more luscious than the one before. Wow. She'd been prepared to be underwhelmed like she'd often been in the past. This was different. Maybe because they were smells she didn't associate with tacos. Like cinnamon. Or barbecue sauce.

The hostess asked for her name.

"I'm here to meet someone."

A low, familiar voice behind her said, "She's here to meet me. I'll take her back."

She spun around to see Dane standing there, looking casually scrumptious. Wait. No. Not scrumptious. It had to be the food. Had he been watching for her?

If she'd been waiting on him, she would have been watching. But somehow knowing that he'd been keeping a sharp eye out for her...enough to have him out of his seat to intercept her...made something warm slide through her.

She followed him back around a corner to where a surprising second room came into view. A huge panoramic window sat on the opposite wall with a view of Mount Elden in what looked like the exact center of the expanse. As if the window had been placed there specifically to frame the famous mountain. "Wow, you weren't kidding."

"It's something, isn't it? This is why I wanted to make a reservation. Fortunately for us, someone else had canceled, and I was able to slide into their spot."

Which, judging by the only empty table in the room, was in the center of the window.

"It's spectacular."

She sat at the table. A waiter immediately slid over, menu in hand.

Dane indicated his glass. "I'm having beer. What sounds good to you?"

He was obviously off duty and planning to enjoy it. Although he'd driven his Jeep, so surely…

"This will be my only one. And it's light, since I'm driving home." It was as if he'd read her mind. She relaxed. Brad had started drinking more heavily toward the end of his life, and she'd never quite forgiven herself for all of their arguments, knowing that played a part in why he had. And he would drive even afterwards. There were a couple of times that she'd refused to get into the car with him and had begged him to get a cab. When he refused, she hailed one for herself and rode home without him.

"I'll just have a strawberry daiquiri sans alcohol, if I can."

"Yes, of course." The waiter left as quietly as he'd come.

"Do you not drink?"

"It's not that I don't. It's just…complicated."

He nodded. "It's okay. No need to explain any further."

"No, I want to. I'm just not sure how to say it. My late husband sometimes drank more than he should have and still wanted to drive home afterwards. It created all kinds of drama and fear. And sometimes I left without him."

"I can't blame you for not wanting to put yourself in a dangerous situation."

"It's still hard to look back at some of it and realize that that was our life. What Cara might have experienced if he'd lived."

"I'm surprised they let him race."

"Oh, he was deadly sober on race days." She drew a deep breath. "And I'm not sure why I went into any of that. Let's talk about the refreshment list for the race instead."

"Okay. I'm ready."

She pulled the sheet she'd retyped just before leaving for the restaurant and used a highlighter to separate the old list from what had been added.

Dane took one look at it and said, "You did all of this today?"

"I was already at work, so all I had to do was go around to the different departments and ask for volunteers. There were quite a few, actually. As you can see."

"I do see. And that should provide everything we need, I think. Especially since I see several other main dishes."

"I asked everyone to bring their donations in disposable pans so there'll be no cleanup needed. They can either take their leftovers home, or they can be divided among anyone that wants some. I think that's the best way to handle waste."

"I agree. Thanks so much for working on this. Do you want me to take it from here? I don't expect you to spend any more time on this."

"It's okay. I can send out reminders and coordinate drop-off times if you're good with that."

She had no idea how hands-on Dane liked to be, or if he was a delegate and hand it off kind of guy. It was nice to see that he was pretty happy letting her run with it.

"If you're sure you don't mind."

"I don't at all."

Their food arriving was her signal to put everything back in the folder she'd carried in and stow it away in a tote bag she'd also brought with her.

She'd ordered barbacoa and corn on soft tacos, knowing she'd probably need to cut them apart and eat them with a fork rather than try to keep the flour tortillas together, but they'd sounded too delicious not to try.

And Dane had ordered the grilled chicken taco with hot sauce and lettuce.

They dug in, and Lou couldn't help making a small sound with her first bite. It was utterly delicious, and she'd never had anything like it before. She looked out the window at Mount Elden and the blue sky and thanked her lucky stars that she'd chosen Arizona as her new home. "This is unlike any place I've ever been."

"I take it that's a good thing."

"A very good thing. I needed a new start, and I certainly seem to have gotten that here."

He smiled, his eyes sliding from her face to her fork, seeming to watch it as it moved from her plate to her mouth. "I'm glad you landed here too. You're very good at your job."

Was that the only reason he was glad she'd joined the team? Not something she could ask. Not something she wanted to ask. Because either she might not like his answer, or she might like it entirely too much. Like when his gaze had lingered on her lips for the briefest second before joining her in looking out over the view.

"Is there ever snow up there on the mountain?"

"Yes, anywhere from November until just before spring, there can be enough snow to close the roads leading up there."

"I bet it's beautiful."

"It is. Very."

She glanced at him to see that he wasn't looking at the view but was looking at her instead. She held her breath for a second, wondering if his comment had been about the mountain or...

It had to be Mount Elden. Because the other possibility made the blood rush through her veins in a way that spelled danger. Especially since Cara wasn't going to be home tonight. It made her think of all sorts of things that should be left alone.

Like that kiss they'd shared by the helipad? Like how she'd wanted it to turn into so much more?

What was she so afraid of? People had sex all the time.

But not her. Brad had been her high school sweetheart. He was the only one she'd ever been with. Sex with him had been great at first. But toward the end of their marriage, it had been almost nonexistent. Mainly because she'd been pregnant, and then afterwards, she'd had her hysterectomy and then had needed to heal at about the time that Brad's drinking got out of control.

Don't think about him. Think about the here and now. And right now there was nowhere she'd rather be than in this restaurant and with this man. No matter what might happen next.

CHAPTER EIGHT

"LET'S TAKE A drive up the mountain." Dane wasn't sure where the words had come from, but she'd seemed so enchanted by the view that he thought she might like to see it a little closer. And after all the work she'd done on the refreshments, she deserved at least a token of gratitude. He could think of no better gift than to offer to do something he knew she would enjoy.

"I would love that." She hesitated at her car. "But what about my vehicle?"

"We'll come back for it. This place is open until midnight."

He wasn't sure she would agree to ride up together, but in his mind, it only made sense. They were going to the same place at the same time. And he found he wanted to spend a little more time with her. Especially after all the thoughts about other men asking her out. What was stopping him from doing that? And Cara wasn't here, so there was no fear of the child getting her hopes up about something that wouldn't happen. He could be careful to phrase it so that it sounded like something between friends.

But right now, he was viewing her as anything but a friend. Which was probably the very reason this was

a mistake. Unless he made sure he kept things light. It wasn't like he was taking her back to his place. Or her own place.

He was taking her sightseeing. And she'd just mentioned in the restaurant how beautiful it was. Even without the snow. He would tweak that to say especially without the snow. Because while it would be more beautiful with the snow, it would be less accessible as well.

They got in his Jeep and started on the path that would lead to the top. And the same way that restaurant window framed the vista, the windshield would frame their journey and anything else that transpired as well.

Like a walk. Yes. Just a walk. Not anything else.

"The road going up can be a little rough. Are you okay with that?"

She glanced at him. "Define *rough*."

"Washboard conditions and some pretty deep ruts."

"Will the Jeep make it?" She sounded slightly worried, which gave him pause.

"It will. It just may be slow going at times."

"I see." She seemed to think for a moment. "Betsy is keeping Cara overnight, so there's not really a time limit. I was only thinking about my car."

"I promise we'll be back before the restaurant closes. It's seven miles up and seven miles back. We should be able to do it in a couple of hours. We ate early, so we might even be able to catch the sunset, although we can't get completely to the summit without hiking."

"Let's see how we feel as we get closer. Maybe there'll be time to get out and walk up at least part of the way."

Dane drove to Lookout Road, which was about half an hour up the highway, turned onto it, and started up.

They talked about work and the medevac team and Chuck.

"I hope he's able to come back to work," Lou said, glancing out the window.

So far the road was good, but he knew that could change at any point. But since this was their dry time of year, he was hopeful that it had been smoothed a little in preparation for monsoon season, which was coming up in July. Once that happened, the road would be a nightmare.

At about the three-mile point, they hit their first stretch of bumps. Small and close together, they resembled the washboard they were named after.

"I was just getting ready to say this was smoother than I expected it to be, but like you said, we're going to run into stretches that aren't so good."

"Are you okay with that? Long bumpy stretches that seem to take forever until we find the next smooth section? The sky is clear today, so the sunset should make it all worthwhile."

"As long as we make it to our destination in one piece, I'll call it a win."

"Making it in one piece is always the goal." He smiled, glad that whatever concern she might have had seemed gone now. "Don't worry. I'll get you there."

He wasn't sure why he made that promise, because you couldn't guarantee you would make it. Or that he wouldn't have to turn around and head back before reaching the spot he had in mind. But if the road didn't get any worse than this, they should be okay.

"I'm going to hold you to that. I'm doubly glad I didn't drink now."

"I wouldn't have brought you if either of us had been impaired. I want our minds clear for what's coming."

And what was coming? He'd made it sound almost ominous. Or euphoric. And it would probably be neither. The most likely scenario was that they would make it up the mountain. There would be a nice little sunset, and then they'd head back to town to pick up her car.

They came to the next set of washboards, kind of like those rumble strips that you drove over before coming to a stop sign.

Only this time there wasn't a good stretch of road afterwards. Instead there were some deep ruts that he had to traverse by driving diagonally to the road. Even his Jeep with its high undercarriage was in danger of scraping if he tried to drive this straight-on.

"Wow. I thought I heard that you guys have a rainy season. Doesn't that help to smooth this out"

He waited until he got through this stretch of road before turning to look at her. "We do have one. And No. It's what causes these conditions. Once the rains come, this road will become much, much worse."

Just then, the road smoothed out again. He picked up a little speed, edging over to let another driver slip past heading in the opposite direction.

"Are you still okay?"

She laughed. "I have to admit, this is a little bit exhilarating."

He slowed long enough to stare at her for a few seconds. *Exhilarating* wasn't a word he'd thought she would equate with this kind of drive. Something heated inside him. Maybe it was the unexpectedness of her words.

"I think so too. Do you want to try driving for a few minutes?"

"Are you kidding me? Not that exhilarating! Maybe after I've been here for ten years."

He traversed another pair of ruts in the road, trying to time it so that one wheel climbed out as another one went into the deep-cut groove. "After ten years, this will either seem boring or like too much trouble to bother with."

"Is that what you think about it?"

"No. I love this. I could come up here every day if I didn't have to work."

"How much further?" She glanced out her window at the road beneath her tires. "It's a long way down on my side. No one has ever gone down over the edge before, have they?" And just like that, her exhilaration seemed to evaporate.

"We're not going over the edge. And we have about three miles left."

"You mean we've only gone four miles?"

"We have." He covered her hand. "But we're more than halfway there."

Surprisingly she gripped his hand and held on to it as they kept climbing. Maybe it was the fear of the lack of road just beyond their wheels, or maybe it was just that she needed something to hold on to, but it was surprisingly nice to have that connection between them.

They'd passed no other cars since that one a mile or two back. He wondered if there were people already at the top or if, because it was a weekday, the tourists were hanging out somewhere else.

It was just Dane and Lou and all of Mount Elden.

He'd left the hard top on since he hadn't known they would be coming up here today. And since the windows were tinted, it afforded them a certain privacy even as they drove. He'd even spent a night in the back of the vehicle while on a camping expedition when his tent had collapsed under the weight of some heavy rainfall. It had been cramped back there, but he'd made it and had slept surprisingly well.

"Just another mile and we should be there." He laced his fingers through hers as the road smoothed out yet again, letting him concentrate on something other than keeping his Jeep on track. There was still a drop-off on her side, but that would reverse once they started back down the way they'd come. At some point he was going to have to let go of her hand, but he could do that when they got out of the car.

Ten minutes later they'd gotten to the end of the road and had needed to stop to let some hikers go by. It still wasn't late enough for the sun to set, and they weren't allowed to park on this section of the area. There was just enough room for them to turn around and head down. But since there was no one else here at the moment, he took the time to stop and let her look out the front windshield.

"Wow, it's so beautiful. You are lucky to live here."

He smiled. "You live here now too. Right? Or are you just passing through?"

There were a few seconds of silence.

"You're right. I am here. At least for now."

It was kind of an evasion of his question, but he wasn't going to press her for an answer. It was a reminder that so much of her life was off limits to him. And maybe

that was the way it should be. She was here. For now. It should give him a sense of peace. Especially since he wasn't looking for anything permanent. Instead, the thought that she might someday just disappear, like his dad had when he died of cancer—like his mom had when she'd been immersed in her own grief—instilled in him a sense of urgency. Dare to Live. Right now. In the moment. Before that moment was gone forever. Along with Lou.

The last time he'd felt like this was when he thought she might die along with him in that chopper. And she'd kissed *him* that time. So what would she do if he...

Tucking his fingers under her chin, he tilted her face up so that she was looking at him. And what he saw in her gaze answered his question: a sense of urgency that rivaled his own. So he did the only thing he could do. He leaned down and pressed his lips to hers.

Lou's response was immediate. It was as if she'd been waiting for him to do this exact thing. And really, she had been. Ever since she'd gripped his hand and felt the warmth and security that his touch gave her. He wouldn't let anything happen to her. Not on the road. Not now. And hadn't she been longing for this to happen? Ever since their last kiss?

Her arms wound around his neck, and she kissed him back, putting everything she had into it. And it was so much better this time. Maybe because there'd been time for this sense of expectancy to build. For her to wonder what would happen if he were to initiate a kiss.

And now he had.

Please don't let him stop. If he paused...if either one

of them pulled away, they would realize just how big a mistake this was.

And *God*, she didn't want to think of mistakes or anything else. She wanted him. And not just his kisses. She wanted him to go to the end and back with her. Just like they were doing with this road. They'd reached their destination, and they would soon need to come down from the mountain. But not just yet.

Please not yet. She just wanted to stay a little longer.

"Lou…" He leaned back slightly to look in her face. "Someone is eventually going to come up behind us, and we'll need to move. I want to find a place where we can—"

Relief washed over her in a flood. "Yes. Just yes."

He pressed his forehead to hers, and she got it. She was having trouble redirecting her thoughts too. He put his hands back on the wheel, but not before giving her another hard kiss. One that promised there was more to come. Then he managed to turn around on the tiny road and head back down the trail, covering the same path they'd already traveled once. The same ruts. The same bumps and the same smooth stretches. Just like their kiss. They were traveling a road they'd been on once before. And it was every bit as scenic and blissful as it had been the first time around. Only this time she had hopes that he might want to take things a little bit further. Or maybe a whole lot further.

A tiny part of her worried that he might hurry and take chances because he was eager to reach their destination. But the fear was not enough to make her call a halt to things. And she found that he was just as careful when crossing difficult stretches of road as he'd been on

the way up. No one spoke. And this time she didn't hold his hand. She wanted all of his attention on the road. So they could get wherever he had in mind all in one piece.

"Can you count down the miles for me?" she asked.

It was like their CPR counts, but this time it was so she knew how much time she had to wait until his lips were once again on hers. Unless he changed his mind somewhere between here and there.

"Five miles." The graveled words sent a shiver through her. There was a promise there that she was terrified would not come to fruition.

"You're not going to change your mind, are you?"

He stopped long enough to run the pad of his thumb across her lips, his glance like molten lava. "No way under heaven. I've wanted to do this for a very long time. I just didn't think it was a…"

He just hadn't thought it was a good idea. She got it. Because she'd thought the very same thing.

And where was that sensibility now?

She had no idea. But what she did know was that she didn't want to find it. Not now. Maybe not ever. She just wanted to feel him against her. In her. And…

He started driving again, not speaking again for what seemed like forever.

"Four miles."

She laid a hand on his thigh, feeling the muscle beneath her fingers bunch up.

"Careful, Lou."

She got it. He needed to concentrate. She'd just been making sure that there was still something simmering on that sexy back burner of his. That he was still going to want her once they got to where they were going. Be-

cause despite his words, she was still afraid something might go wrong.

How had this suddenly changed from wanting him to kiss her to wanting him to do so much more than kissing?

"Three miles."

More than halfway there. Wasn't that what he'd said on their way up the mountain? She could still hear his voice. Only now there was something a lot better than a sunset waiting for them when the countdown ended.

"Where are we going once we get down the mountain?"

"We're not going all the way to the bottom, because I have a better idea."

A better idea? If he suggested they hike back up that mountain, she was going to veto him, because she didn't want to wait that long. And she had a feeling he didn't want to wait either.

"So, how many more miles do we have to go, then?"

"Less than a mile."

Less than a mile?

Oh Lord. Was this really happening?

It had better be, because she was aching to have his arms around her, his mouth back on hers.

He turned off into a parking area that looked to be at a section of trailheads, from what she could tell. There were three other cars in the lot, but since the sun was going down, that made sense. Not many people wanted to hike the trails at night. He parked and leaned over to kiss her. When she clung to him, he backed off. "You have a choice. We can go pick your car up and head to my place. Or we can stay here."

The words *stay here* were said with an emphasis that was unmistakable. An emphasis that meant their destination would be the same, no matter what she chose.

She glanced back and noted that the windows had dark tinting. His back seats were stowed away, and it was wide open back there. Big enough for...

"Can anyone see us?"

"No. There's a curtain between the front seat and the back compartment. It's meant to stay overnight in from time to time."

The thought of making wild love all night long in this vehicle made her shudder. "Stay."

People always thought Arizona was hot. And it was at the lower elevations like Phoenix. But in Flagstaff, it was higher, and the nights actually got chilly. Very chilly, from what she'd seen. Chilly enough to make them seek out each other's body heat. And that would play in their favor.

Dane clicked the door locks and climbed into the back of the vehicle. Then he held his hand out to her. She looked around again to make sure no one would realize what they were doing and then followed him. He pulled a curtain and sent it sliding across the area, leaving it darkly shadowed. She could see the setting sun through the windows, but once it was down, she and Dane wouldn't be able to see anything. But they would be able to feel everything. Touch anything they wanted to. She swallowed. She wanted it all. Everything she could get.

He hauled her to him, set her down on his outstretched legs and kissed her deeply. Her knees were on either side of his thighs, and his hand splayed across

her back in a way that made her breasts press against his chest. "Oooh!"

Dane bit her lip before leaning close to her ear. "We'll have to be quiet. So, so quiet."

The vibrations against her skin made her want to moan again, but she held it inside. Somehow.

He continued. "People might not be able to see in, but the Jeep isn't soundproof. Or motion proof." She caught a glint of his teeth as he smiled.

Had he had someone back here before like this? She pushed that thought from her mind and instead concentrated on how they were going to manage this without being heard and without making the vehicle rock.

Somehow the thought of the Jeep keeping all their secrets made it that much more sexy. That much more taboo.

No one would know when he penetrated her. When he took her body to a high that she'd probably never felt before.

She had never made love in a vehicle. And certainly never where there was a danger of discovery.

But they wouldn't be discovered...unless a thief tried to break into the Jeep. Doubtful. Especially not at this time of day.

His hand slid down her back and over her ass and kept going until both hands hooked behind her knees. Then he jerked her up against him with a speed that made her gasp.

Oh. Quiet. No noise.

This might not be so easy after all. Especially not since a certain hard part of him was now sandwiched against a soft and needy part of her. A very sensitive

part that had just had its first taste of paradise. She allowed herself to fully slide over him as she sat down, her eyes shutting reflexively when she realized exactly how this was going to work.

She wanted her clothes off. And his. Now.

Her fingers reached for his shirt and pushed it up his torso. He helped her, dragging it over his head and tossing it aside. In the dim light, she could make out his form and something dark that followed the curve of his left pec. She thought it might be writing. It had to be a tattoo. It was damned sexy either way.

She traced the arc and felt him shudder under her touch. "I like this."

"Do you?" He paused for a minute. "You know what I like? You and me. In my Jeep. You're a little more fearless than you seem at first glance."

Those words scraped at something raw inside her, but she ignored it and concentrated on the nimble fingers that were gathering her hair into a ponytail and tying it in a knot. "That's better. Now I can…" Warm lips moved along the side of her neck, and she couldn't stop herself from arching into his touch, holding his head in place so he wouldn't stop.

He didn't. He only paused long enough to unbutton the three buttons at the top of her knit top and nuzzled the top of her breast.

A sense of desperation began climbing up her. None of it was enough. He was so close, her nipple tight and needy and crying out for his attention. Why wasn't he taking her shirt off?

The hell with this. She yanked the thing over her head in a millisecond, only stopping when he gave a soft

chuckle. "I was wondering when you were going to do that," he whispered against her skin, his warm breath somehow burrowing beneath the silky lace of her bra and hitting just the right spot.

Then her bra was gone too and his mouth was there, pulling her in and holding her in place while his tongue stroked and curled around her flesh, making her almost cry out. Until she remembered she couldn't. She shouldn't. She'd practically taken a vow of silence. Hadn't she? But what he was doing to her was decadent and crazy. And she suddenly *felt* fearless. Just like he'd said. She ignored the tiny warning light that went off somewhere in her brain and focused on something else. Like climbing off him. Like reaching for his jeans. With a pop she released his button. Then her fingers slid the tab of his zipper down before reaching in to free him.

"My wallet."

Lou's eyes popped open. She'd completely forgotten about protection. She tried to reason with herself that it was because she hadn't needed protection in so long. She couldn't get pregnant. But there were other reasons for using condoms.

Maybe he sensed her hesitation and mistook it for something else, because he reached back and retrieved it himself, pulling a plastic packet out of one of the compartments. She quickly got over her momentary glitch and took it from him, opening it while he pushed his garments down the rest of the way. "Now. Come here."

She did as he asked and held the condom in her palm while he finished undressing her. And it was a study in seduction. Each piece came off with a slow dance of movement that made her head fall back, giving herself

permission to experience everything he was offering. Somehow she thought there would be a furtive shifting of clothes because of where they were and the risk of discovery—and that would be that. But Dane evidently had a different idea. One where his skin came into raw contact with hers. And every spot that he touched came alive, nerve endings buzzing, her whole being clamoring for more. She couldn't remember ever feeling this way with someone. Not even Brad.

He scooted down and let the slope from the folded seats prop him up slightly. She knew what he wanted. Parting her legs, she straddled him, sliding as close to that hard part of him as she could. Then she took the protection he'd given her and guided it down his length, letting her fingers linger over the act, squeezing, releasing, and loving the way he jerked under her touch as if he had been waiting far too long for this. Well, she intended to give it to him. She pushed herself up until she was on her knees hovering over him, her fingers still wrapped around him.

"What do you want, Dane?" Her voice was the softest whisper, and she leaned down until her mouth was an inch away from his.

"I want you. I want to use my tongue, my fingers… my cock. I want to pleasure you until you can't breathe."

He'd already done that. The man took her breath away at every twist and turn of his words with every movement of his body.

She gave him what he wanted, pushing down and taking him in a rush. And yes, true to his words, her breath whooshed from her lungs, and it took her a second to remember to breathe back in. He dragged her head down

and kissed her as if he couldn't get enough, and she reveled in the way his tongue burst into her mouth in a way that mimicked what he wanted to do with his arousal.

He gripped her hips and moved her in sync with his kisses, thrusting deep and retreating over and over until she could keep that rhythm going on her own. His fingers moved between them and found her, teasing that bit of flesh that was at the juncture of her thighs. Every time she rose, his thumb would move forward and stroke over her. And when he thrust home, his digit slid backwards over her. It was a seductive push and pull that took her on a journey up a different kind of mountain. One that promised a fulfillment she could only dream of.

But the higher her need grew, the harder she was finding it to remain quiet. Their subtle movements took on a desperation that said the end was growing near. She could see it even in the dark that surrounded them. A cocoon of need and frenzied craving. She wanted it. Wanted that sweet, sweet ending. Wanted it to wash over her in a rush that would send her catapulting to the heavens. And yet to do that meant…

No! Not yet.

He wasn't giving her a choice, though. She tried to slow her movements slightly to hold back the inevitable, only to have him whisper into her ear. "I need to feel it. Need you to give it all to me." He bit her lobe. "Lou. *God!* Do it. For me." He thrust deep and hard, gripping that sensitive nub between his thumb and forefinger. Everything was tight and straining and…waiting. For her. And then she was done. Her frame rocketed toward release and found it, pulsing feverishly even as he still held her hips tightly in place. The continued pressure

deep inside her was more intimate than anything she'd experienced, increasing the sensations and making her orgasm seem to go on and on. Then he was thrusting wildly as he reached his own climax, mouth still pressed against hers, and she sensed that he had to do that to stay quiet, that like her, it had gotten harder and harder to contain himself.

And then it was done, and she was sliding bonelessly against him, feeling like she was unable to make any of her muscles work. No one had knocked on the window. No one had tried to peer inside the vehicle. No one had even started a car.

They'd done it. Her brain clicked back into gear, turning over random thoughts.

She had no idea what she was supposed to say or do. With legs that felt like rubber, she turned so that she fell off him, trying to feel for her clothes.

She heard something rustle outside. Or at least, she thought she did.

Now that they were done, she was suddenly hyperaware of every noise, of every whisper of the breeze. The fear of discovery washed over her like a flood. He'd said she was fearless? God, he didn't know the half of it. Somehow he'd dragged her into his world. A world where there was a nonchalance about risk-taking that seemed completely foreign to her. A world that didn't worry about condoms or being discovered having sex in a car. She didn't belong there.

"We need to get dressed. Help me."

Instead, he sat up and took her face in his hands, giving her a soft kiss that she was sure was meant to calm her down, but it did the opposite. Now she was scrab-

bling around yanking on whatever she could find, not caring if her clothes were inside out or not. She just wanted to be back in the front seat of the Jeep where she could pretend that everything that had happened back here...hadn't. That just like everyone else who'd come here, they'd simply been out for a scenic drive. Except they hadn't been. And there was no coming back from what had happened here.

She wasn't sure why she was so panicked, but as soon as her body was covered in fabric that she hoped belonged to her, she crawled back into the passenger seat of the vehicle and waited for him to realize that she wanted to get out of there. Now.

Dane joined her a moment later with his pants on, but he wasn't wearing his shirt. He started the car and turned to her. "Are you okay?"

The vehicle's inside lights illuminated the cab, and she could see that Dane's hair was sticking up in a thousand directions. Under different circumstances, she might have thought it endearing, but right now... Her eyes skipped away from his face and caught the tattoo that had been hidden in the dark. Only now she could see that it was actually three written words. *Dare to Live.*

What did that even mean? She had no idea, but whatever it was, she wanted him to cover it up before it seeped into her brain and took hold. "Where's your shirt?"

One brow went up. "You're wearing it, and—" he held up something light and blue that she recognized as her own knit top "—I don't think this will fit me."

Damn. He was right. She'd jerked on his shirt by mistake. Well, there was no way she was going to strip it

off again in the front seat of the Jeep. "Sorry. I'll give it to you later."

She plucked her shirt from him and stuffed it into her purse.

He studied her for a second before finding something in her face that made him frown. And then he put the vehicle in gear and went back the way they'd come, heading in the direction of the restaurant.

She'd be okay once she was in her own car and headed home. But even as she thought it, she knew it was a lie. Knew she was probably destined to make the same mistake she'd made with Brad: fall for someone she had no business being with. Because while Dane might dare to live, she suddenly knew that she was afraid to. Afraid that no matter what she did, disaster would somehow find her and make her pay for being happy.

So all she could do was make it home to the safety of her apartment. And tomorrow she would go and collect Cara and bring her home. Cara, whom she hadn't given one thought to as she'd crawled all over Dane in the dark abyss of that Jeep. She held back a sob of despair. Ever since Brad's death, she'd conducted her life in a way that put her daughter's safety and well-being first. Before even her own happiness. Until tonight, when she'd grabbed at something that could put all of her plans at risk.

If there was any way she could put what had happened here out of her mind, she was going to do it. For her daughter's sake. Even if the process was hard and brought with it a pain that stayed with her for the rest of her life.

CHAPTER NINE

DANE WASN'T SURE what had gone wrong between him and Lou, but he'd never seen a woman so hell-bent on getting away from him. She had returned his shirt. He'd found it in a manila envelope, stuffed inside his work mailbox. No note. No coming to find him and handing it to him in person.

He'd originally thought it was funny that she'd wound up wearing his shirt, until he saw her face.

They'd worked one day together over the last week, and she'd smiled at him and acted like nothing was wrong. But deep inside, he knew there was. He just had no idea how to fix it. Or if he should even try.

The fundraiser was tomorrow, and although he knew she had everything ready in the refreshment department, he had no idea if she would actually be at the race.

Maybe he should go and talk to her. Just like she had when she sensed something was off with him. They'd made it through that and had been fine.

But this was different. And it wasn't just on her side. He'd been struck by how right things had seemed with her. They'd laughed and kissed and made amazing love. And he'd told her the truth. He'd seen her in a completely different light. Willing to take a chance and have fun.

She'd been willing to step onto the playing field without backing down. Until afterwards, when she'd seemed afraid of her own shadow, desperate to pull her clothes on and get out of there. What had happened in the span of five minutes to make that kind of a change? The only thing he could think of was that she regretted what had happened between them and had needed to put some space between them.

Well, she had. He just knew that he didn't like it. Because it was a reminder that rather than talking things through, her default setting was to take flight and disappear anytime something spooked her. No matter what it might cost the other person when she did. Up there on that mountain, he'd almost begun to believe...

Time to set the record straight. Or at least try to.

So he set out to find her and came across her in the cafeteria, of all places. Except she was sitting talking to Jake Norden. And she was smiling and acting like all was right with the world. And maybe in her world, it was. But in his...

He wasn't sure what was going on, but he decided he wasn't going to walk away and hide in his office. He went into the cafeteria and walked over to the pair. He smiled. The biggest, brightest smile he could manage.

"Jake. Good to see you. How's Chuck doing?"

The man leaned back in his seat. "He was actually just released to cardiac rehab. It looks like he's going to make a complete recovery."

"Glad to hear it." He turned to Lou, smile still firmly in place. "Could I speak to you for a minute? About the fundraiser?" He added the last bit just so that Jake didn't wonder what the hell was going on.

Jake stood. "I was just heading out anyway. It turns out that I knew Lou's mom in college. She was an incoming freshman the year I graduated, but we clicked. Lou mentioned her maiden name was Halford, and I asked if she was related to Grace by any chance. Small world."

"Yes. Very."

They said their goodbyes, and Dane dropped into the seat vacated by Jake. "Interesting turn of events. Jake knowing your mom and all."

"Yes, it is. Did you really want to talk to me about the fundraiser?"

"No."

Lou closed her eyes for second before taking a deep breath and meeting his gaze. "Look, I know I owe you an apology. I overreacted after...well, you know. And then because of it, I was embarrassed to face you. I still am, honestly. I've been kind of avoiding you."

He made a face as if shocked. "No...you have?"

"Okay, funny man. You know I have."

"But why?"

"I don't even know. After...you know," she made a swirly motion with her hand to convey her meaning, "I just panicked. I'd never done anything like that before—the car thing, I mean. I thought I heard something outside, and my thoughts immediately jumped to the fear that someone was going to walk up to the Jeep and see us in there or... I don't know. A million other things went through my mind, and instinct took over."

"So you're not upset about...*what happened*." His brows went up. "Since you want to keep beating around the bush." A thread of relief began to wind through his

chest. Maybe she wasn't going to give him the brush-off after all. Although he wasn't sure why it was so important to him. But it was.

"No. At least, I don't think so. Cara is another thing. She didn't even come to mind when I made the decision to spend that time with you. Not until afterwards. Which only added to my panic, because it's not like me. I *always* take her into consideration." She sucked in a visible breath. "I've been so, so careful about my interactions with men. I haven't wanted to get involved with anyone—even on a casual basis—because of what happened with Brad. I have Cara to think about and couldn't bear if I did something that in the end caused her pain."

"I get it. Truly I do. And I'm not asking you to change anything for me." The second those words were out of his mouth, he regretted them. Because he kind of was asking her to change. But now that it was said, there was no going back. He could only try to push through it. "I have to tell you that what we did knocked me for a loop too. Maybe not quite the way it did with you. But I liked it."

She bumped shoulders with him. "I did too. I'm just not sure what to do about it. Can you give me some time to figure things out? I don't want to rush into anything. I *can't* rush into anything."

"I understand. I don't want to rush into anything either. I think we both need to really think through what happens from here." He stood and gently squeezed her shoulder. "You'll be at the race tomorrow?"

She shut her eyes for a minute. "You promised me that it wasn't a race, remember?"

He knew this was a sore point with her. "The word

is in there, and that's what everyone calls it, but like I said, it's not the main goal of the event. Come to it, Lou. See for yourself."

"I will. Will it be something you think Cara would like?"

"I do. There are always a ton of kids there." There were. A lot of them brought their bicycles and pretended they were on a course of their own, although they weren't allowed to be on the actual track while there were dirt bikes on it. But afterwards, they would try to do the event themselves and have fun doing it. He wasn't going to suggest Cara do that because he had a feeling that's not something Lou would want her to mimic. "So...see you there?"

She drew in another deep breath and expelled in what looked like a huge release of tension. "Yes. And Dane? Thank you for coming to find me."

"I expect you to do the same. Come and find me, that is. Tomorrow."

She smiled just enough to kick his insides into high gear and make him want more than just a smile. He wanted to kiss her. But he didn't. He just stood there and waited for her next words, which didn't disappoint.

"I'll find you."

There were dirt bikes everywhere. Some on trailers. Some parked near the course's starting point. At least, Lou thought that was the starting point. She'd thought she would be okay with this, but in reality, she was so nervous it was hard to think. It was like she'd stepped back into the past, into a world she thought she'd left behind.

But had she really left it behind? There was still Silas. He'd won his last race, the one her mom had called her about. She remembered when Brad won his first one. They'd been to prom, and afterward he met someone he knew, and they agreed to meet at a road that was almost never used anymore. It led to a gravel pit. The perfect stopping place, Brad had said. She'd had an inkling of fear, but she was so in love with Brad, and he seemed so…fearless. That fearlessness, strangely enough, had made him seem strong, bold, and had eased her own natural nervousness.

Brad and his friend had left their dates in their fancy dresses at the gravel pit and had gone back to a point on that deserted road. She remembered hearing Brad's Charger revving up its engine and waiting with breathless excitement for the pair to reappear. Two minutes later, with Brad in the lead, they roared onto the site, kicking up dust as they spun around. She'd leaped into his arms once he got out of his car, so proud she thought she might burst.

How naive she'd been back then—filled the sense of invincibility that most teens carry.

She shook those memories away. She now knew that sense of invincibility was a lie. In reality people, died every day due to risky behavior.

This was not the same as a childhood drag race, though. Looking around, Lou noted that these people, for the most part, were grown men and a few women. They were not out to prove something to some date. Or to the world at large. They were here to support an event that funded their hospital.

Keep repeating that, Lou.

She dropped off her cookies at the refreshment table and couldn't hold back a smile. The people on her list had come through in an amazing way. There had to be twelve long folding tables that were stuffed to the gills with food. Plates and utensils had been set up, and there were even people sorting the food into like items. Dane was right. There were hundreds and hundreds of people here. Most had set up folding chairs or blankets all along the huge stretch of black cinders.

Dane had told her to find him, but she had no idea how she was going to do that with so many bodies milling around. In the end, she hadn't brought Cara. She wasn't sure why. There were loads of kids here. Most of the blankets and chair groups had at least one kid's bike sitting nearby. Surely they didn't let them ride with the adults. Her nerves ramped up even higher.

"Hey. I wondered when you would get here."

She spun around to see Dane standing behind her. The man was gorgeous in a white T-shirt and a black leather jacket. Worn black boots stuck out from beneath faded blue jeans. He looked like he belonged on a movie set featuring some kind of tough guys. He was smiling at her. At *her*. A huge bubble of pride grew inside her. She couldn't believe a man like this would even be interested in her.

She blinked as a sense of déjà vu filled her. She held on to her smile until it became real again, when he draped his arm over her shoulders. It didn't feel pushy or out of place. They could be friends for all anyone knew.

But they weren't friends. They were in some kind of nebulous region that separated friends from lovers.

Lou couldn't stop herself from nestling closer as Dane

greeted a friend from work. Once the other man had left, she glanced up. "Do you think Jake will be here?"

He frowned. "I don't know. Do you want to go look?"

"No." She shrugged, a little weirded out that he seemed to mind. "I just realized I don't know a ton of people at the hospital yet. At least not very well."

His arm dropped back to his side, and she missed its weight. She had a feeling she'd said the wrong thing, but she was not good with these kinds of interactions. She wasn't sure where they stood. Since they hadn't clarified it, she didn't know how she was supposed to act.

"Where's Cara?"

She swallowed, having a feeling that that news wasn't going to go over well either. "I-I didn't bring her. I didn't know what to expect so… Betsy offered to watch her for me."

"I see."

He didn't see. His face told her that. But Lou was afraid. She was afraid Cara might start caring about Dane as much as she did.

Because Lou…

She loved him. The track leading to where she now stood was as familiar as that bubble of pride had been a moment ago. Looking back, she could see all the warning signs had been posted in plain sight. Had she missed them? Or had she simply ignored them, thinking things would never progress as far as they had? But they had. And now there were expectations that she wasn't sure she could fulfill.

Someone up at the front spoke into a microphone, calling for all the participants to find their bikes and meet at the starting point.

Dane looked down into her face. "I have to go. Wish me luck?"

He'd phrased it as a question, probably because he wasn't sure how she was going to react. And it bothered her. They'd gone from being comfortable with each other, and him holding her close...to them standing with a little space between them and no longer sure where they stood with each other. Lou didn't like it. At all.

"Of course I do." She took his hands in hers and stretched up to kiss his cheek. "Good luck, Dane. See you at the finish line."

The words had come out automatically, like muscle memory from a time long gone. How many times had she said those words to Brad? So many. So very many. Until he started getting more and more serious about winning and angry every time he lost a race.

"Thanks," he said. "See you there."

With that, he was gone, and she was left standing in her spot all alone. She could remember the last time Brad raced. She hadn't wished him luck, and she hadn't been standing at the finish line waiting for him. She closed her eyes against the bitter tears that appeared. She'd been at home, refusing to even take Cara to the track. She'd watched the race on television and could remember the exact moment she saw the crash happen on the screen. She'd known he wouldn't make it even before the surgeon emerged from the back of the hospital.

She'd never gone to another race. Not even to support Silas.

Until today. *This isn't a race, Lou. He promised it wasn't.*

Her eyes kept track of Dane as he retrieved the dirt

bike he'd let her ride. That seemed like ages ago. But it wasn't. They'd barely known each other a month. And yet she'd fallen head over heels for him.

There weren't a thousand participants. Probably more like fifty, and Dane was on his bike talking to a neighbor. They both laughed about something, seeming totally at ease in this environment.

"Riders… Start. Your. Engines!" The words were loud enough to carry over the noise of the crowds and drawn out with a theatrical flair. Which was also all too familiar.

The bikes roared to life, the vibrations reverberating through her chest and making her shudder. Maybe it wasn't possible to leave this life behind. There would be racing for as long as there were human beings walking this earth. Even in the icy parts of the world, there was the Iditarod and other events that pitted human against human, team against team.

Her eyes tracked back to Dane, who was now looking straight ahead with an intensity that made her swallow. A loud crack of sound startled her, and everyone cheered as the bikes took off. She'd looked away from Dane for a split second, and now she couldn't find him in the cloud of dust that filled the air. The bikes scattered. One of them slid and fell over, the back wheel spinning the vehicle around. Her heart crowded her throat for space. But the man picked the bike up and took off, seemingly unfazed by what had happened. There were so many ways someone could be injured. Or killed. *This* was why she hadn't brought Cara.

The group went around the first turn and headed for the switchback. Since it was on level ground so far, it

was easy to keep track. There were several red bikes, so she couldn't pick Dane out of the pack.

Maybe she should have brought her binoculars. Why? She didn't really want a better view of all the close calls and sliding turns that were taken.

Dane said the event would last less than ten minutes, and she could see why. Everything was happening so fast. Moving faster than she could keep up with.

Like their relationship?

Yes. Exactly like that. Most of the bikes disappeared from sight, having gone over the first hill, and they would soon reappear as they headed up the steeper hill. The one they'd had to walk their bikes up.

But these people weren't walking. They were racing at speeds that took her breath away. And suddenly she knew she couldn't do it.

People were making their way to the left, where there was a large banner stretched across two poles. The finish line.

She couldn't make her feet move in that direction. Couldn't join the folks who were here to support loved ones and friends as they finished the race. She couldn't meet him there, or hug him and pretend that she was happy and carefree. Because she wasn't. She was afraid. Afraid she was stepping into something that would soon spin out of her control and dump her onto the ground, just like that bike had done with its rider a few minutes earlier.

She could not be with someone who got his thrills from hang gliding or jumping from planes or rock climbing. She needed someone safe and steady. Someone who didn't have a Dare to Live tattoo inscribed on his body.

Because to her it would be like a talisman that thumbed its nose at fate. It meant that each day could spell the end of Dane's life and the end of her world if she continued down this path.

Lou needed to get out before she was so swept away by her emotions that it was no longer possible. And she did. She calmly walked back to her car. And drove it to the entrance of the parking lot, where her breathing suddenly erupted into huge sobs that prevented her from going any further. She waited there until her vision cleared enough to let her make the turn that would lead her away from the venue. Away from Dane. And away from any possibility of a future with him.

Dane was smiling as he got off his bike. He hadn't won, but then again, he hadn't been looking to win. He'd been in the middle of the pack and had stayed there, not even trying to spot openings where he could pull out in front. Everyone had made it. No injuries of any kind. That should make Lou happy. Speaking of Lou…

His gaze scanned the people who were greeting various riders, trying to see where she was. She said she'd meet him at the finish line. It took him a minute or two of searching faces to realize she wasn't there. Maybe she'd gotten hung up at the refreshment area. He parked his bike. He could load it up later. Then he went in search of her. The food table had a long line of people waiting for a turn to load their plates. She wasn't there. He hadn't seen a chair in her hand, but maybe she had one set up. Or maybe she'd gotten caught up talking to someone and lost track of time. He spotted one of the

other ICU nurses and headed over to him. "Have you seen Lou?"

"Lou Melia? Yeah, I saw her heading for the parking lot a while back."

"Okay, thanks."

He turned away and went to the seating area. He didn't have to ask the man if he'd seen her come back. Because he knew she hadn't. If something had happened with Cara, he would have expected her to text him. But his phone hadn't pinged once.

Things had seemed okay between them when he'd left, but who the hell knew what wheels had been turning in the back of her mind? He couldn't go after her because he needed to stay and see the event through to the end, since he was officially the go-to person for it.

But even if he could have left right now, he didn't think he would. Even if he could talk her back around, he wasn't sure he should. This was a pattern that was probably going to repeat itself ad infinitum. She would freak out about something and then disappear, leaving him to wonder if she were gone for good this time.

And he wasn't going to stand around and wait for that day to come. He was pretty sure the type of person she wanted to be with was incompatible with the kind of man he was. And just like he hadn't been able to change to go into the family business, he couldn't change to be what Lou needed. What she wanted. Well, he could. For a while. But then it would be his childhood all over again. And he would be miserable. On the other hand, if he did what he wanted, *she* would be miserable.

If he just left her alone, she could find someone safe. Maybe someone like Jake Norden, who was smart—

like…genius smart—and stable. He didn't stop to analyze how that would make him feel, because it would do no good. This time he wasn't going after her. And Dane was pretty sure she wasn't coming back to find him. Despite what she'd said at that café table the last time they talked.

It was time to let her live her life the way she wanted to live it. And he would live his the way he wanted. Right now, the thought of that wasn't very appealing, but it would be. Soon enough. She'd done the right thing in leaving before things got even more serious. And he was not going to sit around and mope about it. He had a career and friends, and that had been enough for many, many years. It would have to be enough now.

Lou had been on two medevac runs in the week since the fundraiser, but neither of those had been with Dane. They'd had that same new pilot—Mike—since Chuck needed to jump through some hoops before he could come back…even if he chose to. And the second member of the team was actually an EMS worker who had just gone through medevac training.

Bill Myers was competent enough and had gotten the job done both times she'd worked with him. But he wasn't Dane.

Wasn't that a good thing, though? Bill was calm and collected and had handled both emergencies like a pro, but Dane thought outside the box, which was part of what made him such a great first responder. Maybe that was because he lived life as a first responder each and every day he walked into the ER. He never knew what he was going to run across. He was a self-admitted thrill

seeker who thrived on intense think-on-your-feet situations. The perfect person for an emergency room setting.

Lou was not. Even though the ICU could be high-pressure, she had a set of tasks that she needed to run through with each patient in order to give them the best care she could. The assessments and initial triage had already been done, and a treatment plan had been made up. All she had to do was follow the plan.

And if she were with Dane? There would be no plan to follow. No protocol in place. It would be living by the seat of her pants every single day, and she was pretty sure she wasn't equipped to do that. Was pretty sure she didn't *want* to do that.

Cara had asked about him a time or two over the last week, but she hadn't pitched a fuss or cried over his absence. Because Lou had escaped before it got to that point. And that was a good thing.

But…was it the *right* thing? She kept coming back to that.

Just because she loved him didn't mean she could be with him. That much she had learned with Brad. If he had lived, they probably would not have survived as a couple. How would it be any different with Dane?

She didn't know. But there was something in her gut that just wouldn't let it rest. And she wasn't sure why.

She probably at least owed the man an explanation. And maybe that would help give them both closure. Or at least her. Maybe he wasn't even that broken up over her sudden departure from his life. He hadn't come looking for her like he had last time.

Lou had been glad for that. At least, she thought she was.

But that closure…she needed it. Maybe once she got it, she could rest easier. Maybe it wouldn't eat at her like it was doing now.

She went over to Betsy. "Do you mind if I take my break a few minutes early?"

Her friend glanced into her face. "No, of course not." There was a pause. "Is it Dane?"

She nodded. Although Lou hadn't told her about the incident in the Jeep, Betsy had guessed most of the rest. Including the fact that she was in love with the man. And after she'd left the dirt bike race, she'd gone to pick up Cara, surprising Betsy, who thought the girl was there for the night. It ended up that her friend had two guests that night. She'd joined the pair as they baked cookies and watched a kids' movie. Then after Cara went to sleep, she and Betsy had had a long conversation.

When she turned to go, Betsy caught her arm. "I'm not one to give unwanted advice, Lou. But make sure you think things through. Don't do or say something that can't be undone."

Tears sprang to her eyes, and she gave her friend a hug. "I have thought about it. But I can only see this ending one way."

She went to the elevator and took it down to the first floor, stepping into the ER to see it was quieter than usual. Maybe because it was the middle of the day and the majority of people were either at work or at school.

She glanced around but didn't see Dane. Going over to the desk, she asked one of the nurses, "Is Dr. Crighton here today?"

"No. He won't be here the rest of the week, either."

"Oh." Dane hadn't mentioned taking time off. But

it would make sense that he would after planning the fundraiser. It had to be exhausting. Still, it was weird that he hadn't even mentioned it.

As if the nurse knew she was surprised by the news, she added, "It wasn't expected. He said he needed to take some personal time and make some decisions."

That sounded ominous. Was he planning on leaving the medevac team? The hospital? She swallowed. She hadn't even thought of that possibility.

She thanked the nurse and then got a coffee and went onto the terrazzo. There were several people out there already. A couple of them waved to her in invitation, but she needed to be alone. She'd screwed up her courage to end things with Dane, but it looked like he'd beat her to the punch.

She hadn't heard from him since the race, and she'd half expected him to at least ask why she'd left early. But in his gut, he probably knew and had already written her off.

She couldn't blame him. She would have written her off too. She remembered the way she'd frantically dressed in his Jeep and had practically leaped over the seats to get up front.

Honestly, if she'd been Dane, she probably would have written her off right then and there. But he hadn't. He'd tried to figure out a way things could end well.

Actually, he hadn't acted like he wanted them to end at all. And she'd been right there with him. Up until the race. When she'd panicked yet again. Was that why she hadn't brought Cara? Because deep down, she'd known that she was going to desert Dane and hadn't wanted her

daughter to witness her chaotic flight? Hadn't wanted her daughter asking why they couldn't stay and see Dane?

Yes. Probably. But was that fair to her? She couldn't protect her from everything. And while she didn't want Cara to turn into a Brad who disregarded the feelings of those around him in order to satisfy his own cravings, did she really want Cara to end up just like her? A fearful individual who always blamed that fear on her late husband?

No. She wanted Cara to be a well-rounded individual capable of analyzing situations and making informed decisions. But how did she do that without exposing her to both sides of the equation? Lou and Brad had been polar opposites who could never seem to come together. And she and Dane?

Lou had been capable of making concessions so that Dane could experience what he loved. And he'd made concessions for her. Like showing her the track and helping her understand what it was all about. And she had no doubt he'd kept the fact that she was out there waiting for him in mind and had taken extra care in how he approached each part of the race. Only she hadn't been there. And that was wrong of her.

Maybe in protecting her daughter, she was doing her a disservice. Maybe Lou was withholding what she needed to make those balanced decisions she'd thought about a few minutes ago. It was possible that Lou's personality and Dane's, instead of working against each other, could complement each other. Provide Cara with both sides of the coin. One side held no value without the other.

So, what did she do? Go find him and take a chance? Or go find him and end things forever?

She suddenly wasn't as sure as she'd been moments earlier. And Betsy had warned her not to say or do anything that couldn't be undone. Her friend was right. Glancing at her watch, she saw that she still had thirty minutes left of her break. So she decided she would make a phone call. One that was a few weeks overdue. She wasn't sure her mom would have the right answer. But one thing she knew she *would* do was listen.

Dane still hadn't come to a decision. He'd taken this last week to think things through and give Lou a chance to maybe contact him and want to talk things out. But she hadn't. Then again, he hadn't sought her out either. And despite telling himself he wasn't going to make that move, that he was going to let her find someone else, he hadn't been able to let it go.

For the first time in his life, he wasn't relieved to have a woman walk away from him. Jana had hung on the longest, but even after she left, there'd been nothing but a profound sense of relief. A knowledge that things wouldn't have worked out between them. And he hadn't cared about her enough to make the effort.

And Lou? Did he care enough to make the effort?

Once Monday came, he would be back on call for the medevac team, and he wasn't sure he could go on as they had in the past.

But why?

Because seeing her would hurt in a way it hadn't hurt before.

Again…why?

His eyes closed as a realization washed over him. It answered so many questions. Why he hadn't felt that relief. Why he didn't want to see her. Why…it hurt.

He loved her. He loved her cautious nature, her need-to-make-certain mindset. Her wanting to live by a prescribed set of rules. But there was another side to her. He'd seen that side when she'd climbed on the back of his motorcycle and let him take her for a spin. When she'd tried to ride his dirt bike. And in the Jeep that night, she'd thrown caution to the wind with mind-blowing results. But the question was, should he ask it of her?

The last thing Dane wanted to do was hurt either her or Cara. And he couldn't ask her to change who she was any more than she could ask him to change who he was.

So how was there any hope at all for them?

Well, for one thing, Dane would fight for her…would go to the ends of the earth for her. He could compromise when he'd never compromised for anyone in his life. Not for his parents or his brother. Not for Jana. But his dad had told him to Dare to Live. And by giving up on Lou, he was not living up to that motto. He needed to accept that dare and try to include her in it. And if she up and left him?

He didn't have the answer for that one. Losing his dad had been the hardest thing he'd ever faced. Could he willingly walk into another situation that might very well end the same way? With Dane alone.

But Lou had faced loss too. She'd lost a husband to a reckless mistake—and yes, Dane had gone back and had reviewed the accident footage and all the media furor and dissections afterwards. He'd come to the conclusion that those analysts were right. Brad Melia had

been almost assured of winning the race, but instead of just staying on course, he'd taken a chance on getting around that curve a little faster to increase the margin of the win and had lost control of the car.

It made sense that she was leery of taking a chance on yet another man who liked a fast pace and fast vehicles. But the difference was, Dane's number one goal was to live. He would not throw that away, and certainly not to win a dirt bike race. Dare to Live was exactly that. Life wasn't always easy, and it didn't always come in elegantly wrapped packages, but that was the beauty of it. He could dare to live…and live life to the fullest.

And that included having someone to share his life with. There were some promises he could make to Lou that might help her see he was willing to take a chance on her…on them. If she could make some promises as well. But he wouldn't know that unless he made the effort to talk to her. And the more time he let pass, the less likely it was that they'd be able to salvage a future he now found he wanted with every fiber of his being. He needed to take his dad's words to heart, and he needed to dare to go after her, even if it was the scariest thing he'd ever done in his life.

CHAPTER TEN

LOU'S MOM'S ADVICE hadn't been profound, and it was something she already knew, but it actually helped her understand her brother a little bit more. She'd told Lou to follow her heart. It was the same advice she'd always given to her kids. And Silas was following his heart. Who was she to deny him that? So she would no longer wish he would do anything other than what he was doing, because he loved racing. And not just because of Brad. Silas himself loved it for himself.

And Brad had also done what he loved. His choices at the end of his life were his and only his. As were Lou's.

So what did she choose? What was her heart telling her?

It told her to choose Dane. And not to try to change him the way she'd done with Brad. If she chose him, she chose him as he was. His dirt-bike-riding, hang-glider-loving, adrenaline junkie self.

And some of his risk-taking had been pretty damned fulfilling. She just had to learn not to panic or shrink back from everything that involved an acceptable amount of risk. After all, she got on a helicopter each and every week. And she still got in it, even after their pilot had had a cardiac event. In fact, Dane's adrenaline

had saved their lives. If it hadn't kicked in and let him take over the chopper with a competence that amazed her, they probably would not be here today. And while he was doing that, she'd been in the back, frozen in place.

Maybe, like she'd thought earlier, they could balance each other out. The could show Cara two sides and make her a more grounded human being. Lou could be the voice of reason from time to time, and Dane could be the voice that got her to step out of her comfort zone.

Like when she'd ridden that dirt bike? Yes. It had been a baby step, but he'd been patient with her.

And if he cared about her as much as she cared about him—and she hoped he did—they deserved a chance to see where it took them. If it meant enough, they'd be willing to work through the hard times by listening and by compromising when they needed to. But to do that, she had to find him. And she didn't want to wait until he came back to work. She wanted to do this now, while she still remembered all the arguments she'd come up with in favor of them being together.

How was she going to do that? She didn't know where he lived. And he didn't know where she lived. But she did have his cell phone number because of work.

So she went to get her phone off the charger, kissing Cara on the head as she went by. Her daughter was in the living room with a big pile of books on the floor, "reading" to her pet bunny rabbit. Would Cara accept Dane into their lives? She was pretty sure she'd be ecstatic, but that was a question for another day. Right now, she needed to know if there was even a chance for that to happen.

She picked up her phone and went to look for his number, only to find she'd missed a call. Her heart leaped

into her throat. Dane had called her? And there was a voicemail.

She clicked the button to go to the message and hit Play before putting the phone to her ear.

"Hey. I know the phone is not the best place for this conversation to happen, but I don't know how else to contact you. And you weren't at the hospital when I went to look for you. Can we meet? Your place or mine? Or you can name the location. Please, Lou. I'd like for us to talk. Call me back."

He'd gone to the hospital to find her?

She glanced back at the phone. The call had been placed four minutes ago. Her hands shook, but somehow she managed to hit Dial on the link from the voicemail.

Would he actually pick up? She didn't know. But what she did know was that he said he wanted to talk. So much so that he'd tried the hospital first. That was a positive sign, wasn't it?

"Hi, Lou."

"Hi yourself. And yes. I would love to talk. But I have Cara. Can we do it in the car? We can get her some ice cream and talk while she's eating? Otherwise, I'll need to call Betsy and ask if she can watch her."

"Cara is part of the conversation I'd like to have. I'm kind of hoping she'll get used to having me around. And that you will too."

She held the phone to her chest for a second as tears swamped her eyes. "I would like that. And I'm pretty sure she already likes you. She asked about you this last week."

"She did? Give me your address and I'll swing by in, say, fifteen minutes?"

Yikes! That didn't give her much time to make her-

self presentable. But maybe she didn't need to. He was going to have to get used to seeing her in sweats with her hair piled on her head, wasn't he? "Yes, as long as you don't mind seeing me in my grubby clothes."

"I'll love your grubby clothes as much as I love your work clothes. Or no clothes at all."

"Dane!" But she wasn't really chiding him. In reality, she was jubilant. And so, so happy. She absolutely could not wait for him to come over. "I'll see you then."

She swept Cara up into her arms and kissed her on the cheek. "Do you want to go out for ice cream with Dane?"

"Really, Mama? I love ice cream. And I like Mr. Dane."

"Me too, honey. Me too. He's on his way to pick us up. Let's watch for him."

She went out onto the balcony with Cara and looked over the parking lot, waiting for his Jeep to appear.

After fifteen minutes on the dot, he appeared. And this time he wasn't towing a dirt bike or a motorcycle. But she wouldn't care if he had been. She loved him and was going to do her best to love the things he loved. Except for maybe rock climbing. She was afraid of heights. But she wouldn't keep him from doing those things.

The bell rang, and she and Cara went down to meet him. Dane swept her daughter into his arms and carried her out to his Jeep. "Wait. I don't have a car seat."

"I do. We can switch it over pretty easily."

Together they wrestled the thing out of her car and into Dane's Jeep, and it wasn't nearly as easy as she remembered. But it was worth it. All of it. Just like their relationship would be worth it, if they could just make it through this part.

They put Cara in the seat, and Lou showed him how

to buckle her in. Seeing the care he took with her little girl made her eyes moisten yet again. Then she was in and so were they, and they headed to the ice cream joint.

Cara got a chocolate cone. Dane got vanilla, and Lou got a twisty mix of chocolate and vanilla. She smiled. They were all different. But that was okay. It's what made them who they were. Then Dane drove out of town and went to the parking lot where they'd made love. The significance of the location wasn't lost on her.

She turned and smiled at him. "Even after all I put you through, you still came back here."

"You put me through a lot in a lot of different ways. And I will forever love this spot."

"Why?"

"Because it's where I fell in love with you. It just took a while for me to realize it. And once I did, I was afraid I was too late."

"Seeing you on that track at the fundraiser… I was afraid I was making a huge mistake by being drawn into a relationship with another man who has no problems taking risks. Because if you haven't noticed, I am the queen of caution."

"I have noticed. And yet you were willing to, er…*be* in this car with me."

"And then I freaked out afterwards."

"You looked pretty cute in my shirt, though."

She laughed, glancing back to make sure Cara wasn't aware of what they were talking about. "I was tempted to keep it as a trophy."

"You can always ask for it back. If you want to."

Her brows went up. "Are you saying what I think you're saying?"

"I want to be in your life, Lou. We can make this work, because it's worth whatever sacrifices and compromises and freakout sessions it takes to keep us together." He touched her face. "I know you're not crazy about some of my hobbies, and I'm not asking you to adopt them as your own. But can you allow me some leeway with them?"

"I can, although I doubted my ability to do that for a while. Which is why I left the fundraiser venue. But somewhere along the way, I realized you're not a reckless man. You're adventurous—in some very nice ways, I might add. But you're not flippant about your life. And I know you won't be flippant about the things that might cause Cara to be hurt."

He held his hand out for hers, and she gladly gripped it. "You know I won't."

"Tell me about your tattoo. Why that phrase?"

He lifted his free hand and rubbed his chest. "Those words were written to me by my dad just before he passed away from cancer. He hadn't lived the way he wanted to live, and I think at the end of his life, he didn't want me to have the same regrets. My mom was always fearful of everything. She never took chances and didn't want him to either."

So many things made sense now. "Oh Dane, I'm so sorry. I can't imagine how hard that was, but I'm glad he gave you his blessing to live the way you want to. And I promise never to hold you back from doing anything you really want to do. I can't promise we won't have a discussion or two if it's something that seems over the top. But I'll listen. And I'll do my best to hear your heart. Because that was my mom's advice to me… to follow my heart. And I am. Right now."

He lifted her hand to his mouth and kissed it. "So am I, Lou."

Turning to the back seat, he started to say something to Cara, then chuckled. "Oops. Okay, maybe we should have taken your car."

She turned around to look and saw that her daughter was fast asleep. The cone had fallen onto the seat, forming a slimy brown puddle on his leather upholstery. "Oh my God, Dane. I'm so sorry."

"I'm kidding. I love seeing her back there. It looks right, somehow. And it also gives me the opportunity to do this." He slid his hand behind Lou's nape and kissed her softly, and she felt his love for her with each touch of his lips.

When she finally eased back from the kiss, she pressed her cheek to his. "Thank you. Thank you for taking us on and giving me a chance to show you that I'm not a lost cause."

"Ditto, sweetheart. I think together, we're going to make a winning pair."

"I do too." She kissed him again. "I love you, Dane."

He glanced back. "Is there a chance for a sleepover in my future?"

"I dare say there's a chance for a lot of sleepovers in your future." She brushed back the hair from his forehead. "For many years to come."

"So we're going to Dare to Live?"

"Yes. Dare to Live. For as long as we live."

She leaned her head on his shoulder and dreamed of years to come and all the happy memories they would make. Because this was where she belonged. With Dane. For always.

EPILOGUE

DANE ROLLED ONTO his stomach and watched his wife read her book, the powdery white sand emphasizing her new tan. They had only a day left of their weeklong honeymoon, but it had been heaven on earth.

Lou had surprised him by not wanting to wait to get married. And when she asked how he felt about her not being able to have any more children, it hadn't mattered to him. At all. Because there were so many ways to have a family, and if Cara was all there would ever be, it was enough. He loved them both like crazy.

They'd even gone to watch Silas race in Alabama before dropping Cara off at Lou's mom's house. And they'd spent this last week in the Florida panhandle.

He leaned over and kissed her under the big floppy hat she had on her head. She sighed and kissed him back. "Mmm…feels good. You want to go for a swim?"

"We can if you want."

She laughed. "I do want." She stood up and reached her hand down to him. He made a face but let her haul him to his feet. This was Dane's first time on a beach, and he'd finally found something he was uncertain about—besides horses. Oh, he could swim. Very well, actually. But…

They got to the water's edge and let it lap over their feet as the waves rolled in. "You're sure." He glanced at her.

"I'm as sure as you can be about these things."

He stared at the water, which was so clear he'd been able to see his feet even when he'd been standing in it up to his neck. Hell. He felt his nerves start to sizzle, sending little warning lights that reached all the way to his toes.

He took a step in. Lou turned so she was facing him, tugging him a few feet farther into the water. "It will be okay, Dane."

"No sharks."

"How the tables have turned." She smiled at him. "It's normally me who's raising the alarm. It's nice to see that my husband actually has a chink or two in his armor."

He was now in up to his waist, still scanning the warm Gulf waters for any signs of life. All he saw were fairly small fish.

Looping her arms around his back, she pulled him against her, tugging his head down so she could kiss him. And that did the trick. He kissed her back, his fear of lurking ocean creatures fading into the background like so much white noise. You were aware of it. But at a different level of consciousness. Her lips left his and traveled to his ear.

"Sharks and stingrays and fish…oh my." The singsong rhythm of her voice said she was joking. But the warm air sliding across his earlobe was no joke. It was downright erotic.

He tilted her head back and gazed at eyes that were bluer than the ocean around them. "You're going to pay for that later. In our room."

She reached beneath the water and pinched his ass, making him yelp. "I was hoping you would say that."

With that, he turned and surged toward the shore, towing her behind him. Not because he'd seen something in the water. But because no matter where they were—on land or in the air or under the water—she could make him want her with just a twitch of her little finger.

And their chairs and towels and sunscreen could sit on the beach a little while longer. Because Dane had things he wanted to see…and places he definitely wanted to be.

Today. And every other day.

* * * * *

If you enjoyed this story, check out these other great reads from Tina Beckett

Expecting Her Best Friend's Baby
Second Chance in Santiago
New York Nights with Mr. Right
Las Vegas Night with Her Best Friend

All available now!

Now read on for a captivating excerpt of the first book in the San Diego Surgeons duet,
Expecting Her Best Friend's Baby *by Tina Beckett*

When physical therapist Therese learned that she had landed her dream job, it should have been the happiest day of her life…until she discovered that her fiancé was cheating on her! With her future left in pieces, Therese sought refuge in the only person she could trust—her best friend, surgeon Seth. But when the comfort of his embrace leads to an impulsive night together, Therese is wholly unprepared for the consequences to be even more shocking than their sudden desire!

PROLOGUE

SETH GRAHAM SLOUCHED on his couch after a harsh reminder about the fragility of life. Right before leaving the hospital, he'd gotten a call that his five-year-old patient had succumbed to a massive infection, despite multiple surgeries. All from a head-on collision that had already claimed the life of his sister and father. Seth's part of the surgery had been to repair the child's nose and a shattered orbital socket. But there had been other, more life-threatening wounds, such as puncture wounds to the abdomen from the car's metal frame, which is where the infection was thought to have originated.

He'd gone down to relay his condolences to Bradley's mom, who'd been by her son's side day and night, and found her crumpled on the floor beside his bed, two nurses crouched down beside her in an attempt to comfort her. He would never forget that sight as long as he lived. Or the way her brown eyes had stared up at him as if pleading for him to change the outcome. To bring her boy back to life. He couldn't. He'd learned that the hard way.

Switching on the television in an effort to combat the images playing in his head, he tried to shake off the memory. Except the comedy that played across the

screen seemed grotesque in the face of what had happened to Bradley and his family.

He froze at a knock at the door, remote still in his hand. He turned off the TV and tossed the remote onto the side table, waiting for a second to see if whoever was at the door would move on his or her way. He hoped so. He really wasn't in the mood to entertain his next-door neighbor, who'd periodically started leaving baked goods outside his apartment. A not-so-subtle hint that she'd like to be more than just neighbors. Seth wasn't interested. He'd had his share of girlfriends over the years, but no one he'd have to see day in and day out if things went south. And they invariably did. He just couldn't commit. And he wasn't sure why.

That wasn't true. He did know why. He just had no interest in trying to dissect those reasons. Bradley's death, though, seemed to hammer home that his current life path held less possibility of heartache than the journey the boy's family was now experiencing. If he was this torn up over a child he barely knew...

The knock sounded again. And this time it was accompanied by a shaky voice. "Seth. Are you home? God, please...*please* be home."

The words had him hauling himself from his couch, not bothering to grab his shirt from the chair next to him. He recognized that voice immediately. But what he didn't recognize was the abject hopelessness he heard in her tone.

Therese was the most optimistic person he'd ever met and had always been the perfect foil for his own melancholic outlook on life.

He yanked open the door and met green eyes that

that were awash with tears. And right now, there wasn't an ounce of optimism in them. "Rese, what's wrong?"

She fell against him, and between sobs, he tried to make out what she was saying but only caught bits and pieces of her words.

"…Oh God…trying to surprise him…wasn't alone."

He gripped her shoulders and gently held her at arm's length. "Slow down, honey. Tell me again."

She stared at him for a long time before her next whispered phrase emerged. "W-what's wrong with me?"

This time he understood the individual words, but not what she meant. Was she sick? She'd mentioned trying to surprise someone. Her fiancé, maybe?

"Does this have something to do with Bill?" He wasn't the man's biggest fan and he couldn't pinpoint the reason. The man was wealthy and successful and, on the surface, seemed like an all-around good guy. But there was something just a little bit oily about him. Seth had convinced himself that he was just jealous of Therese's happiness and had damned himself for it. But it was what she'd always wanted. He remembered her talking about wanting a marriage like the one her mom and dad had even when she was much younger. There had been flashes of attraction between them a couple of times, when time had stood still and he'd sensed she might want to move past friendship, but he always reminded himself that the last person he'd ever want to hurt was the woman standing in front of him. The one whose green eyes relayed a pain and devastation that made his chest ache.

She didn't say anything, but the look on her face said it all. Something had brought her to his apartment, a

crushed, fragile shadow of the woman he knew. Just like his mom had been. Anger crowded out everything else in his chest. "What did he do?"

"I went to his office… I was so excited about the news that I'd been accepted for the job I'd interviewed for at Sunrise Medical Center. I start the middle of next month. You remember? I know six weeks is still a ways out, but I thought he'd be happy for me, but when I went to his office…"

She'd applied for an open position in the physical therapy department. She had asked to use him as a reference for the position. He started to congratulate her, but the words caught in his throat. That's not why she was here. Or why she was upset.

He used his words to nudge her. "You went to his office…"

"I didn't knock. I never have before. He was there." Tears now flowed down her face in a stream. "He was on his couch…w-with Darla. And they…they…"

He searched his memory banks for the name but came up empty. And it really didn't matter. Because it was clear what she meant. Bill was on his couch with this Darla person and they weren't just having a chat. And now he knew exactly why he'd never liked the man. He wasn't just oily. He was an ass.

Seth touched her face. "I'm so sorry, honey."

Her eyes closed for a long time. "What's wrong with me? Why is this happening again? First Doug, then Troy. A-and now Bill."

He knew why she was asking. Seth had taken Rese to her senior prom—after finding out her date, the drum major of the high school's marching band, had cheated

on her with another clarinet player. And then a serious boyfriend she'd had in college had dumped her out of the blue, saying he wasn't ready for a long-term relationship. Except weeks later, Troy had already started dating someone else.

He tipped her chin up. "There is nothing wrong with you. You're beautiful and kind and don't deserve any of this. Don't go home tonight. Stay here. I'll help you go pack your things tomorrow."

"I… I just can't help thinking…"

"No." He leaned closer, shaking his head. "This is on him, not you."

She wrapped her arms around his neck. "Just hold me, Seth. I need to feel okay. Just need to believe that life won't always be like this."

He probably wasn't the best person to restore that belief. But as her face pressed into his neck and the warmth of her skin penetrated the chill he'd been feeling ever since leaving the hospital, his hand came up to cup the back of her head, pressing her closer. And suddenly he felt something soft touch the area just beneath his jawline. It moved a little to the side and repeated.

She was kissing him.

He swallowed hard, but where he should have been pushing her away, he couldn't force himself to. Not because he was afraid of reinforcing her feeling of not being enough, but because a roaring need had just hit him out of nowhere. Hadn't he just been looking for something to take away the heartache of today?

An internal voice warned him that this was not the way. But even as it whispered inside his head, her mouth had reached his and paused there as if waiting to gauge

his reaction. Then her fingers touched the bare skin of his chest, and he shuddered, knowing exactly what was going to happen.

He leaned slightly back and stroked her silky hair back from her face. "Nothing is wrong with you, Rese. Nothing at all."

And then he kissed her with everything he had inside him, hauling her against his body and holding her tight. Consequences be damned. Because right now all he wanted was what she seemed to be dead set on offering. All he had to do was say yes.

Except he didn't need to say it, because she said it for him, the words whispered against his mouth. "Oh Seth…yes…yes…"

CHAPTER ONE

THANKFULLY THERESE WASN'T due to start at the hospital for a few more weeks. She'd needed to get her stuff out of Bill's apartment, which he'd fought, doing everything from buying her flowers to repeatedly phoning her. But she wasn't going back. She couldn't. Her trust was irrevocably broken. And she would never get the image of that woman straddling him on the couch out of her head. In the end, Seth had gone with her to clear out her things. Fortunately, once her ex heard who was coming with her, he'd thankfully vacated the place during that time frame. She'd left her key on the kitchen counter. And that was that.

Oh, how she wished it were that easy.

But it wasn't. There was what had happened with Seth the night she'd found Bill and his assistant. She'd ended up spending the night at his place, and although they'd made love with an intensity that had taken her breath away, he'd opted to sleep on the sofa afterward. He was right, but it had felt like yet another rejection. But the next morning, Therese was so glad he'd made that decision, since she didn't have to face him right away.

She'd woken up in his bed disoriented for a moment, and then horror set in at what she'd done. At how *she'd*

initiated what had happened. She was sure he'd recognized her desperation and had probably felt sorry for her. That thought had cut with a humiliation she couldn't quite shake. She'd be very lucky if she hadn't ruined a lifelong friendship. But when she finally ventured out of the room and found Seth was still home, she'd tried to talk to him about it. He'd interrupted her, saying he understood that emotions had been high and that neither of them had been thinking straight. It wouldn't happen again. And the way he'd said it...it sounded like a promise. Until she could find a new place, he'd offered her the use of his bedroom. And he made it clear he would continue to sleep on the couch.

Unfortunately, after a week's search for someplace that was available immediately and at her price point, she sagged on his sofa, feeling defeated. To continue living with Seth was out of the question. It would be like flirting with fire. What was it they said? Once you broke taboo, it was easier to jump in and do it again. And again. But then she really would lose him as a friend. Because she had already proved that she did not come out a winner when it came to relationships. And she'd known Seth a long time. They'd talked about what they each wanted out of life.

She wanted a happy marriage and a family. Not Seth. He liked women. And they liked him. He'd had so many casual dates that she couldn't keep track of their faces. Including the newest face that had appeared on his doorstep yesterday, wielding a pan of what looked like muffins. She'd taken one look at Therese and turned on her heel with a sniff of disdain, taking the baked goods with

her. Seth had grinned and thanked her for taking care of that little problem.

The last thing Therese wanted was to become one of those "little problems." So she would steer clear of the dark waters she'd stirred up and stick to the shallows, where there was little fear of drowning. Or of finding new heartache. Something she seemed to be good at.

Seth came through the door of the apartment and took one look at her face. "No luck?"

"No." She bit her lip. "I'm so sorry. I really am trying."

"I know you are. The housing market in our area is unreal right now." He sat down next to her. "So don't laugh at what I'm about to say."

She'd never felt less like laughing in her life. And if he offered to let her be his roommate, she wasn't sure what she was going to say. Because she couldn't. He only had one bedroom. And even sitting on the couch with him made her hyperaware that his form was stretched along its length every single night. The only alternative was to go home and live with her parents. And as much as she loved them, she wasn't sure she could do that. Her mom would coddle her once she learned what had happened with Bill, and without trying, she would end up making her feel worse than she already did. Her dad would go storming over to Bill's office and do or say something he shouldn't. And she certainly didn't want either of her parents to guess what had happened between her and Seth.

"I can assure you, I won't."

"It's not ideal, but I have a travel trailer parked at a nice RV park. You can stay there until you find a place.

There would be no hurry that way, and you could find something that really suited you."

She'd never thought about looking at something like that. But she could see how it might be ideal. At least for now. She didn't have any furniture to speak of. "Are you sure? Don't you use it?"

"Occasionally when I want to get away for a weekend, but I haven't used it in a month or two, and it would be much better to have someone in it than for it to sit unused."

How to answer without sounding absolutely desperate and relieved. "I would want to pay rent."

He looked like he was going to say no, until she gave him "the look." The one that warned him to take care with whatever was about to come out of his mouth. "We can talk about that once you've seen it. You might want to run in the other direction."

She blinked. Was it some sort of decrepit metal box? Surely not. Seth liked his comfort, and he liked his toys, such as the sailboat that he'd taken her out on a time or two. "I doubt that. How far is it from the hospital?"

If it was a two-hour drive, she didn't see how that would work either.

"About fifteen minutes...unless it's the height of rush hour. Then it can take a half hour or a little longer."

That wasn't too bad. "Will the RV park let you sublet to someone else?"

He nodded. "But I'd rather not write up any kind of formal agreement. You'd just be there as my guest. Otherwise you'd have to get approval from the park owners, which will include a credit check. And all that will take time."

The credit check didn't matter much, but he was right. She didn't see it being a long-term housing solution, so being his "guest" might be the best answer. And it sounded like he was ready to have his apartment to himself again.

To entertain the muffin lady? No, he hadn't seemed interested in pursuing her. Seth only dated women who knew the score.

He pulled out his phone. "I have pictures of it, if you want to look."

"It's okay, Seth. The other choice is to go back home, and I'd rather not do that unless I have to. I've come to value my independence. So if you're sure, I'll take it. Tonight, if possible."

"Tonight it is."

Six weeks later, she woke up in the most comfortable bed she'd ever slept in, still stunned by what he'd called a travel trailer. Well…it was in the sense that it could be moved elsewhere if he ever wanted it to be. But why would he? The place was immaculate and comfortable, and the RV park was just as welcoming, boasting amenities that ranged from a pool to a Laundromat and a clubhouse. It was also just a ten-minute walk to one of the nearby beaches. She found herself there most days, biding her time until she started her new job. Her old hospital had let her use her weeks of accumulated personal days in lieu of working out her notice. So she was at a loose end.

She could see why he liked coming here. If it were her, she would be here every chance she got. Wandering down the hallway to a good-sized bathroom, she stared

in the mirror at her reflection, making a face at the dark circles under her eyes. The result of all the changes in her life. But things had to get better from here, right?

Maybe she should consider buying her own travel trailer—something a little more simple than this one—and parking it in a year-round park. Living small seemed to be all the rage right now, and lately she'd been obsessed with watching shows that featured tiny houses.

She hadn't seen Seth since he'd brought her here and had watched as she wandered around the unit marveling over everything from the spacious living room to the bedroom on the other end of the trailer. It hadn't taken her long to agree to live there, relieved that he again insisted that she not be in a hurry to find something else. Because it was proving a lot harder than she'd imagined, and the weeks had rushed by. Another reason to keep her eyes and ears open for something like this.

She was due to start work today. But there was just one situation she needed to clarify before she left for the hospital, and then she would be free of her last worry when it came to Bill and their relationship. She glanced at the small rectangular box she'd purchased yesterday evening and wrinkled her nose. What would she do if she found out she was pregnant? Even though she and Bill had talked about starting a family soon, the thought now made her queasy. She hoped the birth control pills that she'd stopped taking just before her ex had been caught cheating had still been circulating through her system. Especially since she'd had sex twice since that time. Once with Bill.

And once with Seth.

That last one sent a shiver through her. If he thought

a woman bearing muffins was a problem, what would he think if…

It was unlikely that she'd have gotten pregnant either time, but not impossible. And the sooner she knew, the better. Especially since her period was overdue. By a little over two weeks.

Just whacked-out hormones, Therese. The result of stress and withdrawal from the Pill. Her doctor had said it might happen.

And if she were pregnant?

You're not. Stop thinking about it!

She wasn't going to worry about that unless she took the test and it verified her worst fears. She grabbed the box from the counter and removed the instructions. She should know in just a few short minutes. What once would've filled her with a sense of anticipation now brought dread.

She'd probably see Seth today, since they were working at the same hospital. It was another thing she dreaded.

She closed her eyes for a few seconds. She could think about that once she took the damned test.

Reading through the package insert, she laid out the items she would need and went to work.

Please, God, let it be negative.

Seth had just come from a patient's room when the elevator doors opened and out stepped Rese and Beth Gaines, the head of HR. He smiled a greeting at both of them and headed their way, stopping short when Beth was the only one who acknowledged him. Rese was busy looking anywhere but at him.

He thought they'd gotten through all of that, especially with the amount of time that had passed. But evidently not. He'd purposely left her to her own devices over the intervening weeks so they could both get their feet back under them. Was she afraid he might say something to Beth that would give away their secret? Not likely. He'd told her he wanted things to go back to the way they'd been before, and he hadn't been kidding. Getting involved with her in any way except for friendship would bring complications that he didn't want or need. And Rese had already been hurt by more than one man.

Besides, he had colleagues from another department who'd been married to each other for five years—and had three children under the age of four—who were on the verge of splitting up, and the tension between the two of them when they wound up in the same space together was palpable. He could only imagine what things were like at home.

Kids only made things harder on everyone. His dad had made that very clear—with his *this damned kid* comments—and Seth had seen evidence of that for himself. It was another reason he didn't want any of his own. He'd always been pretty careful about making sure of that. Almost always, anyway.

Beth came over and shook his hand while Rese stayed where she was. The woman turned to glance back at her with a tilted head, and she finally ventured forward, but it looked like she was trudging through sludge that kept her from moving normally. And the forced smile she gave him looked...macabre.

What was wrong with her? Was it just the fear of discovery? Or something else. Maybe living in the travel trailer was proving unbearable.

Beth let go of his hand and introduced them. Seth nodded. One thing he didn't want to do was lie when no lie was necessary, so he spoke up. "Therese and I have known each other since elementary school. We're pretty good friends, right, Rese?"

She nodded, but again the movement looked stilted and awkward. "Yes. Yes, we are."

There was a shakiness in her voice he could only assume meant she was trying to keep their night together under wraps. Well, so was he, but at least *he* was doing his damnedest to make it look like he actually liked her. Which he did. Rese, on the other hand...well, he couldn't say the same about her.

"Oh, that's right, Seth was listed on your résumé, right?" She turned to him. "Maybe you could finish showing her around the department if you have a few moments? I'm due back for another interview."

"I'd be happy to." Yeah, right. He should be. But something—rather *someone*—was making this whole encounter feel incredibly awkward.

"Great, thanks." She smiled at Therese. "See you later. Thanks again for joining the team here at Sunrise."

"You're welcome." The smile she offered to Beth was real enough. Until she looked back at Seth and that smile morphed into something else entirely. Or maybe it was active dislike. He'd thought they'd parted on good terms, even if there were some residual feelings of awkwardness. But this felt like more than that.

He waited until the elevator doors had closed behind Beth before turning back to Rese. "Is the travel trailer okay?"

"What? Oh yes, it's fine."

"Then what is with you today? Is it Bill? Is he still harassing you?" Her ex had given her a hard time about ending things.

"No, he's not. And I'm fine."

Wasn't the joke that *fine* was a code word for not so fine? And she'd used that term twice now. He probably wasn't going to force whatever it was out of her. But he did want to give her a chance to say so if something was bothering her.

"Are you sure?"

"Yep."

Well, he'd tried. "Okay then. Are you ready?"

"Ready?" She met his eyes for a brief second before looking off in the distance. "Oh, for the tour. Yes."

What else would he have meant?

There was no way he was touching that. Especially when her teeth came down on that luscious lower lip. One he had no business noticing. "Then let's go."

The tour took exactly ten minutes, including introducing her to the staff who were on her floor that morning.

"Thanks," she said when they were done. She acted like she was going to move away, and so he touched her hand. "Rese, let's grab some coffee, okay?"

He didn't want all of their dealings to be like this one. He truly valued her friendship, even if they didn't always talk every single day anymore. But she'd always been his sounding board and the person he'd confided in when something happened with one of his patients.

Like Bradley?

Exactly like that. If he hadn't been in such turmoil about that, their night together would never have happened. He'd have been able to keep his head, like he had the other times they had gotten too close to that line that would take them beyond friendship. Maybe she was worried that he was falling for her. It would explain a lot. He could start by telling her what had happened on his side. And maybe it would put her more at ease.

"Why?"

"I want to talk to you about that night." He realized he'd been wrong in not letting her have her say after things had gotten out of control. Maybe if he had, this wouldn't be so hard now.

Something shifted in her face. If anything, the clouds he'd seen in her eyes got even darker. "I really don't think—"

"Please, Rese. Just have coffee with me."

Her shoulders slumped. "Okay."

He should be relieved that she seemed so loath to spend time with him, but he wasn't. And he couldn't help feeling like there was more to this than what had happened between them. But at least she'd agreed to go with him.

They made their way down to the Sunrise to Sunset café, which was separate from the main cafeteria and only offered coffee, tea and small pastries. He ordered a large black coffee for himself and was mildly surprised when she ordered an iced decaf chai. She just shrugged at the look he gave her.

"Too much coffee makes me jittery."

He did remember that about her. If she went beyond

two cups, she got shaky and didn't feel well. Maybe she'd already had her quota this morning. "I know it does."

They found a table outside that boasted a concrete bench and was shaded from the sun. It was also some distance away from anyone else who was also enjoying their break. She took a sip of her drink and then immediately started in. "I thought we'd settled everything about that...er...night."

"We did, but I wanted to explain why I was so quick to jump in with both feet. I had just lost a five-year-old patient. And it hit me hard. Harder than maybe I realized at the time. And so when everything...happened, I think I saw it as a means of escaping the movie that was playing in my head. I just wanted to forget, you know?"

"I get it. I wanted to do the same." She grabbed his hand. "But I'm so sorry about your patient, Seth."

"Thanks." He let the warmth of her fingers linger for a second or two, then squeezed them and released his grip. "I thought maybe if you knew the context things wouldn't feel so awkward between us. Or am I wrong?"

"No. Not at all. Thanks for telling me."

This time the smile she gave him had a hint of real warmth to it, although there was still a wariness in her face that he didn't completely understand. All he could do, though, was take her at her word. "Is there anything else you want to tell me?"

"Tell you?" She reared back in her chair and stared at him before blinking several times. "Um...no. Nothing."

And just like that, things went right back to stilted and uneasy. He didn't understand it. She'd been fine until he'd asked that question. Maybe he had it wrong.

Maybe she wasn't afraid he was falling for her. Maybe she was afraid of doing just that with him. Oh hell, he hoped not. Because it probably wouldn't end any better than his colleagues' relationship had. Or his parents'. She'd just gotten out of a bad relationship, so maybe she was rebounding. Or maybe he needed to take her at her word when she said she'd been trying to forget, the same as him.

"Okay, then." A thought came to him. "Are you still doing physical therapy that deals with facial muscles?"

"I am. I worked with the plastic surgeons at my previous hospital and did some specialized training in that area. Why, do you have someone you want me to look at?"

"No, not at the moment, but I'm sure I will at some point. Not every PT wants or likes working with those patients. Or with children in general."

"You make it sound like a real problem."

He shrugged. "It can be more difficult than a lot of people realize, and especially with cleft lips and palates there's some overlap with speech therapy."

"I can't imagine someone refusing to work with a child who needs help."

He hadn't meant it to sound like that. "They don't refuse to work with them. It's just not everyone's cup of tea." He smiled at her drink. "No pun intended. I can see how it might be boring to some people. Doing PT on a broken back or a sports injury probably seems more exciting. And rewarding."

"Not to me."

"I'm glad." He took the last swig of his coffee. "Are

you starting actual work today? Or is this just orientation and acquainting yourself with the hospital?"

"Bingo. I assumed I was actually going to see patients today, but they're reworking my cubicle, so evidently my actual first day is tomorrow. I've finished all my paperwork, so I guess I'll head back to the RV park."

"So you're free the rest of the day?"

"Not exactly. My mom is dropping by to see where I'm living."

She made a face, which made Seth laugh. Barbara Cameron was the sweetest lady you would ever meet, but she was also a worrier. "Do your parents know about Bill?"

"Yes. I figured it was better just to rip off the Band-Aid. Plus, it would have been hard to explain why I was moving out of our shared apartment. I didn't tell her everything, though. She doesn't know he cheated on me. Or about…what happened later that night."

"There's no reason for her to know about that at all, is there?"

"No." But the way she drew the word out made him tilt his head at her. "But I think she's going to start wondering why I'm staying in your trailer. The way her mind works, she might figure it out."

"Does that mean you'll tell her?" Seth honestly didn't see how that would help at all. And it might even make Barbara think that things between them could become romantic when nothing was further from the truth.

"Not unless I have to."

Again, he wasn't sure what to do with that. He couldn't think of any reason they would need to tell Barbara any-

thing. But he didn't feel like pressing the matter. Besides, it might make things worse between them when Seth had been trying to make them better. So he just nodded in agreement.

"I hope your visit goes well. Tell her I said hi."

"I will. Thanks." She paused and then added, "I'm sorry if I end up making things awkward for you here at the hospital."

He frowned. "In what way?"

"I... I just never thought things would end like they did between me and Bill. It made me realize you can't control every aspect of your life. But actions have consequences even if you don't mean for them to."

Ah, she was talking about their night together. The only consequence he could think of was that people at the hospital might find out that she'd spent the whole night at his apartment. And since there was little chance of that...

"It'll be okay, Rese. You'll see. Just give it some time. Things normally work out the way they were meant to."

"Do they?" She stared at him for a second before reaching out and gripping his hand again as if it were her lifeline. This time he let her fingers stay where they were. "I really hope you're right."

A shiver of foreboding went over him. Had he tempted fate by saying that out loud? And when he thought about cases like Bradley's, he couldn't see how that had turned out the way it was meant to. He'd only said it to try to make Rese feel better about everything. And when it came to them, he didn't believe one night together could irrevocably change things between them, unless they let it.

And Seth had no intention of letting a moment of weakness destroy a lifelong friendship. So they would get through this. Whatever it took.

She took the next couple of days and the weekend to think about the consequences of that pregnancy test. Really think about them—about how she was going to handle them. Seth's words about things working out as they should had struck deep.

When she and Bill had decided to start trying to have a baby, she'd known she was more excited about the prospect than he was, but she'd chalked that up to nerves. But now she had to wonder if that was entirely true. Had she pushed for this and driven him away?

He should have just broken off the engagement if that were the case. Then he could have done whatever he wanted to. And not wrecked her faith in relationships.

At thirty-eight, time was running out for her to have a biological child. So she would choose to look at this pregnancy as a blessing and go it alone. The problem was what to do about the paternity aspect. If Bill was the father, it was better that he know now than to find out later and have him turn it into a court battle that had nothing to do with the baby. He had not wanted to end their relationship over the affair. Or maybe, being a lawyer, he just didn't like coming out on the losing side. And as she was finding out, Bill didn't forgive easily.

Neither did she. Well, she did, but it didn't mean she would be anxious to go back and repeat her mistakes. She wanted this baby. But it wasn't going to change the fact that she and Bill were through.

And if Seth was the father?

She sat in her cubicle and groaned inwardly, even as she fished out noodles with her chopsticks and took a bite. She'd added a little bit of ginger to hers just in case she got queasy. But so far, her stomach had held steady, for which she was thankful. Maybe she'd bypass morning sickness altogether. It would be one small blessing amid all the other uncertainty.

Her mom and dad already knew. She'd told her mom the day she came to visit her at the camper. And the questions Rese had fretted over were never voiced. Nor was there any dismay over the news of her pregnancy. They were both thrilled. And Therese knew they would give her any support needed.

And Bill? Or Seth? Would either of them lend emotional support, whichever one of them was the father?

Frankly, she could do without Bill's interference.

Nowadays there was a way to determine paternity without an invasive amniocentesis. All it took was a blood draw, which could be done as early as eight weeks. For that she was grateful. But that was still a couple of weeks away, and she would need a DNA sample to match it against. And that's where the problem was. She could ask Bill for the sample. But to do that would be akin to admitting that there was a question as to the baby's parentage. Which meant he would know she'd slept with someone else close to the time of his affair. And he would want to know who. Then the accusations would fly, since he'd always been jealous of her and Seth's friendship.

And if she asked Seth for the sample, there would be no such questions. He would already know the entire

story and the whys behind it. And if it were his baby, she wouldn't need to tell Bill anything.

And if it wasn't, she could simply go to Bill and tell him about the pregnancy without the messiness of a confession.

Messiness? There would be that even without a tell-all explanation. She would be happy to simply have this child and parent it herself. In fact, that would probably be the easiest solution. But was it fair to whoever the biological dad was?

She didn't know. And despite all of the thinking she'd done, she still hadn't come up with an answer, other than the fact that she was going to have this baby. And once she got past this step, she would allow herself to be happy. Really, really happy.

Even that thought made her smile as she took another bite of her noodles. It had been a busy morning, and she had been glad for that as it had provided a distraction from her musings.

She had two cases that looked to last several weeks. One was a complicated orthopedic case that had involved rebuilding a shattered femur, and the other had come from Seth's department and involved a neck and face injury resulting from a bicycle accident. Thankfully the girl had been wearing a helmet, or it could have been worse. Much worse. But she'd crashed through a wooden fence and had severed some muscles and tendons on the left side of her face, and there'd been an indepth surgery to rebuild some of the damaged tissue. They'd had to harvest muscle from another part of her body and put it in her cheek. It had left her with some weakness on that side, making it hard for her to smile

or enunciate some of her letters. Jotting down notes on the latter, she glanced up when she sensed someone standing over her.

It was Seth. And he did not look happy.

She swallowed. Surely he didn't know. Not yet. "Hi. If you're looking for Marinda and her mom, they just left."

Rese could only hope he wanted an update on his patient. But somehow it didn't feel like that.

"I'm not looking for them. I'm looking for you."

* * * * *

Don't miss
Expecting Her Best Friend's Baby
by Tina Beckett

*And look out for the next book in
the San Diego Surgeons duet:*
Forbidden to the Millionaire Doc
by Juliette Hyland

FESTIVE REUNION WITH THE DOCTOR

DEANNE ANDERS

MILLS & BOON

This book is dedicated to all the general practitioners
who provide service in our rural communities.
Thank you.

CHAPTER ONE

ANNA DOBSON SANK back into the car's butter-soft leather upholstery as she stopped at the first of only two red lights in the small mountain town of Rolling Oaks, Tennessee. She knew she couldn't hide forever. In fact, she'd be surprised if the telephone gossip lines hadn't started the moment she'd passed the general store at the edge of town. With a population just over nine hundred, it was very rare that anything went on within the town without it making the gossip rounds.

As the light turned green, she reminded herself that she had no reason to hide anymore. She wasn't the nerdy little girl with glasses too big for her face that made her look like the little "bug" she'd been teased about being. And she definitely wasn't the self-conscious teenager wearing a hand-me-down gown to the prom. Just last year she'd shopped the streets of Paris and Rome. She might have only been able to buy one dress and one pair of shoes, as the prices had been too rich for a doctor barely out of medical school, but she had done it. She'd fulfilled one of her dreams.

And now that she'd finished her first two years working in an ER in Nashville, she was ready to head onto another adventure and fulfill her biggest dream.

She was going to be an ER doctor who traveled around the country helping others and seeing a world she'd only dreamed of as a child. She had been accepted by a travel company with a great reputation and the paperwork had been completed. In a month, she'd be starting at a large urban hospital in Miami, Florida. Nothing could stop her now.

Not for the first time she wished her father was alive to see what she had accomplished, as he had been the force that had kept her going even when things were rough. He'd been the one to tell her not to let anything or anyone keep her from her dreams. He'd been the one who'd huddled over geography books with her as she'd studied about the world outside of their little town.

As she slowed down to make the turn that would take her to the little house she'd shared with her mother since a fire had taken away her father and their home, she saw a sign advertising the upcoming Christmas festival. Her mother had told her that the town had started holding an annual festival with the proceeds being donated to the clinic to replace old equipment. As the clinic had been there since long before Anna was born, she knew that it would be appreciated by the elder Dr. Harris and his son Will, who had followed him into the family business.

Her stomach suddenly began to churn and she thought she might be sick. She'd thought she was prepared for this, but she wasn't.

Her foot hit the brake, stopping the car a bit more abruptly than she'd intended, the tires flinging gravel from the road. How was she going to do this? How

could she pretend that nothing had ever happened between her and Will? It wasn't like she had a choice. Her mother was getting married. And not just getting married. She was marrying Will's father.

Will was going to be her stepbrother.

No matter how long it had been since the night she'd left him, and no matter how much she'd changed and grown since then, Anna knew she wasn't ready to face him. Her feelings for Will from elementary school into their high school years had been a mix of jealousy and admiration. He'd been her nemesis at every science fair. Her competition for top of the class every school year. They'd even battled it out for the valedictorian title, and she still felt that the school should have had some type of tie-breaker contest instead of making the two of them share the title.

Oh, there had been times when they'd gotten along, and the competition between the two of them had mostly been friendly. They had shared a lot of the same interests, after all, such as science and geography, and they'd both shared an enjoyment of discovering the plants and wildlife on the mountains that surrounded their town.

But when they met again at medical school, things had changed, neither of them the small-town teenagers they had been when they'd left for college.

When they'd reunited at Vanderbilt, they'd almost been strangers, but before long, the two of them had bonded over their love of medicine and their dream of helping others. They'd even put most of their competitiveness behind them, instead cheering each other on as

they'd crammed for tests and studied for their medical boards. It had been one of those late-night cramming sessions that had changed everything.

She'd never forget that first kiss they'd shared. It had taken her breath away and curled her toes, and from that moment on, the two of them had been inseparable. While their days had been filled with classes and studying, their nights had been filled with long hours of lovemaking that was still burned into her memories. It had all happened so fast that she hadn't been prepared for what the change in their relationship really meant.

Looking back, she knew that she had pushed all of the consequences of their becoming lovers into the back of her mind, refusing to deal with any of it. But the moment he'd started talking about his plans for the two of them to return to their hometown and work together side by side at his father's clinic, she knew she couldn't ignore it anymore. For Anna, returning home would mean tossing away all her dreams. Wasting all her hard work. Still, that wasn't an excuse for the way she had cowardly snuck away into the night, leaving only a letter to explain why she had to break things off between the two of them.

But her regret over how she'd handled things didn't change the fact that she knew she had done the right thing. Will's dream of returning home as the town's new doctor was just as important as her dream of seeing the world and helping people along the way. The two of them had never had a chance at anything long term. It was just too bad that she had seen it before

Will. Still, she couldn't help but be embarrassed by the immature way she'd left things between them.

This was a nightmare. A nightmare that would never end once her mother married Dr. Harris.

Her mother meant the world to her, especially after the fire. She'd been her anchor when life had been hard. She'd sometimes worked two jobs to provide for the two of them, as their insurance had barely covered Anna's father's business debts, leaving little for them to live on. Now it was Anna's turn to support her mother. But how did she do that when everything inside of her yelled at her to leave this town before she had to face Will?

And Will? How did he feel about the marriage? He'd lost his mother not long after Anna had lost her father. Another thing they'd had in common growing up, both being raised by single parents.

And now his father was marrying the mother of a woman who he probably hated. Maybe that was the answer. Maybe she just needed to concentrate on the fact that this wasn't any easier on him than it was on her. He was probably trying to figure out how to avoid her just as much as she was trying to figure out a way to avoid him.

"I can do this," Anna repeated to herself for the hundredth time since she'd left Nashville that morning. She was an adult now. They both were. Whatever had happened between the two of them was in the past. Will had likely been so busy joining his father's practice in town that he might not have even thought about her in years. Besides, it was just for a few weeks. And

aside from the wedding, they wouldn't have to even see each other.

Easing off the brake, she pulled herself up in her seat, straightened her shoulders, and made herself continue down the winding road that would take her home.

It had been over five years since she'd last been back. For the first three years her mother had bought her excuse of not being able to get time off during her residency. Then there had been her job in the ER of one of Nashville's largest hospitals. Of course her mother had never complained. Instead, she'd made the five-hour trip between Nashville and home to see Anna whenever they both had a weekend free. Anna had tried to make it up to her mother with the trip to Europe, but she knew her mother would have liked for her to be able to visit her, especially on holidays. The fact that her mother's visits had started to decrease should have been a sign that there was something going on in her life. Only Anna had been so busy working as many hours as possible to get the experience she needed for her dream job of traveling around the country as an ad locum that she'd missed it. The guilt she felt for not being more involved with her mother's life was what had had her volunteering to come two weeks before the wedding to help with the preparations.

As she pulled up into her mother's driveway, she realized that no matter how long she'd stayed away, there had been no preparing herself for this homecoming. No way to keep her heart from pounding in her chest as she stared at the small log cabin that had been both a sanctuary from the world and at the same time a re-

minder of all that they had lost. A reminder that her father, the man who'd held their family together, had been taken from them and they'd had to at least try to move on. The fact that her mother was finally doing it was something that Anna should feel good about. She loved her mother. She wanted her to be happy. It was just that she'd never imagined her mother marrying someone else. Her mother and father had loved each other so much that it didn't seem possible that her mother could ever love someone that way again.

Anna knew that sitting there was only postponing the inevitable. She had to face her mom and put the problems this marriage was causing for her behind her. Even with all the stress Anna was feeling about this visit, her mother's happiness was the most important thing right now. Whatever happened while she was here, would stay here. And in three weeks, Anna would be heading out to Florida for her new life.

She unbuckled and opened the door, stepping out as a gust of cold mountain air hit her. After spending all the years away, she'd forgotten just how cold December up in the Smoky Mountains could be. She'd checked the weather before she left and saw that there was a possibility of an early winter storm in the next couple of weeks. Her mother had mentioned it but had said she hoped that the snow would hold off, as the town was eager to welcome tourists from nearby Gatlinburg to the festival.

Holding her coat around her as the wind tried its best to rip it off, she hurried to the porch and then paused at the front door. It felt strange knocking on the door

of the home where she'd spent her teenage years, but it also felt wrong to walk inside without giving her mother some warning. Besides, in three weeks her mother would be living with Dr. Harris, and it wasn't like Anna could just go walking into their home then.

She rang the video bell she'd had installed on her mother's door, then waited. And waited. Her mother's car was in the driveway, and she had known approximately what time Anna would arrive, so where was she? Anna was just about to ring the bell again when the door opened. The sight of her mother, Coreene, standing in the doorway with a blue mask hiding half her face startled her.

"Mom, what's wrong?" Anna asked as she rushed through the door and took her mother by the arm to steady her.

Coreene's eyes filled with tears as she shook her head. "I can't believe it. Two weeks before my wedding, and I have the flu."

Anna couldn't remember a time she'd seen her mother sick like this.

She led her sniffling mother to the couch and helped her sit down before doing a quick assessment. Coreene's eyes were bright with fever, and though her respirations were even, they were a little labored. Anna needed her stethoscope to get a clearer picture, but she'd left it in the car with the rest of her things and wasn't comfortable leaving her mom alone.

"I'm so glad you're here, but I don't want you getting sick, too," Coreene said once she rested a moment in the chair.

"Mom, I work in a hospital, where I'm likely exposed to far worse. Plus, I've had my flu shot. I'll be fine, so let's focus on you. I can't believe you didn't tell me you were sick," Anna said, taking a seat next to her mom.

"I thought it was a cold, but it's the flu," she said. "James just brought me some masks and some medication that's supposed to help. He says I'll be contagious until the fever goes away for twenty-four hours, so I shouldn't leave the house. But there's so much I need to do. I haven't even decorated for Christmas! And I don't have anything to cook for supper because I haven't been able to get groceries."

"It's okay, Mom. I'm here to help now. Let's get you to bed so you can rest, and then I'll go to the store." Anna had never seen her mother have a meltdown like this before. Not that she didn't understand what her mother was going through. Being sick was bad enough. Being sick with a wedding to get ready for made the situation even worse. If there was a reason for a bride to have a pre-wedding meltdown, this was it.

"I was so excited for you to come home. It's the first Christmas you've been home in years, and I wanted us to decorate the tree together. And there's still so much for me to do before the wedding." Her mother stopped talking and began to cough.

"And none of it will get done if you don't take care of yourself. The best thing for you to do right now is to take your medication and rest so you can get well in time to get married. Everything else I can take care of," Anna said as she grabbed a tissue and wiped the

tears from her mother's eyes. "It's all going to be okay. And now that I'm here, you'll have two doctors taking care of you. We're going to make sure you get well as fast as possible."

Anna's mother stood and gave her a watery smile. "Don't forget Will. That makes three doctors in the family now."

Anna made herself return Coreene's smile even though it felt like her face was about to crack into a thousand pieces. Her mother didn't need to worry. Anna would never be able to forget Will.

After getting her mom settled and then going through the empty cabinets, Anna headed back to her car with a list of things they'd need. No matter how much Anna wanted to avoid the people in town right now, her mom needed some nourishing food. If she was lucky, she'd manage to get in and out of the store before anyone even recognized her and back before her mother woke.

But when the automatic doors to the grocery store opened, Anna only had to take two steps inside before her grocery cart had bumped into one of the biggest gossips of all of Rolling Oaks.

"Anna? Anna Dobson? Well, I can't believe it's you."

"It's nice to see you, Mrs. Monroe," Anna said, hoping against hope that the woman would move her cart so that she could get what she needed and get out.

"Oh my, I heard your mother was sick. I'm glad that you've finally come home to help her," the woman said, putting extra emphasis on the word "finally." Anna knew there would be comments about her not coming

home till now, but she hadn't expected to have to deal with them within the first hour of her arrival. And the fact that this woman already knew that Anna's mother was sick just proved that everyone in the town knew everyone else's business. "I guess your momma is going to have to miss the last meeting of the festival committee. And what about the wedding? I told her Christmas wasn't a good time to get married, especially with the festival coming up."

"Mary, is that Anna you've hijacked?" another woman said as she joined them.

"Ms. Bailey? Shouldn't you be at school?" Anna said to the tall, thin woman who had once ruled Anna's biology classroom with a disciplined hand that would have made a military commander proud.

When the woman stepped up to Anna with her arms open, Anna quickly embraced her. Ms. Bailey had always been her favorite teacher, and her classes had been the start of Anna's desire for a career in medicine.

"I'm mostly retired now. I only fill in when needed. It just isn't the same as it was when you and Will were in school. Now none of the kids want to get off their phones long enough to explore and discover the world around them," Ms. Bailey said, disappointment clear in every word.

Anna tried to ignore the way her teacher had grouped her and Will together.

A high-pitched cry came from a cash register a few feet away, a rasping sound that always set Anna's nerves on edge and threw her right into physician mode. Once a medical professional heard the sound of

a child's airway being compromised, they could never forget it.

Without saying another word, she pushed past the two women and sprinted to where a young woman held a small child in her arms. Surprising the woman, Anna began examining the child.

"It's okay, I'm a doctor. What happened?" Anna asked the woman she assumed to be the child's mother as she placed her hands on the child's puffy face. Red hives were quickly popping out on the child's cheeks and his eyes had begun to swell. "Is he allergic to anything?"

"No. He's never had anything happen like this before," the woman said, realizing that there was something wrong with her child. "He was fine. He wanted a cookie before we got in the car, so I opened the package. He only ate one."

Anna looked at the bag on top of the groceries in the cart and found an open box of chocolate and peanut butter cookies. Yeah, that would do it.

While normally a child's cry would get louder when they were scared, this child's cry had become more of a squeak than a howl. Taking the boy from his mother, Anna opened his mouth and saw that the child's tongue was also swelling. Looking around frantically, Anna wished that she was at one of those big box stores that had a pharmacy inside. The child was having an anaphylactic reaction. She needed to inject a dose of epinephrine.

And there was only one place she knew that would have the drug she needed.

"I'm Dr. Anna Dobson. Those women over there will vouch for me. Your son is having a severe allergic reaction, and I need to get him to Dr. Harris's clinic right now," she told the child's mother. Then, hitching the child up on her hip, she began to run.

CHAPTER TWO

WILL STARED DOWN at the lab results his nurse had just handed him. He'd been working in the medical clinic founded by his father for two years now, and he'd never seen so much flu in the community, let alone so early in the season. He thought of his father's fiancée, Coreene. Will knew that his father was concerned that she might not be recovered by Christmas Eve, the night they'd planned to marry.

His heartfelt groan escaped before he could stop it. Thinking about Coreene reminded him that her daughter Anna would be arriving any day now. Will loved Coreene and was thrilled to see his father so happy, but having to face Anna after what had taken place between the two of them in medical school was going to be very awkward.

"I know, right? Before long everyone in the county will have had the flu," his nurse, Dana, said as she left him to call back their next patient.

"Right," he said, not letting on that right then his mind was far from the explosion of flu that was hitting the community.

It was easy to tell himself that after all this time, none of his and Anna's history mattered, but it was

hard for him to believe it. Anna had walked out of his apartment leaving him nothing but a letter for an explanation. At first he'd thought it was just a misunderstanding. She'd had concerns about their futures going down different paths, but they could have worked that out. But after the first few days of his phone calls going unanswered, he'd begun to understand that working things out between the two of them hadn't been an option for Anna. She had made it clear that they were over, and he had to accept that.

He heard the slamming of a door and the pounding of feet, and when the door to the back exam rooms flew open and a woman came flying in with the small child in her arms, his instincts kicked in.

"In here," he said, opening the door to the room that was kept for emergencies. With the closest emergency room forty-five minutes down a curvy two-lane mountain road, there were times when the clinic had to handle the community emergencies until an ambulance from down the mountain could arrive for transport.

"Anaphylactic reaction. Ate a cookie, peanut butter, about five minutes ago," the woman said as she laid the child down on the examining table. "Weight around fourteen kilograms."

"Dana, open the pediatric code cart. You're going to need to draw up two doses of epinephrine 0.3 milligrams," Will told his office nurse as she followed them into the room.

He knew his heart was pounding too fast. While the child badly needed a dose of adrenaline, his own adrenaline level had apparently shot through the roof the mo-

ment the woman had started speaking. As if he had just conjured her up with his thoughts, Anna Dobson was in his clinic. No, make that Dr. Anna Dobson, since it was evident she was in doctor mode at the moment.

"Where's Charlie's mother?" he asked her as he grabbed the adult oxygen mask that was kept set up, and changed it out to a pediatric size, while Anna helped Dana remove the child's clothes. Red, angry hives covered Charlie's face and chest. This was not a simple allergic reaction. This strong of a reaction could be deadly.

"She should be right behind me," Anna said, looking up at him for the first time. As their eyes met, Will didn't know what he expected to see. Not surprise—she had to know that she'd see him when she'd run into the clinic—but maybe happiness at seeing him after all this time? Awkwardness? But instead, there was just the acknowledgment of his presence as a colleague, as if they worked together this way every day.

As he reached over to apply the small mask, he and Anna collided. For a second, Will saw Anna's professional mask fall as their eyes met, and her lips parted in alarm. For that one moment it was as if time stood still as his body tensed in reaction to the contact between the two of them. Then, as if the moment had never happened, it was gone, and they both returned their focus to their patient.

"Hey, Charlie, it's Dr. Will. Everything is going to be okay, buddy. You ate something that has made you sick, but we are going to make you feel better. Okay?" Will knew that the boy was scared and too busy fight-

ing for air to respond, but he hoped that his talking would not only calm the child down but also help to calm himself down. "I'm going to put this mask on your face, and Nurse Dana is going to give you a shot in your leg to make you feel better."

If it had been possible, the child's eyes would have gotten even bigger. None of Will's young patients loved their vaccinations. A shot when you were already scared seemed cruel, but it was going to be necessary.

"Okay, Charlie. Nurse Dana's going to give you the shot now," Will said as Dana swabbed the little boy's thigh and then injected the epinephrine into his muscle as Anna helped hold his leg still. The boy's cries filled the room, reassuring all of them that he was still able to pass air through to his lungs.

"It's okay, Charlie. Remember, I told you all about this on the way over here. It will only hurt for a moment and then you will start getting better," Anna said as she brushed back the damp hair from the boy's forehead. "Your momma will be here in just a minute, and I'm going to tell her what a good boy you were."

The boy's eyes were locked onto Anna's as his cries turned into sniffles. Will took his stethoscope from around his neck and listened to the child's heart and lungs. "Lungs clear except for a little wheezing. Heart rate regular. Dana, can you get us some vital signs?"

"I'm here," Charlie's mother, Jennifer, said, rushing into the room and stopping short when she saw her son. "How's Charlie? I don't understand what happened, Will."

"It's okay, Jennifer, we've given him a shot of epi-

nephrine, the medicine that people carry around with them when they have a strong allergy to things like peanuts, and he's responding well."

"He's breathing easier now," Anna said, backing away from the exam table so that Charlie's mother could get to him. "I didn't mean to scare either of you, but there wasn't enough time to explain everything."

"I understand. I appreciate what you did; I didn't know what to do." Jennifer stopped talking and Will could tell that her thoughts were going where no mother's should ever have to go.

"It can be scary to see something like that happen to your child," Anna said, backing even farther away. Now that her own adrenaline was running out, Will was afraid she was going to bolt out of the room without even speaking with him.

And if he was smart, he would let her. Still, it didn't seem like a very professional thing to do.

"And what a big, brave boy you are," Jennifer told her son.

"Scared," Charlie said between sniffles, his lips quivering. While some of the swelling around his eyes had gone down, there were still hives covering most of his face and chest. He would need to be watched overnight, which would require him to be transferred down the mountain to the nearest hospital in Sevierville.

"I was scared, too," Jennifer admitted to her son, her own lips quivering.

"I think you scared all of us," Will said. "But now that we know you have a serious allergy, we can take care that this doesn't happen again."

Glancing back at Anna, he saw that she had moved even closer to the door. "Dana, can you get another set of vital signs and start weaning the oxygen down? I'm going to step out and speak with Dr. Dobson, but if there are any changes, let me know."

"Sure, Will," his nurse said, never looking up from the tablet where Will knew she was charting all the vital signs and medications. "Do you want me to start an IV?"

He knew the emergency medical techs would request one before transport, but it seemed best to let Charlie relax a few moments before getting stuck with any more needles. "Yes, but give him a few minutes to recover first. The ambulance will want it for transport. Also, I'll need to get an X-ray before I call the emergency room doctor for acceptance."

"Don't forget that Mrs. Davis is still in the exam room waiting for you. Also, I just put Sam Bell in exam room two," Dana said.

"Got it," he said. As if he was going to forget about the elderly lady that made at least one trip to the clinic each week. And Sam? There was no telling what the man had done to his body this time. He turned back to see Anna slipping out the door.

"Anna, can I have a moment?" he asked as he caught up with her in the hallway.

She stopped, but for a moment she didn't turn toward him. Was she really going to just walk out of the clinic without talking to him? When she did turn, her face was almost unreadable, her smile as fake as any he'd ever seen. There was a time he would have called

her out on that. But that time was long gone. No matter how much he had once thought the two of them meant to each other, they were strangers now.

"I just wanted to say thank you, as Charlie's doctor, for your help," he said, now wishing that he had just let her leave. This all felt too awkward.

"I'm glad I was there. Of course, once Charlie's mom had figured out what was happening, I'm sure she would have rushed him in here," Anna said, her eyes looking everywhere but at him. Was she comparing the small clinic that he loved to the fancy emergency room in Nashville where he'd heard she worked?

"But by then things would have been a lot worse. Your taking charge of the situation and getting him here made a difference." Will could tell she was as anxious to leave as he was to end this conversation, the way she shifted her weight from foot to foot something he'd seen her do a million times when she'd found herself unwillingly in the spotlight. Even after years with no contact, he remembered so much about her. Still, there were changes.

"You quit trying to straighten your hair?" he said, surprising himself as much as her. Why couldn't he just tell her thank you and walk away? Instead, he'd now made things even more awkward.

Her hand came up to the riot of mahogany curls that fell down past her shoulders. He'd always thought her curls were perfect. She'd thought they were too "unkempt" looking and had done everything possible to straighten them.

"You can't really take a straight iron into a displacement camp that's being run off generators," Anna said.

"I can see that would be a problem. Your mom told me you had done a few weeks with a humanitarian group during your residency." He needed to let her go. He had patients to see. Yet still, he couldn't seem to do it. "How is your mother doing today?"

"Not so good. She could barely stand up when I got there this morning. She was sleeping when I left, but—" she looked down at her watch "—but I need to get back and check on her."

"And I need to get back to Mrs. Davis," he said, turning to go.

"I guess we'll see each other later. You know, with the wedding and everything," Anna said, her words hesitant.

"I'm sure we will," he said before forcing himself to walk away and leaving her standing there. He knew it was immature of him to feel good about the fact that he was the one to walk away first this time, but at that moment he didn't care.

Anna Dobson was back in town, and seeing her again had brought back emotions that he had thought he'd buried long ago. First there had been the shock of seeing her there in his clinic, then there'd been that haunting, sexual awareness when they'd touched. But underneath it all, there had been the pain of knowing that the reason she'd returned to town had nothing to do with him.

By the time she got back home, Anna had relived every moment she'd just spent at Will's clinic multiple times. She'd been so unprepared to see him there, his blond hair combed back with that little cowlick he'd had since

he was a child still sticking up, and his blue eyes still so bright and familiar.

But he had changed, too. There were a few tiny lines around his eyes and mouth that made her think that he spent a lot of his time smiling and laughing. That thought made her smile. He'd always told her she was too serious, while she'd told him he didn't take things serious enough. And his body? She'd swear she'd felt every hard muscle of him when they'd collided in the exam room. The jolt of electricity she'd felt from the contact had been so strong it had almost made her forget what she was doing. Fortunately, Will hadn't noticed, though she had seen his nurse giving the two of them a curious look.

It was unbelievable that after all the ways she'd imagined seeing Will again, after all her dreading and worrying about it, their first meeting would have happened because of a medical emergency. Though maybe that was a good thing. It was like snatching a bandage off. It was less painful to just get it over with instead of going through the misery of worrying about what would happen when the time came.

But even more unbelievable was the way she'd felt when she'd seen him. Maybe if they had met another way there would have been the awkwardness and the guilt she had expected to feel. But the sight of him, as she'd run into that exam room carrying that little boy who might stop breathing at any moment, had filled her with relief. Instinctively, she'd known that with the two of them there together, the child was going to be okay. That was what had been important. Not the way

her breath had caught when she'd first met his eyes. And not the way her body still hummed from its contact with Will's. The child's well-being had been the most important thing to both of them.

Anna had opened the door and let herself in before she saw her mother sitting at the table. "I was hoping to be home before you woke up."

"Anna, I'm so glad you're here. I need you to do me a big favor. I can't believe I forgot about this. I could have had you take care of it when you went to the grocery store," Coreene said. Anna noticed that her mother's eyes weren't quite as bright as they had been when she'd first arrived, and she seemed to be agitated.

"It's okay. I didn't mean to be gone so long, but something happened at the grocery store and I ended up having to go back a second time." Anna filled her mom in as she unloaded the groceries.

"That poor child. I'm so glad you were there to help. I wish I could have seen Will's face when you ran into that room." Anna knew her mother had always had a soft spot for Will. Anna had always thought maybe that it was because he had lost his mother, and now here Coreene was, about to become Will's stepmother. The whole thing still felt so surreal.

"So, what can I do for you? Is it something for the wedding?" Anna asked as she closed the refrigerator.

"No, it's for the Christmas festival. I forgot about the meeting tonight. I've been in charge of organizing the vendors, and I have all the information for the rest of the committee, along with a map of the festival with each vendor's location marked. If you could take

that to the meeting for me tonight, it would be a load off my mind."

"Can't you just call and let them know you're sick? I could scan everything for you and email it across to everyone tomorrow." Anna waited for her mother to protest. Instead, Coreene's shoulders slumped as she sat back in her chair.

Anna's mother had always been a strong woman, but after Anna's father had died in the fire while he'd tried to save their home and his business, Coreene had been broken. They'd both been broken. But when they'd discovered that the insurance covering the business and home was only enough to pay off their debts and build the small home they lived in now, Anna's mother had dragged herself up and found a way to support their family. Seeing her mom down like this was a strong and unwelcome reminder of that low point in their lives, and Anna couldn't stand to see her in pain. "Don't worry, Mom, I'll take the information to the meeting and take notes for you."

Anna watched as her mother relaxed into the chair. "Thank you, Anna. That's such a relief."

"Now, let's get you back in bed, and then I'll heat up some soup for you before I leave."

"Thank you," her mother said again, giving Anna a weak smile. And while Anna wasn't looking forward to going back down the hill and dealing with a committee that she knew nothing about, that smile made it all worthwhile.

Besides, how hard could it be to put on a Christmas festival in a small town like this? She'd show up and

give them her mother's paperwork, take a note or two, and be home within the hour. After the excitement of the day at the grocery store, it would probably be downright boring.

CHAPTER THREE

WILL WOULD HAVE liked to have gone home and taken a shower before the town's Christmas festival meeting, but with a couple of last-minute walk-in patients, he was lucky to make it there on time. Now, sitting around a table with the other members of the committee, he was just about to make excuses for Coreene missing the meeting when Anna rushed into the room. With a stack of papers in her hands, Will knew that somehow Anna's mother had managed to get her daughter to come in her place, and the look on Anna's face told him she would rather be anywhere else. She was used to fancy cities and fancy people. The people around this table were just ordinary folks trying to make their town better. It wasn't like she cared about their small-town Christmas festival. She'd proven she didn't care about the town by the way she'd avoided it for the last five years.

"Hi," Anna said, as she took the only empty seat at the table.

"Everyone, I'm sure you remember Anna Dobson, or Dr. Anna Dobson now," Will said as an idea struck him. Anna would hate it, but maybe she needed to see just how hard these people worked to keep their only source of health care open. "As all of you know,

Coreene has taken sick with the flu and we don't know when, or if, she'll be able to join us again. I think we should officially invite Anna to stand in as her replacement for now."

"I don't know if that's allowed, Will. If Coreene can't make it, we need to appoint someone in her place," the mayor said, looking around the table at the rest of the committee.

"Well, here is the someone," Will said, pointing at Anna. He almost felt bad about roping her into helping—almost—but a part of him couldn't help but want to see how she would handle things.

"Wait, what?" Anna said, though she couldn't be heard over the other committee members, as they had begun to talk among themselves. Will let them talk, while avoiding looking at Anna.

"I'm just here to take notes for my mom and hand out some maps," Anna said, her voice going up an octave. He couldn't help but smile when the whole table went quiet and turned toward them.

"It isn't anything personal, Anna," Mayor Johnson said. "It's just that you've been gone for a long time now, and we don't know anything about you anymore. This festival means a lot to this community. We have to make sure it runs perfectly."

"I know Anna," a voice said from down the table. "She was in my biology class and then my anatomy and physiology class. She was an excellent student. I always told her she could do anything she set her sights on. And now look at her. She's an emergency room doctor in Nashville," said Ms. Bailey.

"Thanks?" Anna said, though it came out more question than statement.

"And if she has any problems, I'm sure Coreene will help guide her through them," Ms. Bailey added.

"Let's vote on it," one of the other committee members said. "All in favor of making Anna part of the committee?"

Anna's green eyes were wide and her mouth agape as she looked around the room where all but two members voted for her to take her mother's place on the committee.

"I don't... I can't..." she began, her cheeks turning a very pretty pink.

Will felt a stab of guilt for just a moment, but then it was gone. She'd used the excuse of not wanting to be stuck in this town the rest of her life as the reason to break things off with him, but he'd never understood that. Yes, they were a small town, but it was a small town made up of hard working and caring people, something she'd clearly never appreciated. Maybe if she had to do some of the work these people did to help a clinic that she seemed to think had very little merit, she'd see just how much the community appreciated what he and his father provided.

"Then it's settled. Anna will take the place of Coreene for now," Will said. If his smile was a little wicked, the rest of the committee didn't seem to notice.

But when he looked over at Anna her eyes were narrowed at him, acknowledging that she knew he had manipulated the situation to get what he wanted. He had no doubt that she was planning some way to get

him back for this, but fortunately for Will, they were on his hometown turf. He had the advantage.

"Uh," Anna said, and then looked at him again before clearing her voice and addressing everyone. "Sure. I mean, I'm honored to help."

She looked back at him, then at the table. "From what I understand, the festival is a way to help provide money for the clinic. I was in there today with a patient, and I got a chance to see just how much the clinic is needed here. I'm sure Will and his dad appreciate every one of you for what you're doing here."

Her words surprised him, but he managed not to show it as the committee moved on to other issues. By the time they had ironed out the mayor's safety concerns with shutting down the town square, something they had gone over at every meeting, it seemed Anna had been caught up on everything about the festival from the craft booth rentals to the games and Santa's arrival.

"Thanks a lot for that," Anna said as the meeting ended, sarcasm coating each word. "I can't believe that the mayor still has it out for me."

It took a moment for Will to understand what she was referring to. He'd forgotten the petition Anna had started in the eighth grade to have the town square's name changed to the "town rectangle," which did describe the small set of buildings that surrounded the rectangle of land that housed the small courthouse and sheriff's office more accurately. When Mayor Johnson had heard about the petition, she had been horrified at the idea and called Anna's mother immediately. The

fact that Coreene had felt the need to explain the concept of freedom of speech to the mayor, in detail, and then hadn't stopped Anna from soliciting for the petition, had caused friction between them ever since. His own father had thought it was hilarious when he'd heard about it, and they'd both been sad to hear that the question of renaming the square hadn't made it onto that year's ballot.

"I don't think she has it out for you. The festival is the biggest thing to happen in the town, and she wants it to be successful," he said as they both followed the group out. "A lot of us end up at the Coffee Cup before we go home, if you'd like to join us."

"Thanks, but I need to get back and check on my mom," Anna said. "Between the festival and the wedding, she couldn't have gotten sick at a worse time. I want to help as much as possible."

He started to jump to the conclusion that she was just trying to avoid the people of the town, but he knew her first concern would be for her mother. Coreene was all Anna had, much like his father was to him.

Later that night when Will got home to his apartment above the clinic, he went to the small room he'd turned into an office and opened his desk's bottom drawer. Pushing back the row of hanging files, he found the piece of paper he'd stored there for safe keeping and then placed it on the desk. He'd never shared with anyone the contents of the letter. It was too personal for Anna and too painful for him. There had been a time when he'd hoped Anna would realize what she had written wasn't true. Their relationship hadn't been

meant to be only temporary. But after the first two years of his residency without hearing from her, he'd forced himself to put the letter away and move on with his life. Wasn't that what Anna had asked him to do? And even though he understood the reasons behind her leaving, a part of him had never forgiven her for it. She should have stayed and talked to him. Yes, there were problems to work out. He'd grown up knowing he'd take over his father's small-town practice. It was the reason he'd gone into medicine. He'd admired the way his dad took care of their neighbors, and he'd wanted to carry on the practice when his father retired. The town needed him. And he needed the town. It was home. His home.

Anna's dreams had been different than his. She'd felt different about the town, understandably so after all the trauma she'd gone through when her father had died and her family had lost everything.

But still, he should have been given the opportunity for them to talk. To try to work things out.

He spread the letter, wrinkled with age, out onto his desk. And for the first time in years, he read it from start to finish before folding it up once again. He went to put it back and stopped. In the letter, Anna had told him that she was leaving him and ending things between them because she was afraid that if things went further between the two of them, she'd not be able to fulfill her dreams of seeing the world and experiencing life outside their small town. She was afraid that she'd end up living in a town where she didn't feel like

she belonged, one "that always wanted me to be someone I wasn't."

It wasn't hard for Will to understand what Anna
meant. They'd both been the nerdy science kids. They'd
been the kids most likely to succeed. Not the kids most
likely to get invited out with friends, though things had
been better for him because of his father's position in
the town. He knew that.

But what if he could show her that things could be
different? They'd been barely considered adults when
they'd graduated from medical school, each of them
ready to save the world with their brand-new degrees.
Now that they were older, and more mature, maybe she
would be able to see the town differently.

But not him. He knew their chance at a relationship, at least a romantic one, had passed. But for their
parents' sakes, wouldn't it be good for Anna to feel at
home in the town, especially since they had no choice
but to pretend to be the big happy family their parents
expected them to be?

When Anna's phone rang Monday morning, she almost didn't answer it. After seeing Will at the clinic
and then that night at the festival committee meeting,
she'd enjoyed a nice quiet weekend catching up with
her mother. Now, seeing Will's name on her phone, all
the peace and relaxation she'd so enjoyed disappeared.
She'd imagined that if she came home, he'd avoid her
as much as she would avoid him, but that wasn't happening. Instead, she now found herself working on a
festival with him.

On the third ring, Anna's curiosity got the better of her. "Hello?"

"Hey, it's me. Will." His voice sounded as uncertain as hers. "Sorry to bother you, but Jennifer stopped by this morning and wanted me to let you know that Charlie was home from the hospital and doing great. She's got an appointment with a pediatric allergist next week, and the hospital gave her an epinephrine pen to use if he has another reaction in the meantime."

"That's great. I'm assuming that the reaction was from the peanut butter in the cookies, but he does need to be tested to be sure." Before she'd gone to medical school she'd never realized there was so much that a child could be allergic to.

"Yeah, she said she's done a lot of research over the past few days into new ways of treating peanut allergies," Will said, his voice rising over the office noises in the background.

"It sounds like the office is busy, so I'll let you go," she said, anxious to get off the phone. Their conversation was so normal, yet she still felt an awkwardness underlining every word she said.

"Oh, I almost forgot. Jennifer left a cake here for you," Will said.

"A cake? Like for payment? She didn't need to do that. I was just a bystander," she said.

"Not for payment. To thank you," he said, sounding annoyed now. "It's what you do in a close community like this. She just wanted to let you know how much she appreciated what you did."

Anna heard someone call Will's name in the back-

ground. "I've got to go. Looks like someone took a tumble at the post office. I'll see you when you stop by to get the cake."

She sat staring at her phone for several seconds after Will had hung up. Their conversation had almost sounded normal. Well, until he'd gotten annoyed at her for assuming Charlie's mother had thought she would need to pay Anna. But even that had sounded normal. It seemed so easy for Will to act like nothing had ever happened between them. Like they had never been lovers. Like the years since the night she had left him had never happened.

And how was she supposed to react to that? Was she supposed to just pretend nothing had ever happened between the two of them, too? Was it wrong that she was wanted to do just that? Pretend that she was just an old classmate that had come to town for a visit? Could she hide the way her stomach went into a tumbling free fall whenever she saw him?

"What's wrong?" her mother said, coming out of her room.

"The little boy I told you about, the one that had the allergic reaction, his mother baked me a cake and left it at Will's office for me," Anna said as Coreene took a chair across the kitchen table from her.

"Well, wasn't that nice of her. What was her name?" she asked, as Anna got up to make them both a cup of tea.

"Her name is Jennifer, and the little boy is Charlie," Anna said, placing the cup and tea bag on the counter, then pouring the hot water.

"Thanks honey," Coreene said. "I bet that's the Jennifer that married Allen Watts. You remember him. He was in the class behind you."

Yes, Anna remembered him. He'd been one of the sports jocks that had made fun of her and Will. It was hard to believe that he was married to such a nice woman as Jennifer.

"He and his wife are youth pastors at the church downtown. He's great with the kids, I hear," her mom said, before adding honey to her cup.

Anna found that hard to believe, but she knew people changed. Hadn't she? She'd once been the shy, quiet kid that had a hard time making conversation. Now she talked to strangers every day. Maybe Allen had changed, too.

"So, how are you feeling today?" she asked her mother, though from the look of her and the coughing Anna had heard last night, a miraculous recovery was seeming increasingly unlikely.

"I think I'm better. I do appreciate you being here given there's so much left to do. When James asked me to marry him and we decided not to wait, I thought it would be easy to plan a small wedding. I thought a month would be plenty of time. I never dreamed I'd be sick. Now I have two weeks and I don't even have my flowers picked out."

Anna didn't know anything about planning weddings, but she was pretty sure it took months. "Maybe you need to put it off till a later date."

"Oh, no. We've waited long enough. Besides, if we put it off, there will be all kinds of talk. I'm getting

married Christmas Eve, even if I have to wear a mask." Her mother's eyes filled with tears and she began to sniff. "I'd made appointments for me and you to pick out the flowers together, and now you're going to have to go by yourself."

"I…" Her mother wanted her to pick out the flowers alone? Anna didn't know anything about wedding flowers. What if she picked out the wrong ones? What if she messed up the whole wedding?

"Isn't there someone besides me that you'd like to help you? Someone maybe more experienced in helping with weddings? Isn't there a wedding planner that could help?" Wasn't Gatlinburg famous for being a wedding venue? Surely there was someone else that could step in.

"Of course not. There wasn't any reason to hire one. We're not planning for this to be a fancy wedding. It's just a small wedding in the church on Christmas Eve. I hate to ask you to do this alone, but I don't have any other choice."

When her mother's eyes teared up again, Anna knew she was beat. Coreene had always been there for her, through countless spelling bees, science projects, and band contests. And when she was young and couldn't sleep without having nightmares about the fire and losing her dad…her mother had been right there beside her. It had been a horrible time for both of them. As a child, she'd never considered just how hard it was on her mother to lose the man she'd loved since high school and still have to show up as a parent every single day. As an adult, Anna realized that she'd been

so wrapped up in her own life that she hadn't considered just how much her mother had been hurting, and what she had gone through trying to ensure Anna's life was as full as possible. Here was a chance to show her mother just how much she appreciated and loved her. She needed to step up and take it. Anna would show her mother that she could be counted on to be there for her, too. Even if she had to take on organizing the whole wedding, she would do it.

"Don't worry about anything. I want you to just take it easy. I'm going to get some laundry going, and then you can catch me up on everything that you've planned up until now. I can always go into the flower shop and we can do a video chat so you can tell me what you want."

"That sounds nice, but you don't have to wait on me. I can help with the laundry," Coreene said, her voice still ragged from the coughing fits that she'd had the night before and her hand shaking from just the weight of the teacup in her hand. Her mother had a long way to go before she'd be ready for the wedding, but Anna wasn't about to bring up the possibility of cancelling again. Her mother still had time to recover if she was serious about getting rest.

"I'll handle the chores around the house and everything for the wedding that I can. And I've already agreed to help with the festival. All you need to do is rest and get better."

"I'm so glad you volunteered to help. It will give you time to reconnect with some of the people in town who have missed you."

As far as Anna knew, no one in this town but Will and her were aware that the two of them had once been more than friends. And if Will could act like their time together had never happened, so could she.

CHAPTER FOUR

WHEN ANNA STEPPED into the medical clinic to pick up the cake Jennifer had left for her, there were several people she didn't recognize among the overflowing waiting room. Her mother had told her that with the growth of the tourism and jobs in Sevierville and Gatlinburg that there had been several new families that had moved up the mountain, so she assumed the unfamiliar faces were the newer arrivals in town.

When she walked over to the front desk, she was glad to see at least one person she recognized—Ms. Martha Horne, the woman who had run Dr. Harris's office for as long as she could remember.

"Anna, I'm so glad to see you! I didn't have a chance to talk to you the other day when you ran past. How are you?" Ms. Martha said. Though her hair had a bit more silver in it since the last time Anna had seen her, her eyes were just as bright and merry. Anna had always liked the older woman and quickly learned when she'd started working in the emergency room that not all receptionists were as helpful or as kind as Ms. Martha.

"I'm fine, thank you. And I'm sorry about not saying hello; I was kind of in a hurry," Anna said. To be honest, she didn't even remember rushing by the woman,

all she remembered was the sound of Charlie's rasping breath.

"Don't you worry about it. I understand totally. Jennifer was in here earlier and couldn't say enough good things about you. And I'm sure Dr. Will was happy to have your help. It seems the larger the town grows, the more emergencies we have. Not that I'd change anything. It's nice to see all these new couples moving into town."

"I noticed there were a lot of people I didn't recognize here. Mom says that they're even talking about expanding the school."

"As long as it doesn't get too much bigger I'm all for it. I don't want this place to turn into one of those big tourist towns."

"I don't think you have to worry about that. We're a little too far up the mountain for those kinds of crowds." Anna was surprised when she realized she'd said "we're," including herself in the town's population. This wasn't her town anymore.

"You're probably right. Let me let Dr. Harris know you're here. I know he'd want to see you," Ms. Martha said, jumping out of her chair and heading down the hall before Anna could stop her.

A few moments later, Anna saw her heading back with the elder Dr. Harris behind her, a smile as big as the man on his face. "Anna, it's so nice to see you. Come on back. I'm just between patients at the moment."

Anna looked back at the crowded waiting room, feeling a touch of guilt that she was making someone wait,

but didn't see anyone that appeared upset with her interruption. Following him back into the exam room corridor, Anna noticed several changes that had been made to the clinic that she hadn't had time to see on her previous visit. The clinic had been founded over thirty years ago when Dr. Harris had come back to his hometown to set up the practice, and it had been overdue for a remodel the last time she'd been there, so it wasn't the new flooring or fresh paint that surprised Anna. Instead, it was the updated equipment that she saw in the hallways and exam rooms.

"I like the changes," Anna said as she walked into Dr. Harris's office. She'd only been into the doctor's inner sanctum once before, and it wasn't a visit she could forget. After getting accepted into medical school, Anna had come home for a short summer break, and when her mother had told her that Dr. Harris had requested that she stop by, she'd been surprised. She'd been even more surprised when the elder Dr. Harris had ushered her into his office and asked her what her plans were after medical school. It was the first time someone had actually asked her that. She'd always looked up to the doctor, and telling him that she planned on using her doctorate degree to tour the country had been a hard thing for her to do, as she had assumed he was hoping she'd be coming back to Rolling Oaks. She'd never forget the kindness he'd showed her when he'd congratulated her for having a dream and going after it. His kind words had made it a little easier for her to tell her mother that she wouldn't be returning when she finished her residency.

But the office was different, too. "Is it me, or has this room shrunk?"

"No, it's not you. We did a little remodeling a few years ago when I knew Will would be joining the practice. My old office was much bigger than I needed, so we just split it down the middle." Anna had expected the man to walk around to his desk, but instead he reached out for her hands, grasping them in his. "I owe you an apology. I should have contacted you before I asked your mother to marry me."

Anna didn't know what to say. Her mother was a grown woman, and she could decide for herself who she was going to marry. But Dr. Harris came from a different generation, and it was kind of him to consider her feelings.

"I'm not going to deny that this was all a shock to me. I didn't even know the two of you were dating! I still don't know why my mom didn't mention it to me." She tried to keep the hurt that she'd hidden from her mom out of her voice.

"Your mom wasn't sure how you'd take it. She'd never considered dating while she'd been raising you. Much like I didn't while raising Will. But when you moved to Nashville after college, I think she began to get lonely. The two of us began spending some time together, and our friendship grew into something more." The smile on the man's face told Anna everything she needed to know.

"I'm glad you found each other," Anna said, her eyes going misty. "I know if there was anyone that I would trust to take care of Mom, it would be you, Dr. Harris."

Letting go of his hands, Anna reached up and hugged the man.

There was a knock at the door and Anna turned to see Will standing there. He said, "Sorry I'm interrupting, but I need a second opinion on an X-ray."

Dr. Harris looked down at his watch. "It looks like I'm beginning to get behind. Why don't you let Anna see it, since she's here? I'm sure she would be happy to look over an X-ray," Dr. Harris said, pulling away from Anna. "She must see hundreds a day in that fancy university hospital she works at."

"What?" both Anna and Will asked at the same time.

"You don't mind do you, Anna?" Dr. Harris said, There was no way for Anna to refuse the man's request politely, though she knew both her and Will were being manipulated by the elder doctor. "Of course, not. I'd be happy to help you, Will."

"That's great. It will give the two of you a chance to catch up. It's hard to believe, but in a week we're all going to be family!"

The look Anna saw on Will's face as his father rushed down the hall toward one of the exam rooms told her that right then Will wasn't any happier with that idea than she was. So why had he been acting like things were fine between them all this time?

Anger radiated through Will's body. How had his father done that? Why had his father done that? His father had made it plain to him that he wanted his and Coreene's marriage to be peaceful and without any of the drama that had gone on between him and Anna during their

childhood. If his father knew of the drama that the two had had as adults, he wouldn't have ever suggested that the two of them could get along.

"It's okay. I don't need your help. I'm sure of what I saw on the X-ray," he said as he turned to go.

"Then why did you ask your father for a second opinion?" Anna asked, following him as he headed back to his office.

"I was hoping he'd tell me I was wrong," he said, and then stopped before he opened the door. "It's okay, Anna. You can go. Really. I'm good."

"Apparently, you're not, or you wouldn't have asked your dad for help," she said, her jaw tipped up with a challenge. Anna had changed in many ways since the last time he'd seen her. There was a maturity in her emerald eyes and a confidence in her walk that even in medical school she'd lacked. But one thing hadn't changed. She still had a stubborn streak a mile long.

"This isn't a competition to see who's the best at reading an X-ray," he said.

"I didn't think it was," she said. "I thought I was helping another colleague out. It's called a consultation. I ask for them all the time. It shouldn't be a big deal."

She was right. He was taking this as a personal affront when neither his father nor Anna had meant it that way. He could blame it on the fact that he was upset about what he'd seen on his patient's X-ray, but it was more than that. For the last five years he'd lived with the feeling that Anna thought his job here in the clinic wasn't important, or at least not as important as what she was doing in a big city emergency room.

Hadn't that basically been what she'd said when she'd broken things off with him? She wanted to go out into the world and do great things, and that meant leaving Will and his small-town world behind.

He'd accepted that Anna was going to be a part of his life with the marriage of their parents. He'd even maneuvered her into taking part in the town festival, as he thought it would be good for her to be involved in the town. But having her look over his work as if he was less of a doctor than she was—that hit every raw nerve she'd scraped when she'd left him for those bigger and greater things.

"I'm confident in what I am seeing," he told her.

"But you want confirmation. I understand that, Will. I do the same thing. Sometimes I question things I see, too. The fact that you asked your father, someone I would consider a mentor, makes sense. And if your father had any doubts of your not being capable, he wouldn't have asked me to look at the X-ray. He would have done it himself," Anna said. "I'm not here to question your abilities. I have no doubt that I'm going to agree with whatever it is you are seeing. Remember, I spent a lot of time in classes and clinic rotations with you. I've always known you were going to be a great doctor."

It was as if her words eased something inside of him that had been festering for years. Her acknowledgment that she did think of him as a capable doctor meant more than it should. He knew he was a good doctor. He shouldn't need Anna's validation of that fact.

"Come on in, then," he said, giving up. He'd might as well get this over with so that he could get back to

his patient. Though that wasn't something he was looking forward to, either.

Walking around to his desk, he motioned her to join him. He refreshed his computer screen, then found the X-ray he was looking for and waited. For Anna, a hotshot ER doctor from the big city, this would only be another X-ray for her to read. For Will, this was one of his patients, one of his fellow townsfolk. Someone whose health he felt responsible for.

"Whose X-ray is this?" Anna asked as she bent over him, her hair brushing against his shoulder, the fragrance of her shampoo hitting him hard.

Memories of their time together poured through him. He remembered the feel of her hair as he'd run his hands through it. He remembered the smell that had lingered on his pillow long after she had left him.

And he remembered the letter she'd left behind on that pillow. The one that tore him apart until he'd finally realized he had to move on with his life.

"There's a mass on the lower lobe of the right lung," Anna said. "I take it the patient doesn't know and you'll have to tell them today?"

She said the words with a finality that cleared all those past memories from his mind. She wasn't saying anything he didn't know. He'd really just been putting off the inevitable by asking his father to take a look. A second opinion wasn't going to change the results or what Will had to do.

"A friend?" Anna asked, sympathy now in her voice.

"A long-time patient. One of my first. He has a family, two kids. Both in elementary school."

"It looks like you caught it early," Anna said before reaching over him for a pad of paper. "Here's the name of an oncologist at Vanderbilt that I refer my patients to. Call him and tell him I referred you. I can't promise it will help, but I think it will."

"Thanks," Will said as Anna handed him the note and moved away from him. As she walked around to the other side of the desk, the muscles in his body finally uncoiled. He'd blamed his body's reaction to her when she'd run into his exam room with Charlie on the shock of seeing her. Apparently, from the way his body hardened every time she was in touching range, it was still operating in shock mode. Any other excuse was not an option. There was no room in either of their lives for anything else. "I appreciate the help."

"So, can I ask you a question?" Anna said, standing across from him and biting down on her bottom lip, a telltale sign. He'd seen her do this a hundred times when they were kids, usually when called upon for an answer she wasn't sure of. As an adult, the act brought out a whole new reaction, one that he was now doing his best to ignore. A part of him wanted to accuse her of doing it on purpose, but he knew that wasn't true.

"Okay. Go for it," he said, concentrating on shutting down his computer instead of on her lips.

"Does it seem a little weird to you that our parents are getting married?" she asked, and then hurried on. "Not that I object. Your father is amazing. It's just…"

"What part is weird? The fact that our parents are finding love now that they're older? Or the fact that we are going to be stepbrother and stepsister?"

"I don't want to even think about that," she said, her cheeks turning a rosy pink. "Surely no one will think of us that way. We're not children. We're adults. Just because our parents marry doesn't mean that our relationship to each other should change."

He shouldn't tease her. Not after everything that had happened between the two of them. But right then, when he knew he was about to change his patient's life forever, he needed a moment of lighthearted fun to ease the tension, and it had always been such fun to tease Anna. Looking back now, some of his teasing had been cruel, especially when he'd gone along with his friends who'd given her the nickname "bug" to make fun of her glasses. He'd stopped that when he'd gotten older and realized that Anna took it more to heart than it was intended. But they weren't children anymore. And no matter how much he enjoyed teasing her, she'd asked a valid question.

"I guess I would feel different about it if I hadn't seen the two of them together. They share something special. Which makes them lucky, I think."

"What do you mean?" Anna asked.

Picking up the piece of paper with the number of the specialist on it, he held it up for her to see as he stepped around the desk. "No one knows what's going to happen from one minute to the next. Our parents were lucky enough to find love a second time, and I firmly believe that if you find love, you should hold on to it and not let anything get in your way. That's why they're getting married, and I support their decision," he said as they stepped out of his office, then paused

at the door of the exam room where he was about to give a young man in the prime of his life the results of an X-ray that would change everything.

"Okay," Anna said. "You're right. If anyone deserves to be happy, I know my momma does."

If Anna suspected that he'd been speaking as much about the two of them as he was about their parents, she didn't show it. It was just another sign that the time they'd spent together had meant more to him than it had ever meant to her. But then again, he'd known that the moment he'd read the letter she'd left the night she'd walked out of his life.

Will nodded at her and forced himself to open the exam room door.

CHAPTER FIVE

ARMED WITH A list of people to see for her mother, Anna left the clinic, then placed Jennifer's cake in her car before starting down the sidewalk. The sun had come out, and though the temperature hadn't climbed much during the day, the wind had died down. Everywhere she looked, there were signs that Christmas was only two weeks away. Multi-colored Christmas bells hung from the light posts and each of the stores had decorated their windows with Christmas scenery. Even the hardware store that had been owned by Mr. and Mrs. Harvey for as long as she could remember had a six-foot-tall Santa hefting snow with a shiny snow shovel.

When she found the sign over the boutique where her mother wanted her to try on her dress for the wedding, she hurried inside. Coreene had assured Anna that she would like the dress she'd picked out, but she was still anxious to see it.

A voice came from behind the counter. "Can I help you?"

"Oh, sorry," Anna said, feeling ridiculous now. "I'm here to see a bridesmaid dress my mother picked out for her wedding. It should be under Coreene Dobson."

"You must be Anna. Your mother told me you'd be coming in. Everyone is so sorry that she's come down with a cold," the woman said, stepping back into the storage area of the shop before bringing out a vinyl dress bag.

"Everyone?" Anna asked, and then forgot the question when the woman pulled out an emerald-green gown from the bag. "Is that the dress?"

"Yes, it's beautiful, right? I need you to try it on so I can see if it needs any adjustments," the woman said, handing Anna the dress and pointing to a fitting room. "My name is Camilla. And by 'everyone,' I mean everyone in town, of course. Coreene is a very special woman, and she and Dr. Harris make such a cute couple. And with the wedding coming up so fast, it's so unfortunate that she's sick now."

"It is unfortunate, but she's getting better every day," Anna said. "I'm sure she'll be better by the wedding."

A few minutes later, she returned wearing the dress, holding it up off the ground. "I didn't think about bringing any heels with me to wear with the dress."

"That's okay. Let me see what I can find for you," Camilla said.

Moments later, she returned and handed Anna a box with a pair of gold open-toe heels. Slipping them on, Anna stood while Camilla measured the hem and then checked the rest of the dress. After promising to have the dress hemmed and ready for her the next week, Anna left the store with a new pair of shoes and a pair of warm gloves she'd spotted at the cash register.

Her next stop was at the bakery, where she was dis-

appointed to find the owner out for the day. After explaining to one of the salespeople that she needed to speak with the owner as soon as possible, an appointment was made for the following morning.

Her last stop was at the florist. Stepping into the shop, she was thrilled to see that the whole front room had been turned into a Christmas wonderland. If there was anyone in Tennessee that could help her, this was the place. She picked up her phone and sent some pictures to her mother, along with a message updating her on the progress she'd made so far. Seeing all the arrangements surrounding her, she knew their choices weren't going to be easy. There were, of course, the standard poinsettias in planters, but these weren't your everyday planters. Each planter had been painted with white glitter that sparkled like fresh snow. And the arrangements that she could see in the refrigerated area at the back of the shop were even more festive.

"Anna?" the woman at the counter called. "I heard you had come home."

"Shelley?" Anna asked, recognizing the brunette that had been in her class from kindergarten until their freshman year in high school, at which point Shelley's family had moved away.

"That's me. I'll bet you never thought you'd see me again," Shelley said, coming out from behind the counter and giving Anna a view of a very large baby bump.

"When did you move back? And, more importantly, why did you move back?" Anna asked. While the two of them hadn't been super close, when Shelley had told

their classroom that she was moving up to New York, Anna had admitted to the girl that she was jealous.

"I've been back almost two years now. And the reason is I'm carrying around this little baby boy right here." Shelley laughed and then rested her hand on top of her belly. "You remember Daniel Cummins? His family owns the small dairy up the mountain a piece. We reconnected online and one thing just led to another."

"You look happy," Anna said, and then realized how rude that sounded. "Of course you're happy. Have you worked here long?"

Shelley laughed. "Since the day we opened. I own the place. Can you believe it? I never could have done something like this in New York with the property prices so high."

"That's amazing. It's gorgeous." Anna looked around the room again, taking in the Christmas elves displayed in one arrangement, while admiring the classic arrangement of white roses in another. "I don't know where to start, or even where to begin."

"Your momma told me you would be stopping in. Everyone feels so bad about her being sick. We're all praying she recovers before the wedding. It's been the talk of the town, you know," Shelley said.

"Apparently," Anna said. She remembered Shelley as being a shy girl who had avoided attention. How did she deal with the feeling of being under a microscope, someone watching your every move? "After living in the city, doesn't it bother you how everyone seems to know everyone's business here? Doesn't it make you

feel like someone is always watching, just waiting for you to do something to give them something to talk about?" It had always bothered Anna. Her mother had dealt with enough of the town's talk after Anna's father had died and they'd been left almost penniless. It was one of the things that had caused Anna to push to succeed at everything she did.

"Not really. It is different living in the city versus the country. The trip down the mountain can be a bit much during the winter when there's ice on the roads, and I can't just run across town to a shopping mall. But there are so many good things about living here. I know there are a few people in town that love to talk, but they're harmless for the most part. I would rather see it as just having neighbors who are looking out for me." Shelley patted her belly. "And with this one coming, I'm going to need all the help I can get."

Anna forced herself to smile. She wanted to argue with Shelley, but she couldn't. Shelley had lived most of her life here, just like Anna, so the fact that they disagreed was just a sign of how different their lives in this tiny town had been.

While Shelley gave Anna a tour of the shop, Anna called her mother on her video app so that the three of them could decide on the flowers for the wedding bouquets. Coreene had said that the church would already be decorated for Christmas and since Shelley was the only florist in town, she knew exactly which flowers the church was using, so it only took about a half hour for the three of them to narrow down their choices into one that Coreene was happy with.

"I think these are perfect. The church is very traditional with red bows on the pews and poinsettias around the altar, so the white roses with the magnolia leaves are a simple yet classic pairing," Shelley said as she completed the order. "I can also do a simple white rose for the two men. Your mother said Will was to be Dr. Harris's best man."

Anna hadn't really thought about Will's part in the wedding, and her stomach took a tumble as for the first time she realized that meant that the two of them would be walking down the aisle together. A shiver ran up her spine at the thought of her hand resting on Will's arm.

"I know, weird right? After all these years, the two of you back together again," Shelley said, telling Anna that the apprehension she was feeling had to be showing on her face.

"Together?" Anna asked, glad that her mother had already ended their video call and wouldn't notice the flush that was now flooding her cheeks.

"All those years the two of you spent trying to outdo each other at school... I have to say, I always wondered if there was more than just competition between you, and I always thought Will had a crush on you."

"That's...no. It was nothing like that." Anna found herself sputtering out the words.

"Maybe," Shelley said, her smile mischievous now, "but I wasn't the only girl who thought so. Mallory Grimes broke up with him because of you."

"Because of me? What did I do?" Shelley had to be teasing her. When she and Will weren't competing for the best project or the best paper, they had only toler-

ated each other. And as far as Mallory was concerned, the girl had hung on Will like a lovesick puppy. It had almost made Anna ill to see the way the girl wrapped herself all around Will so that he could hardly walk down the school hallways. She'd always assumed Will had been the one to come to his senses and break things off.

"Mallory had a tendency to be jealous back then," Shelley said. "I'm sure that's all it was."

Anna didn't understand what any of that had to do with her. Besides, that was all old business. That was another thing that Anna hated about the small town— everyone knew everyone else's history from the time they were born until they passed on. Sometimes you just wanted to forget things and move on, but that was hard when everyone else constantly wanted to remind you of the past.

Anna and Coreene spent the weekend going through the process of packing up some of the things her mother was planning on taking with her after the wedding. Coreene's fever had finally broken, but she was still weak, and by Sunday she had already become exhausted by the time two boxes were packed and taped closed.

"Mom, you need to sit down and rest. I can do the packing. I just need you to tell me what you want to take with you." Instead of arguing, as Anna had expected her to, her mom took a seat on the couch.

"I'm sorry. I know I'm making this harder by being so indecisive, but it's so hard. Not that this isn't hard on you as well. This is your home, too. I know you never

felt the same way about this place as you did about our home with your father, but it was still your home. And with you traveling around now, you might want to use this as a home base. You know, some place to stay between assignments. Somewhere you could store the things you don't want to haul around the country with you," her mother suggested.

When Coreene had called and told her about the wedding, she'd also shocked Anna by telling her that she was changing the deed on the house to be in Anna's name. Not that it was unwelcome news. Having given up the lease on her apartment in Nashville and putting most of her things in storage ahead of her new assignment starting, she was basically homeless at the moment. An apartment would be provided for her in Miami, but Coreene was right, she would need a place stay between assignments, and it would be nice to have somewhere to store things long term. It would work, except for one problem: Will. Could she really feel free to come and go with him here? Before this visit, she'd worried about seeing him for the first time. And now, after the interactions they'd had, she should feel better. They were both acting like adults. Shouldn't that make this an easy decision? Only it didn't.

Because the more she saw Will, the more she became aware of the fact that there was still an attraction between the two of them—at least there was one on her part. It was a reminder of the time they'd been together that she didn't want. One that would continually haunt her if she made this some type of semi-permanent residence where she came and went on a regular basis.

And then there was the fact that they still hadn't spoken about their past. She'd taken enough psychology classes to know that until they found a way to deal with what had happened and where they'd left things, there would always be an awkwardness between them. While normally that wouldn't be a problem, with their parents' marriage, they had little choice but to address it eventually.

"It's just something to think about," her mother said when Anna went quiet. "You don't need to make any decisions now."

Later that night, once Coreene had gone to bed, Anna looked around at the growing pile of boxes and couldn't help but felt a pang of nostalgia.

The house wouldn't be considered much by some people's standards. It was a typical log cabin–style house that was popular all throughout the Tennessee mountains: small, with only two bedrooms, a bathroom and one great room containing the open kitchen, dining, and living areas. Anna could still remember the day they'd moved in. It hadn't really been the house itself that bothered her. Instead, it was the fact that it wasn't their home. Her bedroom door didn't have the old pencil markings that her parents had made every year on her birthday to show how much she'd grown. There was no big tree beside the house with the tree house her daddy had built her. No large porch where she'd spent hours reading, sitting in the swing her father had made. But the worst thing about it had been the fact that moving into the new house was the first

step toward a life without her father, an idea that had been too painful for her to bear.

She'd cried herself to sleep that night. And the next. And the next. It had taken years before Anna had come to think of the house as a home instead of somewhere they were just visiting.

But looking around the house now, she realized she and her mother had managed to make good memories here. She didn't know what she was going to do with it, but for the first time she acknowledged that just knowing this place was here had given her a security she hadn't known she needed.

With her mother still not recovered, Anna spent Monday contacting all the vendors scheduled for the Christmas festival and confirming that they had all the information they needed. Their payments for rental of the booths—part of which would go toward the purchase of new equipment for the clinic—had already been collected, so all she really had to do was assure them that though her mother wouldn't be present, Anna would be there the day of the festival to support them.

That night, after the last committee meeting before the festival, Anna found herself joining the rest of the group for coffee. And when the mayor began discussing with Will the tent that she had set aside in case of any medical emergencies, Anna couldn't help but listen in.

"Have you thought of expanding the area and having a place where people could come and get some minor testing—blood pressure, blood sugar, that sort of thing?" she asked.

"I suggested it at the first meeting, but the mayor

felt that would take away the festive feeling," Will said, leaning toward her.

"I'm sure having your blood sugar checked isn't very festive, but neither is letting it go untreated. I've volunteered at some fairs where people could stop in and have checks, and it led to people who never would have gone to see their doctor being diagnosed and encouraged to seek treatment," Anna said.

The two of them talked for several minutes about the best way to set something up for the next festival, and she found herself relaxing as they discussed how the latest testing procedures had become less invasive. "You'd need more staff than you have on hand in town, though."

"Are you volunteering?" Will asked, his voice filled with the teasing she remembered.

Anna opened her mouth to agree, but then shut it. She didn't know if she'd still be in Miami next year or if she'd be on the other side of the country. When she didn't answer, the laughter in Will's eyes died, and he turned away from her to talk to someone on his other side. The connection they'd shared for just a moment was suddenly gone.

Later, when the group left the diner and they each went their separate ways, Anna thought about how much she'd enjoyed her conversation with Will. For a few minutes, it had been as if the two of them had been back in medical school, both of them anxious to share the things they'd learned that day. It had been so good to have someone there to listen and support her when she came home so exhausted but also so excited

to go back and do it again the next day. No one had ever understood her passion for learning the newest procedures or newest medications. No one except Will.

The next morning Anna opened up the next box beside her, one she'd dragged out of the attic the day before but then couldn't bring herself to go through. The box was discolored with the black stain of soot, marking it as one of the few boxes that had been spared by the fire. Inside she found an old ornament that she remembered had belonged to her maternal grandmother.

"You don't have to go through that, unless you want to," her mother said. "It's been up there so long that I don't even remember what all is in it."

"I remember the Christmas Aunt Sue came down from Virginia and gave you this." Anna examined the glass ornament of a little girl holding a branch of holly. Some of the red paint on the holly berries had begun to peel from age, or maybe from the fire.

"She said it reminded her of me bringing in the holly branches to decorate the fireplace mantel," Coreene said.

"I remember that. You used to wind them around the stair railing, too," Anna said. "Daddy always fussed because of the mess they made."

"I know. But he still helped me cut them out in the woods every year," her mother said.

For the next hour, Anna and her mother went through all the ornaments in the box, one by one. While Anna had expected that reminiscing over old ornaments that they hadn't displayed since the fire would make her sad, she found her mom and herself laughing instead. Even

when Anna pulled out one of the wooden ornaments that her father had carved for her, instead of tears, she found herself glad that she had those memories.

"Maybe we should have done this years ago, but I didn't ever feel that you were ready," Coreene said as she took out the last ornament, one that Anna had made in grade school for her parents.

"I don't know. For some reason, now seems like the perfect time," Anna told her mother. Looking over to a pile of boxes that they had set aside for donation, she saw the rectangular box that had held an old plastic tree that they had used their first Christmas in the house. "And since this is our last Christmas here, I think I know what we should do with them."

They'd just hung the last ornament on the tree when the doorbell rang. Anna went to the video camera's display and saw Will standing on the porch. Wearing jeans and a long-sleeve denim shirt, both hands tucked into his pockets, he looked nothing like the man she'd seen dressed in his oh-so-proper white lab coat at the clinic. In fact, he didn't look much older than the college kid she'd fallen for all those years ago.

Anna blamed the lump in her throat on the journey down memory lane that she and Coreene had just taken.

"That must be James. I told him to stay away another day, but he wanted to pick up some of the boxes tonight," her mother said.

"It looks like he sent Will," Anna said, trying to ignore the sudden need she felt to go hide away in her room. She was too raw right then to deal with the anxiety she felt every time she saw Will.

Waiting for him to bring up their past was just making things worse. She might have arrived here thinking that they could pretend nothing had happened between them, but it was obvious now that between the festival and the wedding, the two of them weren't going to be able to do that. At some point they had to deal with what happened between them, if not for their sake, then at least for their parents'.

So instead of running from Will yet again, she went to the door to let him in.

CHAPTER SIX

WILL WASN'T SURE how Anna came to be sitting beside him as he made his way back to town. One moment he was making excuses for his father being tied up in the office and sending him instead. The next moment, Coreene had him offering to take Anna to town to help prep for the festival the next day.

Not that it was any trouble; he was part of the setup crew, too. Only now, the two of them sat next to each other with an awkwardness that couldn't be ignored. "Your mother seems to be doing better."

"Her fever is gone, but she still tires easily. She wanted to go to the festival tomorrow, but I advised against it," Anna said, her words said so politely that they scraped against his last nerve.

"My father said that he was going to stay with her tomorrow while you're at the festival," he said. "You know, it was a surprise to me, too, that my dad and your mom were dating. I had no idea. I thought they were just friends." He couldn't help but think that in some ways, it was a lot like his and Anna's relation-ship. Only their parents' relationship was headed for a much happier ending. "My dad has never been seri-

ous about anyone since my mom died. I'm glad it was Coreene that he fell for, though."

"Really?" Anna asked, turning in her seat toward him. "Why is that? You had to know that it would be awkward between the two of us."

Awkward? That was an understatement. Though, the two of them had done an excellent job of hiding it.

"I've known your mother all my life. She's a wonderful woman, and I know I can trust her not to hurt him," he said, holding back the words that would let Anna know just how much he still felt the pain of her leaving him the way she had.

"I like your father, too. He's always been kind to both me and my mother. But…"

Anna paused long enough that Will turned to see what was wrong. "Just spit it out, Anna."

"Doesn't it bother you just a little that we're going to be stepsiblings?" Anna asked.

"Well, we've been everything else. I guess we can try being stepsiblings. Maybe we'll finally find something that works between us," Will said.

"What do you mean by that?" Anna asked. "You want to be my stepbrother?"

"Hell no, I don't want to be your stepbrother. It's as weird for me as it seems to be for you." Will pulled into the parking lot where everyone had agreed to meet and put his truck into Park before turning toward her. "But, let's see, we spent our childhood competing against each other and constantly fighting over one thing or another. Then there was medical school, where every-

thing changed. Enemies to lovers? Isn't that supposed to be one of those romance tropes?"

"We were never enemies. All that childish fighting and competing didn't matter. I never thought of you as an enemy. You were never cruel. Not like some of the other kids at school. You even took up for me." The look on Anna's face told him how much that had meant to her.

While some of the other kids hadn't noticed, Will had seen that Anna had changed after her father died, and she'd become more sensitive to the childish teasing of their classmates.

"The bottom line is that things didn't work out between us. It's in the past, and that's where we need to leave it. What's important now is that we make our parents happy. It seems the least we can do, doesn't it?"

He'd started to unbuckle his seat belt when he felt Anna's hand against his arm. "But can we really do that? Leave it all in the past? Wouldn't it be better if we talked this out now instead of pretending that everything is okay between us?"

He let go of the buckle and leaned back into the seat. He had let himself lose control of his emotions, something that he had always done around Anna. It was like she pushed some invisible button that caused his back to rise. He took a deep breath and turned his head toward her. Her face was flushed with color, the green of her eyes bright and intense, like she was trying to see inside him. Trying to read his mind, something that he was glad she was unable to do. He'd let her inside his head and his heart once before; how could he ever trust her with either one again?

"What is there to talk about, Anna?" Will asked. His hands gripped the steering wheel until his fingernails bit into his palm. He closed his eyes and forced himself to breath. He understood what Anna was saying, but he didn't think going over the past would do anything except cause more pain and anger.

Opening his eyes, he saw something he hadn't expected. Were those tears in Anna's eyes? All the frustration and anger he'd felt just a moment before disappeared.

"I'm sorry," she said, the words filled with a sadness that he knew only too well.

Sorry for being with him? Or sorry for the way she had ended things?

Did it really matter?

"It's in the past, Anna. We've both moved on with our lives." Though, he wasn't sure that was true. The emotions he had felt since Anna had returned to town were ones he hadn't experienced in years. None of the women he'd dated since Anna had ever made him feel that rush of adrenaline he felt whenever she was around. Even now, when the last thing he wanted to do was dig up their past, he felt more alive than he had in years. It had always been that way between them, even before they became lovers.

"You're right. It's the past. We have to move on. For my mom's and your dad's sakes. So, why don't we try something new? What if we try…?" She hesitated, as if not sure how he would take her next words.

"Try what?" he asked, now curious. Their relationship had gone from one extreme to another. What else could there be left for them to try?

"We both agree that the whole sibling thing is too weird to consider. What if we try to be just friends again?" Anna said, her eyes meeting his and holding.

He watched as she bit down on her bottom lip, something he'd seen her do a thousand times. So she wasn't any surer about this than he was. He'd told her once, while they'd been lovers, that he'd always seen it as her tell, and he'd taken advantage of it in spelling bees or class debates. He'd also told her that it made him feel something totally different once they were grown. Then he'd shown her exactly what seeing her worry her bottom lip did to him. From then on, she'd turned the tables against him, using his weakness to bring him to his knees more than once.

His body reacted to the memory at the same time as his brain tried to shut it down. And he'd been the one to say they should put the past behind them? It seemed some of the past was too stubborn to stay where he wanted it.

There was a knock on his window just then, startling both of them. When he turned he saw Mayor Johnson's face pressed against the window, he rolled down the window far enough to hear what she wanted. "Will, what are y'all doing just sitting here? We have a lot of work to do. Anna might not care if this festival is successful, but you should."

Will rolled the window up as the woman walked away.

"I don't understand why she's like that. She seems fine with everyone else," Anna said.

"Marjorie is a difficult woman to understand sometimes. And you do have a history." Will couldn't help but smile when he remembered the petition yet again.

"I was a kid. Besides, I was right. No matter what they call it, our town square is a rectangle. Not a square." Anna's eyes narrowed at him. "And don't change the subject. Like you said, our parents are getting married. We are going to have to spend time together. There is no way they're not going to notice that something is wrong between us. What do you say? Is there any chance that we could be friends again?"

The hope in her eyes cut deep inside him, into that part of his heart that he had sealed off from everyone for the last five years. She was asking for another chance at a friendship that had once blossomed into more, and then had died and shriveled until there was nothing left between the two of them. Did he dare do this? Take a chance of being hurt by her again? It wasn't as if she was going to be here forever. He suspected she'd be leaving as soon as the wedding was over.

"We both want the same thing, right? We're adults now. We have to put our mistakes behind us and move on. Maybe by becoming friends again, we can do that," Anna said. Her eyes widened and she bit down on her lip again.

"A mistake, that's what you think it was?" Anger rushed through him like a wildfire in the mountain tops, then burned out just as quickly when he saw the regret in her eyes.

"I didn't mean it that way," Anna said, her words rushing out and her hands coming up between them as if to hold back his reaction. "I really didn't. I just meant that we didn't think about the consequences."

She was right. But then, he'd thought they were

building something permanent between them. He'd thought they both wanted the same thing. Yes, she'd shared that she dreamed of seeing the world. But he'd thought that they would do that together. He'd even looked into volunteering for Doctors Without Borders. He'd been excited at the prospect. But then she'd ended things between them without giving them a chance to talk things through or make a plan.

Now that he was older, he understood that he'd assumed things he shouldn't have.

And now here they sat, back in the hometown that she'd felt the need to escape, with her asking him to give their relationship one more try. Not the relationship that they'd had. Not the one that she'd destroyed. But a new one. One where they'd only be friends.

Part of him wanted to get out of the truck and slam the door. To walk away and not look back.

No, what he really wanted was to tell her that she'd hurt him in a way that he hadn't been hurt since his mom died. He wanted to shout that she didn't deserve another chance at hurting him.

But what would that accomplish? He'd recovered and he'd gone on to make a good life for himself. He was happy working in his hometown, and he loved helping people that had always been a part of his world. Did he sometimes feel the weight of knowing that something was missing in his life? Did he sometimes think of what it would have been like if the two of them had stayed together? Maybe, but he would never let her know that.

And maybe she was right. The two of them were adults now, not college kids that had been protected

from the world most of their lives. Their parents' happiness was what was important right now. His father was just as much committed to the blending of their families as Anna's mother, and after everything the two of them had been through, they deserved that.

"So, friends?" Anna asked, her words sounding less sure now.

"How about we try that out tonight and see how it goes?" he suggested, unbuckling his seat belt and opening the door. They both climbed out of the truck and then paused, watching several groups of people who had gathered around the area that had been designated for the festival booths.

"Like an experiment?" Anna asked as they started across the street to join the others.

"Yeah, an experiment," he agreed. He liked the clinical sound of that. An experiment was harmless and conducted mostly for research purposes. It was a lot easier to stay detached when he thought of it that way.

"Then let the experiment begin," Anna said as they joined the group gathered in front of the first booth, where a big Welcome sign was being hung.

He saw the mayor moving around the festival, stopping one person then another. When she walked back to where they stood, she pulled a list from her coat pocket.

"Okay, everyone. Tomorrow is the big day, and there's a lot of work left to do. The city maintenance crew made sure all the lights were hung and working this morning, but please let me know if you see any problems with them. The lights have been set up on timers and some computer thing where they are syn-

chronized with the music that will be playing. On each side of the street, the merchants will be open with their window displays lit up. Tonight we need to set up all ten booths. Anna, your mother was in charge of the merchant booths, so take half of the volunteers with you. And, Will, you're in charge of the game booths to the left, so take the rest with you. Most of the work with the booths has already been done, so you should be able to get the setup completed in ninety minutes. We'll meet back here then. Will and Anna, we can discuss how to prepare the medical emergency area then."

Anna turned toward the group of volunteers and tried to smile. She had thought taking her mother's place with the festival would consist of her stacking honey at the Honey Shack display or helping the artist who had volunteered his time to do face painting for the children. She knew nothing about constructing booths. Give her a broken arm and she could cast that in her sleep. But give her two pieces of wood and a hammer, and she was lost. "I'm going to tell you right off, I have no idea what I'm doing."

"It's okay, Anna. We've got this," a guy said from the back.

It took Anna a moment to recognize him. "Daniel?"

The man laughed and rubbed his shiny bald head. "That's me. Of course, I look a little different."

"Don't we all," another man said. "I don't know if you remember me, I'm Jamal Henderson. You were a couple years ahead of me, but we were in band together."

One by one, the group of men and women introduced themselves. Each one seemed to be happy to be there

helping out. When one came up to her and gave her a hug, she didn't know what to do until the man introduced himself as Allen Watts, Charlie's dad. As the group headed over to where the booths had been laid out, Allen relayed how Anna had been there when his son had had an allergic reaction. As others in the group joined Allen to thank her for what she'd done, Anna felt a little embarrassed at the attention everyone was giving her. She was used to being thanked by patients and their families, but this was much more. This was personal. She had history with these people.

Anna quickly turned everyone's attention back on their task and was glad to see that the booths were actually tents with a display table to be set up in the front. Anna thought about the tents she had once helped erect for a mass causality drill. Maybe she wouldn't be as useless at this as she had initially thought.

"If we split up into teams of four, we should be able to be complete all five booths in an hour. I don't know about you, but I don't want to be the last group to finish." She looked over to where Will and his group were already raising their first tent. "And if we beat Will's group, I'll spring for coffee at the Coffee Cup."

Her group of volunteers laughed and separated into groups quickly. She joined the first group and started putting the poles together, handing them off as the tent began to take shape.

They were almost finished with the fourth booth when she looked down the walkway to see that Will and his group only had one more booth to set up.

"It doesn't look like we're going to beat them, boss,"

Allen said to her as she handed him the last pole they needed to complete the booth.

"Maybe," Anna said, "but I'm not giving up yet."

On the last booth, the two groups came together and Anna quickly explained her game plan. As each person hurried to the task assigned to them, Anna headed to where Will and his group were finishing up their last booth. "Okay, so I understand how the booths we're setting up for the vendors work, but I don't understand how these work for games. And what games are we talking about? Like, what game is this going to be?"

Anna tried to hide her smile as someone in Will's group started to explain the games that would be offered at the festival. The group had all but stopped working as another one of them explained the best way to beat each one of the carnival games. She took a quick glance down the walkway and saw that half of her group's last tent was standing, then looked down at her watch to see that they had less than fifteen minutes before they had to meet back with the mayor. They just needed a couple more minutes to catch up.

"Wait a minute. You have the maps of all the festival booths," Will said from the back of the tent where he had been listening. "What are you up to, Anna?"

Anna froze, half of her bottom lip caught between her teeth. Backing up, she waved goodbye to Will, then turned and rushed back to her group as Will called her name.

"We've got twelve minutes. I think we can beat them, but it's going to be close," Anna said to Allen as she joined him at the tent.

"Beat who?" Will said from behind her, causing her to jump.

Anna looked back to where Will's crew had started working again. They had all been kind when she'd interrupted their work, and now she was beginning to feel a little guilty. She'd recognized several of them. And it really wasn't fair not to let Will know what she was doing. "I just thought a little friendly competition between our groups would be good."

Will looked down at her and she squinted her eyes closed, not wanting to see the disappointment on his face. He had always told her she was too competitive. This really wasn't the way to start the friendship she'd told him she wanted. Then she heard a sound she hadn't heard in years. He was laughing. Her eyes popped open and she saw that he was closer than before. Instead of being angry or disappointed, he seemed to find the whole thing humorous. "Only you, Anna Dobson, would decide to turn this into a race."

Before she could say anything, he was moving away from her. In seconds, he was down the walkway and yelling at his crew to hurry.

In minutes, the last pole of her tent was in the ground, and they were unfolding the table they needed to set up at the front. They all turned when a roar of triumph came from the end of the walkway. She couldn't help but groan at her defeat.

"So, I didn't have a chance to ask," Will said when they all headed back to where the mayor was waiting for them, "what did we win?"

"I promised everyone with me a free drink at the

Coffee Cup if we finished first," Anna said. "I guess that means you owe your group a cup of coffee instead."

"I don't think so. I think you owe every one of us a cup of coffee for dragging us into your competition," Will said.

"Okay, you're right. Drinks are on me after we finish. But when this story gets spread around town, make sure that everyone knows I wasn't a sore loser." The people around her cheered, with many of her own group patting her on the back in commiseration.

Later, when they'd all crowded into the local diner to have a drink, something warm settled inside Anna's chest once again. She was surprised to find that it felt good to share memories and reminisce about her childhood with her old classmates. No one had made her feel unwelcome. No one had commented on how long she'd been away without visiting. They just accepted her as if she belonged. As if she'd never been gone. She wanted to ignore it, the connection she'd felt with these people as they'd worked together, but she couldn't.

As she and Will made their way back to his truck, she realized that Will had been quiet at the restaurant. "Are you mad at me? For the whole competition thing? It was just for fun."

"Why would I be mad? I won," Will said, opening the truck door for her before going around to the other side.

"So, why were you so quiet at the diner? You're usually right in the middle of things," she said once he'd climbed inside. She tried to think of something she might have done or said that he could have taken excep-

tion to, but there was nothing. This being "just friends" was going to be more difficult than she thought if she had to constantly worry about what she might have said to upset things.

"I've been thinking about what you said, about us being friends. You're right. We've had our moments over the years. Most of the time we've been friends, or were until…" His words trailed off, but they both knew what he was referring to. "You've always been so driven that sometimes you didn't stop and enjoy the little things, like friendship. It was nice to see you reconnecting with everyone. I know things were tough when you were a kid and we both know that kids can be jerks to each other. But those people tonight, that's who they are now. And you looked happy among them. I liked seeing you happy again."

"I'm always happy." She liked to think of herself as a happy person. She'd worked with enough grouchy and hard-to-get-along-with doctors over the last few years that she'd made it her mission not to become like them. And the new path her career was taking was definitely going to make her happier. It was her dream. The one goal she'd sacrificed everything for.

"Are you?" he asked. His eyes searched hers so deeply that she was afraid he might see the uncertainty his question was causing her.

As if he hadn't expected an answer, he started the truck without saying anything more, leaving her to face the silence of the trip home with nothing but her doubts and insecurities circling around in her head.

Later, as she was getting ready for bed, she thought

of what he'd said. He'd said that it was nice to see her happy again. What made him think she wasn't happy? He knew nothing about her life. Was he referring to how she'd been when they'd been together? Yes, she had been happy with him once, but those times were different. They had been too young to consider their future. They'd been all hormones and emotions. Not once had they talked about their future until the night before she was to leave for her residency.

No matter what Will might have thought, she could still remember everything about that night. Graduation had come and gone, and they'd both been busy packing up the last of their things. They'd avoided talking about the fact that the next day they would be heading in different directions for their residencies. She could admit now that her own doubts about their future had been eating at her for weeks as what she had thought was a college fling had deepened into more. But with all the excitement of graduation, she'd managed to put her doubts and worries aside. And Will didn't mention it, either. It was like the two of them both knew that they weren't ready to talk about their future. It wasn't until that night when Will had talked so passionately about returning to Rolling Oaks that she knew they would never be able to make things work. She couldn't take away his dream of working alongside his father.

She could have waited and let time and distance tear them apart. But why wait for the inevitable? They wanted different things from their lives. So, even though it was the hardest thing she had ever done,

she'd written the letter, explaining that she couldn't continue to see him and left.

But it hadn't been easy. That letter had torn a hole in her heart. For weeks she'd picked up the phone, wanting to reach out to him. And each time she'd forced herself to put the phone down, knowing that it was best that they'd ended their relationship quickly before things had gone any further. She'd had a dream of traveling, one that her father had always encouraged, whereas Will had wanted to return to Rolling Oaks. And who was she to get in the way of his dreams? It wasn't as if the plans she had for her future were any more important than Will's.

The truth was that they had different priorities. His were to his father and their community. Hers were to the memory of her father and the promise of the dream that had pushed her to succeed.

As she lay down in bed, she put away the memories of the way things had ended between them. Instead, she concentrated on the progress they had made that day. They had agreed to put their past behind them and allow the two of them a chance to become friends. Just friends.

She punched her pillow and turned over onto her side, dragging the covers with her. Somehow being just friends after remembering everything they'd once had together didn't sound quite as satisfying as it had earlier in the evening.

CHAPTER SEVEN

DESPITE A NIGHT of tossing and turning, Anna found herself up before the sun without any of her dark thoughts clouding her mood. Today was the day of the festival, and part of her felt like a child on Christmas morning. If part of that was because she was sure to see Will there, she chose to ignore it. She caught herself singing Christmas songs in the shower and couldn't help but laugh. When was the last time she had sung a silly song of any kind, let alone a Christmas song?

She'd grown up like every child, looking forward to Christmas morning. Some of her favorite memories were of Christmas, but some of its magic had died with her father. No matter how hard her mother tried to make the day special for her, they both knew it wasn't the same. As she'd gotten older, she'd realized how much her mother sacrificed for those Christmases. She'd tried to make it easier by making her requests fewer and fewer, telling her mother as she became a teenager that she was too old for Christmas.

But today she was in the Christmas mood. Dressed in jeans and a bright red sweater, she slipped out the door, leaving her mother still in bed. Though Coreene was no longer contagious, she was being cautious and

avoiding crowds until the wedding. Knowing that Dr. Harris would be there later to keep her mother company made Anna feel a little less guilty, but she did hate that the two of them were going to miss out on all the fun.

The sun was just coming up, and the white Christmas lights on the large oak trees were just starting to blink out when she drove through town. Anna wasn't surprised to see that there was already a large crowd of people at the festival site. She'd realized from the first committee meeting that this festival was incredibly important to the town, and it wasn't just because of the money they would make for the clinic. It was also a time to show off their small town. Looking around at all the work that had gone into the process, Anna was surprised to find herself feeling a pride in the little town where she'd grown up.

Looking for someplace where she could help, she headed to where the vendors were unloading boxes into their assigned booths. The festival wasn't a big one compared to the ones in the larger towns down the mountain, but they still had a good variety of artists selling last-minute Christmas gifts. Pulling out her phone, she took a couple pictures of the vendors and their wares. Her mother had asked her to photograph as much as she could. It wouldn't be the same as being there, but maybe it would make Coreene feel more included. After all, it was her mother who had worked with the artists and other vendors to make this happen.

Anna was just getting a picture of a beautiful handwoven rug that was being put out for display when

she felt a tap on her shoulder. Turning, she found Will standing behind her.

"You're up early. Are you feeling okay?" he said.

She chose to ignore his teasing and the fact that he was intimately aware of the fact that she wasn't a morning person. Instead she aimed her phone and took a picture of him. Dressed in a pair of faded jeans and a thick red sweatshirt, he looked good. Really good. Finally looking up from the picture, she saw that Will had turned to talk to someone else. When he turned back to her, she quickly put her phone away. The last thing she needed was for him to notice that she'd been ogling.

"How's your mom? I take it she agreed that she wasn't ready to get out?" he asked.

"She was sleeping when I left, but she seemed excited last night that your father was coming over. I guess he told her he had a surprise for her."

"He told me the same. Left me a message last night that he wanted to talk to me, but it was too late for me to call him back by the time we'd finished up here." They moved apart as one of the men Anna had met the night before pushed between them, pulling a large cart loaded down with boxes. "That looks like the prizes for one of the games I'm responsible for. I'll check on you later."

Anna watched Will join the man and then turned back to where one of the vendors was setting up a display of jewelry that was teetering on the edge of the table. Rushing forward, she grabbed a display case before it could crash to the ground. The woman thanked her, and Anna stopped to admire her work. Anna had

brought Christmas presents for her mother from her favorite department store in Nashville, but she hadn't thought of what to buy her mom for her wedding. Maybe she'd find something today from one of the artist's booths.

For the next two hours Anna rushed around, making sure not only the vendors at the booths were taken care of, but also the food trucks that had been brought into town. When someone began to ring the old bell that sat on the lawn in front of the town hall, Anna looked down at her watch. It was go time. Almost immediately, Christmas music filled the square.

Looking around, she saw that there were people already lining up at the entrance where the mayor stood dressed in a red dress and sky-high pumps. Beside her stood Will and his father, who were talking quietly and then walked away from the mayor and toward her. There was a strange look on Will's face, one of concern, but also one that said he was struggling to understand what was being said.

"What's wrong?" she asked, rushing up to them. "Mom? Is it Mom?"

"No, no. I talked to your mother right before I got here. I told her I was going to stop and pick her up one of the diner's cinnamon rolls as a reward for taking her physician's recommendation to rest another day," Will's father said. "But really, I wanted to stop and speak with the two of you."

"Dad wants to surprise your mother with a honeymoon," Will said, though he didn't look at her as he spoke. "I'm just not sure you're going to like his plan."

Anna couldn't imagine what Will could be talking about. Her mother had explained that they were planning on waiting till spring for their honeymoon, as the clinic was too busy to leave during the winter season. If his father had come up with a way to take her mom away for a few days, she thought it would be a great idea.

"Your mom is really disappointed that she's missed the Christmas festival. She worked so hard to line up all the vendors, and she isn't even up to coming out today. I was just hoping the two of you could help me out with a surprise trip to one of the resorts in Gatlinburg for a few days. We'll still take our honeymoon this March, but I think it would be good for her to get away for a couple of days after the wedding. There's a spa resort that has an opening I can get, I just need some help covering at the clinic."

"Dad, I can handle it. I don't need any help." Whatever it was that Will's father wanted him to do, Will didn't sound like he wanted to go along with it.

"I know you can, Will, but it would make me feel better if you had some help. The clinic schedule is already fully booked for the week after Christmas, and that's not including all the walk-ins we're sure to have, given this is the worse flu season we've experienced in years. I talked to someone at one of the hospitals in Knoxville, and patients are waiting ten to twelve hours to be seen. I won't be able to relax thinking of you being overworked like that."

It took a moment for Anna to realize what Dr. Harris was working his way to asking of her. If he took her

mother out of town, he needed someone to fill in for him. Her. He needed Anna to fill in for him.

He was right. Her mother was worn out, and a couple days at a spa would do wonders for her. Anna couldn't think of anything sweeter or more considerate for the man to do for her mom. If he wanted Anna to work at the clinic for a few days while she was in town, she would do it. She just couldn't understand why Will didn't want her help.

"I'll do it," she said, interrupting Will and his father. Both men turned and looked at her. Dr. Harris surprised her, wrapping her in a hug, but she was most surprised by the look of defeat in Will's eyes as he looked at her.

Anna heard her name being called and looked over to where one of the vendors seemed to be having problems with a sign she was trying to hang. Excusing herself, Anna raced over to help the woman, and then got called over to see an artist who was having a problem with one of the extension cords that had been provided for their art display.

By the time she had taken care of that and checked in on the other vendors, Will and his father were gone. For the next few hours, she went from vendor to vendor, providing refreshments and taking care of the few problems that came up as the crowd around the square began to grow. The few times she caught sight of Will, he was busy interacting with the crowd that had gathered to test their skills throwing basketballs through hoops and rings around bottle necks.

It was after noon before things settled down and

Anna got a break long enough to try the food being sold at one of the food trucks. She'd just bitten into an especially juicy hot dog when Will joined her. She waited while he ordered his food before asking the question that she had wanted to ask all day. "Do you want to tell me why you have a problem working with me?"

"I don't have a problem with you, but I think I remember you saying something about *small-town* medicine not being challenging enough for you," Will said. "And I also remember you saying that you had never wanted to work in our clinic."

Anna ignored the sarcastic tone of his words. She'd written in the letter that she couldn't see herself working in a small-town clinic, where she would become bored. Now that she was older, she could see that at the time she had been young and full of herself. Over the years there had been a lot of things she had wished she could change about that letter. Changing her dismissal of his plans and their importance to him and this town was just one of those things.

Will started walking toward where a band was playing on the front porch of the town hall, and she joined him. It was best that they talk this out now, even if it seemed that it was the last thing Will wanted to do.

"I meant that I didn't want to work here permanently. I'm certainly willing to help out your dad. Especially since we'll be doing all this for my mom. Besides, I thought we had put all that behind us."

For several moments Will didn't say anything. Anna understood that her words all those years ago had to

have stung. Maybe it was only fair that he threw them back at her now.

He stopped and turned so suddenly that she found herself bumping into him. He reached out and steadied her, his hands going to her shoulders, his eyes locking with hers. For a moment they just stood there.

Around them, people danced, and children ran in and out of the crowd as the band played. But for a moment there was just the two of them. When one of his hands reached up and brushed against her cheek, she didn't move. It was as if time stood still.

No, that wasn't right. It was as if time had gone backward. To a time when they had both been young, tired medical students. They'd been studying for hours, and she was still worried about the exam they had the next day. One moment he'd been assuring her that it would be fine, that she'd ace the test as she always did, and the next moment he'd been brushing his hand down her cheek. And then he'd kissed her. Their first kiss. The kiss that had started it all.

He could kiss her now, and even remembering all the pain that had come after that first kiss, she wouldn't stop him. She couldn't. And that scared her.

He stepped away from her, though his eyes were hot with a desire she knew she couldn't be imagining. Maybe it scared him, too. "You're right. We agreed to put the past behind us so that we could be friends. Just friends, right?"

She couldn't speak. What had just happened between them had stunned her. How could she even have considered letting him kiss her? No, it wasn't that she was

going to let him kiss her. She had *wanted* him to kiss her. Right then. Right there. In the middle of the festival for all the town to see.

Because for a moment she'd remembered that feeling of being surrounded by Will. The feel of his arms around her, his lips moving against hers. The way their bodies fit together so perfectly.

But he was right. They'd agreed to put the past behind them. All those memories had to stay back in the past. She had to leave them there. Just like in a few weeks she'd have to leave this town and leave Will…again. She'd hurt him the last time she'd left, hurt herself, too. She couldn't do that to either one of them again.

So even though she still couldn't say the words, she nodded, agreeing with him. No matter how much she might be tempted to want more, from that moment on, she would make sure to concentrate only on their friendship.

Will's phone rang and Anna listened as he advised someone that he'd be right there.

"That sounded like Dana," she said, having overheard his nurse's voice and the crying of a child in the background.

"Yeah, a little girl tripped going down the steps after seeing Santa. Dana says it looks like she banged her mouth as she fell. There's a lot of blood, and neither the father nor the child are handling it well." He stepped away from Anna, removing the last bit of soothing warmth she'd felt from his nearness.

"I'll come, too," she said, unable to stop herself, yet refusing to acknowledge why.

"You don't have to," Will said as she caught up with him. "I might not be an ER doctor, but I do handle things like this all the time."

"I know. I'm not coming because I think you need my help. I was just thinking two sets of eyes and hands are better than one." She laid her hand on his arm, and he stopped beside her. "If you don't want me to come, I won't."

He studied her as if he were looking for some ulterior motive. Finally, he seemed assured by what he saw and began walking again, this time taking her hand as they weaved in and out of the crowd.

Anna saw the jolly ole man himself, or at least someone dressed as him with a couple yards of padding added to their costume. She waved at the smiling Santa as they passed by and thought he might have answered back with a "Merry Christmas," but she couldn't hear him over the wails of a child.

When they arrived at the little tent that had been set up with a couple chairs and a small table, they found a girl of no more than three. It was hard to believe someone so small could make such a noise. A man—the child's father, Anna assumed—stood beside her looking as pale as his daughter. There was blood on his shirt and even more blood on the little girl's frilly red-striped dress.

"This must be our patient," Will said, bending down in front of the child. "I hear you took a spill after you talked to Santa."

"She was hurrying down to me. I had moved back to take a picture to send to my wife—she's a nurse in

Sevierville and had to work today," the man said, his face going even paler. "She's going to kill me if Ellen loses those teeth."

"It's going to be fine. Kids fall and hurt themselves all the time. It's part of being a kid. With your wife being a nurse, I know she'll understand," Will said as he carefully examined the child's face.

Anna opened a package of gauze pads that had been placed to the side and handed him one before squatting down beside the child and taking her hands. "My name's Anna. I haven't gotten to see Santa yet, but I hear he's really nice."

As Anna continued to talk softly to her, the little girl relaxed. Will gently opened Ellen's mouth, and Dana handed him a penlight so he could see the inside better as he cleared the blood away. When Ellen tensed and began to protest, Anna rubbed her hands while explaining everything that Doctor Will was doing.

"It looks like she bit the inside of her mouth, but I don't think she's going to need stitches," Will said, standing to talk to Ellen's father. "The mouth is very vascular, so a lot of times, there's more bleeding than you would expect. I wouldn't give her anything warm to drink for a few days, and there might be some swelling, so if she's uncomfortable, you can give her a child dose of acetaminophen."

As the child's father thanked Will and Dana for their help, Anna took one of the gauze pads and wet it with a small amount of sterile water and began to wipe the little girl's face. Once she was cleaned up, Anna handed her to her father, then began to tidy up herself.

"This is Dr. Dobson, one of my colleagues. She's going to be filling in at the local clinic while my father takes some time off," Will said, surprising Anna.

Had something she said made a difference to the attitude he'd had earlier concerning the two of them working together?

"It's nice to meet you, Dr. Dobson. And thank you. I can tell my wife that Ellen had two doctors taking care of her."

"I hope so. Someone smart once told me that two sets of eyes and hands are always better than one," Will said, his eyes shining with a hint of mischief before looking over at Dana. "And in this case, you had three sets. Hopefully, that will make your wife feel better."

"So, you're going to be working in the clinic with us?" Dana asked as the father and daughter walked away.

"Yeah," Anna said. "It looks like I am."

CHAPTER EIGHT

WILL HAD THOUGHT he was prepared to show Anna around the clinic Monday morning so that she would be ready to start the day after Christmas. He was wrong.

It wasn't that he minded her being there. It was a great idea for his dad to take Coreene out of town for a few days. And even though he knew that he could run the clinic by himself, he also knew that this was the busy season, and an extra pair of hands would be useful. He had no problem staying till the last patient was seen, had done so before many times, but it wasn't fair to expect that of the rest of the staff who had families to get home to. And it wasn't as though his father had never gotten someone else to fill in for him before; they'd had doctors from down the mountain occasionally work in the clinic to cover for one of them.

No, it was the fact that it was Anna who would be there working with him. Not that he doubted her ability. He'd seen her in action when they'd worked on stabilizing Charlie, and he had no problem admitting that she had far more experience in emergency medicine than he did. But most of the cases were routine at the clinic. And there was the real problem. Years ago Anna had said that she thought working at his father's

clinic would be boring. Now he was afraid that she'd be proven right.

Not that he found it boring. They did deal with emergencies such as Charlie's quite often. There were also farming accidents and the occasional tourist injury from a fall, or other medical emergencies that he and his father took care of until the patient could be transferred to a higher level of care. But he had never been an adrenaline junkie, and those emergencies were enough to make him appreciate the slower pace of the clinic.

In his residency, he had concentrated more on his patient's problems instead of chasing the next emergent case. He sometimes wondered what kind of doctors his colleagues had made after they'd finished their programs. Were they still looking for that next exciting diagnosis? Or had they discovered how rewarding it was to help their patients no matter what their problems?

Which brought him back to Anna. She'd chosen emergency medicine over family practice for a reason. She'd likely leave there more certain than ever that Will's clinic was as boring as she had thought all those years ago. For the first time since joining his father's practice, Will hoped that something exciting might come in that day so that he could show her that he was as prepared for whatever came into the clinic as she was. If that was his own competitive side coming out, he couldn't help it.

Walking in through the back entrance, he found Anna standing in the hallway looking into their small break room.

"What do you do with all of this?" Anna asked when she saw him. "This would feed a whole shift of workers at my hospital."

Joining her at the door, he took in all the cookies, candies and cakes that covered the small table where they ate their lunch. "This is just what was left from last week. This week we'll get double this. We each take some home, and we share it with our patients. Dana delivers anything that's left over to people in her church who could use some cheering up during the holiday season. And I'll take some up the mountain this week to Grandma Mason."

"I couldn't believe it when Mom said Grandma Mason was still alive. She has to be over a hundred years old by now," Anna said.

"She'll be a hundred this spring," Will said. "And she's still just as stubborn as ever. I can't get her to come down the mountain to the clinic. She says she's afraid we'll send her to 'one of those big city hospitals.' She's very determined that she is going to die on the mountain in the house where 'God brought me into this world.' There is no reason for me to argue with her."

"I wouldn't, either. She's lived all her life up there. I don't think she'd be happy anywhere else. It would be cruel to make her leave it now. In fact, it would probably kill her. But what about her son? Can't he at least get her to come down to the clinic?" Anna said.

"Major is in his eighties now. He gave up on getting his momma down that mountain years ago, so he gets up to their old farmhouse once a week to bring her supplies. His son and granddaughter live in Geor-

gia, but they visit when they can," Will said. He'd had several conversations with the old woman's son, Major, and they were in agreement with Anna. It would kill the woman to separate her from what she considered her mountain.

"I'd like to go see her," Anna said, surprising him.

"I'm going up Christmas Day if the snow holds off. Major is visiting his kids and grandkids this year, and I told him before he left that I'd try to make my way up there."

"Well, there you are. I wanted to see the two of you before the day got started," his father said before turning to Anna. "Your mother is so excited about our trip to the resort. I hope you know how much we appreciate you covering for me."

"I'm happy to do it. It's nice to see her so happy," Anna said. Will knew that Anna and her mother were close. It was one of the reasons he had agreed that it was time the two of them put their past behind them. It had been five years ago, and they were both different people now. And, most importantly, he wanted Anna to feel comfortable coming home anytime she wanted to. With her mother moving into Will's childhood home, that would be harder for her to do if she didn't feel welcome.

"So, Will, I'm going to put you in charge of showing Anna around and getting her used to the computer system," his father said, then turned to Anna. "I just need a copy of your medical license. We have them posted in the front office."

"Sure," Anna said. "I forgot to ask Mom what day

you would be coming back. I have to be back at work New Year's Day."

"We'll be back Tuesday night, which will give you some time to spend with your mom before you have to leave. I know she'd like that."

The hallway door opened and Dana stepped in. While his father explained his plans to her, Will offered Anna a tour of the clinic. "I know you saw our emergency setup when you brought Charlie in. Right past that is our X-ray room. And then we have a small lab set up across from it. We can run a few labs here, but there is a lot that we send out to a lab in Sevierville."

They stopped by the lab, and Anna stepped in to examine the machines. "This looks like pretty new equipment."

"It is. We got a grant a year ago from the state, and we put it all on new equipment. We might be up in the mountains, but we have to be able to provide the same amount of care as your big city clinics. And with the money from the festival, we'll be able to update even more." Will heard the defensiveness in his voice. Why did he feel like he had to defend their clinic to Anna? She had just been commenting on the equipment.

He looked up to see her arms crossed and her eyes narrowed. Then she reached out and grabbed his arm, pulling him into the lab with her before shutting the door behind them. He opened his mouth to tell her he was sorry when she placed her finger against his lips. His mouth went dry, and he couldn't have said anything even if he had wanted to.

"You might not believe this, but I'm not here to judge

this clinic. I know I said some things that I shouldn't have and that you have apparently taken them personally, but none of what I said was meant as an insult to this clinic. I admire your father and what he set up here. This is where I got my vaccines as a child and all my checkups."

He moved to interrupt her, but she pressed her finger more firmly against his mouth. "No. Don't apologize. And don't keep treating me like I'm some kind of visitor. That room with the X-ray machine you just pointed out to me, that's where it's always been. It's where your dad X-rayed my arm when I fell off the ladder of the tree house my dad built for me. So quit acting like this is the first time I've ever stepped into this place. And don't act like we're strangers. Just act normal around me."

Unable to stop himself any longer, he opened his mouth and nipped the tip of her finger.

"Ouch," Anna said, pulling her finger back.

"Oh, don't be a baby, you know that didn't hurt," he said. If she wanted him to act normal, then that's what he'd do. "And see, I'm not treating you like a stranger. I'd never bite a stranger."

"I'm glad to hear that. So, why don't you just show me what has changed around here, and then we can start seeing patients."

There was a knock, and Will reached around Anna and opened the door.

Dana stood there with a puzzled look on her face. "Is there something wrong in the lab?"

Will looked at Anna, who had turned a pretty shade of

pink. "No. Everything is fine. I was just showing Anna the new equipment. She's very impressed, aren't you?"

"I am. I was just reminding Will that I'm not a stranger to the office," Anna said. "I do know my way around here."

"Well, that's good, because I just put a patient in exam room four, and the waiting room is already filling up," Dana said. "I hope the two of you are ready for a busy day, because I've got a feeling this place is going to keep you hopping."

Anna had worked at one of Nashville's busiest emergency rooms for two years, and yet her feet had never hurt as bad as they did by that afternoon. She'd caught on fast to the charting system, though she had missed the scribe that usually followed her around to the exam rooms at the hospital taking notes while she did her exam. And then there was the typing. She was used to using a voice to transcript system instead of one where she had to type in her own history and physical. But she hadn't had to see as many patients as she normally would in her twelve-hour shifts at the hospital, and she'd actually had more time to spend with them, even with the charting challenges.

She had just taken a bite of Ms. Hammer's pound cake, which Will had recommended, when Dana found her. How was it that the nurse always seemed to know where each of them were? There was certainly no reason for an overhead radio system in the clinic, given that Dana seemed to be able to search her out without any trouble.

Anna remembered the curious look Dana had given them when she'd found her and Will in the lab room together. While there had been nothing going on between the two of them, somehow the woman had managed to make her feel guilty. Maybe it was the way Will had looked at her when he'd nipped at her finger, or maybe it was just awkward to be found behind a closed door in a room the size of a small closet with another co-worker, but Anna had not been able to stop the heat that had flushed her face. Which of course had just made them look even guiltier.

"Will's tied up with Bob Carter in the X-ray room and Dr. Harris has left on an errand, but I just put a man in exam room one who has me worried."

"What's up?" Anna asked before stuffing the last of the cake into her mouth. Will was right. It had to be the best pound cake she'd ever eaten.

"He's a walk-in. I don't recognize him, which is strange in itself, but one of the kids from the high school that works at the diner brought him in. Said he started acting funny, confused. BP is 180/95, RR 92, RR 18, and his oxygen saturation is 98 percent on room air. It looks to me as if his face has a left-sided droop and his speech is jumbled up, too. I didn't think I should wait until Will was finished."

Anna grabbed her bottle of water and took a big gulp to wash down the cake. "No, you're right. We can't wait. Let's go."

There were many reasons that someone would suddenly be confused or acting strange. You had to rule out the worst, something neurological like a stroke,

then you could move on to other things such as metabolic encephalopathy or possible substance or alcohol abuse. Anna knew that with time, most nurses developed good instincts for when something was wrong with a patient. From the look of concern in Dana's face and her assessment of the patient, Anna knew this wasn't going to be one of the less concerning diagnoses. "Were his words slurred? His smile crooked?"

"I didn't stop to do an NIH. I thought it was best to get you first," Dana said, following her down the hall.

"You did the right thing. I would want to do my own anyway," Anna said. While Anna was used to having a nurse triage the patients before she saw them, Dana wouldn't have seen a lot of stroke patients. They entered the room, and Anna found the man on the exam table, a young, scared boy no more than sixteen beside him.

The man looked to be in his fifties, with more than a sprinkle of gray scattered through his dark brown hair. He was well kept, his face shaved, and his clothes were clean and unwrinkled. It didn't take but a moment for Anna to realize what had sparked Dana's concern. The left-sided droop of the man's face was significant.

Sometimes she hated it when she was right. "Hi there, I'm Dr. Dobson. I heard you were having some problems. Can you tell me your name?"

When the man attempted to speak, his words were unrecognizable. Anna continued with her exam. "Can you show me your teeth?"

"Can I go now?" the boy asked. "My boss is going to be mad if I don't get back soon."

"Just tell me what happened. The nurse said you didn't know the man."

"I've never seen him. He came in and ordered two coffees then took a seat at one of the tables while he was waiting. A couple minutes later when I brought the coffees out to him, he didn't seem right. I didn't know what to do, so I called my boss, and he said to bring him over here."

"So about, say, fifteen minutes ago he was fine?" They might not have a name, but at least they would know the man's last known normal time, which was important for determining his treatment.

"Did he pay by card or cash?" she asked. Before he answered, she thought of something else. "You said he ordered two coffees?"

"He paid cash and, yes, two." The poor kid was getting more and more nervous as he stood there.

"I need you to run back to the diner and see if anyone showed up there looking for him. If someone is there or if anyone comes asking for him later, send them to us." The boy was out of the room the moment Anna finished giving him instructions.

Anna turned back to her patient. "Can you smile for me?"

Anna demonstrated smiling and saw the man try to copy her, but only the right side of his mouth lifted. "Nod your head yes or no if you are on blood thinners."

Instead of nodding, the man attempted to speak again, his words too garbled to make out.

"Dana, go get Will. I need to know how you handle strokes. And we need to get this man to the nearest

stroke center as soon as possible. Also, we need to record that his last known normal was fifteen minutes ago. That's important."

"That would be Knoxville. I'll get Will and have Martha call the stroke center we use. They'll page out a stroke alert and get a helicopter headed this way. She'll call 911 and get an ambulance for transport down the mountain to meet the helicopter," Dana said before leaving the room.

Anna couldn't help but be impressed with how confident Dana was in the process. With a stroke, loss of time meant loss of brain. Having a process in place was the key to providing interventions as quickly as possible.

Anna had just finished her neurological exam when Will came in. "What do we have?" he asked.

"Aphasia, facial droop, and some left-sided weakness. We don't have any history or even know his name. Dana said she didn't recognize him as one of your patients." Anna patted the man's right hand, which had been squeezing hers. She knew the man was scared and she didn't blame him.

"I was just about to check his pockets for a phone or wallet. We need to find someone who can give us a history and a list of his medications. I asked him about blood thinners, but I couldn't make out his words. His blood pressure is high, but not enough to treat without knowing what's going on."

"Sir, can you nod your head yes if you are on any blood thinners?" Will asked the man. The man spoke again, his words showing a frustration he didn't have

before. "It's okay. We're going to help you. We think you might be having a stroke. We don't have the medications or facilities to treat you here, so we're going to send you to a hospital in Knoxville."

"I'm going to reach into your pocket for your wallet so we can contact your family," Anna said as Will continued to talk to the man and explain what to expect during his transport. She had just pulled out a small wallet when Dana came back into the room, a small, gray-haired woman beside her.

"This is Mrs. Archer, she's the patient's wife," Dana said. "There's an ambulance on the way, lights on. ETA thirty minutes."

"Can you have Martha call the hospital with the man's ID. It will save time to have him already registered when he arrives," Anna said handing Dana the man's license.

As Will began to explain to the man's wife what they suspected and the need to get him to a stroke center as soon as possible, Anna began entering her assessment into the computer.

The next half hour seemed like hours to Anna, and she wondered how Will could stand there so calmly beside the man and his wife. Unable to bear it anymore, she went to find Ms. Martha to see if she had heard from the ambulance. As she headed down the hall to the receptionist desk, she heard Dana in a room, explaining to someone that there had been an emergency, which had caused a delay. When she heard a woman's voice complaining about the wait, Anna picked the chart that had been placed in a holder outside the door

and did a quick read-through of the patient's reason for coming to the clinic.

Anna knocked on the door and entered the room to find a young woman in her thirties, not much older than her. "Hi, I'm Dr. Dobson. I'm going to be filling in here for a few days. Like Dana was saying, we've had an emergency that's set us back. I'm sorry for the wait."

"That's okay," the woman said. "I just wanted to talk to Will. I need to get his advice on something."

As Dana walked by Anna, the nurse rolled her eyes. It took all of Anna's will not to grin back. "Well, why don't you tell me what brought you into the office today, and let's see if maybe I can help."

It only took a few minutes for Anna to realize that the woman was perfectly healthy. Her complaint of being tired had more to do with the fact that she was working two jobs as a waitress and traveling up and down the mountain sometimes twice a day. "So, it sounds like you have a very busy life. The good news is that your vital signs are great, and your weight is on target. I see in your chart that Will ordered some blood work last month. The results were all good. Is there anything else? Are you sleeping okay? Insomnia? Depression?"

"No, nothing like that. I went over all of that with Will. He suggested that I take a multivitamin, but there are so many out there. I thought maybe he could suggest one. Or order me one." Anna had grown up in the country, where her elders, teachers and doctors were addressed with a Mr. or Ms. and a surname unless the person had another preference. But times had changed.

Still, she didn't like the way that this woman referred to Will instead of Dr. Will or Dr. Harris.

Was there a relationship there she wasn't aware of? It was only fair to assume that Will would have been involved with other people over the last five years. She'd dated occasionally herself, though there had never been anything serious. Her plan of being a travel doctor had always come first.

"I can recommend one I personally take that I think would be perfect for you. I'm sure Dr. Harris would agree with me, but I can step out and ask him if you'd like," Anna said.

The woman let out a deep sigh, then seemed to deflate in front of Anna. "I guess I can try it, and if it doesn't work, I'll just have to make another appointment."

"I tell you what. How about I let Dr. Harris know that I've suggested an over-the-counter vitamin to you, and if he has any other suggestions, I'll have him call you."

Anna had just stepped out of the room when the hallway door opened and two men with a stretcher entered, followed by Dana. Not wanting to get in the way, Anna waited for them to pass, then joined them. Will gave a report to the ambulance crew as they loaded up the patient, and within five minutes, they were hurrying out the door to meet the helicopter.

As soon as they left, Dana offered to walk the wife back to the bed-and-breakfast where she and her husband had been staying. The young woman Anna had seen was their last patient of the day.

"I didn't mean to take over your patient," Will said once Dana and the stroke victim's wife had left the room.

"He wasn't my patient. I was just supposed to be learning my way around the office today. Waiting for that ambulance did make me realize just how spoiled I am. If I'd seen that man in the emergency room, I'd have the results of the CT by now and I'd already have a consult by one of our neurologists. If it was a clot, he would have gone for a removal procedure, or I would have already ordered a thrombolytic," Anna said as she followed Will back to his office where she'd left her backpack.

"There's no way we can offer that type of care. But what we did do today, that made a difference," Will said. She stood while he took a seat. "You have to see that. If we weren't here, there wouldn't have been anyone to help the man. By the time his wife had found him and either called 911 or driven him down to the nearest urgent care center if she'd realized what was happening, then things would have been worse."

"I'm not criticizing the care here. It's the opposite. Dana, Martha, everyone, worked quickly to give the patient the best outcome possible. I was seriously impressed that for a small clinic, you were able to get things done so quickly. You have a good process and everyone followed it." Anna knew that Will was sensitive about the clinic after her words earlier. He was passionate about his practice and Anna admired that. She couldn't say that she had ever felt the same about where she worked. Maybe it was because it was so

much bigger and Anna knew that she made up just a tiny part of it. "And I have to say, there hasn't been a moment that I've been bored today."

Will's smile turned mischievous. "Well, we do have our moments."

"Apparently, you do," Anna agreed.

"And you can see now why my dad was worried about only having one practitioner here. For a clinic our size, we stay busy," he said.

"You would have been okay without me. Dana could have interrupted the X-ray. But with the volume we saw today, and your father seeing patients, too, I can imagine that you'd be working over every night."

"I guess that means you'll be here the day after Christmas?" he asked.

"I guess it does," Anna said, then picked up her backpack and headed out the door. She might actually be looking forward to working at the small-town clinic that she'd once called boring, but she wasn't about to let him see that.

The smile that had lit her face disappeared. She had to be careful. She didn't want Will to get the wrong impression. Her working at the clinic was only temporary. She was about to start her dream of being a travel doc. As soon as New Year's Day came, she'd be headed to Florida.

Because no matter what her heart was feeling, her head knew that this wasn't where she belonged.

CHAPTER NINE

"You know, in the city I would get this catered," Anna said as she followed Will into the kitchen of his childhood home where he was cooking supper for her and their parents after the small wedding rehearsal.

When he'd come up with the idea, she'd been all for the chance to spend time with her mom and her mom's soon-to-be husband. But now she worried that the whole thing could be awkward. It still seemed weird that the next day Will would become her stepbrother.

"Anybody can pull out a credit card and buy someone a meal. Not everyone can do this." Will opened the oven door, and the smell of garlic, fresh oregano and tomatoes filled the room.

"You made your lasagna," Anna said, taking a deep breath and closing her eyes.

"Of course," Will said. "I know it's your favorite."

A flash of heat flushed through her body, and she knew it wasn't from the heat of the stove. The smell of the cooked herbs and spices had brought back a world of bittersweet memories. Will had made this for her before, and she'd asked him if he had a secret ingredient. He'd told her then that his secret ingredient was love. Right before he'd kissed her. That night, the lasagna

had been cold by the time they'd gotten around to eating it. She'd ordered the dish in dozens of restaurants since that night. None had ever tasted as good as Will's.

"What can I do to help?" she asked, looking around the kitchen.

"There are vegetables in the fridge for a salad. You can start on that. I'll work on the bread," Will said.

Anna opened the fridge and began to pull out what she needed. It seemed strange to think that this would be the place she'd be coming to visit her mother on her next visit. But what about Will? This was the kitchen his mother used to cook in. He had to have memories of her here.

"Does it feel strange to you? Thinking about my mom moving in here?" she asked. Opening the cabinet, she found that there were bowls and plates that she recognized as some that she'd helped her mother pack, though she couldn't imagine when her mother had put them there. It must have been Will's father. It seemed like something he would do.

When Will stopped his work with the bread to look around the room, Anna moved closer. "I know you have memories of your mom being here in this room. Is it going to be weird? My dad never lived in the house Mom's leaving, so that makes it easier for me."

"I do have memories here. With my mom, and then later when it was just me and my dad. I don't think your mom's going to change that. I don't think of it as your mom or my dad are trying to replace the people they lost. It's more like they're just adding a new story to their lives. It might be different, but I hope it's a good different, especially for our parents."

They both returned to their tasks, and Anna considered what Will had said. Even though she'd claimed that she was happy for her mother, there had still been a part of her that felt she was being disloyal to her father. She'd thought her mom would always love her dad. But if she looked at it the way Will did, it wasn't that her mom had stopped loving her dad. That love would always be with her mom, and with Anna. But life had changed when Anna's father had died. And with that change came an opportunity for her mother to love again.

They both heard the front door open and heard their parents talking, but then the talking stopped.

"Just a warning that there are children in the house," Will called, making Anna giggle.

The smile he shot her took her breath away. He looked so young and carefree in that moment. She hadn't seen that smile in so long, and seeing it brought back happy memories they'd shared before things had ended between them. She'd spent so much time concentrating on the pain—and sometimes on her regrets—that she had blocked out the memories of the good times when they had been happy together.

"I smell something wonderful," Coreene said as she walked into the kitchen. Her mom's face was glowing. Whether that was from the kiss that Will had interrupted or from the happiness of the wedding rehearsal, Anna didn't know. She was just glad that her mother had finally fully recovered from the flu.

"This was so nice for the two of you to plan this," Will's father said.

"Are you sure the two of you are okay with us leaving you alone for Christmas?" her mom asked her. Anna had reassured her mom a dozen times that she would be fine without her on Christmas Day.

"There's no reason for them to be alone, Coreene. They can spend Christmas together," Will's father said.

"Dr. Harris, that's not necessary. I've spent the last few years working Christmas." Anna didn't look at Will. Having his father force them to spend Christmas together was embarrassing.

"Well, I think it's a great idea," her mother said. "There's no reason for the two of y'all to spend the day alone just because we're not going to be here. Oh, I feel so much better now. I don't think I could have relaxed and enjoyed myself knowing the two of you had no one to celebrate the day with."

Anna looked over at Will, hoping he'd say something, but he just shook his head.

And just like that, Anna knew her mother had won. She and Will would be spending Christmas Day together.

"These are beautiful," Anna told Shelley as she took the two bouquets of flowers from the florist. "I love the rhinestones you added."

"I thought maybe the roses needed a little bling. And since they're saying we might get some snow in the next few days, it seemed these snowflake brooches would be perfect." Shelley said, then winced and rubbed her belly. "I think this baby boy is a little too excited today."

"Are you having contractions?" Anna asked. "You're, what, thirty-four weeks now?"

"I'll be thirty-five weeks on Monday," Shelley said. "And I'm fine. Just some occasional cramping. My doctor says it's nothing to be worried about."

"I could have stopped by and picked these up. You need to be resting," Anna said, still worried by the way the woman continued to rub her belly as if to calm the baby inside. One of the problems in a town this far up the mountain was that women had to drive so far to get to a hospital to deliver.

"And miss this wedding? No way. More than half the town is here. They've had to bring in extra chairs to make room for everyone," Shelley said.

"But Mom said this was supposed to be a small affair," Anna said, turning to where her mom sat at a table that had been brought into the classroom that had been turned into their dressing room. "I don't think she's expecting that many people. Just those in the church and some friends."

The wedding had been planned to take place right before the Christmas Eve service. Except for the church members, Anna had assumed that most people would be at home getting ready for Christmas and spending time with their own families.

"Your mother has a lot of friends here, I'm sure, but Dr. Harris has also taken care of most of the town for the last thirty years. I'm sure his patients heard about the wedding and wanted to show their support," Shelley said, rubbing her belly again, her smile tightening. "And now I'm going to go join them."

Anna watched the woman waddle out of the room, still concerned that Shelley was feeling so uncomfortable when she had several weeks to go before her delivery.

"What's wrong?" Coreene asked, coming up behind her.

Turning, Anna saw her mom standing in a pale pink tea-length dress. Anna had her father's green eyes and brown hair, whereas her mother's eyes were a pale blue, and while there was some silver around her temples, her hair was still mostly a honey blond. Anna wasn't sure she'd ever realized that her mother was such a beautiful woman. Anna had always just thought of her as Mom. Now, though, Anna was taken aback by the woman that stood in front of her. Not just by her beauty but by the strength of her. By the fact that her mother had survived the loss of her husband, always putting Anna first and doing everything she could to make her childhood as full as it could be after the loss of her father.

And now her mom stood here ready to start a new life without any hint of fear of what the future held. Didn't her mom worry that she might have to go through the same loss again someday? Was the love her mom felt for Will's dad so strong that she was willing to take that risk?

"I always thought that I would be walking you down the aisle instead of you walking with me," Coreene said.

Anna didn't know what to say. She'd always assumed the same. She'd never dreamed her mother would find love again after what her parents had shared. "Is it hard? Doing this again?"

"Do you mean, does this bring back memories of me marrying your father?" she asked.

"Yes," Anna said. She shouldn't have asked. This was her mother's day. What was she thinking? "I'm sorry. I shouldn't have asked that."

"No, it's okay. I want to tell you." Anna's mother took Anna's hands in hers, and their eyes met. "I loved your father very much. And, yes, I've relived some memories of our wedding today. But they have been good memories, not sad ones."

Anna nodded, unable to speak as her throat tightened and her vision blurred. She knew if she let the tears flow, her mom's would soon follow.

"I suspect that James is having some of those same memories of his own first wedding." Coreene wiped the stray tear that slid down Anna's face. "We have both lived good lives before today. But today, we get a chance to live those lives together. I'm thankful for that and I hope James is, too."

A broken laugh escaped Anna's throat. "He has no idea just how lucky he is to have you."

Anna sobered then. "I didn't always know how lucky I was, either. The last couple years, I haven't been there for you like I should have. I'm sorry for that."

"I know you have your reasons. You've been busy with your job," her mom said. "I know you love what you do, Anna, but don't let your job become all there is to your life. You are a very special woman. I know there is someone out there that will love you just as deeply as I loved your father and now love James. Don't let yourself get so busy with this dream you have of

seeing the world that you miss out on the things that are really important in life."

"You know, me and Dad always talked about me seeing the world outside of Rolling Oaks. He used to study the maps with me and tell me I could go anywhere in the world if I set my mind to it."

"And you can. But that doesn't mean you have to go there alone," her mother said, leaning over and kissing Anna's forehead as if to take away the sting of her words.

There was a knock on the door, and a woman Anna recognized from the church peeped through the crack. "Coreene, it's time. Are you ready?"

Her momma looked at Anna and smiled. "Yes. I'm definitely ready."

Will stood beside his dad, facing a church filled with people that he'd known his whole life. When he'd arrived at the church, Will had been surprised to find that his father wasn't the calm and collected man he'd always known him to be. Instead, James had seemed nervous. Will had quickly discovered that it wasn't actually nerves. Instead, the man was just overwhelmed with happiness.

Unlike Anna, who had been surprised by their parents' relationship, Will had been there to witness it all. It hadn't been a sudden thing. Instead, he'd watched James and Coreene dance around each other for over a year. He'd seen them go from sharing laughs to sharing secret smiles when they hadn't known anyone was looking. He'd watched their friendship become more.

And he'd watched his dad change from a man whose life had revolved around his job to a man who'd gone on picnics in the mountains and concerts. He'd watched his dad have a life outside of the clinic.

The fact that his own life now was much like his father's had been before Coreene wasn't missed by Will. Seeing his dad change had pushed him to try to make changes in his own life. Or at least he'd tried to make those changes. He'd even joined a dating site, though he'd had no luck finding someone he was interested in there. He'd given up after the third date he'd gone on with someone he had nothing in common with no matter how much the website declared them a good match. He'd told himself that it wasn't like he was running out of years to find someone. He had plenty of time. He was just waiting till he had more time to devote to a relationship before he got serious about someone.

And then Anna had burst back into his life. It had only taken a few minutes of seeing her before he'd had to admit the truth to himself. He wasn't waiting for his practice to settle down. And it wasn't that all those matches he'd been sent weren't perfectly acceptable women. It was that they weren't her.

Anna had held a special place in his life since he was a child. And when friendship had turned into more, he hadn't known how to tell her. The fact that everyone in their high school had figured out that he had a crush on her, yet she was oblivious to it, had told him that she didn't feel the same way. But when they'd met back up in medical school, it had seemed like a sign. Maybe if he'd pressed things with her sooner, things

between them might have been different. Their finally going from friends and classmates to lovers had happened only two months before graduation. It had been his realizing that time was running out before they'd head off to their residency that had finally given him the urgency he needed to show her how he really felt about her.

Not that it had mattered. They'd still gone their separate ways, leaving things between them worse than they'd been before. A part of him wished they'd never had that first kiss. At least then he'd still have had her friendship. Another part knew no regrets for what they'd shared, no matter how badly it had ended.

The doors at the back of the church opened and she was standing there. Anna. As she started down the aisle toward him, his palms became damp and his breathing became labored. He'd dreamed of this once upon a time. Of course, the dress was wrong. In his dream, she'd been dressed in white instead of green, but she still looked just as beautiful as he'd known she would be.

As each step brought her closer, Will tried to drag his eyes away from her. No matter what had happened in his dream, Anna wasn't walking down that aisle to him. She was here for her mother. That was the only reason she'd even come back to town. The pain of that knowledge and the realization that he still had such strong feelings for her made standing there in front of all the people who'd gathered for this wedding almost unbearable.

She was only a few feet away when she looked over at him. Her smile faltered and their eyes locked. For

just a moment, he let her see into his deepest secret: that he still wanted her with a desire just as strong as it had been all those years ago in college.

No, that was wrong. What he felt inside of him right then had grown stronger than it had ever been. While time and the pain he'd felt when she'd left him should have destroyed what he had felt for her, instead it had just sealed it closed until this moment. Now, feeling the depth of his feelings, he understood that he had just been waiting for the time that she would return to him.

The doors opened once more and they both turned, breaking a shared moment that had said more than all the words they'd shared since Anna's return. The sudden loss of the connection between them was like a physical blow as his body tensed, ready to accept the pain he knew was coming as it brought him back to the reality of the moment. This was never meant to be their future. As his soon-to-be stepmother made her way down the aisle, Will pushed back everything that had happened in the last few moments. He forced himself to concentrate on the ceremony, though he couldn't help from glancing at Anna as his father and her mother said their vows. And when he noticed Anna's own glances at him, he made himself ignore them.

Because while he had finally acknowledged to himself that he still had feelings for her, he couldn't let himself forget the pain he'd felt when she'd left him. Anna's plans didn't include him. And they never had.

CHAPTER TEN

ANNA WATCHED AS her mother and her new stepfather rode off with the words *Just Married* and *It's Never Too Late to Find Love* scrawled across their car's back window by one of their friends. As everyone waved and wished them well, Anna felt a sense of loneliness that she hadn't been expecting. Her mother was happy and excited, for she now had someone to share her life with. Anna had no right to express anything but happiness for her. But still, there was that feeling that she remembered from her childhood when she'd lost her father that had been recurring ever since her mother had told her that she was remarrying. That feeling of being alone.

Which was stupid because she wasn't alone. And her mother certainly hadn't abandoned her. Her mother would still be there for her. Just because her mother was starting a new life, that didn't mean Anna was going to be left behind. Maybe it was because it had only been her and her mother for so long that she now felt this way. She'd been the center of her mother's world. Now she wasn't. It wasn't that she was jealous of the fact that she now had to share her mother's love. No.

It was almost as if her mother's marriage was pointing out the lack of someone in her own life.

A shiver passed through Anna that had little to do with the cold wind that had made its way through the coat she'd thrown over her dress as she remembered the look she'd shared with Will. For a moment there had been a connection between them. A link where she'd been flooded with a dozen emotions, some hers, some his, but most shared. There had been hope, desire, longing, need and then fear from the one emotion that she didn't want to acknowledge. When she'd finally managed to pull herself together, she'd felt confused and disoriented. It was as if she'd lived a lifetime of sensations in just a moment. It wasn't something that she ever wanted to repeat, but at the same time, she'd never felt as alive as she had in that one moment.

"What should we do with all of this?" Will asked as he came up behind her. Anna looked around to see that most everyone had left the front entrance of the church and were headed for their cars. How long had she been standing there?

She suddenly felt raw and vulnerable. Turning to him, she avoided his eyes. Instead, she looked at the armload of presents he held. The church had thrown the couple a small reception and wedding shower combined, which meant there were stacks of presents to be taken care of.

"Mom asked me to make sure they were taken to your dad's house. She wanted to wait to open them when she had more time so she could make sure she

thanked everyone," Anna said, her eyes centered on the big pink bow on one of the boxes.

"Sounds good. I'll put these in my truck and come back for the rest of them. There's also the cake," Will said as he started toward his truck.

It took almost half an hour for them to load all the presents into Will's truck, filling it from door to door. Deciding that the safest way to transport the cake was in Anna's car, she followed Will out of the church parking lot and down the few blocks to the home her mother would now share with Will's father.

By the time they'd unloaded everything from the truck and the cake had been packed away in the freezer, the awkwardness she had expected to feel with Will after what they had shared had faded.

"And why again do we need to freeze the cake?" Will asked, his finger dipping into the icing that had been left in the bakery box.

"The top layer of the cake is saved to be eaten on the first anniversary. It's tradition," Anna said as she shut the freezer door, protecting the cake from Will's unending need for sugar. "Didn't you get a piece of the cake at the church?"

"I had two, but I'm still hungry. Aren't you?" Will asked. Anna was about to deny it when her stomach let out an embarrassing growl, answering his question.

"I'll heat up the leftover lasagna," Will said as he opened the refrigerator.

Anna watched as he took out the dish then began pulling out dishes and dividing the pasta into portions. The house was too quiet. The awkwardness she

had expected to feel was there just below the surface. She should have left as soon as they'd finished putting things away.

"It was a beautiful wedding, don't you think?" Anna said, hoping to fill the silence.

"It was. I couldn't believe my dad was so nervous," Will said, placing the first dish into the microwave to heat. "There's some wine left over from dinner last night if you want to pour it,"

"I couldn't believe my mom *wasn't* nervous. I have to say, it feels a little weird going through your dad's cabinets," Anna said. "I know my mom's going to live here, but I think it's going to take some time for me to adjust."

"You'll get used to it," Will said as he took one dish out of the microwave and put in the other one.

Instead of sitting at the table where they'd sat with their parents, they ate in front of the TV and watched the last of her favorite Christmas movie, *Elf.*

"I don't understand how a Christmas movie makes you cry," Will said later as they cleaned up their dishes. "It has a happy ending. Buddy gets a family and the girl. What is there to cry about?"

"Sometimes you cry when you're happy," she said. "It's kind of like there's just too much happiness to hold inside."

"Isn't that what laughter is?" Will asked, then handed her a dish to dry. "But you cry every time we watch that movie. You already know how it ends."

"That doesn't change the fact that it's moving. I mean, Buddy goes looking for his father and ends up

finding a family and a girl who accepts him and loves him just as he is. He even has a little brother that looks up to him. Did you want a brother when you were growing up?"

"No, I don't think I ever thought about it," Will said, looking over at her. "Did you?"

"I asked my mom for a baby sister once. She told me she was blessed to have me and that was more than enough. I didn't know until later that my mom had lost several pregnancies before she had me."

She'd felt terrible when she had realized how much it must have hurt her mom to have to tell her that she couldn't have a sister. And Anna had never really felt like she was missing anything by not having a sister or a brother.

But now she did have a brother. From this day on, Will would be her stepbrother. She'd never get used to that. She managed not to laugh, but she couldn't stop the smile. The whole thing was ridiculous.

"What?" Will said, handing her a wineglass to dry.

"I'm sorry, but the fact that you're my stepbrother is just too much," Anna said, an unexpected giggle escaping. "It's so weird for so many reasons."

It took a moment for Anna to realize Will had gone still beside her. When he reached for the glass she held, she handed it to him without thinking. She watched as he carefully sat the thin glass goblet on the counter and then dried his hands on a towel. All the laughter inside of her died away as he turned to her and gave her a look that sent shivers through her. She'd never seen Will so still. So focused.

When his hands came up to frame her face, she found herself unable to inhale a breath. "I will never think of you as a sister, nor do I want you to think of me as a brother." Will's eyes lowered, and in that moment she knew he was about to kiss her.

There was a warning bell going off somewhere in her brain, but she chose to ignore it. It was like torture waiting for that moment when his lips would touch hers, but when it finally came, she found it was worth it. Her lips were already parted, and she sucked in a deep breath as his lips just grazed over hers.

Her body protested at the tease and her arms came up and her hands raked through his hair, closing around the back of his head as his lips found hers again. This time there was no teasing. This time there was pure desire and need. She returned the kiss with an intensity that matched his. And when his hands traveled down her rib cage and circled her waist, pulling her against him until she was molded around him, she hung on.

They'd shared a passion for each other before, but it had never been like this. Before, it had been like a spark igniting a pile of kindling. This was a full forest fire of emotion racing through her. It was hot and dangerous. And she didn't care.

A sharp knock sounded at the kitchen door, startling Anna. As she turned to see who it was that had interrupted them, her hand came up and knocked against the cabinet, knocking the glass she had been drying earlier onto the floor. The crack of the glass against the ceramic tile floor shocked her out of the haze of desire that she had been lost in.

"Who's in there?" a voice came from the back door as it slowly opened. "I've already called the sheriff, so you better get out of here."

Will let out a mumble that was less than polite as he moved away from her, cautiously avoiding the small pile of broken crystal on the floor. "It's just me, Mrs. Monroe."

Anna stifled a groan. She'd forgotten that Mrs. Monroe lived next door to Will's father.

"That you, Will?" the woman asked as Will opened the back door the rest of the way. "Are you okay? I heard something break."

Too late, Anna realized she had missed her opportunity to escape.

"I'm fine. Me and Anna were just cleaning up and we dropped a glass," Will said as the woman almost pushed him aside to get into the house.

"Anna. I didn't expect to see you here. You feeling okay? You looked a little flushed. If you're running a fever, you should be at home. Your momma might have given you the flu."

If Anna's face hadn't been flushed before, it was certainly a scarlet red now. For once, she agreed with Mrs. Monroe. "I'm fine, Mrs. Monroe. But you're right. I do need to be going home now that we've taken care of things here."

From behind Mrs. Monroe, Will shook his head. He knew she was about to make an escape. "Anna, could you grab the broom and the dustpan out of the pantry for me so we can get this cleaned up before someone

gets a piece of glass through their foot? I'm going to see Mrs. Monroe safely home."

Anna only waited a moment before she rushed to the kitchen closet. But she couldn't find the dustpan anywhere. She had just located it when she heard the door to the kitchen open and Will walked in.

Instead of saying anything, Anna chose to ignore him and instead went to sweep up the glass. She could feel the weight of Will's eyes on her, but he didn't say a word. Finally, the silence was too much.

"Mrs. Monroe made it home okay? I'm surprised she didn't keep your longer with her questions." At least that had been what Anna had hoped for. Whatever had just happened between the two of them had shaken her. They had agreed to be friends. Friends certainly didn't kiss like that. And she couldn't let it happen again.

"She couldn't get home fast enough," Will said. He stood deathly still, like he thought she'd run the moment he moved. He was probably right. "I'm sure the telephone lines will be buzzing soon with the news that she caught the two of us together."

"Do you think she saw anything?" Anna said. Her embarrassment for herself being the talk of the town outweighed by the fear her mother would hear about it. Of course, Anna could always blame it on the older woman's poor eyesight.

"It's possible. I don't know how long she was there. Do you really care?" Will asked.

"Of course I care. The last thing I want is to be the town gossip," Anna said. She ignored the hand Will offered her as she stood. It was rude to refuse his help,

but she didn't think she could stand the feel of his hand around hers right then.

"You know our parents were talked about once people knew they were dating. They actually thought it was funny," Will said, taking the dustpan from her and emptying it into the trash can. "Maybe instead of letting it bother you, you should ignore it. Or even better, we could have fun with it."

"Aren't you afraid of ruining your reputation? You're one of the town's doctors now." Anna moved to where she'd left her keys on the counter. She knew Will didn't care about what the people in the town talked about. He'd never needed to when his father was a well-respected doctor.

"I think my reputation will survive," he said as he walked with her toward the door. For one crazy moment, she hoped he would ask her to stay the night. Fortunately for both of them, he didn't. "I thought we'd leave early tomorrow and head up the mountain to see Grandma Mason. Dana helped me pack up some pound cake and cookies for her."

Anna had forgotten that Will had invited her to go up the mountain with him. They'd promised their parents that they would spend the day together. Right then, climbing a mountain sounded like a much safer way to spend their time together than being cuddled up on the couch watching Christmas movies. "Sure, I'm in. What time should we leave?"

CHAPTER ELEVEN

WILL PARKED THE car at the start of the trail that would take them most of the way to Grandma Mason's home. Their conversation had been centered on the weather and the forecast for a Christmas Day snowfall for the first thirty minutes of the drive. After that, there had been silence. The higher they had gone up in the winding mountain road, the more snow flurries they had begun to see and the heavier the silence became. He had thought he'd give Anna the opportunity to bring up what had happened between the two of them. Now he was regretting that decision.

He'd spent half the night imagining what would have happened if his father's nosy neighbor hadn't interrupted them. The rest of the night he'd spent wondering if Anna would even be home when he got there the next morning, or if she would have left, just as she had the night before they'd left for their residency. It hadn't been until he'd turned the last curve to her home and saw her car there that he had relaxed. She hadn't run. That was a start. A small one, but at least he had a chance now. It was more than she had given him the last time.

"Do you remember the first time we climbed up to

see her?" Will asked as he opened the back door of the truck and pulled out his backpack.

"Tenth grade. You overheard one of the guys in band class telling me this story about a scary old woman who lived in the woods at the top of the mountain. You told us that it was just a story made up to keep everyone off the trail. So I dared you to climb the mountain and see."

"And I dared you to climb it with me," Will said, adjusting the weight of the backpack. Besides the baked goods, he'd packed some medication and a few canned goods.

"I'll never forget the look on your face when you opened the door to Grandma Mason's house and found her there," Anna said, adjusting her own pack that carried the food for their lunch.

"I thought she was dead," Will said. Finding the woman in her rocking chair, eyes closed and not moving had almost scared him to death. Now, every time he climbed this mountain, he wondered if he would find her that way again, only this time not just sleeping.

They started up the thin trail that wound through the heavily wooded oaks that their town had been named for. It wasn't as long a hike as a lot of the trails in these Smoky Mountains tended to be, but there were some treacherous areas where you had to step carefully as the trail followed the edge of the mountain.

"You know the reason I interrupted your conversation that day was because I was jealous, don't you?"

"What?" Anna asked, disbelief in her voice. "No you weren't."

"I was. That was the reason I did most of the things

where you were concerned. I don't know if I'd have even made it into medical school if I hadn't been trying to impress you all throughout high school. It's the reason my GPA was high enough to get me into an Ivy League college."

They continued up the mountain without either of them saying a word. They had walked like that for half a mile when they turned a corner and came to where the trail hugged the edge of the mountain. Anna stopped and took a deep breath. "This view always does something to me. When people talk about picturing their happy place, this place is what I think of."

Will looked out over the side of the mountain. Through a smoky haze, he could see the range of mountains below them. While a lot of trees were bare at this time of year, there were crops of pines that peaked up through the forest. "It's the quiet that I love up here. It's so peaceful. I almost understand why Grandma Mason stays up here."

"I would not go that far. I mean, sure, maybe a day or two up here would be nice. But after that? No, thank you," Anna said. "I love the convenience of the city."

They both started back up the mountain. Soon all he could hear was the chirping of birds, the sounds of their feet against the rocky trail and their labored breaths as they climbed higher and higher. They came to the trickiest part of the trail, where a large pile of rocks had fallen down and covered the path. Once Will made it to the top, he held his hand out to help Anna. She hesitated for a moment, then her hand reached for his. But instead of letting go of her hand after they'd cleared

the rocks, he held it tight. Maybe if he couldn't say the words to show her how he felt, he could show her. They finally reached the spot where the trail wound back into the forest and separated into two paths. They took the path to the right that would lead them the rest of the way.

Dark gray clouds covered the morning sun, and very little light made its way through the trees to the path they followed. Will knew he didn't have to tell Anna to not only watch her step but to also keep an eye out for bears that might be wandering through. After the first time they'd met the woman that lived at the top of the mountain, they'd continued to visit her at least once a month. Sometimes they came together, but at other times, they had brought their friends. Will knew that some of those friends still visited the woman at the top of the mountain because she told the best stories of times long before the tourists came to the area.

"You know, Grandma Mason told me once that you didn't come up here to visit her. That you really came up here to spend time with me," Anna said, her words seeming to echo through the forest.

"Grandma Mason is a very wise woman," Will said. He knew the teenage Will would have denied such a statement, but he'd grown up since then. Besides, he was tired of hiding his feelings for Anna. He was no longer the teenage boy trying everything to get her attention, nor was he the college kid who had been afraid to ask for a commitment from her. Sometime in the middle of last night, he'd made the decision to stop denying his love. He wanted Anna. He'd always wanted

Anna. But if he had any chance of finding happiness with her, he would have to be willing to put everything on the line, including his heart.

They came to a clearing, and there in the middle sat a small cabin, its logs grayed and cracked. Outside on the covered porch sat an old woman with a blanket over her shoulders. She was in a worn-out rocking chair and was looking straight at them as they exited the woods.

"There you are," she said as they approached the steps that led up to the porch. "It's about time you got here."

"Do you really think she knew we were coming?" Anna whispered as she followed him up the steps.

Will shrugged his shoulders. "With her, anything is possible."

"Ms. Mason, you don't need to be out in this weather," Anna said as she took a seat on a bench beside the old woman's rocking chair.

"Anna Dobson, is that you? Just because you got that fancy medical degree doesn't mean you don't call me Grandma Mason just like everybody else," she said, her rocking chair going still. Then she turned to Will. "You bring me some of that pound cake you promised me?"

"I saved a half loaf just for you," Will said, pulling out the foil-wrapped package and handing it to her.

"Edith Hammer might not know how to pick a husband, but it's not her baking skills that ran off the last three," Grandma Mason said. They all waited as she tore open the package and pulled off a piece of cake.

"It's perfect," Grandma Mason said, closing her eyes

and going back to her rocking. They sat there in the quiet as the woman seemed to drift off to sleep. Will and Anna knew better, though. They'd been fooled by her before. Grandma Mason was not going to be hurried by anything, even at the risk of being inhospitable.

"I've been thinking a lot about you two lately," she finally said. Will and Anna looked at each other, not sure what she was about to say next. "You two have always been special. Will, because he has a heart of gold and cares so much for an old lady like me."

"And me?" Anna finally asked after they'd sat there another minute without the woman saying a word.

One eye popped open, and the smile Grandma Mason gave Anna was a little wicked. "You were always the impatient one. Impatient and impulsive. It was a lot of fun to see what you were going to get into next."

"I haven't gotten into any trouble since I left here," Anna said, the defensiveness in her tone hard to miss.

Grandma Mason stopped rocking and opened both eyes, her gaze locked on Anna. Will almost felt sorry for Anna, but she'd brought this on herself. She knew better than to rush the woman. "Well, that's a shame, isn't it? You have to live your life, girl. And life's not meant for working your fingers to the bone. That's not living. That's slowly dying. I know something about that. I don't recommend it."

Anna looked over at Will as if she were waiting for him to come to her aid, but there was no way he was going to disagree with Grandma Mason. But he could at least change the subject. "Anna packed us a really

nice Christmas lunch, and that hike up here has made me hungry. How about we go inside and eat?"

"Well, why did it take you so long to tell me? A Christmas lunch, huh?" Grandma Mason said, jumping up from the rocking chair with more energy than he'd seen her have in years. "I've got a pot of tea on the stove, too. It's been a long time since I've had a Christmas lunch."

Anna and Will followed her into the one-room house. Will had never heard of people living without electricity before he'd been here, but the home had never been wired for it. Electricity had never made it this high up the mountain. Not that Grandma Mason would have used it if it had. Instead of electricity, she cooked and heated the room with a cast-iron stove that sat in the middle of the space.

While Anna unwrapped the ham and potato salad her mom had prepared for their meal, Will went out back to where the wood for the stove was kept. He picked up a few pieces to add to the fire and saw that he would need to chop some more of the logs stacked in the lean-to shed before he left. If the weather channel was correct, temperatures were headed down, along with an increasing chance of snow.

Once Will had added the wood to the stove and the room began to warm, they each took a seat at the small table. As they ate, Grandma Mason asked Anna questions about her job and about Nashville. She surprised both of them when she told the story of her and her husband traveling to Nashville to see Johnny Cash and his wife sing at the Grand Ole Opry.

"I didn't know you'd ever been farther down the mountain than Rolling Oak," Anna said as she began to wrap up the remaining ham. "If you left the mountain then, why won't you leave it now? You could at least come down and stay with your son. I know he'd take care of you."

"That was before the accident, before I lost my Aaron. I'd go anywhere with him. But now, why would I want to leave here? It's the home we made together for our family. It's my home," Grandma Mason said, standing and moving over to the small bed that sat in the corner. "Ain't that why you come up here? All those memories you two made when y'all used to sneak up here."

Was that true? Will did have great memories of the time he and Anna had spent climbing up and down the mountain together. They'd made the trip a dozen times before their parents had discovered where they were going on the days they both seemed to disappear at the same time. But even though reliving those memories were pleasant, that wasn't why he made the climb up the mountain. No, he came to see this weathered old woman with a stubborn streak as long as the Tennessee River.

Will watched as she turned to adjust the one pillow on the bed, kicked her shoes off and lay down. A moment later, her breathing evened out to a regular rhythm. Walking over to the bed, he laid an old, knitted afghan over her.

"She'll sleep for a couple hours, and we need to start back down," Will said to Anna as he unloaded the last of his pack onto the table. He'd brought her enough

medication to last her until the next month. With the canned goods he'd brought and what she had stocked on the shelves in the corner, she would be able to last for a few weeks in case the weather turned bad and no one could make the trip up the mountain.

They opened the door to a gust of wind full of tiny snowflakes. They'd just made it out of view of the cabin when Anna stopped. "Did you notice her color?"

"Yes," Will said. He'd noticed the blue-gray tint of her skin, especially around her mouth.

"She's been in heart failure for several years. I bring her medications to help, but..." He didn't have to say the words. They both knew it was just a matter of time before her heart wouldn't be able to pump any longer.

"Someone will visit her one day and find her...gone," Anna said, her voice wobbling with the last word.

"And I bet they'll find her with a smile on her face," Will said.

"But still..." Anna began, and then stopped.

"She's where she wants to be. Not everyone gets that privilege. We have to respect her wishes," Will said. "It would kill her if someone took her off the mountain. We both know that. Even her son knows that, though he's not happy about it."

On the way down the trail, Will tried to think of a way to bring up what had happened between the two of them the night before, but he kept thinking of Grandma Mason. He understood that he had to be willing to let the old woman go her way, even if that probably meant she'd be alone when her time came. It was what she wanted.

But what about Anna? She'd told him over and over that she wanted to travel the world, to see what life was like beyond their little town. He'd been so certain that forcing Anna to see what the two of them could have together in their small town was what he needed to do. But if the kiss they'd shared hadn't made a difference to her plans, maybe it was best if she didn't know how much he cared about her. Maybe it was best that she didn't have to make the choice between her dream and him. Maybe she was right that they should concentrate on just being friends. They'd shared a kiss. That didn't necessarily mean that she wanted more.

By the time Will dropped Anna off at her house, he'd tried a dozen times to bring up the subject of that kiss. He'd ricocheted back and forth as if he were a pinball in a pinball machine trying to make up his mind on what he should do. Anna had chosen to pretend nothing happened between them. So, did that mean that kiss had meant nothing to her? They weren't high school kids, where a kiss was assumed to mean that you were involved with someone. They were adults. Adults that should have discussed the situation together, instead of him sitting there watching her walk away from him, again.

For years he'd asked himself if things would have been different if he'd gone after Anna that morning she'd left him. Could they have talked things out then? And if he had gone after her, what would he have said? Would he have finally had the nerve to say the three words that had been locked inside him for years? Would he have finally told her that he was in love with her?

But that was in the past. He had been given another opportunity with Anna. He could get out of his truck and march up to the door before she closed it and say those words. Finally take a chance. He wanted to do it. He could call to her to wait and she would. His hand reached for the door, squeezing the handle tightly. And then? Uncertainty froze him in place. Was he really thinking that three little words would change anything when she'd made it clear before that he wasn't enough to even consider changing the plans she had for her life?

He let go of the door handle and watched as Anna closed the door behind her. No matter how much he wanted to confront Anna, he couldn't seem to make himself do it. So instead, he'd drive back to his apartment and spend another sleepless night as he silently counted the number of days before Anna would be leaving him once again.

CHAPTER TWELVE

FROM ANNA'S TIME working in an emergency room, she knew that the day after Christmas was one of the busiest of the year. People ate things they shouldn't or, like the patient in front of her, too much of everything.

"You know you're supposed to watch your sodium intake," Anna said to the woman whose ankles were swollen and whose blood pressure was, according to her medical records, at an all-time high.

"It's my husband's fault," the woman said. "He insists on brining the turkey for a day before he smokes it. He knows I love his smoked turkey."

Anna didn't bring up the fact that she'd probably been okay if she'd stuck with just the turkey. Having experienced many holiday meals herself, Anna knew there had likely also been a ham and many more dishes high in sodium on the woman's table Christmas Day. And they both knew that next year, nothing would have changed. So instead of lecturing the woman, Anna increased her Lasix prescription and encouraged her to forego the higher sodium leftovers that she was sure were packed away in the woman's fridge.

The day continued with Anna taking most of the walk-ins while Will saw those patients who had a prior

appointment scheduled, keeping them both busy. Anna was glad for the fact, as once more, she found herself passing him in the hallway. When he stopped and looked up from the chart in his hand, Anna had mumbled something about a patient waiting for her and hurried away.

On their trip to see Grandma Mason, they'd managed to avoid the big elephant in the room, the kiss they had shared the night before. She'd put on her best poker face and kept their conversation to the weather and Grandma Mason as much as possible.

Still, that hadn't kept her from thinking about it, worrying about it and, when she couldn't help herself, reliving every detail of it. How she'd managed not to grab Will by the shirt and force him to kiss her again before she'd climbed out of his truck, she didn't know. It was like she'd lost all control of not only her mind, but also her body. That one kiss they'd shared had taken her right back to their college days when they'd been unable to tear themselves apart from each other. Where only a look from Will had Anna hot and ready for him.

Through the years, she'd blamed her overworked brain and out-of-control hormones for the way she'd responded to Will those last two months of medical school. The pressure of making it through the program had ended more than one person's career before it had even started, and she'd had friends drop out of the program even in their last year. The stress of it all meant patience was in short supply and tempers could flare up at any time. It made sense that the stress had them reaching out to each other to help relieve the anxiety of the moment. It all made sense, she'd told her-

self over and over, but had she ever really believed it? Whether she had or not, that kiss they'd shared Christmas Eve after the wedding had shattered all her excuses. It wasn't stress making her respond to Will now. It wasn't stress that had her reliving that first moment his lips had touched hers or the way she'd felt molded against his body. No matter what she had told herself since that night, there had been a rightness there in his arms that she had never been able to experience with anyone else. And just acknowledging that scared her.

"Hey, Anna," Dana said, stopping in the hallway beside her. "Are you okay?"

No, she was not okay. She wasn't sure she'd ever be okay again. But that wasn't something she could talk to Dana about. She couldn't even discuss it with her mother. "I'm fine. It's just been a busy day."

"Well, I'm afraid it's not over. There's a patient I had planned for Will to see, but she's specifically asking to see you," Dana said, her fingers drumming against the chart in her hand.

"It's okay. I'm caught up," Anna said, then held her hand out for the chart. When Dana continued to hold on to it, Anna knew there was more to just a patient wanting to see her instead of Will. "Is there a problem?"

"I just want to make sure that you are okay seeing her," Dana said, her hands still fidgeting with the chart. When Anna continued to hold her hand out, Dana handed her the folder. "I can tell her you're busy and she'll have to see Will."

Looking down at the name on the chart, Anna knew it wouldn't matter what Dana told her. If the mayor

wanted to see Anna, that was who she was going to see. Why she wanted to see her, though, Anna couldn't imagine. "Did she say why she was here?" Anna asked.

"She refused to say. All she'd say is that she wanted to see you instead of Will."

"It's not a problem. I'll be glad to see her. What room did you put her in?" Anna asked.

"She's in four. Do you want me to go with you?" Dana asked.

"No, I'll be fine." Anna watched as some of the tension in Dana disappeared, and her hands came to rest at her sides. Had Dana thought Anna couldn't handle the mayor? Working in an urban emergency room had prepared her for almost anything. She'd gone toe to toe with more than one outraged patient without backing down. She was definitely capable of handling Mayor Johnson.

"Good afternoon, Mayor," Anna said when she entered the room and found the woman looking extremely uncomfortable sitting on the exam table. "What brings you in today?"

The mayor opened her mouth and then closed it. Anna waited as the woman seemed to be working herself up to saying something, but Anna couldn't imagine what could be so difficult for her to say. Unless…

"Is it a woman thing?" Anna asked, understanding now why Mayor Johnson would have chosen to see Anna instead of Will.

"No, of course not. I see a doctor in Knoxville about those things. It's just…" The mayor swallowed as if something large and uncomfortable was lodged in her throat. Anna almost felt sorry for her.

"It's just…" Anna prompted.

"It's my hearing. I think I'm losing my hearing," the woman blurted out, her face going pink, as if she'd just admitted that she was pregnant with the county sheriff's love child. "You can't say anything about this, right? It's protected, my information?"

"Of course it's protected. And I'd never say anything anyway. But I don't understand the problem. I take it this is something new?"

"Yes. I wanted to go to a specialist in the city, but they can't get me in for three months. I can't wait that long. If it gets out, everyone will be saying I'm getting old and unable to do my job."

"I'm sure that wouldn't happen. You've been mayor for as long as I can remember." Anna walked over to the cabinet and picked up an otoscope. "I'm sure whatever the problem, no one is going to want to replace you. Even if you are losing your hearing, there are lots of options open."

"You don't understand. You're young and have all this energy. You've got a fancy doctorate degree and you're probably involved with some hot doctor in Nashville. You have everything. I only have this town and my job." The woman seemed to shrink in front of Anna. Did she really think their lives were that different? Anna's whole life revolved around her job. She'd put it before everything else, to the point that she'd even lost track of her own mother's life. And as far as her being involved with someone? The only hot doctor Anna had ever been involved with was right down the hall, but she wasn't about to mention that to the mayor.

Just because the mayor had felt the need to share with her, that didn't mean Anna was going to reciprocate. "Let's start by examining your ears."

The mayor pulled away from Anna as she went to put the disposable end of the scope into her ear. "Just relax, this won't hurt."

Anna examined the interior of one ear, then moved to the other, looking closely at the eardrum in each. "Have you been sick lately with a cold or maybe the flu?"

"I had a bad cold about two weeks ago. It went away on its own. Why? Did the cold damage something in my ear?" the mayor asked, then straightened on the table. "I'm not one to run to the doctor every time I get sick."

"The cold might have gone away, but there's still a lot of fluid behind both your ear drums and so they're inflamed. I'm surprised you haven't had pain with it, to be honest. I'm going to give you a prescription for an antibiotic, and I need you to take all of it."

"So, I'm not going deaf?" the mayor asked. "I just need some medication?"

"Yes, but you'll need to come back in to see a doctor once you've finished the course of antibiotics, just to confirm that the fluids have gone. Is that going to be a problem?" Anna asked, summarizing her findings on the chart and making note of the need for the patient to be seen again in two weeks. "I'll send the prescription over to the pharmacy for you."

The mayor hopped off the table, all the vulnerability she had displayed earlier gone. "Thank you. I… I appreciate your help."

"Not a problem. That's why we're here. Just make

sure you keep that appointment." Anna handed her the form to take to the front desk so they could make a follow-up appointment.

Anna waited as the woman grabbed her bag, then took her discharge paperwork and marched out of the room. As she watched the mayor walk up to the receptionist, Anna wondered if that would be her someday. Would Anna end up just like her, with nothing more than her job to live for? No friends or family? No one to come home to? No one to share kisses with?

No, that wasn't all there was waiting for her. She still had her dream of seeing the world. Working for the travel company on her first assignment in Miami would make that a reality, not a dream. It had been Will and remembering what they'd once shared that had taken her focus off of her dream. She just needed to refocus. She just needed to get back to her real life, the one where there weren't any hot doctors waiting to kiss her.

Her phone rang and she pulled it from her jacket. Seeing the name, her stomach dropped to her toes. Though her recruiter was the last person she wanted to talk to at the moment, she forced herself to answer the call as she searched for the excitement she'd just felt a few weeks ago when they'd discussed her move. Where had it gone? And how could she possibly get it back when, instead of thinking about where she was headed, she could only think about what she was leaving behind.

Will walked into work on Monday morning not feeling any better than when he'd walked out Friday afternoon. He'd finally gotten up the nerve to invite Anna

on a real date that weekend only to overhear her on the phone discussing her plans to leave for Miami. While he'd been messing about trying to find the perfect moment to bring up what was happening between the two of them, she was still planning to start a whole new life that didn't include him at all. It was just more proof that the kiss they'd shared had changed nothing. She would be leaving him, again.

"Morning," Anna said, coming into the break room, where he had stopped to pour himself his first cup of coffee for the day.

"Good morning," he said, unable to keep the grumpiness from his voice.

"It doesn't sound like you're having one. What's up?" Anna asked, joining him.

He knew he had no right to feel betrayed, but right or not, that was how he felt. "Nothing. It's just another Monday."

"Hopefully, it won't be as busy as Friday," Anna said.

He looked up at her and was surprised to see that she didn't look much better than he felt.

"Morning, everyone," Dana said as she rushed into the room. "I sure am hoping this snow keeps some of the walk-ins at home today."

After spending most of the weekend moping around his apartment, Will had been surprised to see just how much snow had accumulated. It was one of many things that was good about living in the apartment over the clinic. The commute was easy no matter what the weather was.

Will saw Dana looking at him and then at Anna. "What's wrong with the two of you? You look like you've lost your best friend."

He looked over to where Anna stood staring off into space, her coffee cup still sitting where she had poured it. Dana had no idea how close she was to the truth. Without a word, Will walked out of the room and into his office.

A large calendar sat on his desk, covered with the odd note here and there. He placed his cup on the edge of the desk and silently counted the days until January 1, when Anna would be leaving—two more days, that was it. Then he straightened his shoulders, turned to grab the lab coat hanging on the back of his door and ran straight into Anna.

"Sorry, I didn't hear you come in," Will said, his hands coming up to her shoulders to steady her, then jerking back.

"Dana asked me to tell you she put your first patient in room one," Anna said, her eyes studying him. "Are you feeling okay?"

"I'm fine," he said. He started to walk past her when her hand reached out for his arm.

"Did I do something?" Anna asked. He looked at her then. Her eyes were filled with concern.

Yes, she'd done something. She'd ripped his heart out of his chest and just continued on with her life. But doing it once hadn't been enough. And in two days, she would do it again. Walk out of his life and leave him alone again. And he couldn't even blame her. She'd told him very clearly that all she wanted from him was

friendship. He'd been the one to kiss her and open up the old wound inside of him.

"I'm sorry I kissed you." The words came out before he could stop them. It wasn't what he'd meant to say. He'd meant to tell her he was fine. But why should he lie about it?

"I..." Anna cleared her throat and looked away from him. "I...know."

She knew? What did she know? That what he'd felt at that moment was stronger than anything he'd felt before? That the only thing about the kiss that he regretted was that it hadn't been enough to make her want to stay with him?

"So, things are okay between us?" she asked, the worry in her eyes melting the last of the anger he'd felt earlier away.

"Yeah, we're good," he said. "I need to get to work before Dana comes looking for me."

A few hours later, Will realized that Dana had been right. They were in for a slow day at the clinic. The snow had continued to fall at an alarming rate. It had gotten so bad outside that it was not only keeping their walk-in patients at home, but it was also causing their scheduled patients to cancel their appointments. As he watched the snow fall outside his office, he was reminded of his childhood when snow like this meant the possibility of the school closing. Those unexpected snow days had been a time of celebration for him. Now he looked on the snow as an inconvenience. Some things were not as much fun as an adult.

But did it really have to be that way? With his dad

out of town, he was the boss. The clinic wasn't busy. Why couldn't he declare a snow day for himself? For the first time that day, he felt a smile begin to form.

He grabbed his and Anna's coats from the break room. If he only had two more days with her, he was going to make them count. He followed the sound of Anna's voice to the empty waiting room, where she and Dana were looking out the window watching the snow. "It's looking like we might as well close up, don't you think? Nobody in their right mind would come out in this."

"You don't have to tell me twice," Dana said. "I'm out of here."

Will waited until Dana was out of the room, then handed Anna her coat. "Here, put this on. I want to show you something."

The moment their coats were on, he took her hand and pulled her out the front door.

"What is it?" Anna asked, stopping once he had shut the door behind them. "Couldn't you have shown me from the window? It's cold out here."

He let go of her hand and stepped away from her. Bending down, he grabbed a handful of snow, molded it into a ball, then turned and let it go. The look on Anna's face when the snowball hit her directly in the chest was priceless.

CHAPTER THIRTEEN

ANNA WATCHED AS the wet ball of snow slid down her
coat. What had just happened? One moment Will was
moping around the office, and the next thing she knew,
she was getting pulled out into the cold and hit with a
snowball. From the moment she'd arrived that morning, she'd known that they were going to have to talk
about what had happened between the two of them.
She'd spent the weekend pacing inside the house, trying to make some sense of her life.

She was so confused. Her first instinct was to pack
her bags and get out of town the moment her mother
and Will's dad returned. Either way, she had to leave for
Miami on New Year's Day. But leaving without talking to Will seemed too much like the last time she'd
panicked and left him. She was an adult now, and she
had to handle situations like an adult.

Another snowball hit her in the chest, and she looked
up. Will stood in front of her, a wicked smile on his
face as he molded another handful of snow. Right then,
he didn't look anything like the man that had stood in
his office and said he regretted kissing her. He regretted
it? So it hadn't meant anything to him? It sure hadn't

felt that way. She would have sworn he was just as affected by that kiss as she was.

Thinking about the kiss and the way Will had brushed it away so easily, Anna bent down and grabbed her own handful of snow. If he wanted a fight, he'd get one. Dodging the snowball that he'd thrown, she aimed and hit Will straight in his smiling mouth. When he laughed, it just made her angrier. She grabbed more snow and then the fight was on. Instead of waiting for Will to retaliate, she quickly grabbed two handfuls of snow, squashed them together and let them fly. Back and forth, they volleyed snowball after snowball till they were both wet and breathing heavy.

"Okay, I give up. It's a tie," Will called, placing his hands in the air, palms forward so she could see they were empty.

Her arm was getting tired, and she'd lost the feeling in her right hand several minutes earlier. She'd had no idea that she could feel so violent. But her anger had died quickly, and as usual, it had turned into a competition between the two of them. He was probably trying to be diplomatic by declaring their fight a tie, but Anna wanted the win. Without taking her eyes off Will, she bent and gathered one last handful of snow.

"You don't want to do that, Anna," Will said, moving forward, his hands still in the air.

Oh, but she did. She really, really did. Pulling back her arm, she was just about to let the winning snowball fly when Will rushed toward her. She tried to dodge him as she aimed and threw the snow, but he was already in front of her. As her throw went wide, her feet

began to slide out from under her. She made a grab for Will's coat, but it was too late. Her feet slipped and before she knew what had happened she was flat on her back in the snow with Will on top of her.

"Ouch," she said, her hip hitting something under the snow. She'd have a bruise there for sure. Looking up, she found Will's face just above hers. The pain of the fall was quickly replaced by a pain in her soul. There had never been anyone in her life like Will. And deep inside, where that pain seemed to be growing, she knew there never would be.

"Are you okay?" His hand came up and brushed her hair from her face. She closed her eyes and let herself enjoy the warmth of his body against her.

"I'm fine," Anna said, her voice low, her breath coming fast as the weight of him pressed into her. All around them, the world was white and silent, her pounding heart the only thing she could hear. Things seemed so much simpler at that moment. There were just the two of them. No decision about work. No guilt about the past.

With him there next to her, she forgot about the cold and the hard ground. She felt neither. All she could feel was the weight of him pressing into her. The feel of his hard body awakened a desire that she had kept locked away from the night she'd left him. Her breath caught and she found herself shifting under him, wanting to get closer.

"This morning, while we were talking, I didn't mean to say that I shouldn't have kissed you, though it is true," Will said. His hand stilled on her face and the pain in her chest got stronger. "You asked for us to be

friends and I crossed that line. But what I should really have said this morning was that though I shouldn't have kissed you, I don't regret it. I don't regret anything where you are concerned. Not our past or present."

Anna opened her eyes. His words eased some of the ache in her chest, but when she saw the sadness in his eyes it returned. He was right. She'd said she wanted them to be just friends. It was all they could be. His life was here. She didn't even know where she'd be in the next month. So why did she feel this pain? He was all but saying that he accepted that she'd done the right thing the night she'd left him. But instead of being happy that the two of them could finally move on from their shared past, she felt empty.

He was waiting for her to say something. But what was she supposed to say? That she was glad that he saw now that they could only be friends? And what about his admitting that he didn't regret kissing her? Didn't that mean that it meant something to him too? "I don't regret kissing you, either. I don't regret anything as far as you are concerned."

"I don't know what you two have going on right now and I don't care," Ms. Martha's voice came from above them. "I've just had an emergency call. It's Dan Cummins. Shelley has gone into labor, and they can't make it down the mountain because the bridge is iced over."

"So, you do this often?" Anna asked. She'd grabbed everything she thought they might need and shoved it into backpacks while Will had gotten snow chains on his tires. Anna's peaceful moment with Will had

come crashing to a halt the moment she'd heard the word "labor."

"Never," Will said, pulling out of the parking lot. His knuckles were white where they gripped the steering wheel. Was that because of the fact that the trip up the mountain was going to be a dangerous one? Or was it because they were about to have to deliver a baby? She was pretty sure it was a mixture of both. The butterflies in her own stomach had more to do with the realization of what she'd just admitted to Will. But it was what she hadn't admitted that scared her the most.

"But you had a delivery setup at the office, so this has to have happened before."

"We keep it in case of an emergency. There was a time when my dad did a lot of the deliveries before it became so easy to go down the mountain to the specialist," Will said. "Is it warm enough for you?"

The heater in the truck had been turned on to high and she was finally getting the feeling back in her hands. She had peeled her coat off and set it in the back seat with Will's to dry out. "How far to Shelley and Dan's place?"

"It's just past the dairy farm. We'll need to park this side of Miller's Bridge and hike the rest of the way. On a normal day, we could make it in twenty minutes," Will said. But today wasn't normal. They'd be lucky if they got there within an hour. The slow speed of the truck as they crept out of town was torturous.

"So, have you done this?" Will asked. "Delivered a baby?"

"I've caught a few babies in the emergency room

when there wasn't time to get the mother up to the Labor and Delivery Department. I'm used to the nursery team making it down in time to take over the baby, though." From the worried look on Will's face, she decided not to mention that most of those deliveries had been more of her catching the baby versus a controlled delivery.

"Okay then," Will said, then stopped as the wheels of the truck seemed to lose traction. He eased off the brakes and Anna held her breath until she felt the tires grip the road once more. Will cleared his throat and Anna handed him a water bottle. He took a swallow, then began again. "Okay then, I think we should team up. You have more experience in the delivery department, so you're in charge there. And since I do have some pediatric experience, I'll take care of the baby at delivery."

"Sounds like a good plan."

The truck got quiet after that. As they drove, Anna stared out the window where the trees outside were blanketed in snow. Every so often, she'd spot a house where white swirling smoke escaped the chimneys. She thought of the families that were probably huddled around those fireplaces. Were they sharing stories? Playing cards? Watching their favorite movies? Most of the houses up the mountain from town were small older homes. Some of them had been handed down through generations; the families were content to continue living the same life as their parents and grandparents before them. She envied that, the contentment they experienced. She felt like she had been searching for that her whole life.

No, that wasn't true. There was a time when she had

been content. A time when she and her parents had lived up among these people. Where they too had lived a simple life, with her mom teaching in the local school and her father carving furniture in his workshop to be sold in the stores down the mountain. For the first time, she thought about what life might have been like if her father hadn't died. Would that have changed things? Would her life have gone in a different direction if her father had been there to advise her? Would things have been different between her and Will?

The truck came to a sharp stop and Anna was thrown out of her musings. Looking around, she saw that they had made it to the bridge. "Are you going to leave the truck on the road?"

"It will be fine. No one is going to be on these roads right now." Will reached into the back seat, then handed Anna her coat. She was glad to find that it was mostly dry now.

Once they'd gotten their coats zipped and their hats and gloves on, they got out and grabbed the backpacks Anna had packed. Anna looked around them for a trail, but she couldn't see one. "Do we try the bridge?"

"No, there's a trail that leads up the mountain to where the road double-backs. We can take that up and then follow the road another mile." Will pointed to their right. "It's been a long time since I've hiked up here, but I remember the way. Just take it slow until we get back to the road. There's no telling what could be under the snow. I don't want you to fall and hurt yourself."

"I've hiked in the snow before. Don't you remember when we were on the school newspaper and I decided

we needed a picture looking down on the school from the mountain?" Anna's mother had been so mad at her when she'd found out. But even Coreene couldn't deny that the picture of their small school covered in snow had been perfect.

"I remember. I went with you because I was afraid you were going to break your neck, which you could have if I hadn't been grabbed your arm when you bent over and started to slide off the path."

They spent the next thirty minutes climbing up the mountain and talking about the various situations they'd gotten themselves into as kids. When they reached the road, they followed it past the dairy until Will stopped and pointed out a house a good hundred yards off the road.

"We've almost made it," he said between breaths. They'd been walking for almost an hour with a lot of that uphill. "Do you need to stop?"

Her lungs burned from breathing the cold air and the muscles in her legs were protesting. But she knew they didn't have time to stop. It was Shelley's first baby and usually those took longer, but it had to have been two hours since Martha had received Dan's call. They didn't have time to stop. "No, I can do it."

Leaving the road, they followed the long drive that led to a two-story home with a large porch running all the way across the front. Smoke billowed out of two fireplaces, one on each side of the house. If reaching the house to help Shelley hadn't been enough, the thought of sitting in front of a warm fire right then would have been.

The door swung open the moment they stepped on the porch and a disheveled Dan came out to greet them. "Thank goodness you're here. Martha told me that you were on your way, but I didn't know if you'd make it on time."

"Where's Shelley?" Anna asked. Before he could answer, she heard the sound of loud panting coming from down the hallway and followed it. She peeped in the door, not sure what she might find. "Shelley? Can I come in?"

"Please, get in here," Shelley said between pants. "I didn't believe Dan when he said you were coming. I love that man to death, but if he had paced across this floor one more time, I think I would have had to kill him. He's been more nervous about this than me, and I'm the one having the baby."

Anna started to laugh but thought better of it when Shelley's eyes narrowed. "How far apart are the contractions?"

"They're two minutes apart. Please tell me that you or Will have done this before. I just turned thirty-five weeks. I wasn't expecting this to happen. I wanted an epidural." If it sounded like Shelley was whining, well, she had earned the right. "Tell me you can give me something…"

Shelley's voice gave out as another contraction hit her. Anna knew she couldn't give her anything for the pain without it going to the baby. So instead, she took her hands in hers and squeezed. "Shelley I want you to breathe with me, okay? Slow, deep breaths in through your nose and out through your mouth."

Anna sat down on the bed beside Shelley, their eyes locked as they repeated the breathing exercise. Once the contraction was gone, Anna palpated Shelley's abdomen. "Your doctor said the baby's head was down right?"

"Yes. He's been in that position since my last ultrasound about three weeks ago. Why? Is there a problem?"

"No, it feels like the head is still down and engaged. I'll be able to tell better when I check you. And I can feel him moving. That's good. I don't have anything to monitor the heartbeat, but there isn't any reason to think that there is a problem. You've been doing your kick counts right?" Anna stood and moved over to where she'd dumped her coat and backpack.

"Yes, every day since I was about twenty weeks. It seemed he was especially active last night, before all this happened," Shelley said, laying her hand on her belly protectively.

"Everything seems fine," Anna said, trying to reassure her friend. "I could feel the movement myself."

But when this was over, Anna was going to recommend that Will get a handheld Doppler machine, which could monitor the heartrate manually. As Anna began to unpack her backpack, the two men entered the room. "Dan, I want you to go over there and sit down by your wife. When the next contraction starts, I'm going to show you how to coach her through it."

"Okay," Dan said, joining Shelley on the bed, "I can do that."

"Will, if you could maybe clear everything off the dresser and finish unpacking our bags. I'm going to check and see how dilated Shelley is. Shelley, this isn't

going to be a precise measurement—you know I'm not an obstetrician—but we need to see if you're making progress. Can you tell me how long you've been in labor?"

"I'm not sure. I've had some cramping for several days, but I thought it was those false labor contractions. They weren't close together until this morning. They were five minutes apart when I decided we should go to the hospital, so Dan went and checked the roads. He wanted to make sure it was safe. By the time he came back and told me the bridge was iced over, they had gotten closer. That's when I told him to call you."

"So it's been about three or four hours. Okay, that's good," Anna said. She continued talking to Shelley, asking questions and trying to put her at ease as she positioned her on the bed and then put her gloves on. Anna was relieved when she examined the cervix and discovered Shelley was getting close. "You're making great progress. Like I said, obstetrics isn't my field, but from the experience I do have, I'd say you're at least seven to eight centimeters. I don't think it will be much longer."

Another contraction started and Anna showed Dan how to breathe with Shelley. When that one passed, Anna got busy preparing. She pulled a chair over to the side of the bed and unwrapped a sterile towel, then began opening packages containing sterile scissors and a plastic cord clamp. Beside those, she placed a suction bulb and then opened more sterile towels. She placed two of those on her improvised sterile tray.

As she opened a suture holder and then a suture, Will

said, "Dan, I'm going to take care of the baby when he's born. You said you were warming blankets in the dryer. Can you point me toward the laundry room so I can get them when the time comes?"

"It's okay. He can take you there and show you," Shelley said. "And maybe get me a glass of water, if that's okay?"

"I think it would be fine for you to have some water as long as you're not feeling nauseated. Do you need anything else, Anna?" Will said.

"A glass of water would be great," Anna said. She wasn't sure what Shelley wanted to discuss with her, but it had been plain that she didn't want to do it in front of the men.

"I don't know how I'm ever going to pay you back for this. I would send you free flowers for life if you lived here. But I guess if Will can't get you to stay, then my flowers won't persuade you."

"What do you mean? About Will getting me to stay?" Anna asked. Another contraction hit and Anna covered the instruments and supplies she'd been working on with another sterile towel. Moving back to Shelley's side, Anna went through the breathing exercise with her. Anna noticed that Shelley's contractions seemed to be getting stronger.

"I saw the way he looked at you when you came down the aisle at the wedding. That man is in love with you. And you seem to like him, too. So what's the problem?"

"Let me get this straight. You're about to have a baby and want to know about my relationship with

Will? I think the pain must have done something to your mind," Anna said.

"I'm just curious," Shelley said, before she bent over grabbing her stomach. "Oh God, Anna. It hurts so bad, but I really feel like I need to push now."

By the time the men came back, Anna was at the end of the bed directing Shelley on how to pant through the contraction. "That's good. Just like that. I just need to make sure you're fully dilated before you start pushing."

"What? We're about to start pushing?" Dan asked, heading to Shelley's side.

"No, I'm the one about to push. You just get to sit here and look pretty. And did the two of you have to climb up the mountain to some spring to get that water?" Shelley said, for the first time acting how Anna had always thought laboring women were meant to act—crabby and short-fused.

"I can't feel the cervix, so I'd say you're fully dilated. If you feel like pushing the next contraction, it's okay. It's your first baby, which means you could be pushing for a while, so if you don't feel the urge, you can wait." Anna noticed her hand was trembling when she removed her gloves and went to ready another pair. She'd been totally confident that she had things under control until now.

"You're doing great," Will whispered into her ear.

Glancing up, she saw that he had taken a spot by her side. He'd let her take total control of the situation, and she had no words for what his faith in her meant at that moment.

"I'm getting another contraction. And I need to push, Anna. I really need to push."

"That's fine. That's natural. Dan, help her get her hands behind her knees and support her back for her," Anna said, donning her gloves. "Take a breath when you need to and then push again."

Shelley took a breath and bore down again. "Shelley, you're amazing. You're doing so good. I can already see the top of the baby's head."

For the next fifteen minutes, Anna coached Shelley through the contractions. With each push, Anna saw more and more. "The baby's crowning, Shelley. You're almost done. Just another push or two."

Another contraction hit and Shelley began to push. "Okay, that's good, he's almost here. I need you to listen to me. When I tell you to stop pushing, I need you to stop and pant. It won't be but for a few seconds, but it's important for the baby and you."

Will moved over to her side, a blanket spread out to receive the baby as soon as it was born. "If the baby is crying and has good color, I'm going to place him on your chest. We don't have a warmer like they have in the hospital, so we're going to use your body heat," he said.

"Shelley, stop pushing," Anna said as the baby's head delivered and her heart almost jumped out of her chest at the sight of the umbilical cord wrapped around his neck. She remembered what she had learned in her obstetric rotation and tried to lift it around the baby's head, but it was too tight to reduce. There was another way, but she'd only seen it done once.

"Dan, help Shelley pant. It's really important that she stays in control right now," Will said as Anna reached for the surgical clamps. "The baby has a cord around his neck and Anna's going to have to clamp it and cut it. Shelley, when Anna tells you to push, you need to push with everything you have. Got it?"

She could hear the confidence that Will had in her in his words. Not waiting for Shelley and Dan's agreement, she picked up a surgical clamp. First she freed the cord enough to get one side under it, and then she clamped it shut. She'd just cut off the baby's blood flow from Shelley. She grabbed another clamp and clamped it close to the first, allowing just enough room for her scissors to fit between them. As soon as the scissors cut through the cord, Anna placed her hands on the baby's head. "Push, Shelley, push!"

As Shelley pushed, Anna guided the baby's shoulders out, and a moment later Baby Boy Cummins was born. Anna quickly handed him to Will.

The room was deathly quiet as Will dried the baby boy off, rubbing his back with the blanket. The baby had been cyanotic and too still when she'd handed him to Will, and unable to help herself, she started to cry. Was there something else she could have done?

"Is he okay?" Shelley asked. "He's okay, right?"

Then Anna heard it. It started as a soft cry and quickly turned to a full-on fit.

"He's fine. He just had to catch his breath for a moment. Being born was a lot of work for him, too." Will reached over Anna and handed the baby to Shelley. "Yes, place him skin to skin. Just like that. Good. Now

cover him with the blankets so he doesn't get cold. I'm going to listen to his heart and lungs, but from what I can see, you have a perfectly healthy baby there. I'd say he's somewhere between seven and seven and a half pounds, though I'm not sure how we're going to put that on the birth certificate."

Anna laughed. She wasn't even sure how you got a birth certificate with a home birth, but she knew one thing for sure: she was going to find some way to make certain that both her and Will's names were on the thing. Because without him there to help her, she wasn't sure she could have done any of it.

Anna found Will in the guest room down the hall a short while later, his eyes closed as he stretched out in the bed. She hadn't been this tired since the grueling years of her residency.

"Are they okay?" he asked, sitting up when she entered the room.

"They're perfect," Anna said as she sat down next to him. "I thought they might need some time alone. And I…"

Her voice trailed off as she turned to look at him. "I was so scared, Will. When I saw that nuchal cord and I couldn't get it to go around the baby's head, I just panicked. I knew I had to clamp and cut that cord. There wasn't any other way to deliver. But once I did that, I knew I had to get the baby out fast."

She tried to hold in the tears, but when Will stood and took her in his arms, she couldn't hold it together any longer. If something had happened to Shelley's baby because of Anna's inexperience, she didn't know

what she would have done. The deliveries in the emergency room had all been uncomplicated. Going through this tonight with Shelley had scared her. She was so glad she'd had Will there with her.

"And you did. You got the baby out, and now he and his mom are doing great," Will said, his hands running up and down her back as her body relaxed against him.

"I don't understand why I'm crying. I should be excited. We delivered a beautiful healthy baby."

"It's okay. It's been a long day." Will lifted her head and brushed his hand against her wet cheek, his touch so gentle.

Without thinking about it, she reached up and brushed her lips against his. His hands stilled and she started to back away. But when his arms went around her, pulling her closer, she stepped in until their bodies melded together. When Will's head bent toward hers, she met his lips with a hunger she'd felt building for days.

She knew the emotions of the last few hours were helping to fuel this fire between the two of them, but it was more than that. His hands ran down her body as if he were trying to memorize each curve and dip. Still, it wasn't enough. "I want more."

Before she could let herself think of all the pain of their past, she threaded her hands into his hair. When his hands slipped under her shirt, she found herself removing it. Her bra came next. Then his shirt joined hers. She felt as if her body had gone from freezing point to boiling in a matter of seconds.

"You are so beautiful," Will said, as he stared down

at where his hands palmed her breasts. "I've missed this, missed you."

His words broke something inside of her. Her heart wanted to promise him things that her head couldn't allow. She knew this couldn't lead to anything. The problems they'd had before hadn't gone away. But did there have to be promises of something more? Couldn't they just enjoy this one moment before it was gone?

She rocked her body against his hand when he reached for the zipper of her pants, letting him feel the urgency inside her. They made quick work of removing the rest of her clothes, then his.

"I'm not sure this was what Dan meant when he said we could use the guest room," Will said as he pulled her down to the bed with him. Anna felt heat flush her cheeks as she remembered there was another couple down the hall. "It's okay. They're much too busy with their new baby to worry about the two of us."

Anna relaxed as Will's hands slid down her body, and his lips found hers before traveling down her neck, then lower. She let her own hands explore, noting the way his body had changed over the years, becoming more defined than before. Her body responded to every taste and lick of his tongue, her core tensing until she thought she'd shatter at any moment.

And then Will was inside her, filling her over and over with each thrust, demanding that she give more and more until her body shuddered as wave after wave of pleasure rolled over her, until thrusting one last time before following right behind her.

CHAPTER FOURTEEN

WILL HELPED ANNA put on her backpack right as the sun began to come up. He'd spent the night holding her as she slept, dreading the rising sun and the reality it would bring with it.

They'd checked in on Shelby and the baby, reassuring themselves that they were both doing well before packing up their things so they could head back down the mountain.

"Are you sure you want to go out there?" Dan asked. "It will be slow going."

Will couldn't deny it. The snow had slowed, but there had to be close to two feet on the ground. He wasn't looking forward to the trip, but it was Anna's last day in town, and he needed to get her back home. It didn't make it any easier when all he could think about was the way she'd felt in his arms just a few hours ago. Now he had to face reality and the fact that this would be the last day they had together. "We really need to get back to the office before Martha sends a hunting party out for us."

"I don't know how to thank the two of you for everything," Dan said. "If there is ever anything I can do for you, either of you, let me know."

They'd only made it halfway down the drive when Anna stopped in front of him. "That has to have been the craziest thing I've ever experienced."

"I'm so glad you haven't found your visit boring," Will said, without the sarcasm he would have used a week ago.

"Admit it. That was amazing," Anna said as they started back down the driveway. He couldn't help but hope she wasn't just talking about the delivery they'd done.

"Yes, it was amazing," he said. "Bringing new life into the world has to be amazing every time."

"So, why didn't you go into obstetrics?" Anna asked.

"Why didn't you? You did a great job with Shelley." It was true. He'd been in awe of the way she'd taken charge and helped Shelley throughout her labor, coaching her and supporting her. Then there had been the delivery. He'd watched her hesitate only a moment before she'd clamped the cord that had been around the baby's neck.

"I don't know. I've always had this dream that I'd travel the world helping others," Anna said. "I guess emergency medicine seemed to work best for that. What about you? Was general medicine always what you wanted to do?"

He thought about her question as they left the driveway and started back up the road. The snowfall was finally letting up, and they were traveling at a brisker pace than they had the day before. "After my mom died, I spent a lot of time at the clinic with my dad. I got to see how he helped people. It wasn't glamorous,

but there were times when I'd get to see something exciting happen. But mostly, I saw people get better. Not all of them, of course. But I knew that what my dad did was important for the community. I admired that. And when I got older, I realized that one day my dad would have to retire and there wouldn't be anybody there to care for the people I'd come to care about."

"So you felt that it had to be you? It sounds like the decision was already made for you," Anna said.

"I've always known that you thought that, but it isn't true. I had a talk with my dad before I started medical school. He told me to keep my options open. I know he would have supported me if I had come home and told him that I wanted to go into obstetrics. I made the decision to take up general medicine. And I made the decision to come back here to practice."

For the next few minutes, they didn't talk. They reached the path that would take them down the mountain and back to the road where they had parked the truck. They were halfway down when Anna started talking again. "I'm sorry. It was wrong for me to suggest that you had only gone into the practice because of your dad. I've seen how you are with your patients. They love you. They bring you cakes. The town has a festival to buy new equipment for the clinic. You belong here. I can see that."

When they'd been in medical school, Will had always felt that Anna thought he was settling by going into general medicine instead of specializing. It had only been after she'd left him that he'd realized that to her, he was making a choice that she couldn't be a part

of. It was almost as if she blamed the town for the reason she had to leave him. "I have to admit that it's not normally as exciting as it was yesterday, but I know I'm needed, and that's important to me."

"I know. I just… I wish things could have been different," Anna said.

Will wanted to push, to ask exactly what she wanted to be different. Was she saying she wanted things between the two of them to be different? Or that she wished *they* were different?

From the beginning of their relationship in medical school, they'd both had their minds set on what their future would be like. Anna had always known that Will planned to go back to their hometown. Will had always known that Anna planned to specialize in emergency medicine and travel the world. They had known that their lives were headed in different directions. But they'd chosen to ignore it. Looking at it now, Will could see that Anna had been the bravest of the two of them. She'd known they had no future and broken things off. Now Anna was making plans to move across the country. And he would still be here when she left the next day. Nothing had changed.

When they made it to the truck, Will looked at his watch. "I'll call and let Martha know we're on our way as soon as I can get service. The snow has almost stopped now, so people will start getting out as soon as the road's clear."

"I just want a cup of coffee and a shower," Anna said, as he started the truck. "And heat. I want heat, coffee and a shower."

"You should head home once we get back to the office. I can handle things today." He couldn't help but think things would be better that way. He wasn't sure he could spend another day in the office with her working beside him. It was too close to what he had secretly dreamed of all those years ago in medical school. He hated to admit it, but deep down, he'd always thought that he would be able to change her mind. He'd thought that she would forget about her dreams for him. Not once had he ever considered that he could change his own plans for her. And now it was too late.

He pulled out onto the road, maneuvering until they were headed back down to town. While the roads were still covered with snow and ice, he was glad to be on his way back home. He slowed even more to make a sharp turn as the mountain road wound downward and had just begun to accelerate again when something from the side of the road caught his eye. He heard Anna's scream at the same time he felt the impact of the deer that had run out in front of them. He tried to control the spin they'd been thrown into, but the tires lost their traction, sending them off the road and into the trees. He heard the crunch of metal as the truck traveled down the mountain. He flung his arm out to protect Anna. He couldn't let anything happen to her. He saw the tree in front of them, but there was nothing he could do to stop the collision he knew was coming. The impact threw him to the side and he felt his head hit the door's window. There was the horrible grind of metal against the tree along with the explosion of the truck's airbags. Then there was only silence.

* * *

Anna sat up and stared at the large tree that sat halfway inside the hood of Will's truck. What had happened? The smell of burned rubber filled the truck, and she pushed against the deflated airbag in front of her. She'd seen the deer and had known they couldn't avoid it. Then the truck had gone into a spin, and before she realized what was happening, they'd been headed off the side of the mountain. It had only been the tree that had stopped them from going farther. "Okay, you've proved your point," Anna said, wincing when she moved her shoulder. "There is nothing about your life that is boring."

She heard a moan and looked over to see Will holding his head. "Will? Oh God, Will. What's wrong? Where are you hurt?"

There wasn't any danger of the truck moving any farther down the mountain with the tree in front of them, so she took off her seat belt and slid over to his side. "Will, look at me?"

"I'm okay," he said. "I think I hit my head on something."

Anna looked around the truck where medical supplies and other items had been tossed around. Carefully, she placed a hand on each side of his head. "I need you to be still and don't turn your neck. Any chance you have a C-collar in here?"

"No, sorry. All I have is a first aid kit and the supplies left over from delivering the baby," Will said, his voice trailing off.

She looked around and saw a generic first aid kit on the floorboard.

She forced herself to remain calm when all she wanted to do was cry. Her instincts told her that there was something wrong with Will. The pain and the drowsiness weren't good signs. "Will, I need you to open your eyes for me,"

His eyes opened and she took a deep breath. "Tell me what you feel. You said your head hurts. What else?"

"I'm okay, Anna. It's just a bump on the head. I'll be fine. I'm just very tired. I need to rest, and then I need to come up with a way to get us out of here."

She knew that at the very least, Will had a concussion. She didn't want to think about the worst possibilities. And she didn't even have a penlight to check his pupils. Not that it mattered. Her doing a neuro check on him wasn't going to change anything. What she needed was to get him to a hospital. She looked around for her phone but couldn't see it. "Will, where's your phone?"

"In my pocket," he said, opening his eyes. "There's blood on your face."

Anna reached into his pocket and pulled out his phone. "It's just a scratch from the glass. I'm fine."

"I really don't like this feeling," Will said.

"What feeling?" Anna asked as she pushed the button on the side of his phone that would take her to the option to make an emergency call. She hit the button to call 911 and waited. Nothing. They were too far down the mountain to get service. She needed to be higher. "What feeling, Will? I need you to tell me what you feel."

"I'm just so tired," Will said. "I just need to close my eyes for a second."

Anna couldn't hold back the tears any longer. She tried to wipe them away, but they just kept falling. "Will, I'm going to have to leave you. I need to get to the road so I can use the phone and get help."

"I know. I've always known you had to leave me. It's okay. Please don't cry." Will's eyes opened and the look she saw in them made Anna's heart turn inside out. "I'll still love you, no matter where you go. And someday when you finish chasing that dream of yours, I'll be waiting here for you."

Anna's hand went to her mouth as she tried to hold back the sobs that threatened to take over her body. She knew he didn't know what he was saying, but still... he'd said he loved her.

But that didn't matter. Not right then. Will was showing all the signs of having a traumatic brain injury. He might even need surgery. She had to do this. She had to leave him. "Will, I'm only leaving you for as long as it takes to get help. I'm just going to climb up the mountain so I can call 911 so that we can get you out of here. I'm coming back. As soon as I get someone on the phone, I'm coming back. I promise."

Unable to stop herself, she bent down and brushed her lips across his. "I'm not leaving you." Then, without looking back, she slid over to the door and pulled on the handle.

The weight of the door pressed into her shoulder as she used all the strength she had to get it open. Once it was, she looked down and was relieved to find the tires of the truck were still on the ground. Then she looked up at the road. They had slid farther than she thought.

Normally the climb would not have been that challenging, but with the ground wet from the snow, she knew she'd have to be careful. It would only take one misstep for her to slide down the side of the mountain.

She took one more look back at Will, wiped the tears from her eyes so she could see and began to climb. She took the first step, grabbed hold of a tree root and pulled herself up. She took another, then another. Every couple of steps, she would look up to check her progress. She wouldn't allow herself to look down to where she knew Will was waiting for her to return. What if he woke up and thought she'd just left him there? What if he fell asleep and never woke up?

No, she couldn't think like that. He would be okay. He had to be. She grabbed the base of the next tree and pulled herself up another few feet.

The moment she made it to the road, she pulled out Will's phone and tried to make the call again. When the 911 operator answered, she had to fight through the tears so that the man could understand what she was saying. She told him about the wreck and Will's injuries, then gave him the directions as best she could. When the man told her to stay on the phone and to remain where she was, she protested. She had promised Will that she would come back to him after she made the call. But when the man explained that without clear directions, her being there to flag down the emergency vehicles was the fastest way to get Will the help he so desperately needed, she quit arguing.

Her legs suddenly became too weak to hold her, so she sat down on the side of the road and waited. As

the minutes dragged on, she tried not to think about Will waiting alone in the truck for her to come back to him. She knew she was doing what was best for him. But hadn't she done the best thing for him once before? She'd known the night she'd left the letter for him that it was best for them to end things.

And how had that turned out? With her alone in Nashville and him alone here. Was that really what she wanted? He'd said that he'd be waiting for her when she had finished chasing her dreams. Was there a chance he really meant that, or was he just confused because of the head injury?

She heard the motor of a diesel truck right before it turned the corner and recognized the driver the moment he got out of his truck. Paramedic, volunteer fireman and tow truck driver, Eddie had been driving these back roads and helping people for as long as Anna could remember. As she went to meet him, she heard another truck. This time it was the chief of the fire department. Before she could explain to the first two men, another truck drove up, this one with two more volunteer firemen. As the last group to arrive began to unload a stretcher and an emergency kit, Anna walked the men over to where the truck had gone off the side of the road. When they very politely asked her to give them room to work, their way of telling her to get out of their way, she stepped back while they discussed the best way to safely get Will up the mountain. A few minutes later, she saw two of the medics tie some lines onto the bumper of the tow truck, and then they

started down the mountain with a heavy-duty back board between them.

The minutes ticked by as Anna waited for the men to return. Finally, she saw one, then the other. On the back board with a C-collar safely around his neck, lay Will.

"How is he?" she said, rushing toward them. "Will, can you open your eyes?"

She started to panic when he ignored her plea, but she saw that his breathing was regular and his color was good.

"We've got an ambulance waiting for us in town," Eddie said, taking her arm and leading her to his truck. "The medics are going to take him down, and we'll follow them."

Just as Eddie had said, an ambulance waited at the clinic, where a crowd of people had formed. Anna got out of the truck as soon as Eddie stopped. As the ambulance crew transferred Will over to their stretcher, Anna explained who she was and received permission to ride in the back with Will.

Finally, after what felt like hours, the ambulance pulled out of the clinic parking lot to take Will to the hospital, where she could make sure he got the treatment he needed.

CHAPTER FIFTEEN

WILL OPENED HIS eyes and looked around the hospital room. He wasn't sure how long he'd been there. It could have been days, or it could have been weeks. It seemed every time he closed his eyes, someone was trying to wake him up. His memories of the accident were all jumbled up, but he did remember Anna bending over him and telling him she had to leave him, but she would be back. But after that, he had no memories at all. Had she come back for him? She had to have, or he wouldn't be there.

But how long ago had that been? Maybe he'd only been out for a few hours. Even if it was the next day, New Year's Day, she would stop by to tell him bye before she left town.

The door to his room opened, and Anna walked in carrying a large cup and a paper bag. Her eyes widened when she saw him and he started to get up.

"What are you doing?" she said as she sat the cup and bag down on the bedside tray before rushing over to him. "You can't get up yet."

Her arms came around him, steadying him as the room began to spin. She helped him back into the bed,

but when she started to move away, he tugged her down beside him.

"You came back for me," he said. His voice was hoarse, as if he hadn't used it for a while. Just how long had he been out? "What's the date?"

"It's January first," Anna said. "And of course I came back for you. Did you think I would leave you halfway down that mountain?"

"It's New Year's Day." He'd slept through the last hours they'd had left to spend together.

"It is." Anna stood and walked over to where a large vase of flowers sat on the windowsill. When she turned, he saw that tell of hers as she bit down on her bottom lip. "The flowers are from Shelley and Dan."

"How are they doing?" Will asked. He'd almost forgotten about the baby they'd delivered.

"They're fine. Your father should be there now, checking on them for me. I gave him a few suggestions of things that we should have on hand in case we have to do another delivery," Anna said as she started back over to the bed.

"We?" Will asked, his heart speeding up with every step she took toward him. Anna moved back over to the bed and sat down beside him. His head still ached, and he knew he was probably still somewhat confused from the head injury.

"Do you remember anything about the wreck?" Anna asked, ignoring his question.

He tried reaching for his memories, but he could only remember small pieces of what had happened. "I remember you were crying."

"I knew you were hurt, but I didn't know how bad. I don't know if you remember the neurosurgeon coming in to see you, but he says you have a small subdural hematoma and won't need surgery."

Will remembered a man examining him, but that wasn't what was important right then. "You were crying. You said you were leaving me and you were crying."

"I had to leave you in the truck to get help. I didn't have a choice." Anna said, her eyes once more filling with tears. "I don't want to ever do that again."

"Don't cry, I'm going to be fine," Will said, somehow knowing deep inside that the words were true. He'd recover from the injuries he'd received in the wreck. He just wasn't sure his heart would recover when Anna left him for the second time.

"Do you remember anything else? Anything that you said to me?" she asked, her eyes full of hope as she stared up at him, making him search through his memories once more.

Then he remembered. Yes, Anna had cried. She'd been crying as she'd tried to care for him in the front seat of his truck as it lay half destroyed against a broken tree that had probably saved both of their lives. He'd told her not to cry. "I said that I'd still love you, no matter where you went. And that someday when you finished chasing that dream of yours, I'd be waiting here for you."

"Did you mean it? When you said you loved me, I mean?" Her voice was soft and cautious, as if she were afraid of his answer.

"Of course I meant it. I've loved you most of my life. And I meant what I said. I know how important your dreams are to you. I won't take those from you. I will wait for you, if you want me to." The nervousness he felt at that moment wasn't from the accident. The thought of Anna leaving him was like a physical blow, but he knew he'd wait a lifetime just on the chance that she'd come back to him.

"I don't want to ever leave you. Not again," Anna said as she turned to him. Her body shivered and he pulled her closer to him, wrapping his arms around her. "I've been so stubborn. So caught up in this fantasy of this dream I had that was going to make me happy, when all this time, I've always been my happiest when I was with you."

"What are you saying? That you're giving up your dreams for me?" Will wanted nothing more than for Anna to stay with him, but not at the cost of her own happiness. "I never wanted you to give up your dreams for me. I love you too much to ask that."

"I'm saying that everything I've been out there looking for is here because it's you. I see that now. You're what I need to make me happy. That even if I do go out into the world someday, I want it to be with you. I love you, Will. I've always loved you. I'm finally following my dreams, and they've led me right back to you, where I belong."

"We don't have to stay in Rolling Oaks," Will said, unable to believe what she was saying. "I can travel with you, if that's what you want. We can go anywhere you want, as long as I know you love me."

"Maybe we can travel later, when the kids are grown," Anna said, surprising him even more, "but for now, I think I'd like to be home, with you."

Kids? He liked the sound of that. He pulled her closer to him, then looked down where two bright green eyes stared back at him with the love he'd always longed to see. Anna had finally come home, to him.

* * * * *

If you enjoyed this story,
check out these other great reads
from Deanne Anders

Single Dad's Fake Fiancée
The Rebel Doctor's Secret Child
Unbuttoning the Bachelor Doc
A Surgeon's Christmas Baby

All available now!

MILLS & BOON ®

Coming next month

EMERGENCY ROOM REUNION
Amy Blythe

He glanced at her mouth—again. And he wasn't the only one guilty of that look.

But she wasn't going to make the same mistake twice. 'We shouldn't have... That night you came in with a broken tibia, I didn't think you were staying.' Her words were running away from her, but she couldn't stop them. 'It felt like goodbye, like there was nothing to lose, but now you're *back* back, and there's something to lose. Oh god.' It hit her like a ton of bricks, the real answer to her question. 'You came back to give it another go?'

'No.'

'No?'

'I just wondered if there was still something.'

'How is that different?'

'Because there's no pressure,' he said, eyes pleading. 'Because you kissed me back and it was like nothing else.' His tone seemed to dare her to contradict him, to disagree, and she couldn't do it.

Without meaning to, without consciously making the choice to touch him, she reached out, grazed her

fingertips to the back of his wrist. This was real. He was really here, really telling her he wanted her still, after all this time.

Continue reading

EMERGENCY ROOM REUNION
Amy Blythe

Available next month
millsandboon.co.uk

COMING SOON!

We really hope you enjoyed reading this book.
If you're looking for more romance
be sure to head to the shops when
new books are available on

Thursday 18th December

To see which titles are coming soon, please visit

millsandboon.co.uk/nextmonth

MILLS & BOON

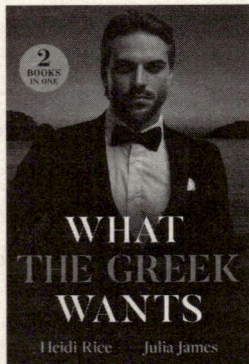

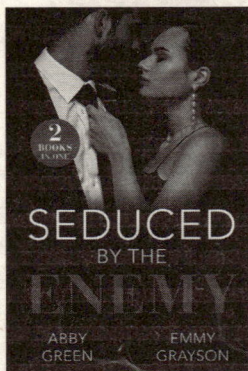

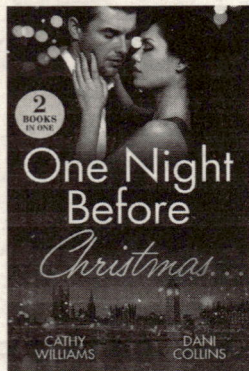

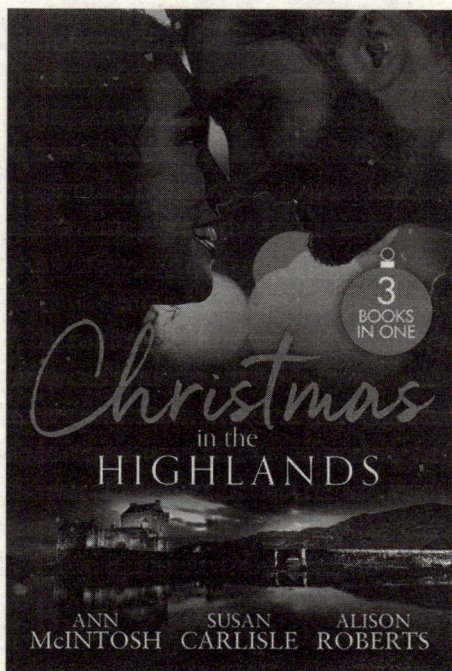

LET'S TALK
Romance

For exclusive extracts, competitions and special offers, find us online:

- **f** MillsandBoon
- **X** @MillsandBoon
- **O** @MillsandBoonUK
- **d** @MillsandBoonUK

Get in touch on 01413 063 232

OUT N

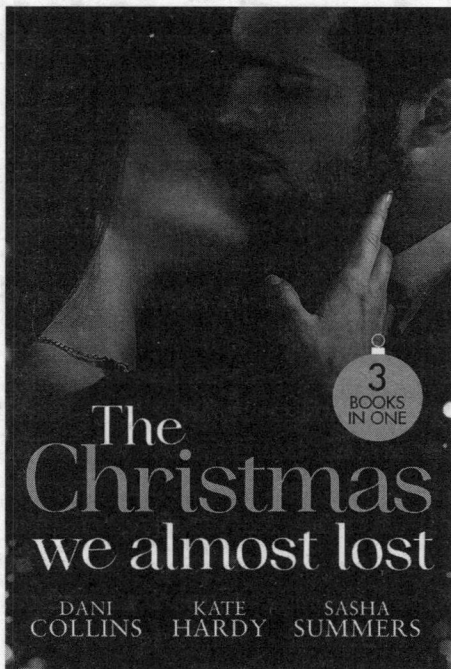